HISTORICAL

Your romantic escape to the past.

Lady Beaumont's Daring Proposition
Eva Shepherd

A Deal With The Rebellious Marquess
Bronwyn Scott

MILLS & BOON

LADY BEAUMONT'S DARING PROPOSITION
© 2024 by Eva Shepherd
Philippine Copyright 2024
Australian Copyright 2024
New Zealand Copyright 2024

First Published 2024
First Australian Paperback Edition 2024
ISBN 978 1 038 91081 3

A DEAL WITH THE REBELLIOUS MARQUESS
© 2024 by Nikki Poppen
Philippine Copyright 2024
Australian Copyright 2024
New Zealand Copyright 2024

First Published 2024
First Australian Paperback Edition 2024
ISBN 978 1 038 91081 3

MIX
Paper | Supporting
responsible forestry
FSC® C001695

Published by
Harlequin Mills & Boon
An imprint of Harlequin Enterprises (Australia) Pty Limited
(ABN 47 001 180 918), a subsidiary of HarperCollins
Publishers Australia Pty Limited
(ABN 36 009 913 517)
Level 19, 201 Elizabeth Street
SYDNEY NSW 2000 AUSTRALIA

Cover art used by arrangement with Harlequin Books S.A.. All rights reserved.

Printed and bound in Australia by McPherson's Printing Group

Lady Beaumont's Daring Proposition

Eva Shepherd

MILLS & BOON

After graduating with degrees in history and political science, **Eva Shepherd** worked in journalism and as an advertising copywriter. She began writing historical romances because it combined her love of a happy ending with her passion for history. She lives in Christchurch, New Zealand, but spends her days immersed in the world of late Victorian England. Eva loves hearing from readers and can be reached via her website, evashepherd.com, and her Facebook page, Facebook.com/evashepherdromancewriter.

Visit the Author Profile page
at millsandboon.com.au

Author Note

Lady Beaumont's Daring Proposition is the final book in the Rebellious Young Ladies series and features Lady Emily Beaumont, the most serious member of the group of four friends who met at Halliwell's Finishing School for Refined Young Ladies, and Jackson Wilde, a man who does his best to never take anything seriously.

The book is partly set in London's East End, which was a deprived, overcrowded area where disease ran rampant during the Victorian period. While the squalid condition in which people were forced to live was often dismissed as being due to laziness and vice, some socially conscious people worked hard to change the conditions of the poor.

I based Emily on these caring people. She works in an imaginary hospital called the Hope Charity Hospital, where Jackson Wilde finds himself after yet another lively night out. What starts out as a mutual dislike doesn't stay that way for long, and this unlikely couple soon embark on an involvement that changes their lives and those of many people around them.

I hope you enjoy reading Jackson and Emily's story, and I love to hear from readers. You can reach me via my Facebook page, Facebook.com/evashepherdromancewriter, or through my website, evashepherd.com.

Chapter One

〜〜〜〜〜

London 1895

The night Jackson Wilde, Viscount Wickford, had his life changed for ever started out like any other. He dined at his London club, played a round or two of snooker. He then proceeded to visit various drinking and gaming establishments throughout the city, deliberately selecting ones his father, the Duke of Greenfeld, would describe as dens of iniquity and lascivious vice.

As the night turned into early morning, the dens became more iniquitous, the vices more lascivious and the décor decidedly seedier. Friends with more refined tastes than Jackson—and you didn't have to be particularly refined to be included in that category—dropped off as the night wore on, until, somehow, he found himself in the dark back alleys of the East End, alone and completely lost.

Well, not completely alone. He'd spotted several large rodents scurrying along the gutters and a few mangy cats out on the prowl, presumably in pursuit of the scurrying rodents. But apart from those undesirable companions the area appeared completely deserted.

He looked up one narrow alleyway, the walls so close they appeared to almost touch. Then he turned and looked back in the direction he had come, taking in the identical red brick walls, appearing black in the light of a half-moon, and the broken cobblestone paths, glistening from a recent rainfall.

'They all look the same,' he said to no one in particular, his voice echoing off the walls.

'And they all smell the same,' he added under his breath, not wanting to offend the rats and cats who called this alleyway home, but unable to ignore the acrid stench of coal smoke, the putrid stink of rotting garbage and rat droppings, and the other less savoury smells whose origin he'd rather not know.

A loud snore drew his attention to a pile of rags in a doorway. It seemed he was not the only human inhabitant after all. He approached the sleeping vagrant but was stopped in his tracks by the overwhelming smell of raw alcohol. This man obviously needed to sleep off whatever demon drink had got him into this state, even more than Jackson did, and was unlikely to provide any useful advice on how Jackson was to wend his way back to his Kensington townhouse.

There was nothing for it. He was going to have to acquire that backbone his father always told him he was severely lacking and work his way methodically through this warren. It shouldn't be too hard. After all, he'd aways managed to find his way out of the maze at the family's Norfolk estate. And had been even better at getting himself lost so his father couldn't find him, and make good on his promise to once again beat some sense into his wastrel excuse of a son.

His not so fond memories of his father were interrupted by a shrill scream, piercing the night air.

'Did you hear that?' He looked towards the sleeping vagrant, who merely snuffled in his sleep and rolled over, as if such sounds merely provided the usual background noise to his slumber.

The woman's scream came again—louder, shriller, more desperate. Orientating himself towards the sound, he sprinted through the labyrinth, hoping and praying he was heading in the right direction.

Another cry ripped through the air, along with the sound of men's laughter.

He was close.

He turned yet another identical corner and found the source of the distress call. A young woman was pinned up against a wall, surrounded by a group of baying males. Her terror delighted the taunting men, whose faces were contorted with looks of cruel pleasure.

'Come on, darling,' one man said, pulling her towards him. 'You promised us a good time. So now deliver on that promise.' He grabbed the front of her dress, her cries for help drowning out the sound of tearing fabric and the accompanying men's laughter.

'Stop,' Jackson called out as he rushed forward, fists raised. Later, when he had time to consider his actions, he would admit it might have been better to take a moment to assess the situation and devise a plan of action. Boxing had been his strongest subject in school. It was, in fact, the only subject he excelled at, but even a man who had shown some prowess in the ring should have known better than to take on five or six assailants all fired up and looking for trouble.

But at the time he didn't have the luxury of hindsight, and thinking things through had never been one of his strong suits. So, instead, he threw a punch at the nearest man, and had the satisfaction of seeing him fall to the ground, before his four or five companions turned in his direction.

'Run,' he yelled to the young woman. She took action immediately, sliding past the distracted men and disappearing around the corner.

As he faced the furious men, it became increasingly clear he should heed his own advice, turn tail and run as fast as he could, but in the time it took to come to that conclusion it was too late. The huddle of men surrounded him, making escape an impossibility. No option was left but to fight.

His fists flew out again, landing with a painful crunch in a second man's face. Jackson smiled as he watched the cur stagger backwards. But it was to be the last time he smiled for some time. Fists continued to fly in every direction, most of them landing on Jackson's face, chest, stomach and anywhere else the men could reach in the ensuing melee.

Somehow, the cobblestones defied gravity and rose up to meet him, smacking him in the face with a powerful force that made the men's punches feel like soft slaps. In the mayhem, self-preservation took over. He rolled into a tight ball, protecting his head, and prayed the men would show some pity and leave him to nurse his injuries.

Sinner that he was, he did not expect his prayers to be answered. They weren't. Boots replaced fists as the men indulged themselves in a kicking contest, treating him like a rugby ball stuck in a scrummage.

'That will teach you for ruining our fun,' one panting man said as he finally ran out of energy. 'Now, where did that little whore go?'

'If we don't find her, we'll be back to finish off the job,' another man added, giving Jackson a final kick in the middle of his back for good measure.

And with that the alleyway fell silent. Jackson could only hope they did come back. That would mean the young woman had managed to escape and her safety would provide some compensation for having the life almost kicked out of him. But if they did return, Jackson did not wish to remain such an easy target. He would at least try and make them work for their sport.

With much wincing, groaning and moaning, he pulled himself along the alleyway, seeking somewhere, anywhere, to hide. At a pace that would put a snail to shame he dragged himself to a corner, hoping the dark night would disguise the tell-tale trail of blood. He wedged himself between the wall and a pile of rotting rubbish, its fetid smell mixing with the metallic scent of his blood. In this uncomfortable refuge he drifted off, not caring if it was to sleep or to death, just wanting to free himself from the unbearable pain wracking every inch of his body.

Jackson forced open his eyes. Through narrow slits, he looked up at the most glorious sight he had ever beheld. He was in heaven and a bewitching angel was watching over him. If he'd realised heaven would be so, well, heavenly, he would have paid more attention during those interminable sermons his father had dragged him to every Sunday.

The old preacher at their local church would have had Jackson's undivided attention if he'd revealed that heaven was populated with chestnut haired beauties, with velvet brown eyes, honey-coloured skin and decidedly kissable red lips. His gaze moved lower. And the preacher most definitely had omitted to mention that angels also had devilishly curvaceous bodies. If he had, Jackson was sure to have remembered.

He tried to smile at the beatific sight, but his swollen lips would not allow it, so instead he contemplated what was potentially a sacrilegious thought. Was it wrong to lust after angels? That was a subject the preacher never raised. But surely, for Jackson, heaven would not consist of cherubs sitting on fluffy clouds and playing harps, but would be full of alluring women, eager to satisfy his every whim.

There was only one way to discover the answer to this deep, theological question. He needed to put it to the test.

'Kiss me, my angel,' he said through thick, swollen lips.

Thick, swollen lips?

Wouldn't his suffering be relieved when he reached heaven? He vaguely remembered the preacher mentioning something about that.

The halo of soft light surrounding the celestial being grew brighter, becoming almost painful and forcing him to close his eyes. Excruciating agony ripped through his entire body as he emerged further into consciousness. Even his toes and fingers were screaming out in pain.

He made a concerted effort to sit up, but his angel placed her lovely hand on his shoulder to stop his progress.

'You mustn't move,' she said.

'Aren't you going to kiss me and relieve me of my suffering?' He repeated, more in hope than expectation.

'You will behave yourself while you're here, Jackson Wilde,' she said in a voice that lacked the compassion he would expect from an angel. 'And you will treat the nursing staff with the respect they deserve. No one will tolerate any of your misbehaviour. I can tell you that right now.'

Despite the pain, he forced his eyes open again and attempted to get a better look at his chastising angel. She came fully into focus. With a complaining groan he sunk back down on to the bed, his response more a reaction to his predicament than the state of his body.

Lady Emily Beaumont was frowning down at him. No one, except a man whose mind was groggy with excruciating pain, would ever mistake that strait-laced do-gooder for an angel. He closed his eyes to block out the disapproving sight.

His father had been proven right. Jackson had been sent straight to hell.

Emily could hardly credit it. Even with his face bruised black and blue, his blue eyes almost swollen shut, and his dark blond hair encrusted with blood, Jackson Wilde was still a handsome man.

But good looks such as his had no effect on her whatsoever. Not when she knew exactly what sort of man he really was. She had met men like him before. Men who cared about no one except themselves, and whose only purpose in life was to have a good time.

He was the sort of man any sensible young woman would avoid at all costs. Unfortunately, most young women were not nearly sensible enough and could not see what was patently obvious to Emily. Men like him were not to be taken seriously. They used women for their own amusement and, when they tired of them, they moved onto the next one.

Kiss me, my angel, indeed.

Even in this state he could not resist the temptation to flirt and charm. That just showed the man's true character.

And yet, despite his reputation, every debutante seemed

to be under the illusion she would be the one to tame Jackson Wilde. The one he would marry, settle down with—the one to change his ways.

Emily shook her head in disbelief as she looked down at the Viscount as he drifted off to sleep on the hospital bed.

He was not a man she had hitherto shown much attention, but at the few Society balls they had both attended, she had witnessed young women all but throw themselves at him. It was as if he cast some sort of spell over those innocent debutantes and easily had them dancing attendance on him.

They all chose to ignore his reputation and the antics reported about him in the scandal sheets. All because he was good looking, debonaire and would one day inherit a dukedom.

She scanned his face, covered in a mass of cuts and contusions. It was obvious what had happened to him this evening and how he had got into this state. He would have tried out his charms on the wrong woman, and some man had given him his comeuppance. Hopefully this would teach him a valuable lesson, although in reality there was little chance of that. Men like him never changed.

And if he tried to flirt with her again, he would soon discover she was no gullible debutante, or chorus girl impressed by his wealth and status. Nor was she a bored married woman looking for some excitement. She was a woman who would not be toyed with.

Emily would like to think this immunity to men such as him came from innate intelligence and the ability to see through the attractive façade to the real, shallow, selfish man beneath, but she knew this was not so. It was wisdom that had come from bitter experience. A bitter experience she would never repeat. So Jackson Wilde could try all his charming tricks on her, flirt and flatter as much as he liked, he would find it was all simply a complete waste of his time and energy.

He opened his eyes again and once more tried to smile at her, stopping immediately when the crack on his bottom lip parted, causing Emily to join him in wincing.

'So, is this heaven or hell?' he asked, rather nonsensically.

'You're in the Hope Charity Hospital. An institution that treats the deserving poor.'

He attempted a laugh, which quickly turned into a cough. 'And the occasional undeserving rich.'

'You were brought in early this morning by some local men. Matron has assessed you and says you have little more than bruising and cuts, but you were unconscious when you arrived, so they want to keep an eye on you to make sure there is nothing more serious. Once a bed is available, you'll be moved to the ward.'

'In the meantime, can I assume you or one of the other nursing angels will be bathing my fevered brow and tending to my every need?'

Emily stared at him in disbelief as he actually attempted to wink his swollen eye.

'I have already told you, while you are here, you will respect the nursing staff,' she said, enjoying being able to assert her authority and put this self-entitled man in his place. 'You will not charm them, flirt with them, or,' she waved her hand in the air as she attempted to grasp the words, 'do anything else inappropriate.'

His attempt to smile was thwarted when the crack in his lip parted further. 'Believe me, as much as I'd like to do something inappropriate, I don't think I'll be able to for quite some time. So your virtue, and that of the other nurses, will be safe for now.'

'I'm not a nurse.'

He slowly eased his eyes open a little wider, as if assessing her. 'If you're not a nurse what are you doing here, tending to me?'

That was a good question. Matron had informed her, in a rather sniffy tone, that one of *'Emily's people'*, a man dressed in formal evening clothes of white shirt, white bow tie and black swallow tail jacket, had been brought in and she should go and see to him as the nurses were all busy. Emily had resented the implication. The nurses and other staff at the Hope Hospital were *her* people, not this man. She may have been born into the aristocracy, but she much preferred to identify with those who gave their time to helping people less fortunate than themselves, rather than idle, privileged men like the one in the bed who thought of nothing more than endlessly enjoying themselves.

But Matron ran the wards and to have questioned her authority would have only confirmed that ferocious woman's suspicions that Emily was merely a dilettante, passing her time with no real commitment to the hospital. Plus, she had to admit, she was curious to discover the patient's identity. Few of Emily's so-called people would venture into the East End. When they did, it was usually for disreputable reasons.

'Well, I can tell you how I did not end up in here,' she said in her most reproachful voice. 'It wasn't because I got into a brawl and came out the loser.'

'No, I'm sure if you got into a brawl, you'd be the victor, no matter how brawny the opponent.'

Emily straightened her spine, determined to not let this

insult affect her. So what if she had never been the belle of any ball she had reluctantly attended? So what if she was four-and-twenty and still unwed? She had found a place where she was needed, where she felt valued, and she would not let this ne'er do well undermine her confidence or accuse her of being anything less than feminine.

'Well, if you're not going to tell me how *you* got here, can you at least tell me how *I* got here?' he said. 'My last memory is of rotting away in a God-forsaken alley behind a pile of rubbish.'

'You were lucky. Some men found you and carried you into the hospital.'

He spluttered an attempt at a laugh. 'I think we have a different definition of lucky.'

'At least you will now get the treatment you need and will soon be able to leave and be tended at home by your family physician.'

He touched his face and winced. 'I think it might be best if I hide out here until the worst of the damage is healed.'

'What's wrong? Are you worried that your lady friends will be less than impressed by you, now that you've lost your good looks.'

'Why, Lady Emily, I'm flattered that you believe I possess good looks, and that you assume I have more than one lady friend I wish to impress. You make me sound like quite the lothario.'

She didn't have to *make* him sound like a lothario. That was exactly what he was. Jackson Wilde was known to run with a fast set that surrounded the Prince of Wales. The stories of what Queen Victoria's son and his friends got up to were a topic of constant salacious gossip and difficult to ignore.

'Well, perhaps you should take your present condition as a warning,' she said. 'You might not remember how you came to be in Hope Hospital, but you must have some memory of how you came to be in this condition.' It was none of her business, but strangely she wanted to know, if for no other reason than it would confirm all her suspicions about him.

'I'm afraid that will have to remain a secret.'

'I suppose it involves a woman.'

He attempted to laugh again. 'Doesn't everything bad that happens to a man involve a woman, in one way or another?'

It was just as she suspected. 'In that case, you probably got no more than you deserved.' That was a bit harsh, but his smug manner was irritating. He'd been up to no good. That was obvious. And with a woman he should not have been with. He'd taken a beating because of it, and still he acted as if it was all a bit of a lark.

'That's the same thing those men said as they laid into me with their fists and boots.'

'And I don't suppose even that will convince you to change your ways?'

'Never. It will take a lot more than a beating and a stay in a hospital to change the habits of a lifetime.'

Why was she even bothering? If a beating wouldn't change him then he was hardly likely to listen to a lecture from her. Men like him were incorrigible. It didn't matter how many women they hurt, what mayhem they caused— they just went on blithely breaking hearts and destroying lives without a backward glance.

'Are you going to introduce me to this patient?' a voice behind her said.

Emily turned to see that Dr Gideon Pratt had entered

the cubical and was standing just inside the green curtains. She smiled at him in welcome. Gideon was everything she could possibly want in a man and as far removed from the likes of Jackson Wilde as it was possible to get. While Jackson had a reputation as a libertine who spent all his days and nights in pointless pleasure, Gideon was hard working and dedicated to improving the conditions of the less fortunate.

She was so grateful he had come into her life and reminded her that there *were* good men in the world. After her devastating first Season—and the humiliation of falling so hopelessly for that reprobate Randall Cochran—she had thought she would never meet a man she could trust. That was until she met Gideon.

'I didn't realise you were rostered on today,' she said as he approached the bed.

She was always well aware of Gideon's roster and made a point of being on the wards when he was working. She also constantly hoped he would suggest they spend time together on his days off. Something that was yet to happen.

Perhaps that was why he was here, because he was seeking out her company. That could almost be seen as a romantic gesture, something else that Gideon had hitherto not been one to indulge in. Not that she expected it of a man who was both serious and level-headed, but still, it might be nice, just on the odd occasion.

'I'm not rostered on, but I heard that a special patient had been admitted, so I thought it best I come in and offer my services.'

'Yes, you're right,' Emily said, impressed by his dedication. 'There was a rather nasty accident at a local foundry and several men were rushed in with severe burns, but I believe the nursing staff have it under control.'

Gideon tilted his head and nodded it towards the bed.

'Oh, and we've had one man admitted with some relatively minor injuries,' she explained. 'But there's certainly nothing special about him. As soon as there's a bed available he'll be transferred to the ward.'

Gideon gave a small laugh as if she was making a joke, something she certainly was not doing.

'Are you going to introduce me to this patient?' he asked again.

'Why? Shouldn't you try and find the special case you were referring to?'

Gideon actually rolled his eyes at her, as if she was playing some sort of game.

'Oh, I see.' It was apparent that *Jackson Wilde* was the special patient he was referring to, and that *special* label had nothing to do with his medical condition.

Gideon moved closer to the bed and his demeanour as he looked at the Viscount was full of respect and admiration. For a moment Emily wondered if he was impressed because Jackson Wilde was a titled man, then dismissed that as unfair. Gideon was not like that. He had presumably heard a man of substance had been admitted and merely wanted to pay him extra attention, but only in the hope of securing further financing for the hospital. He was always thinking of others.

'It looks like you've been in the wars. How did a man such as yourself end up here?' Gideon asked.

Before Jackson could answer and say something offensive about getting into a brawl over a woman, Emily leapt in. 'He was admitted early this morning. It's obvious he's been in a fight of some kind.'

'Well, you're in the right place,' Gideon said. 'The care you will receive in this hospital will be as good as any you will get anywhere else in London.'

Emily smiled at Gideon. He was right. Gideon *was* a talented doctor, and Emily was constantly heartened to have the affections of such an impressive man. She was also somewhat chastised by her momentary doubt in his inherent goodness. It was shameful that, even for a moment, she had thought him impressed by Jackson Wilde's title. Of course he would be interested in the Viscount, because of the good he could do the hospital. And he was right. She too should be thinking of the financial support he could provide the hospital, rather than lecturing the man on his miscreant behaviour.

'Would you be so kind as to fetch some water, cloths and bandages,' Gideon said, turning to Emily. 'And ask a nurse to come and clean the patient's wounds while I examine him.'

'Matron has already performed an examination and said there's nothing much wrong with him.'

Gideon raised his eyebrows but made no comment.

'Of course, I'll see if I can find an available nurse,' she said, knowing that questioning a doctor was frowned on almost as much as questioning the matron.

'And please inform the nursing staff that we have an important patient who must take priority.' He sent her a smile that suggested he expected her to be in complete agreement.

Emily looked down at Jackson Wilde and wondered whether special treatment would be a waste of effort. Men like Jackson Wilde frittered away their money at the gaming tables or spent it lavishly on chorus girls and actresses. They were not known for being benevolent donors to worthy causes. But if anyone could get this man to change his ways it was Gideon. Even if it was just by setting an example of how a good man behaved.

Chapter Two

Well, well, well. The do-gooder was in love with the doctor.

While it was no concern of Jackson's, watching their courting ritual was at least going to provide him with a much-needed diversion from the pain that was wracking his body.

'I haven't formally introduced myself,' the doctor said, standing stiffly beside the bed and bowing his head. 'I'm Dr Gideon Pratt.'

'I'm pleased to meet you,' Jackson replied, equally formally, and equally ludicrously given the circumstances. 'I'm Jackson Wilde.'

The doctor continued to smile down at him, apparently waiting for more, so Jackson added, 'Viscount Wickford.'

The smile grew wider. 'The eldest son of the Duke of Greenfeld, I believe.'

'The very same.'

'I'm delighted to make your acquaintance and only sorry it is not under better circumstances. But you can rest assured I will inform Matron to treat you with the attention you deserve, and we will endeavour to provide you with as much privacy as possible. Perhaps when you are transferred to the wards the nursing staff can see if a private room is available, and, if not, I will arrange for some screens to surround your bed.'

'Is that usual procedure?'

'No, but we don't usually have men of your stature in this hospital.' He sent Jackson a smile that could best be described as fawning.

'Then I insist you make no special arrangements on my behalf. I'm just pleased that I'm going to get some medical treatment.' At least, I'll be pleased when you stop attempting to ingratiate yourself to me and actually provide said medical treatment.

'That is very gracious of you, my lord,' he said with another bow. 'And I promise you will receive the very best of care. Dare I say it, possibly better than you would get from even the most esteemed physicians.' The smarmy smile turned into a more serious, professional expression, as he finally inspected Jackson's head and neck. 'I believe these injuries are little more than contusions, cuts and scrapes.'

Just as Lady Emily had said, Jackson wanted to add, and just as the matron had observed.

Dr Pratt palpated Jackson's chest and he responded with a loud cry of pain.

'I'm so sorry, my lord, but it does appear you also have a few cracked ribs. Unfortunately, there is not much that can be done, but you will have to remain in the hospital until they start to heal. But once you return to your home, I will be more than happy to continue treating you as your private physician.'

Jackson chose not to respond to that suggestion. 'In the meantime, please do not let me keep you from your other patients,' he said instead. 'Didn't Lady Emily say something about a foundry accident? Perhaps those men need your extra special help as well.'

'A nurse will soon clean up your wounds and bind your ribs,' the doctor continued. 'And, as I say, when you are well enough to be moved home, I am more than willing to accompany you and continue to provide my medical expertise, to you and your family, now, and at any time in the future.'

Once again, Jackson chose to ignore this request, but as the doctor appeared to have no intention of moving from his bedside, he asked a question he really did want an answer to, and it certainly wasn't about anything as boring as his injuries or who would treat them. 'Am I right in assuming you and Lady Emily are more than just colleagues?'

'Yes, Lady Emily and I are courting,' the doctor said, puffing himself up with what looked more like self-importance than admiration for his betrothed. 'She's the daughter of the Duke of Fernwood, you know.'

Jackson nodded. 'The Duke and Duchess must be delighted,' he said, unsure if that would be the case.

The puffing deflated slightly. 'Well, we haven't officially announced our courtship yet, but as Lady Emily is, shall we say, no longer a debutante, they are hardly likely to object.'

Jackson had spent enough time at the gaming tables to know when a man's face shows he is calculating the odds. Dr Pratt would be aware that a duke would want his daughter to marry another titled man, not a doctor, but was apparently hoping her age would mean her parents would be happy to offload their unwed daughter to virtually anyone, including a man with as little status as him.

'So when do you plan to inform them?'

'When the time is right. And I'm sure once we are married her parents will come to see that a marriage to a doctor with a thriving, highly profitable medical practice is an agreeable outcome for all concerned.'

'And you have a highly profitable medical practice, do you?'

'Not yet, but that is my intention, once I have sufficient private patients to set up my own clinic.'

Jackson stifled a sigh. That explained why he had been elevated to the status of a special patient. It wasn't just the usual fawning over an aristocrat. The man was touting for business.

'Does that mean you intend to leave the Hope Charity Hospital once you have established this thriving, highly profitable medical practice?'

'Of course,' the doctor responded with a frown, as if surprised he should even be asked such a question. 'Don't get me wrong, I'm grateful to the hospital. It was thanks to the kind patronage of the hospital board that I was able to undertake my medical training. That is why I work here. I'm bonded until I pay them back for my fees, but obviously I wish to set up on my own, and Lady Emily deserves nothing less than to be the wife of a man who can keep her in the style into which she was born.'

These sounded much more like his ambitions than Lady Emily's. The doctor's calculating expression raised Jackson's suspicions. Was he using Lady Emily to advance his career? Did she know? Did she care?

Lady Emily pushed aside the curtain and came back into the room, now wearing a nurse's apron over her dark blue day dress and carrying a large ceramic bowl, a pile of cloths and several bandages. She placed them on the bedside table and smiled at the doctor.

Their interactions were interesting and diverting, but whatever the true nature of the relationship between the doctor and Lady Emily he had no reason to concern himself with her affairs. She was old enough and certainly assertive enough to not need his help. And if Jackson was foolhardy enough to inform her of his suspicions regarding this Dr Pratt, he was certain his interference would not be welcome.

And surely there were worse men that a woman could marry than one who intended to use his wife as a means to advance his career. A man such as himself, for example. No, he had no need to worry on Lady Emily's account.

'The nurses are busy attending to patients with more serious conditions,' Emily said, drawing Gideon's attention away from the Viscount. 'They said they would get to this patient the moment they had a chance.'

Gideon's eyes grew wide with surprise.

'My apologies, Your Lordship,' he said to the Viscount, causing Emily to swallow a grimace. She knew Gideon was only thinking of the hospital, but she did wish he would not use such a deferential tone of voice. The Viscount's title did not make him the superior man—his behaviour definitely made him inferior to a man as good as Gideon, one who dedicated his time to the care of others. If there was any justice in the world, Jackson Wilde would be deferring to Gideon.

'Then perhaps, on this occasion, you could tend to our patient, Nurse Emily.' Gideon smiled at her as if he had made a joke that would amuse her.

Instead, her teeth gritted together at the condescending way in which he called her Nurse Emily. Gideon knew she would love to be able to train as a nurse, but her parents' objections made that impossible. And the board would never go against the wishes of people of such renown as the Duke and Duchess of Fernwood. Instead she had to help out where she could. But perhaps she should not be so hard on Gideon. He was merely making a joke. Perhaps not the funniest of jokes, but that was of no matter. Gideon had many fine qualities, but an ability to make her laugh was not one of them.

'All you need to do is clean his wounds and tightly bind his ribs,' he explained, despite it being obvious what was required, even to someone with no nursing training.

'Yes, I can do that.' She looked down at Jackson Wilde, who attempted to smile at her and give her another of those salacious winks. Suddenly this did not seem like such a good idea.

'If the patient has no objections, of course,' she said, hoping Jackson Wilde would say yes, he did object. While she loved it when she got the opportunity to help the nursing staff, she would really rather not get that close to this particular patient. `

'No objections whatsoever,' he said. 'Providing Lady Emily does not see doing such a menial task as beneath her.'

'Of course I don't,' she shot back, affronted that he would think she was someone that put herself above the dedicated nurses who worked tirelessly on the wards.

His swollen lips curled as much as they could into a smile, and Emily wondered whether she had walked straight into a trap. It was obvious he enjoyed teasing her. In future she would not rise to the bait.

'Good, I will leave you to it, Nurse Emily,' Gideon said, smiling as if he had once again made a delightful joke. 'And I'll come back and check on our patient once he has been cleaned up.' He bowed to Jackson. 'Goodbye for now, my lord. Goodbye, Nurse Emily.'

Gideon departed. Emily continued to stare at the still waving green curtain, uncomfortably conscious that she was once again alone with Jackson Wilde.

'I don't think the doctor will be getting a job as a vaudevillian comedian anytime soon,' Jackson Wilde said. 'Someone should tell him that if a joke isn't funny the first time, it doesn't get any funnier if you repeat it. Don't you agree, *Nurse Emily*?'

Emily dipped the cloth in the warm water and wrung it out tightly, venting her annoyance at both men on the cloth. 'Dr Pratt is an excellent doctor and you are lucky to have him treating you. You wouldn't find a finer doctor anywhere in London.'

'Yes, so he says.'

Emily was tempted to further take out her annoyance on his head, to give it a firm scrubbing to wash away the blood, but that would be appalling behaviour. Worse than that, she did not want him to see how much his criticism of Gideon affected her. Instead, she lightly dabbed at the wounds, slowly removing the encrusted blood.

'So, you and the doctor?' he said, causing her hand to still momentarily.

'I don't know what you are talking about.'

'You seem to have a mutual appreciation for each other.'

'Yes, I admire the doctor immensely,' she said, wringing out the cloth and turning the water pink.

'Perhaps one day he will be one of London's most prominent physicians with a thriving medical practice treating the great and good of the city,' Jackson said, a slight note of derision in his voice.

'Gideon—Dr Pratt is not like that,' she fired back. 'He is a man dedicated to caring for the poor and the needy, not the rich and the privileged. He is a man of high principles. That's something I suppose you would not understand.'

'No, it certainly is not something I understand. I just hope that you do.'

She paused, the flannel suspended above his head, wondering what he meant by that. Deciding it was of no importance she continued cleaning his wounds. He was merely playing a game with her for his own amusement, and she would not let him question her faith in Gideon. He was a good man. Unlike the men she met during the Season, unlike Randall Cochran, that dissolute scoundrel she had once had the misfortune to think herself in love with, and unlike the Viscount. They were all men who cared nothing for anyone else but themselves.

'So do your parents approve—'

'I haven't introduced him yet, but I'm sure they will see just what a wonderful man he is once they get to know him.'

'I was actually going to say, do your parents approve of you working in a charity hospital?'

'Oh.' She dabbed gently at a cut above his eye, annoyed that she had revealed so much. 'Well, they didn't approve at first, but when I informed them that the Queen's daughter, Princess Alice, had been interested in nursing and had been a good friend of Florence Nightingale, and Princess Helena did charity work for the British Nurses Association and the Red Cross, they reluctantly gave their approval. As

I kept reminding them, if it's good enough for Queen Victoria's daughters, surely it's good enough for the daughter of the Duke of Fernwood.'

'Although I suspect the good Queen's daughters are still expected to attend social occasions. I don't believe I've seen you at any balls since your first Season.'

'No, and you won't be seeing me at any more if I can help it.' She bit her lip as if to take those words back. 'I didn't mean I would be avoiding you. I just meant that I would rather not attend any more balls.'

'I took no offence. So, you prefer these, shall we say, somewhat grim surroundings to the glitter of chandeliers and parquet floors?'

He looked around the small cubical, and she could imagine what the stark surroundings looked like through his eyes. She took in the plain, cast-iron bedframe and the white sheets that had been repeatedly boiled until they were threadbare. She was suddenly unable to ignore the strong tar odour of the carbolic soap used to scrub down all surfaces.

She frowned at the apparent criticism. 'Yes, I do,' she stated emphatically.

The hospital might be a bit grim, but it was somewhere she felt she belonged. From the moment she had entered the ballroom, for the first event of her first Season, Emily had known she would never truly fit in. The conversations were superficial, the titled people she mixed with were so self-important, and the other young ladies had made fun of her because she was so hopeless at the required flirtatious behaviour.

And then she had met Randall Cochran and everything had changed. He was so handsome, so charming, and she had loved the attention he had shown her. She had even thought herself in love with him. Until she discovered exactly what sort of man he was.

Her chest tightened and that familiar sense of dizziness swept over her as she remembered that humiliating overheard conversation. She'd gone searching for Randall, knowing he was in the card room, but hoping to lure him back to the ball room for yet another dance.

'So much for your boasting. You haven't even kissed Lady Emily yet,' a friend of Randall's had said, stopping Emily in her tracks.

'The Season is still young,' Randall had responded. *'The silly chit is already falling in love with me, fluttering those big doe eyes at me every chance she gets. All I have to do is play with her a little longer, charm her, flatter her, and before long I'll have her begging me for it.'*

'And then you'll be forced to marry her,' his friend had said.

'That fate hasn't befallen me yet. That's the beauty of this plan,' Randall had said. *'I get to take the wench, then I make the family pay me to keep it a secret that I've ruined her.'* He'd laughed loudly. *'Most men have to pay an enormous sum for a virgin. Whereas I'll get a willing virgin for free, and even come out of it all the richer.'*

This had elicited much laughter and back-slapping among his friends, and had sent Emily scurrying back down the corridor. It had all been too humiliating. He had been right. She *had* thought she was falling in love with him, *had* relished every one of his compliments—had even fantasised about him kissing her and caressing her. She had arrogantly considered herself an intelligent woman, but had been revealed to be a gullible half-wit, more naïve than the most credulous debutante, one who is completely susceptible to the charms of a seducer.

After that awakening, she had avoided being in Society whenever she could, and had dedicated herself even further to charity work. And would continue to do so. Discovering the man she thought she loved was a debauched liar had also made her swear off all men. But then she met Gideon, a man she could trust, and with whom she could be content.

'I most certainly prefer these surroundings to even the grandest of ballrooms,' she added, determined not to feel any shame over what had happened between her and Randall Cochran. She had done nothing wrong. It was the rakes of this world who should be ashamed, but she knew they never would be.

He nodded slowly, watching her carefully as she tended his wounds. 'I can't say ballrooms are my favourite place either,' he said gently.

He watched her for a moment. 'You're very good at this. Do you have aspirations of training to become a nurse?'

She looked into his eyes to see if he was teasing, but could see no sign of it.

'Sadly no. While my parents see charitable work as acceptable for a woman of my background, they would never countenance me taking paid employment. I help out on the wards whenever I can but the board members have also made it clear they would prefer it if I focus more on administration work, fundraising, that sort of thing. Activities they consider much more ladylike.'

She looked towards the door, not wanting to mention that nurses were expected to resign if they married. That was something both her mother and Gideon had pointed out to her, but to inform Jackson Wilde of this unfortunate fact would only lead to more questioning about her relationship with Gideon.

'Well, you would make an excellent nurse.'

She could detect no condescension in his voice, but once again she scrutinised his expression for a sign of amusement. 'Thank you,' she finally said, finding no such look.

'So you believe your parents will be happy for you to marry a doctor?'

Emily chose not to answer but to continue with her work, aware that he was watching her carefully. It was not a subject she wished to discuss, and she could not see why it would be of interest to him. Boredom probably.

And she certainly was not going to tell him that Gideon was yet to formally ask for her hand.

'It's quite obvious the doctor is entranced. I'm sure it won't be long before he's down on bended knee, declaring his undying love.'

Once again she chose not to respond. A man like Jackson Wilde would never understand her relationship with Gideon. It was not one based on silly, intangible concepts like love and romance. They had a meeting of minds. They both wanted the same things from life, and she had immense respect for him. That was a much better foundation for a successful marriage than passion and romance ever could be. Wasn't it?

'And once you're married you can continue your life of service to the poor and the needy,' Jackson said, his words suddenly dripping with sarcasm.

She stopped her work and glared at him. 'I don't know why you're being so cynical. I am proud of the work I do at the hospital and proud of Gideon—Dr Pratt. He works long hours at this hospital and is dedicated to providing the highest level of care to his patients.'

'Yes, I've noticed he's been dedicating himself greatly to my care since I was admitted, although I don't believe he's spending quite so much time with the other patients.'

'That's because he's not rostered on today,' she shot back, outraged that he would dare to criticise a man as honourable as Gideon. 'And, well, if you must know, he's hoping you will make a generous donation to the hospital, which will help other people in need who can't afford treatment.'

'There's no denying the man is a saint,' he said.

'Well, compared to some men who think only of themselves and having a good time, yes, he is a saint.'

She expected him to be chastened by her outrage, but he merely continued watching her, assessing her. 'And does the good doctor expect you to continue working here after you're married? Has he told you of his plans for the future?'

'We haven't actually discussed that in any detail, but yes, it is what we both want.'

'Perhaps it is a discussion you should have before you tie the knot, so you are certain you both want to spend your lives working side by side, making the world a better place, curing the sick, helping the needy and all that. You wouldn't want to find yourself married to a man who, say, wants to become rich and successful, tending the wealthy, while his wife stays at home doing whatever it is wives do when they stay at home.'

'Don't be ridiculous,' she fired at him, shocked that he should be trying to plant doubts in her mind about Gideon. 'And who are you to give marriage advice?'

He nodded his head slightly. 'Quite right, Lady Emily, I'm sure you know exactly what you're doing.'

She squeezed out the cloth, wringing out the last of the pink liquid.

'I need to change this water,' she said, picking up the bowl and carrying it out of the ward, fighting to calm herself after that strange, unsettling exchange. Jackson Wilde had tried unnerving her by flirting. Now he was trying another tack, questioning her relationship with Gideon. It was all just mischief-making for his own entertainment. Gideon was a good man. He would make an excellent husband. His dedication was as unquestionable as her own. Jackson Wilde was merely riled at being in the company of a man who was in every way his superior, that was all.

Repeating these words to herself she rushed down the hall, emptied the bowl in the deep concrete sink in the sluice room, pumped out some fresh water and put it on the stove. Watching the water boil she continued to mentally repeat all the things she wanted to say to Jackson Wilde, about how wrong he was, how men like him knew nothing of women like her, or men like Gideon. They were merely wealthy wastrels and she would not let him get under her skin.

Once the water had boiled, and her own mood had cooled down, she picked up some clean cloths and towels and returned to the ward. She gave him her most professional smile, letting him know that she was completely under control, then placed the bowl on the bedside table, sat down and observed her work.

'That looks good, and I don't believe you're going to require sutures,' she said, taking in his skin, which was now free from blood but covered in an array of multicoloured bruises.

'Right, I'm now going to have to remove your jacket and

'shirt so I can bind your ribs,' she said, keeping her voice as impassive as possible.

'I'm more than happy for you to undress me.'

She frowned at him, letting him know she would tolerate no more nonsense from him.

'Sorry,' he said with a light laugh. 'You've already told me not to flirt with the nursing staff. But it's what I do in the company of pretty women. I'm afraid I just can't help myself.'

She frowned again, making it clear his flirting and false flattery had no effect on her whatsoever.

She carefully edged his jacket off his shoulders, undid the buttons of his formal white shirt, which was covered in mud and blood. She then slowly slid it off his shoulders and down his arms, taking care not to cause him any discomfort, while fighting to ignore any discomfort of her own.

His chest and back were as bloody and bruised as the rest of him, but even in that state it was impossible to ignore the breadth of his shoulders, the athletic muscles of his chest or the line of dark hairs on the hard ridges of his stomach. Despite his dissolute lifestyle, his physique suggested he also spent time in more physical pursuits—boxing perhaps, or horse riding.

She swallowed, realising that she was staring. What on earth was wrong with her? This was appalling. She should be focusing on tending to his bruises and cuts, not admiring his chest, not speculating on how he got such powerful muscles. And she most certainly should not be thinking about the ultimate destination of that line of dark hairs.

Once more she rang out the cloth, as if trying to wring out her inappropriate thoughts, and took the time to regain her composure. Turning back to him, she adopted the required professional detachment as she gently ran the flannel over his chest, removing the dried blood. She would focus on the job at hand. She would not think about the feel of his muscles under the stroking cloth, nor would she compare them to iron covered in soft leather, and she certainly would not wonder what his naked skin would feel like without the barrier of a damp cloth.

Damn it all, despite her resolve, she knew she was blushing, and that the heat was not confined to her face. With each stroke of her flannel, her body burned hotter, her heartbeat pounded faster, breathing became increasingly difficult.

She had assisted nurses before in cleaning up patients, but never had touching a man caused her to react in this manner. It was all too humiliating, and she just knew that the effect he was having on her would not be lost on the Viscount.

She flicked a glance up to his face, expecting to see a mocking leer, but his expression was far from derisive. Even with his eyes swollen, she could see the intensity in his gaze. It was a look every bit as unsettling as the feel of his chest under her touch.

She swallowed and lowered her gaze.

'That's got you cleaned up,' she said, trying to adopt the brisk, efficient but cheerful tone the nurses used with their patients. Unfortunately, the quivering in her voice sounded neither brisk nor efficient, and certainly not cheerful.

'I'm going to have to bind your chest in bandages now,' she said, wishing it was not so, but unable to think of any way out of this situation that would not make her feel more uncomfortable than she already did.

Not speaking, he merely nodded. It might have been better if he had made some silly, flirtatious quip. A joke, even an inappropriate one, would be far preferable to the way he was looking at her now. A strange feeling shimmered through her as his gaze held hers. It was unlike anything she had felt before—unsettling but strangely exciting.

She blinked rapidly and looked away, trying to regain control of the situation and her absurd reaction. He was merely a patient who needed her care.

'You'll need to sit up so I can wind the bandages around your back,' she said, annoyed that the quivering note in her voice was getting worse.

He did as she asked. Drawing in a slow, steadying breath, she placed the bandage on his chest, leaned over him and rolled it across his front and around his back. Damn it all, this felt even more intimate than stroking his chest with a cloth, but there was no way to complete the task without her body coming dangerously close to his.

She drew in a steadying breath, inadvertently inhaling his intoxicating scent. What was it? Sandalwood, and something else. Something decidedly manly, leather perhaps. Whatever it was, it was causing unsettling reactions deep in her body, as if her heart wasn't just pounding in her chest but had taken her over.

You don't even like this man, Emily reminded herself as her inner arm inadvertently brushed against his naked shoulder. *He's everything you despise in a man. Selfish, frivolous and dissolute. He's a womaniser who cares for nothing and no one.*

Forcing herself to focus on the action of tightly binding his chest, she tried to drive all other thoughts out of her mind. She would not think of the touch of his skin, the hardness of his muscles or the way his warm breath gently caressed her neck as she moved in even closer towards him.

'How's the patient doing?'

Emily jumped back at the sound of Gideon's hearty voice behind her, the bandage falling from her fingers.

She had not heard him come into the cubical. The heat on her cheeks burned hotter, as if she had been caught doing something shameful. But she had nothing to be ashamed of. All she was doing was tending to a patient, just as Gideon had asked.

Jackson Wilde's eyes left hers and he looked up at the doctor. 'The nurse is doing an excellent job,' he said, his husky voice presumably the result of her touching his injuries.

'Very good,' Gideon said, still in that hearty manner. 'Let me just inspect your work.'

Gideon leant over her and looked at the bandages, thankfully oblivious to her burning cheeks and awkward manner.

'I'll just finish this off, shall I?' With brisk efficiency he wound the last of the bandage around Jackson Wilde's chest and fixed it in place.

'Excellent job, Nurse Emily,' Gideon said, causing Emily's shame to intensify. He was such a good man, so much better than Jackson Wilde. She should not disparage him just because he was once again making a silly joke that no one laughed at. She sent a castigating frown at Jackson Wilde, so he would know that if he was going to make fun of Gideon she would not countenance it. But he said nothing, merely continued to watch her in that disconcerting manner.

'Right, all that's needed now is for you to get changed into pyjamas and we can put you on the ward,' Gideon said, turning to Emily.

Her stomach clenched and fire burned hotter on her cheeks. She picked up the basin, put it down—gathered up the cloths, put them down—put the cloths into the basin, picked it up.

'I'll just clear this away, and see if I can find someone to help...help do that,' she mumbled, pointing a shaking finger at Jackson Wilde, before turning and rushing out of the cubical.

Once the curtains closed behind her, she paused, shut her eyes briefly and drew in a deep, slow breath. She did not know what had just happened, but it must never happen again. Gideon was the man she wanted to marry. She was not attracted to Jackson Wilde. He was exactly the sort of man she could never be attracted to. She had shown herself up once before over a charming degenerate. It was a mistake she would never make again.

Repeating those commands to herself like a protective prayer, she stood up straighter, then walked briskly down the hallway in her most professional, no-nonsense manner. She was determined to forget all about what had just happened, even though she was unsure exactly what it *was* that had just happened.

Chapter Three

~~~~~~~~~~~~~~~~

Jackson had no doubts about what had just happened, but the question foremost in his mind was *why* it had happened. Yes, she was an attractive woman, and yes, she had come intimately close to him, but it was Lady Emily Beaumont for God's sake. Emily 'Do-gooding Moralising' Beaumont. He was not and never would be attracted to a woman such as her. She was everything he avoided—uptight, reproachful and judgemental. And she wouldn't even know the meaning of the word fun, never mind how to have any.

In every conceivable way she was not the sort of woman he had the slightest bit of interest in. The women he liked had a touch of wildness to them. They were women who loved to indulge themselves, who lived for a good time. If he wanted to be with someone whose greatest satisfaction came from lecturing him on his dissolute ways, all he had to do was spend some time in his father's company.

And yet, when she touched him, even through the thickness of a flannel cloth, a strong wave of desire had consumed him. He had wanted her, desperately. Even now he could feel the touch of her gentle stroking hand on his body, smell her enticing natural feminine scent, one unadorned by any artificial perfumes.

It was ridiculous. He must have taken a worse beating

to the head than he had previously realised. He did *not* want Lady Emily Beaumont. And even if he did, which he didn't, he couldn't have her. She was one of those untouchable women who had to save themselves for marriage.

He looked up at the doctor who was prattling on about something, probably himself and what a brilliant physician he was. This was the man she hoped to marry. This was the man she was saving herself for. This cold fish. What a waste. The man was so full of himself he hadn't even noticed what should have been immediately apparent. If he cared as much about Lady Emily as he did about ingratiating himself to Jackson, he would have noticed the obvious signs in his beloved's appearance when he arrived. He would have seen how her cheeks were flushed a bright pink, how her breath was coming in short gasps, how she was unable to make eye contact with the man she professed to want to marry.

This buffoon, who couldn't even see what was right in front of his face, was the one who would take her to his bed on their wedding night, the man who would undress her, would caress and kiss that lovely body, who would—

Jackson released a low grown.

'What is it, my lord?' the doctor said, his face etched with concern. 'Is the pain too great to bear? Do you require laudanum?' He rushed to the curtains and yanked them apart. 'Nurse, laudanum, now,' he shouted down the corridor.

'I don't need laudanum and I don't want it,' Jackson called out. The powerful drug would probably quench his improper desires, which under the circumstances made the offer tempting, but he did not want his brain muddled. He had seen the damage laudanum did, and it was one of the few vices he was determined not to indulge in.

'Are you sure, my lord? There is no need for you to suffer any unnecessary pain.'

If the doctor knew the thoughts that had been going through Jackson's head when Lady Emily had been ministering to him, he was sure he'd be wanting to inflict as much pain on his patient as he possibly could. But, thankfully, the doctor was too blind or too brainless to see what should have been obvious to any man in love.

'Yes, I'm sure. I'm not in any undue pain.'

A nurse came in, carrying a vial of the dreaded drug.

'The patient says he does not need pain relief,' the doctor said, halting the nurse's progress. 'But while you are here you can change him into his pyjamas so he can be admitted to the ward, and please inform Matron that he will require screening from the other patients.'

'Please inform Matron of no such thing,' Jackson interrupted. 'I insist that I be treated exactly like all your other patients.'

'In that case, Matron requires me to help with the men from the foundry,' the nurse said, then caught the doctor's expression. 'But first I'll get the pyjamas.'

She bustled off, and the doctor returned to smiling at Jackson. 'I'll see you again when you are on the ward and we can continue this conversation,' he said, with a bow of his head, before departing.

Jackson had no idea what they had actually been talking about, and had no desire to see the doctor again, but he remained grateful that the man was neither a mind-reader nor particularly perceptive. He could only hope he remained that way.

* * *

Emily emptied the bowl and watched the pink water swirl down the drain. This would not do. Her behaviour was ridiculous. Jackson Wilde meant nothing to her. Nothing. Gideon was the man she cared for.

Despite knowing this, she could make no sense of the effect he had on her, but it was over now, and she would waste no more time thinking of it. He would soon be transferred to the wards. He would be under the care of the nurses and she would not need to see him again.

'I hope I didn't upset you,' Gideon said as he entered the room. 'I forgot myself when I suggested that you help the patient change into his pyjamas. It is something for a nurse to do, not a lady of your delicate sensibilities.'

Emily tensed. She could say that she was not delicate, that she was more than capable of carrying out all the jobs performed by the nurses, but she had just proven that to be incorrect. Although she was sure, if it had been any man other than Jackson Wilde, she would not have flinched. But she could hardly say that to Gideon.

'You'll be pleased to know a nurse has taken over and the Viscount will soon be on the ward.'

Emily forced herself to smile. 'That's good, I'm sure he will get excellent care from the nurses.'

'That is what I wish to talk to you about. I have informed the Viscount that I will be providing him with personal care, and I would like you to tend to his needs when I am absent.'

Emily's eyes grew wide. 'Why?' That one word held so many questions, all of which seemed to be whirling around in Emily's mind, making her confused and somewhat lightheaded.

'He is an important patient,' Gideon said, frowning at her, as if such things should not need explaining. 'We need to make a good impression on him. He could be so helpful for our future.'

Emily was unsure if that was the case. Jackson Wilde might donate to the hospital, and possibly even become a patron, but there was no guarantee.

'Don't worry, Emily,' he said, patting her arm. 'I won't be expecting you to undertake any nursing duties. Just keep an eye on him and let me know if his condition changes so I can attend him immediately.'

She continued to stare at him in bafflement.

'All you'll be required to do is talk to him, provide him with an enjoyable diversion while he's here. Perhaps you can read to him on occasion.'

Her already wide eyes grew wider. 'Divert him? Read to him?'

'Yes,' he said, seemingly unaware that the prospect of doing such a thing horrified her.

'And remember, if his condition does change, contact me immediately. Even if I'm not on the ward, send word for me rather than calling for one of the other doctors.'

She looked to him for further explanation. He said nothing, as if no explanation was required.

'Why?' she repeated, as it was seemingly the only word she was capable of forming.

He smiled as if sharing a private joke. 'Let's just say it will be better if he receives care from the same physician. It will be better for the long-term outlook of the patient.'

Emily could not understand his argument. Surely if any patient needed immediate medical attention the nearest doctor would be the best one to summon, but she knew

Gideon always had his patients' best interests at heart, so she did not question this request.

'Right, I'll wish you *adieu*,' he said. 'And remember, contact me if there are any problems with our important patient.'

Emily nodded. On the wards she knew she should do as the doctors requested, but she would not be following that particular command. She would not be providing Jackson Wilde with a diversion. She most certainly would not be reading to him. And if there was any change in his condition, the nurses would be perfectly capable of coping with it. It would be up to them whether they contacted Gideon, or did what is normal procedure and alerted the nearest doctor.

She hated that she would be going against Gideon's wishes, but what option did she have? For some unfathomable reason, Jackson Wilde unsettled her unlike any man had ever done before. She would never be able to explain this to Gideon. It was something she couldn't even explain to herself, but under the circumstances it would make sense to have as little to do with Jackson Wilde as possible.

Emily was still leaning against the sink, contemplating this unsettling situation, when a young woman entered the sluice room looking somewhat lost.

'I'm afraid the public are not supposed to be in here,' Emily said.

'I know, I'm sorry, but can you help me? I've gone and got meself lost.'

'Of course,' Emily said, escorting the young lady back into the corridor. 'Who are you looking for?'

'I don't know his name, but last night some friends of mine brought in a gentleman who had taken a right beating. He was in ever such a bad way.' She lifted up a battered hat, the rim torn, the crown squashed. 'This here is his topper. I want to return it to him, and, you know, make sure he's all right after what happened.'

Emily stiffened. She knew exactly to whom this young woman was referring. There was only one such patient that fitted that description.

'Were you present when it happened?' Emily asked, curiosity getting the better of her.

'Yes, you could say it was my fault and I feel ever so awful about it.'

A strange sense of satisfaction washed over Emily. She was right about him. He was a man beneath contempt. He was just another wealthy man who came down to the East End in search of a woman desperate for money. It was appalling, and it proved Jackson Wilde was even more despicable than she had previously thought.

Emily clung onto her disapproval with something akin to pleasure. Disapproving of Jackson Wilde was so much safer than any of the other turbulent reactions she was having to him.

'I'll take you to him.' Emily knew she could just as easily give the young woman directions to the ward, but she was curious to see Jackson Wilde's reaction when he was confronted with his night-time misbehaviour in the cold light of day.

They entered the ward, where men dressed in identical blue and white striped pyjamas were either sitting up or lying down on the rows of white, cast-iron beds. A few nurses, dressed in their black and white uniforms with white head-covering, were moving from bed to bed, administering to the patients.

They approached Jackson Wilde's bed at the end of the ward. He too was dressed in the same striped, well-worn pyjamas, and the sight of a viscount in such humble clothing was somewhat incongruous, and strangely satisfying.

He attempted to lift himself up to a seated position and tried to smile at his visitors, his strained expression showing both actions were causing him pain.

'The doctor said you are to remain perfectly still while your ribs heal,' Emily commanded. 'You have a visitor.'

She stood back to watch his discomfort. There was not the slightest spark of recognition as the young woman approached the bed. Typical. Men like him used women like her, then returned to their own privileged lives without a backward glance.

'Oh, your poor face,' the young woman said, leaning over him and lightly stroking his cheek. 'I'm Kitty. We didn't have time for no formal introduction last night, what with everything that was happening,' she added with more compassion than he could possibly deserve.

'I'm Jackson Wilde, and I'm very pleased to see that you are looking so well. I was worried about you, Kitty.'

She smiled at him as if he had just bestowed a blessing upon her, and Emily was unable to suppress a rebuking tut.

'Jackson,' Kitty said, her voice soft. 'That's such a lovely name.'

Emily sighed with exasperation. Did this man cast a spell over every woman he encountered? And couldn't women see what sort of man he really was? Thank goodness she was witnessing this exchange. If nothing else, it had brought her back to the reality of the man's true character.

For one, brief, irrational moment she too had almost

succumbed to his charms, but never again. And in the unlikely event she did start to fall for his magic, she would only have to remember this encounter with Kitty to pull herself back from that particular precipice.

'It's just a shame all my customers aren't as much of a gentleman as you,' Kitty continued to coo. 'It would make my life a whole lot easier.'

Emily crossed her arms, her jaw tensing as her teeth clenched tightly together. This conversation was unbelievable, and Jackson Wilde was lapping up the attention as if he was actually a man worthy of adulation.

If she needed any further confirmation on the type of man Jackson Wilde was, which she didn't, Kitty had just provided it. He was indeed a man so base he visited the poverty-stricken prostitutes of the East End to satisfy his craven desires. The depths to which he was capable of sinking was beneath contempt.

Kitty gently stroked that awful man's face again. 'If there's anything I can ever do for you, you know you only have to ask, and I mean anything,' she said with a wink. 'And of course, for you, it will always be free of charge.'

'That's a very kind and generous offer,' his said, his swollen lips moving into what appeared to be a smile. 'But as you can see, I'll be out of action for quite some time.'

'Oh, I don't know. I've had customers in worst condition than you and I've always found ways of giving them satisfaction.' She gave a small laugh. 'But I'll leave you now to get better. When you get out of here, remember— if you want me, just ask on the street for Pretty Kitty, everyone knows me by that name.'

'Pretty Kitty. I will remember and it's a name that suits you perfectly.'

Kitty gave a small, coquettish giggle while Emily shook her head slowly, hardly able to believe the exchange she was witnessing.

'Oh, and here's your topper,' Kitty said, placing the battered top hat she had been clasping in her hands on the bedside cabinet. 'It took a bit of a beating as well.' Then she placed a light kiss on his forehead, careful to avoid the bruises and cuts. 'I'll leave you in this lady's care, but don't forget, when you get out, ask for Pretty Kitty.'

'I won't forget.' He looked up at Emily. 'And if I do, I'm sure Nurse Emily will remember everything we've just said.'

Emily bit down her censorious *hmph*.

'I'll show you out, Kitty,' she said instead.

Once again this was unnecessary, as she was sure Kitty could find her own way out of the hospital, but Emily wanted to let this young woman know she owed Jackson Wilde nothing. If he was degenerate enough to come to the East End in search of women, then a beating was the least he deserved.

'He's such a gentleman,' Kitty said as they walked down the corridor.

Emily merely *hmphed* in response.

'I dare say he saved my life, and I feel so bad about it.'

Emily stopped walking. 'Saved your life? What do you mean?'

'Well, I was set upon by this group of toffs.' Kitty shuddered slightly. 'I should have known better than to go with them. They had that look in their eyes, the one punters get before something bad happens. But I needed the money ever so desperately, so I ignored all the warnings and it didn't take long for things to turn nasty.'

Kitty grimaced, then smiled and pointed back at the ward. 'And then Jackson appeared like a white knight on his charger. Except of course he was running, not on a horse, but he was straight into the fray without a thought for his own safety.'

She beamed a smile at Emily, then frowned. 'I ran off, just like he said for me to do. I was ever so scared. But I came back later with some men from the boarding house where I live. We followed the blood trail and found him in a terrible state. The men brought him in here and I was ever so worried he wouldn't make it. But he looks right chipper today, doesn't he?'

Emily almost wished she had not heard this story. It was so much easier to see Jackson Wilde as the villain not the hero.

'I'm very pleased that you are all right,' Emily said, not wanting to talk about Jackson Wilde any more. 'It must have been a terrible ordeal for you.'

'I'm all right, thanks to him. I just wish there was something more I could do for him than just offer my services for free, but I can't afford no flowers or nothing.' She looked at Emily and blushed slightly. 'Sorry, Nurse.'

'You have nothing to apologise for,' Emily said. She had been involved in the Hope Charity Hospital for long enough to know the desperate circumstances of women like Kitty, and what drove them to this particular work.

'Although in his case it won't be no hardship to offer my services,' Kitty added with a laugh. Seeing Emily's frown, she pulled her face into a more serious expression. 'You will treat him really special, won't you?' she pleaded.

It was the second person today who had made that request, and neither knew just how much they were asking of Emily. 'Yes, he will get the best possible treatment from everyone at the hospital.'

Satisfied with Emily's answer, Kitty said goodbye, leaving Emily to wonder whether she owed an apology to Jackson Wilde.

Chapter Four

Jackson lay back in the bed, smiling to himself, as Lady Emily approached. He shouldn't take such pleasure in shocking her, but how could he help it? It was what he did best. He'd spent most of his life shocking his father, so such behaviour came naturally to him. And when it came to holier-than-thou types like his father and Lady Emily, he really didn't have to try terribly hard to cause their mouths to curl down in disdain, or their nostrils to flair as if assaulted by an offensive smell.

And that was precisely how Lady Emily had looked at him when hearing of his involvement with Pretty Kitty.

'Have my night-time antics appalled you?' he said once she reached his bed. 'Has my dalliance with Pretty Kitty caused your low opinion of me to descend to even greater depths?'

He waited in anticipation for the inevitable lecture. After many years of being berated by his father, there were few insults or rants about his scurrilous behaviour that riled him, but a telling-off from Lady Emily was likely to be an interesting experience. He was certain she would look simply divine when fired up with self-righteous indignation.

'She told me what happened.' Her ramrod posture and

the downward curl of her lips did not suggest that Kitty's revelation had done anything to improve her opinion of him.

He raised his eyebrows, or at least attempted to, facial movements having become somewhat of a trial. 'I hope she didn't go into too much detail, and, if she did, I hope she praised my performance, deserving or otherwise.'

'She did praise you.'

'Well, I always like to leave the ladies satisfied.'

This comment was rewarded with a delightful blush colouring her cheeks.

'Why did you lead me to believe that you were one of Kitty's clients? And why are you doing so now?'

He attempted to smile at her. He would not apologise for any misunderstanding. She was the one who was so quick to judge and condemn him. Usually she'd be justified in doing so. Fortunately, or unfortunately, in this particular case, he had, for once, done nothing wrong.

'I don't believe I led you anywhere, you went there all by yourself. And as for continuing to do so, well, you wouldn't deny a sick man some entertainment, would you?'

'I am not here for your entertainment.'

'That is a pity. I could do with a bit of a diversion. Perhaps we should call Pretty Kitty back.'

'Stop this now,' she said, her loud voice drawing the attention of the men in the neighbouring beds. 'Stop this,' she repeated, lowering her voice. 'I am sorry I judged you unfairly, but, well, given your reputation you can hardly blame me.'

'You're right, the fault is all mine.'

'I didn't say that. I just mean, well, a lot of men like you do come down to the East End looking for women like Kitty. And those men care not one fig for those women or the desperate circumstances that have led them into that life. Those women often have children to feed, a slumlord demanding rent, debts to money lenders that have to be paid. And their customers are often men who live comfortable lives and could easily free these women from the terrible circumstances in which they find themselves. But they don't. Do they? Instead, they use them to relieve their carnal needs.'

She continued to glare down at him as if expecting him to argue, but she would get no argument from him. He agreed with everything she said, and he hoped that Kitty did find a way out of her unfortunate circumstances. And perhaps Lady Emily was right. Despite his father's disdain for him, the old Duke did provide Jackson with a generous allowance, one that he usually squandered at the gaming tables and on various other forms of entertainment. There was nothing to stop him from contacting Kitty when he left the hospital. Not to claim his reward, but to help her so she, and perhaps all the other women like her, was never placed in such a precarious position again.

'Thank you, Lady Emily, for that enlightening lecture. I'm assuming that moral guidance is provided free of charge, along with the medical treatment.'

'I'm just explaining to you why I was so incensed when I thought you were Kitty's client.' She narrowed her eyes at him, and he suppressed a smile, knowing that yet another blast of moral indignation was coming his way. 'So, what were you doing in the East End if you weren't, you know.' She shrugged, her cheeks turning a slightly darker shade of pink.

'Seeking out female company to relieve my base carnal needs?'

'Yes,' she said, her cheeks darkening further until she resembled a rather pretty beetroot.

'I was lost and, shall we say, slightly under the weather.'

'You were drunk.'

He smiled at the satisfaction evident in her voice, and waited for the next lecture he could see she was itching to give.

'Drunk might be going a bit far, but let's just say I had imbibed a little bit more than was sensible and it had caused me to become somewhat disorientated.'

Her demeanour became amusingly indignant. 'I believe you are splitting hairs. Drunk means you had imbibed too much.'

'Perhaps. But if I hadn't, I wouldn't have got lost and I wouldn't have stumbled across Pretty Kitty and her attackers. So, you could say, in this instance, the demon drink turned me into Pretty Kitty's guardian angel, and I should be encouraged to drink as much and as frequently as possible so I can continue to perform such good works.'

'Your lack of logic is staggering.' She huffed out a sigh, lifted her head and looked straight ahead, as if seeing something of interest on the wall behind his bed. 'But you are right. Kitty was lucky you saved her, and—' she paused '—and I am sorry I jumped to conclusions and judged you so harshly.'

'You've nothing to apologise for. I've been judged harshly before, but never by anyone who looked so delightful when they frowned at me.'

As expected, her lips turned down and her eyebrows drew closer together.

'There it is again, that lovely frown.'

The frown grew deeper and he waited for another lecture on not flirting with the nursing staff. But, instead, she forced her face into an uninterested expression.

'As you are going to be here for a few days, is there anyone you would like me to contact? Your father, or some other relative?'

It was Jackson's turn to frown. While being lectured by Lady Emily was amusing, there was nothing amusing about being castigated by that tyrant. While he was immobilised in this bed he would prove far too easy a target for his father's venom. 'No, I think I will use this time alone for some quiet contemplation.'

'But won't your family and friends be worried?'

'They will all assume, like you, that I have found some female company to while away my frivolous time.'

Her lips pursed tightly together. 'I didn't—' She stopped abruptly. 'Well, hopefully you'll soon be completely better and back to…doing whatever it is you do.'

'Doing whatever you assume I do.'

'Hmm,' was the only response she gave.

Jackson's attention was drawn to the man approaching from the end of the ward—he stifled a groan. 'Oh, look,' he said, not bothering to disguise his irritation, 'it's the good doctor. Again.'

She turned to face the sanctimonious doctor and, to his immense annoyance, sent him a delighted smile. What on earth did she see in that prig? Perhaps it was exactly that. Do-gooders were presumably attracted to sanctimonious prigs.

'How is my patient doing now?' he asked, smiling in that now familiar self-satisfied manner.

Much the same as I was when you asked me an hour or so ago, Jackson wanted to say.

'Excellent. I certainly can't complain about the level of care I'm receiving,' he said instead.

The doctor beamed at Lady Emily. 'Yes, I informed Nurse Emily to provide you with extra special personal attention,' he responded, laughing at the repetition of his little joke. His very little joke, a joke that was getting smaller and smaller every time he made it.

Jackson watched with satisfaction as Lady Emily's smile became tense.

'And there is nothing I like more than some extra special personal attention from a lovely young lady,' Jackson added, unable to stop himself from teasing. 'Especially when she offers it so freely.'

The doctor smiled at him as if he had been the one to receive the compliment, although it was apparent his innuendo was not missed on Lady Emily. She was now doing an impression of someone who would rather be anywhere other than standing uncomfortably beside his bed.

'Well, I'll leave you to consult with the patient,' the blushing Lady Emily said before quickly walking away.

Jackson wanted to call out to her, *Please, do not leave me alone with your beau*. There were only so many times he could listen to the doctor telling him what an excellent physician he was. If he was told one more time that Dr Pratt should be treating Jackson's entire family, extending out to the most distant cousin and every titled person of his acquaintance, he would explode and inform the doctor in no uncertain terms that he'd rather take his chances with the least experienced of quacks rather than put up with his fawning presence for a moment longer.

'I'm afraid I am rather tired,' he said instead, doing his

best impression of a waning patient. 'I think I'd like to rest now.'

'Of course, of course, my lord,' the doctor said, backing away from the bed. 'I'll leave you for now and will be back to check on you later.'

Rather than respond, Jackson closed his eyes, and didn't open them again until he was sure he was alone.

Chapter Five

Jackson Wilde remained on the ward for another month, until the doctor declared he was fit to be moved and could return to his own home. Despite Gideon's imploration for her to spend as much time with the Viscount as possible, Emily did the opposite, and spent as much time off the wards as she possibly could without drawing comment.

Despite that, she couldn't avoid hearing the nurses' gossiping about their favourite patient. Needless to say, those otherwise sensible and professional young women were all entranced by the charming Viscount. With much giggling they would good-naturedly vie to be the one to administer to him, especially when it came time to give him his bed bath. Even Matron, usually such a no-nonsense woman, had made a passing comment about what a personable young man he was.

Kitty visited regularly, and when word got around about his saving her from a band of thugs, the awe in which Jackson Wilde was held only grew among the nursing staff. With each retelling, his role became more heroic, causing the sighing and swooning to increase, along with Emily's exasperation.

She just knew the man was in his element. All those young—and not so young—women thinking him irresistible. Thank goodness she was not one of them. After that one, brief lapse of good judgement she was now completely immune to his allure.

When the day of his discharge arrived, all the nurses, including the ones not on duty, lined up to say goodbye, as if he was some sort of dignitary who required a guard of honour. Unfortunately, Emily had no choice but to attend this shameful act of adoration. The chairman of the board had pointed out that it would be in the hospital's best interest if all members of the board said their farewells to the Viscount, particularly as he had indicated he intended to make a generous contribution to the running of the hospital. While not officially on the board—being a woman excluded her from such a position—her social rank meant Emily was treated as an unofficial member. It had taken a lot of hard work for her to get that recognition, so she wasn't going to jeopardise it by staying away from this irritating send off.

Gideon was also present, which provided some compensation. He had visited Jackson Wilde every day since his admission, sometimes several times a day, even though that particular patient required little further in the way of medical treatment, other than bed rest.

For his departure the Viscount was dressed in a dark grey day suit, having allowed one of the nursing staff to contact his valet the day before his discharge. The man had arrived in a fluster, horrified to see His Lordship in such a place, his snobbery evidently more entrenched in him than in his master.

The valet had attempted to remain at his master's side, so he could provide everything he deemed necessary, but had been sent away by Jackson Wilde, who, so the nurses reported, had told his valet he was receiving excellent care from a team of nurses who tended to his every need like a flock of heaven-sent angels. This had caused further swooning and sighing from the nurses, and teeth grinding from Emily.

According to the nurses' reports, the valet had countered that he should remain so he could dress his master prior to his discharge, but the Viscount had said the nurses were more than capable of doing so. Once this tale had spread there was much teasing among the nurses and friendly arguments over who would be the lucky woman to do so. All Emily could think was thank goodness it was not to be her. The memory of how she had reacted when she had cleaned his injuries was embarrassing enough, she did not want to risk repeating such aberrant behaviour.

And now, finally, he was to depart and life at the Hope Hospital could return to normal. While the nursing staff and board members waited in an excited line, Gideon walked beside the Viscount. Emily hoped she was the only one to notice the irritation on Gideon's face as Jackson Wilde took his time walking around the ward, pausing at each bed and exchanging a few words and lots of laughter with each man.

'Goodbye, Jackson,' one of the men called out, as Gideon finally steered him towards the waiting line of hospital staff and board members. 'Hope all goes well for you.'

'Give my best to your wife,' he responded with a wave. 'And thank her for the cakes. They were delicious.'

Both Gideon and Emily stiffened at this exchange. Emily because it was apparent Jackson Wilde had been charming the female visitors, along with everyone else, while Gideon's reaction, she suspected somewhat unkindly, was because of the informality of this conversation between a workman and a peer of the realm.

Gideon had complained several times to Emily that Jackson Wilde should not have been on the same ward as the other men, and that Matron should have made more effort to either find him a private room or screen off his bed. He'd even bravely suggested this arrangement to Matron and had, not unexpectedly, received a short shrift for his troubles, and been informed in no uncertain terms that she ran the ward and such decisions were hers and hers alone.

Emily should not fault Gideon for this adherence to Society's rigid expectations on how members of the aristocracy should be treated. He was not the only one to think so. Why, even Jackson Wilde's valet had been shocked to see his master in a public ward. She knew Gideon wasn't a snob. How could he be? He worked every day among London's poorest people and had dedicated his life to their welfare.

Matron was first in the line-up and she simpered like a young girl when Jackson picked up her hand and lightly kissed it.

'Thank you so much for your kindness,' he said. 'It has been an honour to meet you and all your hard-working staff.'

Matron blushed slightly, almost causing Emily's mouth to fall open. He had made that stern, somewhat frightening woman actually blush. Unbelievable.

'The honour is all mine,' Matron replied and gave a small curtsey.

Excitement rippled up the line as he thanked each member of the nursing staff in turn, with the women preening and giggling as if this were a social occasion, where harmless flirtation was de rigueur, and not a serious place of work. Emily noted he addressed each nurse by her first name, although this should not really be a surprise. They were women. Of course he'd be on familiar terms with each and every one of them.

As he moved closer to Emily, she forced herself to continue smiling politely for the sake of appearances. It was a smile that should not have to be forced and she *was* pleased he had made such a rapid recovery. She should also be pleased that he was leaving and she was unlikely to ever see him again. And yet, the strange feeling in the pit of her stomach did not feel like pleasure. She wasn't sure what it was, and refused to analyse it, but it was definitely neither happiness nor relief.

'Lady Emily, it has been a pleasure,' he said, finally reaching her in the line-up.

'Viscount Wickford,' she said with a small curtsey, putting her hands behind her back so there was no danger of him repeating the overly familiar gesture he had made with Matron.

She had no need to take such precautions. He merely bowed his head before moving onto the next person in the line-up, giving her even less attention than he had the nursing staff and patients. And that was as it should be.

It was now quite obvious he had forgotten all about their encounter when she was washing his wounds. And thank goodness for that. It was all now in the past and over and done with, and of little consequence to either of them.

Despite Emily thinking about it constantly for the last month, it was apparent he had now completely put it out of his mind, if it had occupied any space in his thoughts in the first place. While it had been a strangely intimate exchange for her, for him it was apparently of no consequence. Good. That was exactly how it would be for her as well, once she was able to shake off the strange heaviness in her chest.

'And thank you, Mr Greaves,' he said, shaking the chairman of the board's hand. 'You should be proud of this hospital and your magnificent staff.'

The chairman returned his hearty shake. 'And I can only thank you again for your pledge of a donation. Very generous. Very generous, indeed.'

Jackson Wilde brushed his hand in front of his face as if it was of no account. 'And have you given any thought to my proposal?'

'I have indeed,' Mr Greaves replied. 'And I think it an excellent idea.'

The Viscount turned to face Emily. 'As it was Lady Emily who gave me the idea, I believe she should be involved in the project from the very start.'

Emily stared from one man to the other. Proposal? Idea? This was all news to her. 'I'm sorry, what are you talking about?'

'The Viscount has made an interesting proposal to the board,' Mr Greaves said, smiling at her like a kindly father. 'He has suggested we extend our services to further help the local community.'

'How?' Emily asked, but what she really wanted to know was why did she have to be involved, or at least why did she have to be involved with Jackson Wilde.

'I believe now is not the time to discuss this in detail,' the Viscount said. 'Perhaps Lady Emily and I can soon meet for afternoon tea, where I can give her the bank draft for my donation and go over the finer points of this new proposal.'

'An excellent idea,' Mr Greaves answered for her.

With that, Jackson Wilde turned and waved his farewell to all the staff. Everyone else waved enthusiastically as if seeing off a loved one on a long sea voyage. All except Emily, who remained somewhat stunned, wondering what on earth Jackson Wilde was up to.

A few days later a note arrived at the hospital, inviting Emily for afternoon tea with Jackson Wilde so they could discuss something of interest to them both. Emily would like to have thrown it away, but the meeting had been arranged with the consent of Mr Greaves. She had no option but to attend.

On the day of the meeting, she resisted the temptation to make an extra special effort with her clothing or hair. Why should she? It was a business meeting, nothing more, and she wanted Jackson Wilde to know that she placed no importance whatsoever on his opinion of her. She had no wish to impress him, and it was essential he realise she was not like virtually every other woman he came into contact with—bedazzled by his good looks and charms, and desperate for his attention.

She was a sensible, serious woman who was being courted by a man of substance, and that was how she expected Jackson Wilde to treat her. She would broker no flirting. This was to be all business.

She arrived at the tea shop slightly before the arranged time, determined to be seated and waiting in a composed manner when he arrived, but found him already waiting for her. It was so incongruous to see him seated among these women dressed in their finery, with their lacy dresses and hats bearing feathers, ribbons and flowers. It was like seeing a lion seated among a flock of exotic birds.

The bell above the door alerted him to her arrival. He stood beside the table and watched as she lingered at the entrance. The image of a lion returned. She couldn't shake off the idea she was approaching a dangerous animal and needed to be on her guard. It was a disturbing concept that wasn't diminished by the way he was watching her, as if he did indeed wish to devour her.

This was simply a business meeting, she reminded herself. To prove that she would not be intimidated, she strode across the room, her head held high, her nose in the air, but the rapid beating of her heart and the jangling of her nerves belied her attempt at aloofness.

'Lady Emily,' he said when she arrived. 'You're looking as lovely as ever.'

She merely nodded her head, reminding herself that flattery and charm were as natural to him as flight was to a bird.

He pulled out a chair for her and she took her seat. As he brushed past her, she inhaled his scent of sandalwood and leather. The uninvited image of his naked chest invaded her mind. She swallowed and pushed it away. That was the last thing she should be thinking about at a business meeting.

As he took his seat across from her, she smoothed out the wrinkle-free white linen tablecloth, moved the rose patterned teacup slightly to the left and then back again. Then, taking a steadying breath, looked at him across the table.

Apart from a bit of tell-tale yellow colouring around his eyes, his face had almost healed up completely. Once again he was that devastatingly handsome man she had met on occasion at Society balls. The man she had hardly spoken to because he was always surrounded by a coterie of twittering debutantes. His dark blond hair was raffishly curly, with one escaped curl teasing his high forehead. Those blue eyes sparkled, as if he was constantly thinking of a joke, or laughing at the world, and those full lips, no longer bearing a painful split, were slightly curled at the edges, as if he was amused by her presence.

Well, handsome is as handsome does, as the wise proverb warns. A man's looks, his charms, his easy smile, these were of no importance. All that really mattered was a man's true character. She had learnt that lesson well in her first Season. It was a lesson she did not need to be taught again. When it came to men, what was in their heart and soul mattered, not superficialities like good looks and charm or a smile that took one's breath away. That was why she hoped to one day marry Gideon, a good man, a man much more worthy than Jackson Wilde could ever be.

With that thought firmly in her mind, her confidence returned and she stared him unflinchingly in the eye.

'Mr Greaves said you have a banker's draft you wished to pass on to the hospital. Have you brought it with you?' Her tone of voice made it clear she would tolerate none of his nonsense. It also signalled she would linger no longer than was entirely necessary.

'Straight to a discussion about money, I see,' he said, those lips quirking further, the edges of his eyes crinkling. 'It seems you and Pretty Kitty have more in common than I would have thought.'

Emily frowned at him and cursed the heat rising on her cheeks.

His smile grew wider. He was obviously enjoying her discomfort.

'Yes, I brought the banker's draft, but I have also discussed with the board another proposal, which I think you might be interested in. I've ordered tea so we can have a nice long discussion about it.'

'That won't be necessary. I'm merely here to pick up the donation. If you've got a proposal it would be best to discuss it with the board.'

'If my proposal is to be a success, it will require some fundraising, for which I will need your help.' He smiled again, that annoyingly slow smile she just knew was designed to unsettle a woman.

'Mr Greaves agreed that you would be perfect for this role, although, may I suggest, it might be a good idea to learn to woo donors a bit first, not ask outright for their money.'

He was teasing her, but Emily was in no mood to be teased, and especially not by him.

'I do not wish to woo you or anyone else. If you don't want to give me the money, then we have nothing else to talk about.'

A woman at the next table looked from her to the Viscount and back again, her lips pulled into a moue of disgust.

This caused him to laugh, and Emily's cheeks to grow even hotter.

'Well, I've ordered tea,' he said. 'You might not want to woo me, but you can at least stay until you've had your tea and heard what I have to say. Then I promise, I will discretely slip the bankers draft to you, so you don't shock the ladies present.'

Emily said nothing, wishing her burning cheeks would calm down.

The waitress placed the teapot on the table, along with a three-tiered stand full of cakes, sandwiches and scones. Emily doubted she would be able to eat anything, not while her stomach remained in such a tangled knot.

'Thank you, Betty,' he said to the waitress, receiving a delighted smile and a small curtsey in response.

'Anything else you want, just let me know,' Betty said.

'You know the waitress?' Emily asked, unsure why she should be surprised. She was a young woman, after all, and a pretty one at that.

'I do now. I introduced myself when I was ordering tea. Do you disapprove?'

'I couldn't care less,' she responded, aware that if she actually didn't care she would not have inquired. 'So what is this proposal?'

He held up one finger as if to still her inquiries. 'Shall I pour?'

She flicked her hand in agreement.

'Before we discuss my proposal, don't you think we should make some polite conversation? I believe that is the usual manner in which business discussions are conducted.'

Emily said nothing, merely sipped her tea.

'For example, you could enquire after my health.'

'How is your health?'

He smiled that annoyingly charming smile. 'Thank you for asking. Yes, I am mending well.'

'And how did your family and friends react when they found out you weren't in the company of a young woman but in fact had taken a rather brutal beating?'

His smile faltered slightly, then returned as bright as before. 'My father was bereft that such a terrible thing had befallen his beloved son.'

She stared back at him, the cup halfway to her lips. Everyone in Society knew how much the Duke of Greenfeld abhorred his son's behaviour. Had that gruff old man actually been concerned for the welfare of his son and heir? It seemed unlikely.

'You had better put that cup down before you drop it,' he said. 'I am of course jesting. My father reacted in the expected manner. I can't remember all that he said, but the gist of it was something about me burning in hell, being a damnable disgrace, a suggestion that I deserve to die among harlots, guttersnipes and beggars.'

'That is so unfair.' Surely if the man knew why he had taken that beating he would not judge him so harshly. Although the Viscount was still smiling, only his lips were doing so. His eyes held no laughter, only a hint of pain.

She placed her cup in its saucer and reached out across the table towards his hand, before realising what she was doing and quickly retracting it.

'But my father is correct. I do want to mix with such types, well, the harlots anyway. And that is why we are here today.'

All pity she might have felt for him instantly evaporated.

'Don't look so shocked, Lady Emily. My proposal has the full backing of Fergus Greaves.'

She doubted that very much. The chairman of the board was an upstanding man of virtue, with impeccable morals.

'Along with giving the hospital a banker's draft, to show my appreciation for the exemplary care I was given during my stay, I also wish to provide some money for Pretty Kitty and her, shall we say, colleagues.'

'And you expect me to pass the money on to them,' she said, her voice growing louder with her outrage. 'And Mr Greaves agrees with this?' Emily was unsure if it was possible to be more offended. 'Well, I will be no party to this.'

She threw her serviette on the table and rose from her chair.

'Please, sit down, Lady Emily. If for no other reason than you are drawing attention to yourself.'

She looked around and saw the ladies had all stopped in their chatter and turned towards her, with a mixture of curiosity, outrage and enthralment.

She sat down, knowing she had already made herself the subject of gossip, and not wishing to give these women any more fodder.

'That's better,' the Viscount said, and Emily scowled at his condescending manner. 'When I was in hospital you mentioned that women like Pretty Kitty often have no option but to ply their particular trade, and I, perhaps more than most men, am now painfully aware of how dangerous that profession can be.' He gently touched the healing bruise beside his eye.

Emily remained poised on the edge of her chair, waiting for him to finish speaking so she could make a quick but discreet exit, one that would not draw the attention of the assembled ladies.

'What I have suggested is working with the hospital board to help these young women find another way of earning a living.'

'You mean, like a training school?' she asked, still wary

that this might simply be another way in which he was teasing her.

'Exactly. One where they can learn different skills.'

'*You* want to set up a school for fallen women? Isn't that a bit like the poacher becoming the game keeper?'

He placed his hands over his heart. 'Lady Emily, you wound me terribly.' Then he smiled at her, that disarming smile she was determined to resist.

'I've talked it over with the board, and Fergus believes it will be just the sort of project you should be involved with.'

'Why me?'

'It was you who gave me the idea.'

She raised her hands, palm upwards in question.

'If I remember correctly, you informed me that men who visited the East End to relieve their carnal needs didn't give a fig about the women they sought out or the terrible lives they lived. They merely used them then return to their comfortable lives and forgot all about them.'

Emily blushed slightly. That sounded exactly like the sort of lecture she would give him.

'Well, this comfortable man agrees with you entirely and he wants to think about more than just his carnal needs for once.'

The heat on her cheeks grew more intense and she wished he'd stop talking about carnal needs.

'At the moment I am dependent on my allowance from my father, and that alone will not be enough to get the school started and pay its ongoing running costs. It will require fundraising, and who better than a woman of your diplomacy, tact and social skills to undertake such a project.'

'I doubt very much if Mr Greaves said any such thing.'

'No, you're right, he didn't. But he agreed with me that

as the daughter of a duke, and someone with friends who are in the highest positions in Society, you will be well placed to host events to help raise the funds we need.'

She stared at him, even more shocked than she was when he first mentioned giving money to Pretty Kitty. 'You want me to take on the role of a Society hostess?'

'Yes, for a good cause. I know you enjoy balls as much as I do, but if the point of the exercise is not to exchange idle chit chat, nor to jostle to make the most advantageous marriage, but to help people who are in desperate circumstances, then it is hardly too great a sacrifice, is it?'

'No, I suppose not,' she said slowly, mulling this over.

'The school will be a project you can commit yourself to entirely from the very start,' he said, his voice full of appeal.

'Hmm,' she said, not entirely convinced.

He shrugged one shoulder and looked uncharacteristically abashed. 'Forgive me if I'm wrong, but I got the impression at the hospital that you sometimes feel a bit surplus to requirements, and that the nursing staff and board treat you as someone merely dabbling in good works.'

She tensed, knowing he was unfortunately correct. Even Gideon on occasion did not appear to take her commitment seriously.

'Well, this will be your idea. You'll be fully involved from its inception and everyone will know it.'

It wasn't actually her idea, but she could see the attraction of being involved in such a worthy project from its beginning.

'Hosting a ball or two might be hard work but you're not afraid of hard work, are you?'

'Of course not,' she said, offended by his words. Then

she saw his smile and knew it had been a deliberate ploy to win her over. But he was right. If hosting a ball was what was required to better the lives of women like Kitty, then she would do it.

'I'd be happy to do whatever it takes to raise the necessary funds.'

'Good. So we host a ball, charge for the tickets and perhaps have an auction to raise even further funds, then use all that money for the school.'

'You want to charge for the invitations? Like a public ball?'

'Yes, exactly, but we make the price so prohibitively high that the great and good of this city feel compelled to buy tickets, just to prove to everyone that they are able to afford them. And as the money is going to charity, they can all feel like worthy people while doing nothing more than enjoying themselves.'

'Yes, I suppose that would work,' she said. 'And I dare say I could get my mother to help. She loves nothing better than organising a ball. And my friends, Irene, the Duchess of Redcliff, and Georgina, the Duchess of Ravenswood, I'm sure would also help.'

She lifted up her tea cup, then placed it back in the saucer. 'And I am good friends with Amelia Devenish. She's the wife of the media magnate Leo Devenish. Their newspapers and magazines are read by all of Society. I'm sure they'll be happy to provide publicity.'

'And if the guests know the ball will be covered in all the Society pages they'll be desperate to attend, all wanting to be seen as bountiful people who are dedicated to helping the less fortunate.'

'Exactly,' Emily said, smiling back at him. 'And maybe

we can ask people to donate goods to be auctioned off. And hopefully, once again, people will be vying to show just how generous they can be.'

'Excellent idea, Lady Emily.'

'No, you were the one with the excellent idea. I'm sure the training school will make a huge difference to women like Kitty.'

'It is all thanks to you,' he said, picking up a cream cake and placing it on her plate. 'I would never have thought of it if you hadn't told me about the plight of such women.'

Emily felt it prudent not to point out that she hadn't just told him about their plight—she had given him a lecture, and all but held him personally responsible. Instead, she took a bite of the delicious cake.

'It will of course mean you and I will have to continue to spend time together while we get the school up and running,' he said, and took a satisfied bite of his scone.

Emily swallowed down her cream cake, her throat suddenly tight. In her excitement for the project, that was one factor she had not considered.

Chapter Six

'A ball. My little girl wants to host a ball, and she wants me to help. I am so happy.' Her mother rushed over to the roll top desk in the corner of her parlour and pushed up the lid. 'Oh, why couldn't you be like this during your previous Seasons, or even earlier in this Season before all the most eligible men were taken?' She pulled out a piece of paper from the drawer. 'But never mind. There's still time, we just have to invite—'

'That's not the point of the ball,' Emily interrupted. 'As I've already said, it's to raise money for a worthy cause.'

'Yes, yes, I know, but it's still a ball, and there's no reason why you can't find a husband while you're doing all your good works.' She opened her ink well, dipped her pen, looked up in thought, then began writing—her pen scratching furiously over the paper.

Emily released a loud sigh, which was ignored by her mother, who was now absorbed by the list she was compiling. There was no point continuing to argue. Her mother would never give up hope in finding her a suitable husband, but she was right, in a way. The ball would be a perfect time to introduce her parents to Gideon. He had been wanting to meet them for some time, and Emily had always hesitated, not wanting to subject him to their scrutiny and possible objections. But the board members would also be present at the ball. They were all eminent men she knew her parents would approve of, and when they saw the high esteem in which they held Gideon, she was sure they would have no objection to him courting their daughter.

Having informed her mother, Emily's second task was to assemble her friends so they too could assist with the organising. To that end, the four women gathered at Amelia's house, anxious to hear why Emily had summoned them. They had been friends since they met at Halliwell's Finishing School for Refined Young Ladies. At that time, they'd been four square pegs expected to fit into unsuitable round holes. It was only the bonds of their friendship that had enabled them to survive the school, which Georgina had renamed Hell's Final Sentence for Rebellious Young Ladies.

They'd remained friends ever since and continued to support each other through the good times and the bad, and there was nothing Emily valued more than their friendship.

'I'm to host a ball and I want your help,' she announced as they took their seats in the drawing room. They all looked at her with surprise, as she knew they would.

'*You* want to host a ball?' Georgina said, eyeing her sideways. 'You? The woman who, if I remember correctly, said at the end of the first Season, *"Absolutely nothing and no one will drag me to another ball,"* and has managed to avoid virtually all of them since.'

'That's right,' she declared. 'But this ball will be different. I'm raising funds for a training school for, well, for fallen women. It was Jackson Wilde's idea.' Damn it all, Emily heard her voice falter at the mention of his name. Something that was not missed by her friends either, who simultaneously raised their eyebrows.

'Yes, I'd heard the Viscount spent some time recovering in the Hope Hospital,' Irene said. 'I'd wondered whether the two of you became acquainted.'

Was it Emily's imagination or did she hear an emphasis on the word *acquainted*?

'Yes, he was a patient for a while,' she said, keeping her voice as neutral as possible. 'I spoke to him on one or two occasions but had little to do with him, really. He was one of Gideon's patients.'

She waited for her friends to excitedly ask questions about the man she had informed them she hoped one day to marry. There was a pause in the conversation.

'More tea?' Amelia asked, signalling to the footman.

'Gideon of course provided him with the best of care and said that the Viscount was so impressed that he will probably ask him to become his private physician. Not that he will, of course. Gideon is dedicated to the work at the hospital.'

'He doesn't want to set up in private practice?' Irene asked, her tone suggesting disbelief. She had met Gideon when she had visited the Hope Hospital to see Emily, and Gideon had actually put aside his work to spend time politely talking to her friend.

'No, of course not,' Emily said. 'He's dedicated to the charitable work at the Hope Hospital.'

The three women nodded, although not as enthusiastically as Emily would have liked. Irene didn't seem to take to Gideon when they met, which was a disappointment, as he was nothing if not completely courteous to her. He had even taken time out of his busy workload to give her a tour of the hospital.

'I'm going to introduce him to my parents at the ball. So it will kill two birds with one stone, as it were.'

She hadn't exactly hoped for squeals of delight from her friends, but a bit more than their muted response would have been nice. After all, introducing a man to one's parents was an important event—one that was a precursor to an official courtship, then an engagement and marriage. Instead, all she got was some polite smiles, a few nods and murmurs of 'that's nice'.

'Well, I wish the two of you every happiness,' Amelia finally said, and the other two raised their tea cups in a toast.

'To Emily's happiness,' Georgina said.

To which Irene gave a, 'Hear, hear.'

'So did you say this was all Jackson Wilde's idea?' Georgina asked, returning to a subject that seemed to animate them more than her coming official courtship.

Emily recounted the tale of Pretty Kitty and the beating he had taken, which, not surprisingly, the three women listened to with wide-eyed interest. Then she explained how this had led to a discussion between her and Jackson on the terrible lives of such women. She used the term discussion, even though she knew that in reality she had harangued the Viscount. Though, on this one occasion, he was actually completely innocent of any wrongdoing.

'And now the two of you are going to raise money for a training school for fallen women,' Georgina said, her hand over her heart and an approving smile on her lips. 'What a wonderful tale.'

Emily was tempted to point out that while, yes, it was good of Jackson Wilde, Gideon gave all his time to the hospital. He worked tirelessly for the poor and never expected any thanks.

'And I suppose it means the two of you will be spending a lot of time together now?' Irene asked.

'Yes, for the fundraising,' she said, adopting a brisk and unemotional tone. 'And we'll be working with the board to find suitable premises. Then I believe the Viscount will be organising tradesmen to turn the premises into a school.'

'It looks like you've transformed him, Emily,' Irene said, beaming with delight. 'You've tamed the rake.'

'Nonsense,' she shot back at this ridiculous suggestion from a woman she had hitherto thought quite sensible. 'He may be giving his time, effort and quite a bit of his allowance to the school, but he's no different to the way he's always been.'

She could hear the disapproval in her voice, but she did disapprove of him and could see no reason to disguise it. The man didn't meet a woman he didn't want to flirt with. He had no doubt left the hospital and gone straight to one of his mistresses. Nothing about this man had really changed.

'Still, what the two of you are doing is admirable, and I will help in any way I can,' Amelia said.

The other two nodded.

'Good,' Emily said, pleased they had got back to the real reason why she was here. And it wasn't to discuss Jackson Wilde. 'Mother has of course leapt into the fray, but it would be good to have your help, otherwise the only people she will invite will be eligible men. And, Amelia, the more publicity your papers are able to give the event the better.' She looked round at her friends, whose expressions were gratifyingly enthusiastic. 'We want people to think this is an event they absolutely must be seen at, and they also must be vying to be seen as the most generous donor present.'

'Leave that to me and Leo,' Amelia said. 'Our newspapers will turn this ball into the event of the Season.'

'Perhaps we should make it fancy dress,' Georgina added. 'Then it will be something quite different for people to get excited about.'

'Excellent idea,' Emily said, as Amelia called for the footman to bring papers and fountain pens so they could begin their organisation in earnest.

'We could also set up a photography studio in one of the side rooms and people could have their portrait taken in their costume,' Amelia said.

'In exchange for a generous donation,' Emily added, which was greeted with a chorus of, 'Yes, absolutely.'

The tea going cold, the four women set about preparing for what they fully intended to be the Season's most memorable ball, one that would have people dipping eagerly into their pocket books, or writing out enormous bank drafts.

Emily smiled to herself as she watched her friends enthusiastically volunteer for the various tasks. Who would have thought, when they first met at Halliwell's Finishing School, that one day they'd all be so respectable?

Now her three friends were all happily married and in love. And she would soon be married as well. Perhaps she wouldn't experience the grand passion that her three friends had, and might not be as besotted with the man she married, but that hardly mattered. In Gideon, she had found the man she wanted. Their relationship might be a tad lack-

ing in romance, but he was a man who made her feel safe,
a man who she could trust, who was honest and reliable.

No woman could ever want more from a man than that.
Could she?

Chapter Seven

On the night of the ball, Emily's nerves were jingling with a mixture of excitement and worry. Would it be a success? Would they raise the money necessary for the school? Would everything go as planned? Would Jackson Wilde dance with her? No, that last one hardly mattered. What she should be thinking about was how her parents would react when she introduced them to Gideon. It was so important that they like him and accept the fact that their daughter would be marrying a doctor.

Strangely, of all the things she should be anxious about, that was the thought causing her the least concern. It must be because she simply knew her parents would admire and respect Gideon for the man he was, despite his lack of title and wealth—just as she did.

'Can you please try to sit still, my lady,' her lady's maid said as she worked on Emily's hair.

Emily had chosen to wear a simple pale gold Regency gown, which she'd had since she was a child, and had often worn when playing dress up. It had belonged to her grandmother. It was hard to believe such a matronly woman had once worn a dress of such fine material that clung to one's curves, emphasising the bustline.

Her lady's maid had spent time analysing family portraits painted during the Regency period and was sure she had perfected the style, with a bun at the top of the head, and ringlets around the face. She had insisted Emily spend the night with her hair tied up in strips of cloths to create the required ringlets, which to Emily's mind was going a tad too far, but her lady's maid was a perfectionist and it would have been mean of Emily to deny Mabel her fun, so she complied.

'Lovely,' Mabel said when she had finished, then frowned. 'But you must leave that alone, my lady.'

Emily realised she was pulling at the low-cut neckline. Did Grandmama really expose so much cleavage when she was a young woman? That too was hard to believe.

'Perhaps a simple string of pearls tonight, my lady,' Mabel said, opening Emily's jewellery box and placing them around her neck before she had time to answer. Emily was not so sure. It looked as if she was deliberately drawing attention to her decolletage, and it really wouldn't do to have anyone think that. After all, she was hosting this ball for a serious reason, not to flirt or to try and attract a man's interest.

She gazed at her reflection in the full-length looking glass and had to admit Mabel had done a wonderful job. She did look rather splendid. And tonight *was* supposed to be about having fun. The more fun people had the more generous they would be, so she really *should* get into the spirit of the occasion.

She thanked Mabel, pulled on her elbow length gloves, picked up her matching gold fan and joined her parents in the ballroom, where her mother was giving last minute instructions to the servants and extra staff who had been hired for the evening. Not that she needed to, they all seemed to know exactly what they were doing, but that was what her mother did when she was nervous, so there was no point trying to stop her.

Her father took her hands and smiled at her. 'You look enchanting, my dear,' he said, kissing her on the cheek. 'And what do you think of my costume?'

Emily laughed as he stood back, lifted his head high and placed one hand inside his jacket. 'Well, Napoleon, it looks like tonight you and I will be enemies,' she said.

'Yes, I think we should have had a family discussion about what we were to wear instead of keeping it a surprise,' he said with a laugh. 'Your mother decided to come as Marie Antoinette. Everyone is going to think that it is a sign of marital disharmony.'

She looked over at her mother, who was giving orders to a young maid. She was wearing an ornate costume that could not contrast more dramatically with Emily's simple gown. Her mother's hair was swept up into an enormous bouffant and powdered grey, and she was laden down with what appeared to be every one of the family jewels.

The first guests to arrive were her friends Amelia, Irene and Georgina, and their husbands. The four women spent some time admiring each other's costumes. Amelia and Leo were dressed as Cleopatra and Mark Antony, Georgina and Adam as Romeo and Juliet and Irene and Joshua as Robin Hood and Maid Marion.

It really had been a good idea to have the fancy dress theme. Emily was rather looking forward to the occasion. Usually a sense of dread descended on her when she was forced to attend a ball.

The friends did one last inspection of the room and all agreed that everything looked exactly as it should. The chandeliers with their countless candles sent flickering light around the room. The parquet floor was polished to perfection. The orchestra was seated on the balcony, and servants were waiting to tend to the guests' every need.

'And we were right to go with large bouquets of white and pink lilies,' Georgina declared. 'Their scent is simply divine, and they look magnificent.' That had actually been Georgina's idea, but she was obviously expecting some praise, so the others obliged.

'It is perfect and is sure to be a success,' Irene said, gently patting Emily's arm. 'Amelia's gushing articles in all the ladies' magazines means everyone who is anyone will be here tonight. I'm sure you'll raise even more money than you need for your school.'

Amelia and Georgina both nodded at this comment. Emily smiled at them, knowing they were right. The amount people had paid for the tickets already meant the funds had swollen to a respectable degree, and her friends' husbands had donated significant amounts of money, and pledged to continue supporting the school.

But, strangely, that was not what she was most anxious about. It was seeing Jackson Wilde again. This time she would not be tending to him as a patient, nor would she be in the role of a woman taking part in a serious business meeting or discussing fundraising activities. Tonight she would be a woman dressed in her finery, at a Society ball.

The board members were the next to arrive, and Emily had to supress a giggle. Mr Greaves was dressed as a Roman gladiator, seemingly not worrying that his legs, bearing the blue veins and knots of old age, were on display for all to see. His wife was dressed more sensibly, as a woman from ancient Rome, in a floor-length white gown with a shawl draped over her shoulders.

The room started to fill up with milk maids, Shakespearean characters, pirates, several Henry VIIIs and a surprising number of geisha girls and women in harem costumes.

Gideon arrived dressed as a Roman senator, in a full-length white toga and a laurel wreath in his hair. He greeted Mr Greaves, who good-naturedly joked that tonight Gideon would be the one in charge.

Gideon then bowed formally to Emily. 'You look lovely tonight,' he said. Before she could thank him, he looked around the room. 'I saw you talking to the Duke of Redcliff and the Duke of Ravenswood.'

'Yes, their wives and I are good friends.'

'Excellent. Perhaps you can introduce me to those gentlemen.'

'They have already pledged to donate sizeable amounts to the school,' Emily said, somewhat confused, as Gideon had hitherto shown no interest in the organisation of the ball or the fundraising efforts.

A matching look of confusion crossed his face. 'Nevertheless, I should like to make their acquaintance.'

That did make sense and Emily wondered why she had questioned his motives. Of course Gideon would want to meet her friends and their husbands. She led him across the room to where the Dukes of Redcliff and Ravenswood were in conversation with Amelia's husband, Mr Leo Devenish.

While they made their introductions, Emily looked around at the guests, all chatting and laughing in small groups as they showed off their dazzling costumes. The ball was already a great success and it had hardly begun.

Her gaze was caught by Jackson Wilde, walking towards her from the far side of the room. She quickly suppressed a gasp. Was he dressed as Mr Darcy? Had he known she would come in a Regency gown? She was sure she had mentioned it to no one, not even her friends and family.

And, oh, my, he did look magnificent in his long black jacket, tight leather breeches, tucked into knee-length boots, and a high-collared white shirt with an intricately tied cravat.

The conversation between the four men died away. The sound of the music quietened as he walked towards her. All she could hear was the pounding of her heart. With each step he took, bringing him closer to her, the room became warmer, the air thinner, as she struggled to catch her breath.

The four men all turned in the direction she was staring and it was evident her friends' husbands were pleased to see Jackson Wilde. After greetings were exchanged, he bowed to her. 'May I have the honour of this dance, Lady Emily?'

'Oh,' was the only inarticulate response Emily was capable of giving.

He looked to Gideon. 'I'm sure the senator can spare you for one dance.'

'Yes, of course. Dance with the Viscount,' Gideon said with a wave of his hand. 'While I continue this fascinating conversation with Their Graces.'

Was it a look of irritation she saw cross the two Dukes' faces? She would not have taken them for snobs and could see no other reason why they would object to talking to Gideon. But she had no time to contemplate their reaction as Jackson Wilde linked her arm through his and escorted her out onto the dance floor, where they joined the other couples waiting for the waltz to begin.

When he placed his hand on her waist and took her gloved hand in his, her breath caught in her throat. The warmth of his touch seeped into her body. That was something she had not considered when choosing this costume. The fine muslin material provided little in the way of a barrier between a man's hand and her skin. It was as if he was caressing her naked flesh, sending her temperature soaring.

She placed her hand tentatively on his broad shoulder, feeling the strength under her fingers. A memory of his naked chest flashed into her mind. She fought to drive out the image of those hard muscles, and how they had rippled under the stroking of her flannel as she had cleaned his wounds.

She swallowed, closed her eyes and took in a long, steadying breath. This would not do. It was just a dance. All she had to do was move with him to the music and make some polite conversation.

Conversation. That was it. A bit of mindless chit chat would drive out any further thoughts of his naked body and put a stop to all these disconcerting sensations. She looked up into those blue eyes and anything she might have said disappeared before the words had fully formed. How could she think of idle chatter when he was holding her with that gaze. She stared back, suddenly aware that his eyes weren't just blue, but contained swirls of grey, making them more complex than she had first assumed. Just as she suspected Jackson Wilde contained more complexities than appearances would suggest.

The music started and she surrendered to the grace of his movements as they glided across the parquet floor.

There was no denying that being in his arms felt good. Very good. Too good.

As if drawn by an invisible thread too strong for her to resist, with each step she moved closer and closer to him, until his chest was almost touching hers. Warmth radiated off his body, that scent of sandalwood and leather enveloping her, making her almost giddy.

Say something, anything, she commanded her useless brain. *Break this spell*.

Desperate to do so, she attempted a polite smile. The smile quivered and died. The look in his eyes was unlike any she had seen before, and it could never be described as polite. His gaze moved to her lips, which parted on a soft sigh.

Despite what she might think of him, despite how offended she was by the way he lived his life, being in his arms was undeniably an intoxicating experience. And that was how she felt, as if she had imbibed far too much of the punch. It was easy to see how he had gained his reputation as a ladies' man. Surely no woman could remain unaffected when in the arms of such a commanding, desirable man. And the way he was looking at her made *her* feel desirable, like a beautiful woman capable of entrancing a man such as him. She could not be blamed for her reaction. How could she not be dazzled by him? How could any woman not wish for him to do more than just dance with her, more than just look at her? How could any woman resist becoming this man's mistress?

Emily stumbled over her dancing slippers, causing him to wrap his arm around her waist to stop her fall. What on earth had she been thinking? Intoxicated? Becoming his mistress? Where had such a ludicrous idea come from? This was getting out of hand.

Put an end to this. Now. Do not think of his hand on your waist. Do not think of his strong muscular shoulders or firm chest. And definitely do not think of those dazzling blue eyes or those full lips.

She coughed to clear her constricted throat. 'The ballroom…' She coughed again. 'The ballroom looks wonderful, don't you think? And I'm so pleased the weather remained fine.'

Emily released a held breath. She had done it. She had made some boring small talk. Perfect. Nothing could bring a person back to reality faster than a dull conversation about the weather.

He smiled down at her, those blue eyes crinkling at the corners, and, damn it all, it gave every appearance of being a knowing smile. Was he aware of the effect he was having on her? Was he laughing at her? She gazed back into his eyes, searching, but could see no hint of mockery in their depths. Instead, she noticed their warmth, like the blue of a summer sky on a languid afternoon, and she felt bathed in their light.

She blinked rapidly to push out that absurd image. He was merely looking at her. There was no summer sky, no bathing in light, no languid afternoons. She needed to take control of this situation. But how? If small talk didn't work, she was completely out of ideas.

He spun her around again and she felt so light in his arms, so feminine. Perhaps she should just surrender to the moment. Enjoy this brief dance and then forget all about it, just as he would surely forget about holding her so close as soon as the music stopped.

And so she did. As one, they swept across the floor and, just as she had completely given herself over to the dance, the music soared up into a crescendo and it was all over.

His hand dropped from her waist and he offered her his arm to escort her off the floor, over to where Gideon was standing, watching them.

Gideon.

While she was in Jackson Wilde's arms she hadn't even thought of Gideon. This was all too, too bad. Had Gideon been shocked by her behaviour? When she arrived at his side she quickly scanned his face, hoping she would not see jealousy or hurt.

He bowed to the Viscount, giving no signs of any such reactions. Perhaps he had nothing to be jealous of. Perhaps those intense looks, the silent exchanges, had all been in her imagination.

'My lord, what a pleasure it is to see you again,' Gideon said to Jackson Wilde. 'And I'm pleased to see you looking so healthy. It's always good to see a patient respond so well to my attentions. And I'm sure I need not remind you that I am more than happy to attend you as a private patient.'

'You're right,' the Viscount said. 'You have no need to remind me.' He bowed to Emily. 'Now if you'll excuse me, I'm sure you will want to dance with Lady Emily.'

'Such a gracious man,' Gideon said, even before Jackson Wilde was out of earshot, seemingly oblivious to the slight, or preferring to ignore it. He turned to Emily and smiled. 'I think now would be a good time to introduce me to your parents.'

'Yes, of course,' Emily said, still feeling somewhat disconcerted by the dance, even though it had been no more than a waltz around a ballroom surrounded by onlookers.

She gazed across the room to where Jackson Wilde was now speaking to a group of men, which included several members of the House of Commons.

Gideon slid her arm through his. 'Emily?'

She turned to face him. 'Yes?'

'You were going to introduce me to your parents.'

'Oh, yes, sorry, of course.'

'Your mother is smiling at us,' Gideon said as they crossed the crowded room. 'That has to be a good sign.'

'Yes,' she agreed, surprised to see he was right. Her mother was smiling at her with approval, something that rarely happened at a ball.

'I see you were dancing with Viscount Wickford,' her mother said before Emily had a chance to introduce Gideon. 'He looks so dashing tonight in that Regency costume. You two looked as if you were made for each other. Is that why you chose that costume? So you would be a match for Viscount Wickford?'

'Of course not,' she said, quickly glancing at Gideon. 'I had no idea what anyone would be wearing tonight.'

'Oh, such a pity,' her mother said, although Emily could not for the life of her think how that should elicit pity.

'But it looks like dancing with the Viscount has put some colour in your cheeks,' her mother added.

Emily cursed her burning cheeks and sent her mother a warning look, letting her know this was neither the time nor place to discuss the Viscount or any reaction she may or may not have had to dancing with him. A look that merely caused her mother to smile back at her, as if unaware she had done or said anything that deserved her daughter's censure.

'Mother, Father, may I introduce you to Dr Gideon Pratt.

He is a doctor at the Hope Hospital. Dr Pratt, my parents, the Duke and Duchess of Fernwood.'

'It's a great honour to meet you, Your Graces,' Gideon said with a low bow.

'Jolly good work you're doing at that hospital,' her father said. 'Well done.'

'And I don't just work at the hospital,' Gideon said. 'I am also setting up my own private practice and intend to soon have a thriving surgery, treating many of the most respected members of London Society.'

Emily frowned. This was the first she had heard of such a plan. 'But he will still continue to provide his excellent level of care to the patients at Hope Hospital,' Emily said, her statement almost a question.

'Perhaps,' Gideon replied, still smiling at her parents. 'Although I will be fully committed to providing the highest level of care to my private patients.'

Emily's mother smiled politely while looking between Emily and Gideon, as if unsure why they were being introduced and why this man was telling her about his profession.

'Well, don't let us keep you young people,' her mother said. 'The orchestra is once again playing. I believe you should be on the dance floor and enjoying yourself, especially after all the hard work you have put into making tonight such a success.'

Gideon bowed again as if her mother had bestowed a compliment on him, when he'd taken no part in organising tonight's ball. Then he took Emily's arm and led her away.

'I believe that went very well,' he said.

'Yes, I suppose so.'

'Once we've had this dance, I believe I should take the

opportunity to circulate with as many of the guests as possible.'

'Oh, yes, of course. That's very good of you. We've already raised a lot of money for the school, but if you circulate and tell them the good work that the hospital does, then hopefully some of the guests will also be willing to act as patrons for the hospital.'

'Yes,' he said distractedly, as they started to move around the dance floor. 'There really is the cream of Society here tonight, all gathered in one spot. It's simply wonderful.'

'Well, if by the cream you mean the richest and the most influential, then yes, you're right.'

He gave a small laugh as if she had made a joke, which she hadn't.

'Yes, the very best people, all in one place, and I simply cannot let this opportunity pass me by.'

Pique rose within her. This was a side of Gideon she had hitherto not seen. Or was she misunderstanding his intentions? She needed to know for sure.

'Did you mean what you said about a private practice, or were you just saying that for my parents' sake?'

'There will be plenty of time to discuss that later,' he said. 'Let's just enjoy this dance.'

They continued to move around the floor in silence. Emily had so many questions circulating in her mind— about Gideon's plans, his ambitions, their future together— and she really did want them answered, sooner rather than later.

'Gideon, before you start circulating again, can we please have a quiet word? Perhaps out on the terrace,' she said the moment the music had finished.

This caused him to smile brightly. He took her arm and

led her towards the French doors at the end of the ballroom and out onto the terrace overlooking the garden.

'So are you going to tell me what you meant when you told my parents about your plans for a private practice?'

He closed the French doors, cutting off the sound of the orchestra and the chattering guests. 'I believe tonight would be the perfect time for me to formally ask your father for your hand in marriage,' he said, as if he hadn't heard her question. 'We could even announce it here tonight, in front of all of Society.'

'Oh,' she said, lowering herself on the cold concrete seat and giving a forced laugh. 'Shouldn't you ask me first?'

He stared at her in confusion. 'Ask? But I thought we had an understanding.'

'Well, yes, perhaps, but it would be nice to actually get a proposal,' she said with a small, somewhat awkward laugh. 'After all, I'll only ever get one.'

He continued to look down at her, his brow furrowed. 'I wasn't aware that you were like that. You're usually such a practical, sensible woman, one who doesn't care for such romantic twaddle.'

Emily shrugged. She thought so too, but, surely, under these circumstances, a bit of romance was called for.

'But if that is what you require,' he said with a condescending smile as he sat down beside her. 'Lady Emily, will you do me the honour of becoming my wife?'

Emily stared at him, willing herself to say yes. Wasn't this what she always wanted, to be married to a sensible, serious man, dedicated to his profession, one who was committed to helping others and making the world a better place? But there were still those unanswered questions. 'Gideon, we need to—'

'Or do you need more romancing?' he asked, once again giving her a somewhat condescending smile. Before she was aware of what was happening, he took hold of her shoulders and smashed his lips against hers. Emily clamped her lips tightly together. She pulled back against his hold as he crushed himself more tightly to her chest.

No, this was definitely not what she wanted. A bolt of realisation hit her. She knew not only did she not want his kisses. She did not want Gideon, did not want to become his wife.

Placing her hands on his shoulders she pushed hard and turned her head, so his lips were no longer on hers.

'Sorry,' he said as he released her, looking more smug than apologetic. 'Although now that we are engaged I believe you can't condemn a man for taking a few liberties. But I appreciate that a chaste woman such as yourself needs a bit more coercing into such intimacies. You need have no fear on that account. I am a gentleman and can wait until our wedding night.'

Coercion? What did he mean by coercion?

'Oh, Emily, we are going to be so happy together. Once my practice is established, I'll be able to keep you in the comfort to which you are accustomed. We'll be able to mix with the *crème de la crème* of Society. I promise you, I will make you the very best of husbands.'

'But what of the hospital, the school?'

He smiled and took hold of her hands. 'Once we are married you won't need to fill your time with charity work. You'll be too busy being my wife.'

'I don't want to marry you,' Emily blurted out.

'Don't be silly. We had an agreement. That's why you

held this ball, so you could introduce me to your family, your friends and to Society.'

'I said I don't want to marry you,' she repeated, her voice stronger.

He continued to smile at her as if this was some sort of game.

'You're not the man I thought you were,' she continued. 'I thought you were as dedicated to the hospital as I am, not an ambitious doctor wanting to make money.'

His smile turned into a confused frown. 'What? You expected me to want to spend my life working among the wretched of this great city? I didn't fight my way into medical school and dedicate all those years to study to spend the rest of my life in the East End.'

'That *is* what I expected of you. That is the man I thought you were. I thought you were a better man.'

'I am a better man, and will be an even better man with you at my side. I intend to be one of the most eminent doctors in London. A man you will be proud to call your husband.'

'I would be proud of a man who dedicated his life to those who needed his help, not a man who wants to become rich and well thought of by people whose opinion I care nothing about.'

His eyebrows drew close together, as if he was trying to decipher a language he couldn't quite grasp.

'What are you saying?'

'I'm sorry. I don't want to marry you.'

He continued to stare at her, shaking his head slowly. 'So why did you lead me on? Why did you make me think that we had an understanding? Why did you make me think we were courting? Why did you introduce me to your parents and your friends?'

'I'm sorry,' she repeated, pulling her hands out of his grasp and placing them in her lap.

Emily could not believe she had done it again. She had deluded herself about a man. Again. And she *was* sorry, not just for herself, but for what she had done to Gideon.

'I'm sorry, Gideon. Sorry that I thought you were a man different to the one you really are. Sorry that in my mind I made you into the man I wanted you to be, not the man you really are. None of that is your fault.'

'Is it because I kissed you? I shouldn't have done that,' he said, desperation entering his voice. 'You need not worry about such things. We will need to consummate the marriage to make it legal, but once we've done that we can come to an arrangement. After all, I am a gentleman, I won't force you to do anything you don't want to.'

'I don't want to marry you,' she repeated, her voice rising.

'But—'

'But nothing. I have given my answer. You said you were a gentleman, so just accept that I have turned down your proposal and there is nothing you can do or say to change my mind.'

He frowned at her, as if incapable of understanding this simple declaration.

'I don't want to marry you, Gideon,' she repeated. 'I think you should go now.'

His lips drew into a hard, thin line. 'I cannot believe you have turned down the chance to become the wife of a man who will one day be a successful doctor.'

Emily looked down at her hands clasped in her lap, wishing he would just leave.

'You must know that a woman your age is unlikely to get another offer of marriage.' He stood up and began pacing. 'I had wondered why the daughter of a duke had ended up being left on the shelf. Now I have my answer. All I can say is thank goodness you let me know what you're really like now, before I ended up married to a dried-up old spinster who is terrified of a man's touch.'

Emily clenched her hands tighter and stared straight ahead, out into the dark night, not wanting him to see how deeply his barbed words had pierced her.

'You, madam, are a bitter old maid, who will only become more bitter with each passing year.'

With his cruel words still ringing in her ears, he strode back into the ballroom, leaving Emily shaken and trying to grasp how this had happened. How, for the second time in her life, she had completely misread a man's character, only to discover he was nothing like the person she'd imagined, and had hoped him to be.

Chapter Eight

Dr Pratt reappeared in the ballroom, alone, his face like thunder. When he'd departed to the terrace, arm in arm with Lady Emily, shutting the doors firmly behind them, Jackson's heart had sunk. The doctor had looked so pleased with himself after being introduced to the Duke and Duchess of Fernwood, giving Jackson the strong suspicion that he was about to propose.

During the long minutes they had been absent, he had attempted to distract himself with conversation, doing what he was here to do, drumming up support for the school. He had no reason to concern himself with what was happening out on the terrace. Lady Emily was a grown woman capable of making her own choices. Just because Jackson thought the doctor a complete twit did not mean she saw him that way. But, if he had proposed, Dr Pratt's furious expression made it clear what her answer had been.

Satisfaction washed through Jackson. He watched the doors. Lady Emily did not return. The doctor stood against the wall for a moment, as if gathering himself. Then he smiled, strode across the room to a group of men chatting beside the supper table, and bowed politely in introduction.

Jackson's attention turned back to the French doors. She had still not returned. Had the doctor left Lady Emily in a state of distress? There was only one way to find out. He rushed across the dance floor and pulled open the glass doors leading onto the terrace.

She was sitting against the wall, staring into space.

'Is everything all right?' he asked, knowing it wasn't.

She looked towards him. Even in the dim light from the ballroom, he could see tears sparkling on her black eyelashes. 'Oh, yes, perfectly all right, thank you,' she said, sitting up straighter.

'May I join you?'

She shrugged in answer, so he moved from the doorway, closed the doors and took a seat beside her on the stone bench.

'You don't look as if everything is all right,' he said, looking out at the garden, dimly lit from the light spilling out from the ballroom.

She drew in a shuddering breath. 'Gideon proposed,' she said quietly.

He merely nodded.

'I turned him down.'

'I take it he was disappointed that you are not to become his wife.'

She gave a small, humourless laugh. 'Yes, I believe he is disappointed that the Duke of Fernwood's daughter is not to be his wife.'

'I'm sure that's not true. I'm sure he cared about much more than your title,' Jackson said, aiming to comfort her, but suspecting she was correct.

She turned to face him, blinked away her tears, and stared him straight in the eye, her defiant pose contradicted by a slight trembling of her lips. He wanted to take her in his arms and tell her she did not have to be strong, not in front of him, but taking her in his arms was the last thing he should do.

'He actually said that a woman of my age should be grateful he proposed.' The wobble to her voice revealed just how deeply those words had wounded.

How dare he?

Jackson's jaw clenched and he exhaled loudly through flared nostrils, then forced himself to rein in his anger. It would do Lady Emily no good if he lost his temper with that craven maggot.

'You shouldn't listen to anything a man with a broken heart says,' he said, fighting to keep his voice even.

She gave another mirthless laugh. 'Broken heart? I doubt that very much. If his heart is broken, it's because he fears losing his dream of owning a private medical practice tending to members of the aristocracy.'

Jackson made no comment, again suspecting that to be the truth.

She bit her lip and looked at him, those liquid brown eyes appealing for his understanding. 'He also said I was a dried-up old spinster who will only get more bitter as I get older.'

'The cad. You mustn't believe a thing that ba—' He swallowed down the word he wanted to use and instead turned on the seat and clasped her hands. 'He is the bitter one. He was just lashing out at you in anger. You are most definitely not bitter. Nor are you old, and you're certainly not a spinster. You're an enchanting young woman and the only reason you are yet to find a husband is because no man is good enough for you.'

She laughed as if his words had been said in jest, but it was no jest. She was indeed a beautiful young woman, one who deserved to be loved and respected by a man much more worthy of her than that Pratt fellow could ever be.

'No, I think he might be right. He tried to kiss me tonight and it was awful. It was my first kiss and I hated it.' Colour exploded on her cheeks. She once again blinked away the tears that were threatening to fall and lowered her head.

He lightly placed one finger under her chin and gently lifted it. A man like Pratt had no right to make this admirable young woman feel bad about herself.

'That's probably because it *was* awful,' he said. 'But it just shows that you either didn't want Dr Pratt to kiss you, or he was a terrible kisser, or both.'

She shrugged one shoulder. 'How would I know if he's a terrible kisser or not?' Her eyes moved to his lips. 'I'm four-and-twenty and no man has kissed me before. All I know is his kiss revolted me so much I couldn't stop myself from pushing him away. He was the man I thought I wanted to marry and I couldn't even bear being in his arms. Perhaps his horrid description of me was right.'

'No, he is wrong.'

Before Jackson had time to consider the wisdom of what he was doing, he took her in his arms and kissed her lovely lips. To his delighted surprised she sunk into his arms and kissed him back.

This was most definitely not the reaction of a spinster, nor of a woman who hated being kissed. This was glorious. Just as he had fantasised. He had wanted to kiss her from the first moment he saw her angelic face looking down at him when he awoke in hospital. And when she had tended his wounds he'd wanted to do a lot more than just kiss her, but he'd had enough sense to know not to. Now it appeared all sense had deserted him.

Stop. Now, the small part of his brain still capable of reason told him. *Men like you do not kiss women like her. Not unless you intend to face the consequences.*

He couldn't undo the kiss, but if he had a modicum of decency he would make it a short, light kiss, just to prove to her that she was no dried-up old spinster.

But he didn't stop. Instead he deepened the kiss. His tongue ran along her soft bottom lip. She moaned lightly, her lips parting. She was not objecting to what he was doing, quite the opposite. Her hands wound around the back of his neck, holding him closer as she kissed him back.

His tongue gently entered her mouth, tasting her, savouring her, as she melded in closer to him—her full, soft breasts against his chest. If there was any doubt about the passion of this woman, it had now been firmly stripped away. She was a woman made for the giving and taking of physical pleasure. But he should not be the man either giving or taking. She was a respectable young woman. Respectable young women saved themselves for marriage to respectable men. And no one could ever accuse Jackson of being respectable.

This was wrong. He had gone too far already, and he must not go any further, as damnably tempting as it was to do so.

With the greatest reluctance he withdrew from her lips and, still holding her close, looked down at her lovely face. Her red lips were plump from their kiss, her face flushed a pretty shade of pink, her eyes still closed. Had he ever seen a more tempting woman? If he had, he certainly couldn't remember when, but it was a temptation he should have resisted, and one he must never sample again.

She slowly opened her eyes and gazed at him, her warm brown eyes almost black in the subdued light. Her lips parted and she released a slow sigh, her breath gentle on his cheek.

As if emerging from a trance, she blinked several times, then her hands dropped from behind his neck. She placed them demurely in her lap and once again looked straight ahead, out at the darkened garden.

'I probably shouldn't have done that,' he said, aware of the husky note in his voice. 'But at least we've proven Dr Pratt completely wrong. Whoever you do eventually marry is going to be a very lucky man indeed.'

'Thank you,' she said, causing him to smile. He was unsure whether she was thanking him for the compliment or the kiss, but neither was required.

'You deserve someone much better than Dr Pratt,' he said quietly.

'Maybe,' she responded.

'You do, Lady Emily. You deserve a good man, one who is worthy of your love. I believe that such creatures do exist, although I'm yet to meet one.'

Her small laugh filled him with almost as much satisfaction as that kiss had done. After all the terrible things that cretin Pratt had said to her, it was good to hear her laugh.

'Thank you,' she repeated. 'You are very kind.'

It was his turn to laugh. 'I don't think your parents or Society would see it that way.'

This truly was a peculiar situation in which he found himself. He had just kissed a woman to make her feel better, to make her realise just how attractive she actually was. One could almost see it as a noble, unselfish act.

He smiled at this delusional idea. With her thigh almost

touching his, the taste of her still on his lips, her feminine scent sparking inappropriate reactions deep within him, what he had just done and wanted to do to her right now could never be described as unselfish or noble.

And if they remained out here for much longer, alone on this darkened terrace, she would discover just how ignoble and selfish he really was.

'I believe it might be best if we returned to the ballroom before tongues start to wag.'

And we should do so while I am still able to exercise some self-control.

She didn't answer so he forced himself to stand and offer her his hand. It was essential they return to the ballroom, where his behaviour could be modified by the company of others.

'Lady Emily, would you do me the honour of the next dance?'

She looked up at him, nodded and without comment placed her hand in his.

He led her into the centre of the ballroom and quickly looked around, expecting to see no sign of Dr Pratt. But no, there he was, smiling and ingratiating himself to the Earl of Bosworth. Jackson swallowed down his ire. He had insulted this remarkable woman, left her hurt and reeling, and now he didn't even have the decency to leave.

He could only hope that the next man Lady Emily was attracted to was a far better one than Dr Pratt. That of course completely ruled out Jackson.

Despite that kiss, despite discovering there was a sensual woman trapped inside that stern exterior, that sensuality was not his to explore. She was still the moralistic, judgemental Lady Emily, and he was—well, he was Jackson Wilde.

He would enjoy one last waltz and that would be it. They would then go their separate ways. He placed his hand on her slim waist and suppressed a low groan. He could almost feel her skin through the flimsy fabric of her gown. Unlike the usual ornate fashions women wore, clothing seemingly designed to make them inaccessible to men, this gown created little in the way of a barrier. In one quick movement, he was sure he would be able to lift it over her head, exposing her delightful body to his appreciative gaze. He wondered what she was wearing underneath, and if those items would be as easily removed as her gown.

She looked up at him, a question in those deep brown eyes. A question that she would be horrified by if she heard the answer. So he said nothing, instead they moved off in time to the music.

Do not think of her naked body, he reminded himself, which of course made him think of her naked body. *Do not think of that kiss*, which made the taste of her suddenly rich on his lips. *Do not think about her scent. Do not inhale and allow that fresh, sweet scent of a woman to send your mind drifting off into inappropriate places. Distract yourself, do something, anything.*

'The ball has been a great success,' he said, wincing at a comment that would be inane at the best of times, but was particularly asinine after what they had just shared.

She smiled up at him, a smile that appeared both amused by his inane attempt at conversation, and somehow knowing, as if she was well aware of the complexity of his feelings.

'Parts of it have been particularly successful,' she said with a little grin.

Was she teasing him? Tonight really was a night full of wonders.

'Why, Lady Emily, whatever do you mean?' he replied, wanting to be the teas*er*, not the teas*ee*, if such a word existed.

'I'm talking about the flower arrangements, of course,' she said with a cheeky smile. 'What did you think I meant?'

'Exactly that. The flower arrangements are indeed tonight's highlight.'

Her smile grew wider as he twirled her around. 'Mmm, the scent of them fills the senses and makes one almost heady with sensual delight.'

He raised a surprised eyebrow. She had moved from teasing to outright flirting. He had assumed she would never do something as frivolous as flirt. Would tonight's surprises never cease?

'Yes, some scents can transport one and arouse one's emotions,' he said, remembering her fresh, womanly scent undisguised by artificial perfumes. He had been consumed by it when he had kissed her, and now he longed to bury himself in that scent once again.

'And the supper was particularly successful as well,' she said, with that teasing smile, as if she knew exactly what affect her words were having on him and was relishing the power it gave her. 'I can almost taste the delicious flavours on my lips,' she added, running her tongue along her bottom lip.

Jackson released a moan, which he covered with a small cough. Was she trying to torture him? If that was the intent, he was prepared to give as good as he got.

'You're right,' he said, preparing for the duel. 'Some tastes are designed to be savoured, to be explored, and delighted in. When something is truly delicious you want to slowly lick it all over, exploring every part of it with your tongue and your lips until you've had your fill.'

That resulted in a satisfying blush colouring her cheeks.

'Don't you agree, Lady Emily?' he asked, unable to disguise his amusement at her discomfort.

She swallowed, drawing his attention to the creamy skin of her neck. 'Yes,' she croaked out, making his smile grow larger. That did the trick. There would be no more teasing, no more torture, no more talk reminding him of the delights of how she tasted on his tongue and lips.

They continued dancing in silence and a tinge of guilt attempted to undermine his sense of self-satisfaction. Perhaps he had been wrong to tease her so. She was new to this game and he was a seasoned campaigner, but, oh, it was good to see her blush, and he couldn't deny he liked seeing a woman who was usually so strong and assertive looking at him in that coy, abashed manner.

The dance came to an end and he took her arm to escort her off the dance floor, where crowds milled at the edges, talking excitedly.

'Oh, and of course your kiss was simply sublime as well,' she whispered with a quick wink as they joined the throng, leaving him no opportunity to retort without being overheard.

He laughed and knew that, despite his best efforts, she had won.

Chapter Nine

As if she'd been drinking champagne, Emily bubbled inside. There were so many emotions she suspected she should be feeling; upset over the collapse of her hoped-for marriage, shock at being kissed by a notorious rake, embarrassment over kissing him back with such unrestrained enthusiasm, but she felt none of these. Instead, gleefulness fluttered through her, making her giddy. And she simply refused to analyse the reasons why. She would just surrender herself to these glorious, unfamiliar sensations.

Like a debutante at her first ball, Emily wanted to twirl around the room, to laugh, flirt, dance and enjoy herself.

It was hard to believe such a transformation could take place, all because of one kiss. But oh, what a kiss. In reality, it was nothing more than the touch of his lips on hers, and yet it had set off such unimaginable reactions within her. It was as if her body had been sleeping until that moment, and he had awakened it. He had given her a small taste of the pleasure a man and woman could give each other and it was delicious. So delicious she longed to feast until she had her fill.

Emily had known such delights existed in theory. Her friends on occasion waxed lyrical about their wonderful husbands and it was obvious even to Emily that they were expressing appreciation for more than just the men's characters. Now she had been given a hint of the decidedly enticing possibilities Jackson Wilde could provide, she knew a hint would never be enough.

The music started up again, and Emily looked up at him expectantly.

'We've already had two dances. I believe if we have another dance, we will set tongues wagging,' he said.

What did Emily care about that? Let them wag.

'Perhaps we should sit this one out,' he continued. 'As committee members we do have to set an example of how respectable people conduct themselves.'

Was he serious? He was Jackson Wilde, what on earth was he talking about, being respectable, setting an example?

'But—'

His laughter cut her off. 'I'm sure you must be in need of refreshments. I know I could do with a drink.'

He linked her arm through his and escorted her over to the supper table, where he poured two glasses of punch from the large bowl and handed one to her. Emily shouldn't have done it, but she couldn't stop herself from lightly stroking her fingers along the back of his hand as he handed her the glass.

His eyes widened, and Emily wondered if she was making a spectacle of herself. Gideon's cruel words crashed in on her. Was she proving to Jackson Wilde that she really was a spinster, just as Gideon had said? One kiss and she was swooning all over him. Was he laughing at her?

But no, she would not think that. She had seen and felt his own reaction when he'd held her close. He had wanted that kiss as much as she did, and he was still at her side.

There was nothing to stop him from dancing with any one of the pretty, single young women present tonight.

Jackson Wilde had kissed her, danced with her, wanted her. He was no gentleman. He had proven that time and time again. If he was still by her side, it was not due to politeness but because that was exactly where he wanted to be.

'Have you had your photograph taken?' a geisha girl asked, breaking in on her thoughts.

'Photograph?' Emily asked.

'Oh, it's such fun, and such a good idea,' Lord Nelson added as he handed the geisha girl a glass of punch. 'And a wonderful memory of such a splendid evening.'

Emily looked to where Lord Nelson was pointing.

'That was Amelia's idea,' she told the Viscount. 'She arranged for a photographer to set up in the morning room as another way to raise money for the school.'

'As it's all in a good cause, shall we?' Jackson suggested, offering her his arm once more. 'An indelible image of tonight is exactly what we need.'

Even greater happiness filled her. He wanted an image to remember this night by. It was a thrilling thought. While having her photograph taken would be fun, Emily knew she did not need a memento to remember what had happened tonight. Nothing could ever make her forget that remarkable kiss. But he was right, it was in a good cause, and it would be lovely to have tonight captured for ever.

They wended their way through the crowd and joined the excited queue.

'Isn't this simply marvellous,' the milkmaid standing in front of them said. 'I had my portrait taken at a studio once, but tonight the photographer has brought all his equipment here to us. Such fun.'

'Indeed, it is, my dear,' the pirate on her arm answered. 'Aren't these modern gadgets just the thing? And I read the other day that some clever chap has even invented a way of filming people while they are actually moving. Marvellous.'

'Oh, yes, we do live in a fabulous time, don't we?' the milkmaid responded, shaking her head in wonderment. 'Maybe one day people will be able to film balls such as this. Won't that be simply wonderful?'

Emily returned her smile, although, considering some of the things that had occurred this evening, she was uncertain whether she would want a complete photographic document available for all to see.

When their turn came, Emily and Jackson entered the adjoining room, which had been transformed into a photography studio, with black curtains obscuring the furniture and creating a booth. They stood in front of the large cardboard backdrop—depicting a pastoral scene of fields and weeping willows—and beside a pedestal bearing a large fern in a porcelain pot.

'Elizabeth Bennet and Mr Darcy, I believe,' the photographer said.

Jackson and Emily exchanged conspiratorial smiles. That had certainly not been her intention when she had dressed this evening. She had merely chosen a costume that was easy to acquire and comfortable to wear. She'd had no idea that Jackson would also be dressed in the Regency style, but it was a lovely coincidence, almost fortuitous, one could say.

'As you are representing a famous couple, perhaps you

could stand a little closer together,' the photographer added, looking at them over his camera and tripod, moving his hands in a manner to suggest the closing of a gap.

Emily and Jackson shuffled nearer to each other. Jackson smiled at her, looking as awkward as Emily felt.

'Now, please turn to face each other, and, Mr Darcy, if you would place your hand on Elizabeth's waist. And, Miss Bennet, if you could put your hand on Mr Darcy's arm. That should capture the romance of their story.'

They exchanged amused looks, but willingly did as instructed.

'And if you could gaze at each other as if you are besotted, just as Miss Austen's famous characters would surely do.'

As one, they rolled their eyes, and despite their laughter did their best impression of two people in love.

'I'm afraid you will not be able to laugh, and it is better if you do not smile,' the photographer said, a small note of impatience entering his voice. It had no doubt been a long night for him and he would be starting to tire of making excitable guests do as they were told. 'You need to remain perfectly still while I capture your image.'

Somewhat chastened, Emily did as instructed and looked up into Jackson Wilde's blue eyes, with what she hoped was an adoring expression. As she held his gaze, this became an increasingly less difficult task. They were such enchanting eyes, she was sure she could stay as she was, staring into them, for an eternity.

He gazed back at her with equal intensity, holding her captive. His gaze moved to her lips. Was he remembering their kiss, just as she was? Were his lips tingling as well?

Was he wishing they were doing more than gazing at each other, that they were once again locked in an embrace?

She closed her eyes and released a sigh of pleasure, imagining his lips on hers. As if conjuring memory to reality, his lips lightly stroked hers.

'I said, don't move,' a voice called out as Jackson's arm slid further around her waist and she was gently pulled up against his body.

'I said…' The photographer's voice faded as she moulded herself into him, loving the feel of his hard muscles against her soft breasts, his strong arms holding her tightly. Gently, she rubbed herself against him, kissing him back, needing to feel him, taste him—to have him.

His hands moved further around her body, capturing her hips and holding her firmly. Heat flooded through her body. Her heart beat fast within her chest, and a deep throbbing pounding within her core. She wrapped her hands around the back of his head and kissed him with a fervour she did not know she possessed.

'When something is truly delicious you want to slowly lick it all over, exploring every part of it with your tongue and your lips until you've had your fill.'

His words on the dance floor entered her mind. It was what she wanted him to do now. She wanted to feel his hands, his lips, his tongue on every inch of her body, exploring all those parts his kiss had brought to life.

He pulled back from the kiss and looked down at her, his hooded eyes intense.

She stared up at him, bewildered by what had just happened. Why had he stopped when it was obvious that they both wanted this? Then reality crashed in. The sounds of music, talking and laughing from the adjoining room filled her ears. She was in a public place and had lost all sense of reason and propriety. She continued gazing into his smouldering eyes, and realised she really didn't care. She wanted him to kiss her again and hang propriety, hang reason.

His arms dropped to his side. It seemed he had more sense than her. Damn him, why did he suddenly have to become so sensible?

'You are so beautiful,' he whispered. And she did feel beautiful. Beautiful and desirable, desired by an attractive, virile, breathtaking man. And it felt good. Very good.

'That was splendid,' the photographer said, adjusting his camera.

She turned to face the photographer, as if trying to remember who he was and why he was here.

'I managed to take several shots while you were,' he paused. 'They're perhaps a little bit risqué but have wonderful artistic merit. They should be ready in a week or so and, if they turn out as well as I expect, I'd love to be able to exhibit them. With your permission, of course.'

'No,' Emily and Jackson Wilde said as one, turning to each other with matching looks of disbelief.

'Oh, well, perhaps you'll change your mind when you see them.'

'They will not be for public display,' the Viscount said, his voice firm.

The disappointed photographer nodded and prepared his camera for the next subject, as Jackson Wilde took Emily's arm and led her back to the ballroom.

'How was it?' a waiting Henry VIII asked.

'Words simply can't explain its wonders,' the Viscount said, sending Emily a quick wink and causing her to giggle. Emily couldn't remember the last time she had giggled like a young girl, and it felt rather lovely. In fact, a lot about tonight felt decidedly lovely, at least the bits that had involved her being in Jackson Wilde's arms, either when he kissed her or when they danced together.

'As we have already behaved in a somewhat scandalous manner tonight, I don't think it will do our reputations any more harm if we dance together one more time,' Jackson said, leading her back onto the dance floor.

He was right. Their behaviour tonight *had* been scandalous. It had also been the most fun Emily had had in her life and she did not want the fun to stop. There was no denying Jackson Wilde was a wholly unsuitable man. No respectable woman in her right mind would get involved with such a man. He lived a dissolute life and his salacious antics made him a regular feature in the scandal columns. In so many ways he was exactly the sort of man she should avoid, and yet in so many other ways he was also perfect for what she had in mind.

She wanted him. At least, she wanted his kisses and his caresses. She would be a fool to want more than that, and Emily had made enough of a fool of herself over a man. She shuddered slightly at the memory of Dr Pratt's insulting proposal.

She was not a dried-up old spinster. Jackson Wilde had shown her that. And she wanted him to show her so much more. But, before that happened, she was going to have to have a serious discussion with him to ensure that this time she got it right. Never again would she be duped by a man. Never again would she allow herself to be deluded into thinking he was someone he was not, or that the relationship was anything other than what it appeared to be.

But that was a discussion for another time. The rest of this night would be for enjoying herself. And, as he continued to whirl her around the dance floor, that was exactly what she did.

Chapter Ten

Two days later, Jackson stood in the middle of the drawing room at his Kensington townhouse and stared down at the piece of crisp white paper in his hand.

Lady Emily's feminine handwriting informed him she wished to meet with him to discuss the ball, and intended to visit his home at three o'clock, nothing more. Jackson turned it over, looked at the blank back, then turned back to the written words and read it once again, trying to discern some meaning, any meaning, from the brief letter. Did she want to discuss the kiss—or, to be more accurate, those kisses—and their ramifications?

He blew out a held breath. For Jackson, such a discussion had the potential to be life changing. She could demand a proposal. It was quite within her rights to do so, and he would be honour-bound to accede to her demands and make her his wife. That was something he should have thought about before he kissed her, and it certainly should have occurred to him before he kissed her in front of a witness, and, more than that, he should have taken the time to consider the potential outcome of kissing her while a photograph was being taken. But thinking had been one thing he had done far too little of during the ball.

There was also the possibility he had nothing to worry

about. Perhaps she merely wanted an innocent meeting to discuss the proceeds from the ball, how much money they had raised and how that money could best be used to gain the maximum benefit for the girls and women of the East End.

Innocent?

He gave a snort of laughter and shook his head. It was merely a few kisses, but in the eyes of Society there was nothing innocent about a man kissing a young lady. Nor could he use the word innocent to describe the thoughts he'd had about Lady Emily since the ball, all of which had involved sensual antics that were enticingly sinful.

He placed the note on the table and looked at the clock ticking on the mantelpiece. In a few minutes she would arrive and all his questions would be answered. It was best he put aside any thoughts of their kisses, or the fantasies he had harboured in the two days since he had last seen her. Although, to do so demanded a level of mental discipline that was illusive to a man such as himself. Her kisses had been a revelation, nothing less. He had discovered, in the nicest way possible, that the woman he had dismissed as judgemental and preachy was surprisingly sensual, and a rather good kisser.

But that had all happened during a fancy dress ball. People often let their hair down, sometimes literally, at such occasions. The next day they would be back to their highly respectable, buttoned-up selves, and there was a very good chance that Lady Emily would be no different.

Plus, she had just been hurt by Pratt. That could make even the most prudent and restrained woman act out of character. And unfortunately for Lady Emily, she had been in the company of a man who was more than capable of taking advantage of a woman in that state.

Perhaps that was why she wanted to see him. To demand an apology. If that was what she required, she would have it. Not that he was really sorry. How could he ever be sorry to have tasted her kisses? But if it was an apology she demanded, then it was an apology he would give, and he would attempt to make it heartfelt.

He looked over at the abandoned note. Perhaps she wanted to tell him that what happened at the ball was best forgotten. Perhaps she would be back to prim and proper Lady Emily, the woman who thoroughly, and quite rightly, disapproved of him. For one night they had played the roles of Mr Darcy and Miss Elizabeth Bennet, and now it was back to being Jackson Wilde and Lady Emily Beaumont, two people who could barely abide each other. Yes, that also made sense. She wanted to ensure they put what happened firmly in the past and never mentioned it again.

Whatever she wanted, there was no way he could know until the lady herself arrived and enlightened him. In the meantime, he had to exercise some patience and wait. He crossed the room and sat down. Then stood up and returned to leaning on the mantelpiece, looking at the ticking clock.

This was ridiculous. He was nervous. He could tell himself the only thing he had to be nervous about was his dread of being dragged kicking and screaming up the altar, but that was not the only thing causing his agitation.

He was nervous about seeing her again. And that in itself was bizarre. They had shared two kisses, nothing more. Kisses that were quite chaste compared to his usual encounters with young women. And yet, they were kisses that affected him even more than some of his adventurous liaisons with the fairer sex. How was it possible that a woman he hardly knew, a woman he had assumed was nothing more than a moralistic, judgemental do-gooder, could leave him nervous like a schoolboy about to have his first tryst with a girl?

He paced around the room, the clock's ticking growing louder and louder with each passing second. The note said she would arrive at three o'clock. It was now three o'clock. Where was she? He tapped the clock to ensure it was working correctly just as a footman knocked on the door to the drawing room.

'Come,' he called out.

'Lady Emily Beaumont, my lord,' the footman said.

Jackson nodded, and leant against the mantelpiece, adopting his most devil-may-care posture. It would not help his waning masculine pride if he let her see that her visit had flustered him in any way.

She entered and, damn it all, a jolt of raw attraction shot through his body.

Framed by the doorway she looked simply radiant. Dressed in a simple grey skirt with a lacy high-necked white blouse, her hair tied in a neat bun at the back of her head, she looked more attractive than any woman who donned ornate hairstyles, sparkling jewels and lavish clothing designed to attract a man's eye. The skirt nipped in at her small waist and flared out over her rounded hips—the simple blouse clung to those luscious breasts he had felt against his chest when they had kissed. Breasts he had fantasised about ever since.

How could he possibly be blamed for kissing such a woman? What man could resist her? Certainly not a man like him.

He waited for her chaperone to follow her in. No one

else entered. His agitation wrenched up a notch. This would not do. If he couldn't be trusted to keep his hands and his lips to himself when they were in a public place, how was he to be expected to keep his hands and various other body parts to himself when they were alone in the drawing room of his townhouse?

'Please leave the door open, James,' he said to the footman, and saw the man's eyebrows raise almost imperceptibly before he nodded and departed, leaving the door fully ajar.

She turned and looked at the door, then back at him, her head tilted in question.

'You are an unaccompanied young woman alone in a man's home. If the door is closed, and no servants can observe what is happening between us, your reputation could be compromised.'

'I believe that ship has already sailed.'

Was her statement designed to put the fear of God into him? Or, to be more precise, the fear of marriage? Whatever the answer, it still did not mean he would risk a closed door. She may think the worst that could happen between a man and woman when they were alone was that they could exchange kisses. He knew different, and for his own protection, as much as hers, that door had to stay open.

'Despite what took place at the ball, I believe for propriety's sake it best that the door remain open so the servants can see at all times what occurs between us,' he said, sounding like he was the prim and proper one.

She crossed the room and shut the door.

Jackson suppressed a low moan. A shut door when he was alone with a woman sent a signal to his servants that he was not to be disturbed under any circumstances. Did she really care so little for her reputation? And did she really want to put him in this taxing position?

Well, Jackson, he told himself. *Now is going to be a test of your mettle.*

Whatever his mettle actually was. His father had always said it was something Jackson did not possess. Somehow, he was going to have to suddenly find it in abundance.

'Won't you please take a seat,' he said, still standing by the mantelpiece and indicating the divan furthest away from him.

Unlike his command to not shut the door, this time she did as he asked. The cotton of her skirt rustled gently as she crossed the room. When she took her seat, he heard that captivating sound of silk stockings rubbing lightly against each other. It was a sound that never failed to entice him. But enticed he could not be, not with a shut door. Not with the guarantee they would not be interrupted by his well-trained servants.

She patted the seat beside her. 'And won't you join me? It's a little hard to talk when you're standing so far away.'

Damn, why didn't he point to one of the wing-backed chairs where she would be carefully contained away from him. Now he would have to sit dangerously close to her, within kissing distance of those lips and caressing distance of that luscious body.

She waited, so he did as she asked, crossing the room and joining her on the divan.

He looked down at her hands, clasped tightly in her lap as if to stop them shaking, while she stared straight ahead into the middle of the drawing room. He wasn't the only nervous one. Of course he wasn't. This must be extremely difficult for her. That would be why she shut the door, so the servants would not overhear this difficult conversation. That would be why she didn't bring a chaperone. His actions had put her in this precarious position, and he needed to put this right.

What would a decent man do in these circumstances? Would he raise the subject of their kisses first or would he wait politely until the young lady mentioned it? He had no idea. He was no gentleman and had never kissed a respectable young woman before. He had no idea what etiquette demanded.

That was a lie. He knew exactly what etiquette demanded. He was supposed to make a proposal of marriage.

Jackson's stomach and heart sank. Oh, God. That *was* why she was here. She was waiting for his proposal. And now he was about to prove everything his father said about him was true. Like the lowlife he knew himself to be, he was going to try and weasel his way out of a situation he should never have got himself into in the first place. He was once again going to fail to take responsibility for his actions.

With his father's glare of distaste in his mind, he braced himself. 'About what happened at the ball,' he said, trying desperately to think *what* he was going to say about it.

'Yes, that's what I've come to talk to you about.'

He swallowed. 'You have?'

'Yes.' She drew in a deep breath. Jackson did the same and waited for his life to be ruined.

'I enjoyed our kisses very much,' she said. 'And I have decided I wish to become your mistress.'

His held breath released from his lungs in a loud exhalation. Had he heard her correctly? 'You what?' he asked, his voice coming out in an unmanly gasp. 'You what?' he repeated in a deeper, more controlled voice.

'I wish to become your mistress.'

He had heard correctly, but it was no less startling on repetition.

'You don't need to look at me like that. You've had mistresses before, haven't you?'

'Ah, yes, one or two.'

'Well, from what I've heard there's been considerably more than that. But that's all for the good.'

'Is it?' He would have thought in Lady Emily's eyes that would be all for the bad.

'Yes, it means you are experienced and know what a woman wants.'

'Well, I suppose—'

'And after what happened between us at the ball, and after all those cruel things that Gideon said, I came to a decision.'

'You did?' he asked, starting to sound like a monosyllabic idiot.

'Yes. I decided Gideon was correct. Or perhaps not correct, not yet anyway, but the way he described me could very well become correct if I don't do something to change my fate.'

'I wouldn't believe a word that man said.' What was he doing? Was he arguing against the idea of them becoming lovers? Was he going mad? Wasn't that what he wanted? Did he not want her in his bed? Hadn't he repeatedly imagined her laying naked beneath him, that long chestnut hair spread over his pillows, her arms reaching out to him. Her legs parted—

He coughed and crossed his legs. Now was certainly not the time to let those images play out in his mind.

'I agree that he was lashing out in anger,' she continued, her voice still matter of fact, as if they were discussing something unimportant, such as a delay in the morning mail delivery, and not a subject of monumental importance. 'But what he said, and those kisses we shared, made me realise that I do not want to become a spinster.'

Jackson could point out that if a woman doesn't marry then she does indeed become a spinster as a matter of course, but suspected now was not the time to point out matters of semantics.

'He also said I would become increasingly bitter, and I admit there is a danger to that,' she nodded to herself. 'I admit I was very imbittered about how he had deceived me into thinking he was a different man just so I would marry him, or, at least, how I had convinced myself he was a different man, and exactly the sort of man I wanted to marry.'

She shrugged as if pushing all those thoughts away. 'But that is not what I'm here to discuss. Realising I had been so wrong about Gideon made my decision clear-cut. It is obvious that I am no judge of men, so it is best I don't marry and risk being stuck in a situation I will live to regret.'

She turned to face him in the seat. 'But I don't wish to remain a virgin for the rest of my life.'

Jackson swallowed. 'You don't?'

'No. And, unlike Gideon, I know exactly what sort of man you are.'

'You do?'

'Yes, you have never tried to hide your true self from me or anyone else. You are a man who drinks too much, who gets into dangerous, sometimes life-threatening situations, one who has had more women in his life than he can probably remember.'

'Hmm.' It was an accurate description, but this was the first time anyone had suggested that these flaws were useful attributes.

'You are most certainly not the sort of man I would ever wish to marry.'

'I'm not?' Wasn't that what he wanted to hear? Yes, of course it was.

'I believe we could come to an arrangement where you are the one to relieve me of my virginal status and show me what it is like when a man makes love to a woman.'

He stared at her, still in a state of disbelief. She had just made an outrageous proposition, and had done so in a completely unemotional manner. This left him stunned.

'I know it is what you want as well,' she continued, while he tried to gather his thoughts.

'From the way you kissed me, and the reaction you had,' she cast a quick glance down at his groin, negating his belief that she was entirely innocent about what could happen between a man and a woman when left alone together behind a closed door. 'I know that you were, well, shall we say, not adverse to the idea of taking things further when you kissed me.'

He still stared at her, trying to come up with reasons why this was not a good idea, while his body was telling him to stop arguing and do exactly what he had been thinking about for the last two days.

'And those kisses made it apparent that you know how to satisfy a woman.'

He'd liked to hope that was correct, and he'd certainly had no complaints. Far from it.

'Well?'

'Believe me, Lady Emily, I would enjoy nothing more, but—'

'Good, that's settled, then.'

'I would enjoy nothing more,' he repeated, hoping this time she would let him finish. 'But have you thought this through? You don't want to marry Dr Pratt, but that does not mean you will never marry.'

He was doing it again. What on earth was wrong with him? Had he suddenly developed a conscience, a sense of morality? And if he had to acquire these undesirable traits, why did he have to do so now?

'As I said, I have also made up my mind about that as well. I shall never marry.'

'You can't say that. You had one bad experience with that Pratt fellow but there are other men.'

'You're right.' She stood up and Jackson quickly did the same, shocked at what he had just turned down.

'I don't wish to argue with you and I'm sorry to have wasted your time.'

'Oh, God, no, you haven't done that. It's just I don't think you had really thought this through, but I'm pleased you have now seen the wisdom of saving yourself until your wedding night.'

She rolled her eyes and he couldn't help but agree that he sounded like some moralistic matron giving advice to a debutante.

'I *have* thought this through and my mind is made up,' she said, picking up her reticule. 'I thought this arrangement would be advantageous for both of us. I thought you'd be agreeable to an involvement with me, one where you taught me about physical love without any expectations of it becoming anything more than a passing involvement, one with no commitments or expectations. But if you are unwilling, I will have to try and find someone else.'

'What? No. Good God, do not do that.' He took hold of her hands and gently pulled her back down onto the divan. Did he see a small smile quiver at the edges of her lips? Had that been a genuine threat? He could not take the risk. The world can be a dangerous place for a woman, and would be lethal to one such as her in search of a lover.

'So you will do it?'

He nodded.

'Then perhaps you should kiss me,' she said. 'To seal the deal, as it were.'

He took her chin in his hand and looked down into those brown eyes. 'Lady Emily, you must be the strangest, most unusual, unique woman there has ever been.'

And then he did what he'd been longing to do since she entered the room. He kissed her. The moment her soft, lush lips were against his any thoughts that this was a bad idea evaporated. It was now a very, very good idea. The best idea anyone had ever had.

But he didn't want to just kiss her lips. He wanted to kiss, caress and explore every inch of her divine body, and, miracle of miracles, she had given him permission to do so.

His lips left hers and he kissed the soft, creamy flesh of her neck, loving the taste of her and the silky feel of her skin.

She let out a gentle sigh as he nuzzled the soft, sensitive skin behind her ears. She was permitting him to strip her naked, to take her, and by God he was desperate to do so.

His fingers moved to the buttons of her lacy blouse, opening the top one at her throat. He kissed the base of her collarbone as he moved to the next ridiculously tiny button. Then he stopped.

It was what he wanted. That was something about which he was certain. She said it was what she wanted as well, but did she really know her own mind? What she said she wanted and what she really wanted could be two different things. He had to take this slowly, very slowly, and see how far she really wanted to go, before her sense of what was proper took over. Then he would have to deal with his own unsated desire for her in the time-honoured fashion of frustrated men.

But there would be no harm in kissing her one more time before she came to her senses. His lips returned to hers and, despite his admonition to take it slowly, he kissed her harder, with more demanding need, just holding back enough to see if she would be frightened by the force of his passionate desire. He detected no fear. Quite the reverse. She kissed him back with matching intensity. Her lips parted. Her tongue stroked his lips. Her breath became small gasps. He could feel her heart pounding against his chest—in desire, not fear.

Could he risk going a bit further? Still kissing her, he undid one more button on her blouse. What he really wanted to do was rip them apart, but he forced himself to move at a speed that gave her ample time to object. No objection came. He moved to the next one, and the next. When the final button was undone, he pushed open her blouse and slid his hand inside, pulling down her cotton chemise.

Unable to resist, he withdrew from her kisses so he could feast his gaze on her breasts. They were just as he had imagined them, full and pert, the nipples pointing at him expectantly as they rose and fell with each quick breath.

Even if she stopped him now, she had given him a glorious sight to fuel his fantasies. The question now was, would she finally object, or could he go even further? He looked from that arousing sight of her breasts and into her eyes. His self-control was becoming seriously undermined. If she was going to stop him, he could only hope she did it soon, before he was completely lost.

She nodded in answer to his unasked question. He cupped her full breasts, loving the feel of their weight in his hands. He kissed her again, expressing his desire for her with his lips and his hands. Her nipples tightened under his touch as he slowly rubbed his thumbs over the hard peaks.

Her moans urging him on, he traced a line of kisses down her neck. She tilted back her head, offering the silky flesh to him. His lips slowly moved lower, kissing across the soft mounds of her breasts still cupped in his hands. Lifting one breast to his lips, his tongue swirled around the edge of the hard, sensitive bud, causing her breathing to come faster and faster, as his thumb continued to stroke its twin. When he took the hard tight nub in his mouth she cried out in ecstasy, and he knew she was now incapable of stopping him. She did want this, of that there could be no question.

'Beautiful,' he whispered, as he shifted to the other nipple, nuzzling and licking.

Any lingering doubts he might have had that he was pushing her too far, too fast, was removed when her hands wove through his hair, holding him to her breast, showing him she had completely surrendered herself to his caresses.

But selfish cad that he was, he still wanted more, much

more. Her breaths became fast gasps as he licked and suckled. He reached down and pulled at the bottom of her skirt, pushing it up above her knees. His hand slid between her legs, moving up the stockings, past the garters, to the naked skin of her inner thighs.

His body was saying, go on, take what you want—but part of his mind was reminding him she was a virgin. This was all new to her and he might be pushing her further than she was prepared to go.

To his immense satisfaction, her legs parted slightly, giving him easier access. His own breath now came as fast as hers, as his hand moved up her soft skin, under the fabric of her drawers. She put up no objection, even when he reached the cleft between her legs.

But he had to know for certain. His lips released her breast and his hand moved away from her legs. 'Are you sure?'

Her eyes opened slightly. She nodded, then closed them again.

Still watching for the slightest sign that this was not really what she wanted, he lightly ran his hand back up her legs and under her drawers, pausing at the cleft. Her back arched and her body moved to its own rhythm, letting him know that she wanted his touch—more than wanted it, had to have it.

And by God he was more than willing to give it to her.

One arm wrapped around her back, holding her close. He ran his fingers lightly along her feminine folds, parting them gently. Her rapid gasps told him he did not need to hold back. He pushed one finger slowly inside her and gave a low animal growl as the tight sheath closed around him.

What he wanted to do now was throw all decency to the

wind, to wrap her parted legs around him, enter her hard and fast and relieve his own pounding, painful need to be deep inside her. He drew in a long, steadying breath and once again reminded himself she was a virgin. This was her first time and it was his first time with a virgin. He'd heard somewhere it could be painful for a woman on her first time, and the last thing he wanted to do was hurt this lovely, enchanting creature.

Once again nuzzling the soft skin of her neck, he further parted her cleft and pushed a second finger inside her, spreading her wider. As his palm rubbed against her bud, he watched her gorgeous face. Her mouth was open, her head tilted back. Her face, neck and breasts were flushed pink. With each stroke, she gasped louder, faster, until the gasps became deep moans. Her back arched as she rubbed herself against him, her hand over the top of his, urging him to increase the pressure and the pace. He did as she silently commanded, moving faster and faster, pushing harder and harder, until a shiver swept through her body, and her sheath clenched around him tighter. Then she sunk back onto the divan, gasping for breath.

Jackson withdrew his fingers and wrapped her in his arms, her heart pounding against his chest, her head nuzzled against his shoulder, her panting breath warm on his neck.

'Thank you,' she murmured, causing him to smile.

She leant back from him and gazed into his face. 'That was wonderful,' she said. 'But, well, I'm still a virgin. Aren't I? I came here with the intention of losing my virginity and I'm not leaving until I do.'

He had to laugh. She really was the most surprising, captivating, tantalising woman he had ever met.

She looked down towards his groin. 'And we both know it's what you also want.'

'Of course it's what I want,' he said, his husky voice unrecognisable to his ears. 'But once you've lost your virginity there is no getting it back. Are you certain?'

She rolled her eyes as if he was starting to irritate her, reached down and undid the top button of his trousers. He grabbed her hand, pulled it away and lightly kissed her fingers. 'If you really want me to take your virginity, perhaps keep your hands away from that area, or I won't be much use for that purpose.'

'Oh,' she said, narrowing her eyes in question.

'I'll explain later.'

'Good,' she said, lying back on the divan, her skirt still around her waist, her blouse open, her breasts on display for him. Was there ever a more glorious, more sensual, more arousing sight than that? By God, he wanted to do as she asked and take her now, without preamble. But this was her first time. It should be special.

'Would you like to retire to my bedchamber?'

'And risk having you change your mind? I don't think so.'

'Believe me, wild horses couldn't make me change my mind now.'

She smiled at him, the cheekiest, most seductive smile he had ever seen.

'If this is really what you want,' he said, reaching up under her dress, pulling down her lacy drawers and tossing them to the floor. 'Then believe me, I am more than happy to oblige.'

With an unseemly haste he pulled open his buttons and pushed down his trousers. This was not the way a young woman should be deflowered. It should happen in a bed, and it should happen on her wedding night. But, as she was the one to insist, and as he was a mere man, and a randy one at that, there was no point even pretending he would waste any more time debating what should and should not happen.

Wrapping his arms around her, he lowered her back onto the divan and covered her body with his own. Her legs parted. She draped one over the back of the divan while the other wrapped itself around him. He released a deep growl as he positioned himself at her entrance.

Kissing her lips, he slowly eased himself inside her and felt her sheath close tightly around him.

'I promise you, I'll be gentle,' he murmured in her ear, before kissing her neck and easing himself further inside her. Would she tense up? Was that what virgins did? Would she push him away? Would she come to her senses and realise what a bad idea this really was? He moved as slowly as his rampaging desire allowed, uncertain as to how she would react.

She did not tense up. She did not push him away. Instead, her legs wrapped around his waist, opening her up further to him. To his surprise her hands cupped his buttocks, pushing him towards where he wanted so desperately to go. He did not need to be asked twice. He pushed himself fully inside her.

She gasped, causing him to quickly withdraw. He lifted himself up, looked down at her face and brushed a loose strand of hair back from her forehead.

'Did I hurt you?'

'No, not really,' she said, opening her eyes. 'Don't stop.'

He entered her again, just as carefully as his pent-up

desire would allow. Her fingers once again dug into his buttocks, and her nails caused a strangely arousing pain. He pushed further inside her, and released a low, primal groan as her wet folds fully encased him. Watching her lovely face, her lips parted wide, her breath coming in loud, insistent pants, he pushed himself even deeper inside her, loving the sensation of her rubbing against every part of his sensitive shaft. No longer thinking, he withdrew and pushed himself into her again and again, faster and faster, deeper and deeper, his arousal growing bigger and harder with each thrust.

Her panting became loud moans, even screams, as she writhed beneath him in time to his thrusting. Using every ounce of self-control he possessed, he held himself back until her core rippled around him and she released a louder cry as she gripped him tightly. Withdrawing from her he reached his own climax, hoping no embarrassing tell-tale sign would be left on her clothing.

Collapsing onto her, Jackson had never felt such euphoria. Sex was always enjoyable, sometimes spectacular, but this had been different. He'd felt such a connection with her, as if they had really been joined, not just physically. Why that should be, he had no idea. It could not be because he was her first. At least, he hoped not. He was not one of those men who saw it as an accomplishment to deflower a virgin, but, he had to admit, he did feel pleased that she had wanted him to be the one to do so.

But whatever had caused it, he had felt something, something different, something more than just the usual sensual gratification, as wonderful as such gratification always was. They continued to lie in each other's arms, breathing heavily, their hearts still pounding against their chests.

Jackson was sure he could stay like this for ever, but when his heartbeat resumed its normal pace, he gently kissed her neck.

'Well, you're no longer a virgin,' he murmured.

She gave his buttocks a playful squeeze. 'And I'm certainly not bitter.'

'No,' he said and lightly kissed her lips. 'You're as sweet as honey.'

'And twice as sticky,' she said, causing him to laugh. 'Nobody ever told me how sticky it all would be.'

Still laughing, he held her close and kissed her again. Now that he had willingly done as she asked, a small part of his mind was asking, what happens now? She had not only said she wanted to lose her virginity, but to become his mistress. After what he had just experienced, he could only hope and pray that she would not change her mind about that either. One taste of the lovely Lady Emily Beaumont was never going to be enough.

Chapter Eleven

She had done it. No one could now accuse her of being a bitter old spinster, because she was no longer a virgin. Not that she would be able to tell anyone about what had happened on the Viscount's divan, but still, she would know. She smiled to herself, a gleeful, mischievous smile, as she basked in her risqué secret. This behaviour was so unlike her, and it felt glorious.

She had made the decision to lose her virginity to the Viscount on the night of the ball, but it had taken two days to work up the courage to ask him. And she almost hadn't come today.

But every time she remembered that kiss and every time she had thought about Gideon's cruel words, her determination had grown. She would not remain a virgin. She would not become a bitter old spinster, and that kiss had proven Jackson Wilde was the perfect man to prevent that happening.

She bit her bottom lip so she wouldn't laugh out loud as she remembered the unemotional way in which she had made her outlandish proposition. He would never know that inside she had been a turmoil of emotions and jangling nerves. Remaining stoic had been the only way she had been able to stop herself from fleeing out the door in mortification at what she was asking. But she had known if she did flee, she would live the rest of her life in regret. And now that she knew what she risked missing out on, she could only say a silent thank you to herself for not letting nerves and emotions win the day.

'I hope I didn't hurt you,' he said, his arms still around her, his glorious weight still on her, his thighs caressing the inside of her legs.

'Not at all,' she said, smiling contentedly.

'I have heard it can be painful for a woman the first time.'

'You've never been with a virgin before?' she asked, somewhat incredulous. The fact that she was offering him the chance to deflower a virgin had been one thing that had given her courage, certain that he would not turn down such an opportunity. Wasn't that what Randall had said?

'Most men have to pay an enormous sum for a virgin. Whereas I'll get a willing virgin for free, and I even come out of it all the richer.'

She pushed that painful memory away. She would not let Randall ruin what had been such a wonderful, rapturous experience for her.

'No, never,' he said.

'So this was a first for both of us.'

He smiled and held her closer. 'Yes, I suppose it was. And the first time is never the best.'

'It gets better?' She found that hard to believe. 'In that case, let's do it again.'

He lightly kissed the top of her head. 'If I was eighteen, I'd probably be able to oblige, but I'm afraid I'm an old man of eight-and-twenty, so you're going to have to wait.'

'Oh, all right.' She tried not to sound too disappointed.

He lifted himself off her. 'What excuse have you given your mother for coming to my home without a chaperone?'

'I told her I was attending a board meeting.'

'Then I suspect it best if you return home soon, if you are to avoid arousing your mother's suspicions.'

'Yes, I suppose so,' she said, watching as he stood up, pulled up his trousers and did up the buttons. All the while he watched her in return, and she could see in his eyes that he liked what he was looking at. But he was right. She had got what she came for—to be away from home for too long would cause her mother to ask questions.

She pushed down her skirt and pulled up her chemise.

'So, do you want there to be another time?' he asked, and he almost looked sheepish.

'Yes,' she said, looking back up at him, that one word holding so much expectation. Of course she wanted there to be another time. How could she experience something so divine and not want to go back for more?

'Perhaps next time it should be in a bed, and not quite so furtive,' he said, picking up her lacy drawers from the floor and handing them to her. She stood and wriggled back into them.

'Not that I actually object to furtive,' he said with that sensual smile, reminding her body of all they had just shared. 'But we could take our clothes off next time, not just the essential bits.'

She fumbled with the buttons of her blouse. 'Yes, that would be nice,' she said, her words sounding wholly inadequate.

'Allow me to help.' Before she could answer he lightly pushed aside her hands and slowly did up the buttons at the front of her blouse. Her body instantly reacted to the touch of his hand, the warmth of his body so close to hers, and that masculine scent of leather and sandalwood.

'Next time, we should be a bit more discreet as well,' he added, his fingers lingering on the last button a moment before he stepped back.

'Oh, will the servants gossip?' She looked towards the door.

'No, my servants are used to turning a blind eye to the comings and goings in this house.'

'Good,' she replied, her heart giving an irrational lurch. There was no reason why she should react in such a manner to that statement. His reputation as a womaniser was the very reason why she had come here today. It meant he had experience with women. It meant he was a man who was honest about who he was, and a man with whom she would never be so imprudent as to want anything more from him than what he was prepared to offer. That did not include a commitment of any kind.

No, this all suited her perfectly, and he was perfect for what she wanted. There was no rational reason to care about any other woman he'd had in his life, or would have in his life in the future.

'I also pay my servants handsomely,' he added. 'They know there is no advantage in endangering their position by selling gossip to the gutter press or any other interested parties.'

'Good,' she repeated. This time there was no doubt in her response. As much as she had enjoyed herself, and as much as she refused to believe she had done anything wrong, she would hate for her parents to hear what she had been up to. It was shameful enough for them to have an unmarried daughter with no prospects, but to have one who had all but thrown herself at a man like Jackson Wilde would be a shame they would not be able to bear.

'But I unfortunately do have neighbours, and they *do* take an unhealthy interest in the comings and goings of this house,' he added.

'Oh,' once again she looked towards the door, as if expecting to see these nosy neighbours glaring at her.

'I do, however, have a small set of private rooms located in a shopping arcade that specialises in hats, ribbons, that sort of thing, for young ladies. It is perfect for such liaisons. You will be able to pretend you are on a shopping expedition then discreetly slip down the alleyway that leads to my rooms.'

Emily listened as if merely taking an interest in this plan. She ignored the tightening in her stomach and refused to speculate as to how many other young ladies he had entertained at his private rooms, rooms chosen exclusively for such liaisons.

'If you wish we could meet there on occasion,' he said.

Oh, yes, she wished, she wished a great deal.

'I believe that would be a satisfactory arrangement,' she said, once again using that detached voice to cover a turmoil of confusing emotions. She moved to the looking glass over the mantelpiece to fix her hair.

He stood behind her, smoothing the loose strands back into the bun at the back of her neck. She watched him in the looking glass. He really was devastatingly handsome. His dark blond hair had fallen over his high forehead and she was itching to push it back, to run her fingers through his tousled locks. His blue eyes had narrowed as he concentrated on his task, the laughter lines visible at the edges. Her gaze moved down to his full lips. Lips that had kissed her lips, and her body, and sent waves of ecstasy coursing through her. She could hardly wait until they were kissing her again.

As if hearing her thoughts, he leant down and kissed her neck. She closed her eyes and sighed.

'Until next time,' he murmured and took a step backwards.

She blinked several times to pull herself back into reality.

'Yes, until then.' She quickly scanned the room to ensure she had not left behind any items of clothing, then walked out the drawing room, her head held high as if they had merely just concluded another meeting about the school.

The footman was waiting at the front door. He escorted her down the steps to her waiting carriage, held out his hand and helped her in. The Viscount was correct. The man was the very soul of discretion, and she could read not a trace of judgement in his impassive expression. But why should he react in any other way? This was no doubt a regular event for him, as it was for the Viscount.

She looked back towards the three-storey cream townhouse, at its black railings leading up to the portico and oak door.

Did every young lady who entered that house to spend time with the Viscount experience what she had just experienced? Did he turn each and every one of them into a woman desperate for his touch, aching to have him inside her again, filling her up, making her his? And afterwards, did they all feel as if the earth had been somehow tipped off its axis? Did they all feel as if they had been changed in some fundamental way? She suspected they did, that he was an expert at making them feel that way, and she was not special at all.

That was why he was such a successful womaniser. And that was why she had chosen him, so she had no right to judge him or to expect any more from him than what he had just given her.

She would not think about those other women. She would just be content at how wonderful it had all been. And it was going to happen again. A little shiver ran through her at the thought of his hands, lips and tongue on her once again, of him taking her again, bringing her up to that soaring height and sending her crashing over into that blissful state.

As the carriage took Emily home, she couldn't stop herself from smiling. It was so hard to believe. She, Lady Emily Beaumont, was now Viscount Wickford's mistress. Or, at least, one of his mistresses. Her smile quivered slightly, before she forced it to return, just as brightly.

She would not allow herself any regrets. It had taken too much internal debate to come to this decision for her to let any doubts creep in now. But the Viscount was right. Now that she had lost her virginity there was no going back. Men from her social class wanted women who were chaste, and should she actually meet a man she wanted to marry, she would not lie to him.

She released a huff of exasperation. It was all so unfair.

Gideon's revelations as to his true character had left her with two choices; marry a man she neither loved nor respected, or remain on the shelf and become a woman pitied by all. Neither of those choices appealed.

She sat up straighter in the carriage. But she had boldly taken a third option, one forbidden by Society's rules. And for that defiance she could not help but harbour a secret pride.

She nodded, as if to underline her conviction. No, this was the best solution. She would officially remain a spinster, but she would experience pleasures that would otherwise be denied her.

She sighed, long and slow, and closed her eyes.

And oh, what pleasure she had had experienced. His kisses had been sublime, but making love to him was more than she could possibly have imagined. And she would soon be making love to him again. It made the sacrifice of never marrying worth it.

Didn't it?

Of course it did.

On arrival at her family's Belgrave home, Emily quickly checked herself in the hall looking glass. Her cheeks were still a little flushed, but that could be explained by the wind. As could her hair, still slightly dishevelled despite the Viscount's attentions. She pushed a few stray locks back into her bun. Her finger slowly moved down her neck as she remembered his farewell kiss.

She wasn't sure how she would explain her lips, which appeared somewhat plumper than usual. If asked, perhaps she could say she was doing something risqué like trying on lip rouge. Her mother would be shocked, but it would be nothing compared to how shocked she would be if she knew the real reason for her changed appearance.

She inspected herself one more time, looked down at her blouse and skirt to ensure all buttons were in the correct buttonholes, and, satisfied that all was as it should be, entered the drawing room, where her mother was taking tea and working on her embroidery.

'You're looking rather pleased with yourself,' her mother said, signalling to the maid to pour Emily a cup. 'Did the meeting about the school go well?'

'Oh, yes, very well.'

'The results were as good as you expected?'

'They certainly were, much better than I could ever imagine.' Emily said with a nod of thanks as she took the cup from the maid.

Her mother gave her a long, appraising look, the tea cup poised in her hand. 'You're looking rather, I don't know, different. Did you see Viscount Wickford at your meeting?'

'What? No. Well, yes, he was there, I suppose, but, no I didn't see him.' Heat rose on Emily's cheeks. That was something she was going to have to get under control if she was to conduct a clandestine relationship. She could not blush, stammer or act in a generally awkward manner every time the Viscount's name was mentioned.

'Hmm, I see,' her mother said, causing Emily's cheeks to burn brighter. 'I had noticed you spent rather a lot of time with him at that fundraising ball of yours.'

Emily fought to maintain a calm demeanour, determined to prove to herself she really was up to the task of subterfuge. 'Yes, well, he was part of the organising committee. It's only natural that we would spend time together. We had much to discuss.'

'Hmm, I see,' her mother repeated in that annoying manner. 'Only natural, indeed. Perhaps we should host another ball before the Season is over so the two of you can continue your...' She paused and waved her hand in a circle. 'Your discussions.'

'No need. I'll be seeing him at the board meeting to-morrow,' Emily said, pleased that her voice remained even and her cheeks were now cooling. She could do this after all. To the rest of the world she would continue to be the same sensible woman everyone expected her to be, while maintaining a secret life that would shock Society to its very core if they ever found out. She took a sip of her tea, rather liking this new, decidedly naughty side of herself.

'Hmm, I see,' her mother said yet again. 'Another meeting so soon. Did you not get everything discussed today that you needed to talk about?'

'Obviously not,' Emily answered and waited for her mother's inevitable response.

'Hmm, I see,' she said, causing Emily to smile.

Emily had not been lying to her mother. Not entirely. She did have a meeting the next day with the board, and Jackson Wilde would be there. This was going to be a test for both of them, but Emily in particular.

The meeting was to discuss the purchase of an abandoned warehouse, which Mr Greaves believed would be perfect for conversion into a school. The board members had been invited to inspect the premises, along with the primary fundraisers, Emily and the Viscount.

When her carriage arrived outside the warehouse, she paused and took a few deep breaths before alighting. At all times she would have to act as if the Viscount was nothing to her. She would continue to see him as merely a man she didn't entirely approve of, a man about whom she was putting aside her objections regarding the way in which he lived his life, for a greater good; that is, a school for disadvantaged women.

Too much was riding on her ability to remain dispassionate when dealing with the Viscount in public. While she would be publicly shamed if Society knew she was yet another woman that Jackson Wilde had taken as his mistress, there was more at stake than just her embarrassment.

Her parents would be mortified. The board would be scandalised. It might even put the future of the school in jeopardy. Knowing this was about more than just herself, she stepped down from the carriage, lifted her head high and strode into the warehouse.

The Viscount and the board members had already assembled. They were standing in the middle of the immense building, with its towering ceiling showing exposed wooden beams, brick walls and large dust-covered leadlight windows.

It was hard to see how this building could possibly be transformed into a school suitable for female students learning skills such as cooking and needlepoint.

Emily greeted each man in turn with a polite nod, and made a point of not holding the Viscount's gaze for any longer than that of the other men present.

'I was just telling everyone that the ball was a resounding success,' Mr Greaves said. 'Lady Emily, Viscount Wickford, you are to be congratulated.'

This was greeted with 'hear hears' from the other board members, and the Viscount received several pats on the back, while Emily merely tilted her head slightly in acceptance of the praise. But what they had achieved did feel good, very good. This was what she wanted to do with her life. She wanted to make a difference and improve the lives of others, and the school would do that.

'Thanks to your efforts,' Mr Greaves continued, 'we have more than sufficient funds from the tickets, the donations and the pledges of patronage to purchase these premises outright without a bank loan, to pay for the conversions, hire tutors and for the school to continue for the foreseeable future.'

This earned the Viscount some more back-patting and nods of approval in Emily's direction. Mr Greaves led the party around the warehouse, pointing out features and where partitions could be placed for school rooms, and how, once cleaned, the windows would provide ample lighting for all the classrooms. Offices already existed on the mezzanine floor. They would require nothing more than clearing out and appropriate furniture being installed for them to be converted to a board room, offices for senior staff members and a staff room for the tutors.

The board members and the Viscount discussed the premises as they walked around the building. But, despite the talk she had given herself before she entered the warehouse, Emily could not quite forget she was in the presence of her lover and felt it best to keep quiet, in case her voice inadvertently revealed her inner turmoil.

The Viscount, on the other hand, had no such problems. He was chatting away to Mr Greaves and the other board members, making suggestions and comments, and even the occasional joke, which everyone except Emily laughed at.

But what else did she expect? That he would fall apart just because he was in the company of his latest mistress? While this was all new to her, it was far from new to Jackson. He'd had countless illicit affairs and would be a master at living a double life.

And if she was being painfully honest with herself, what happened between them probably meant little to him. It had been her first time, and its significance could not be greater, but for the Viscount she was merely one more woman in a long line.

The tour came to an end. The board members said their goodbyes and climbed into the row of black carriages lined up outside the warehouse. Emily released a sigh of relief as she headed to her own waiting carriage. She had done it. She had got through her first public meeting with the Viscount and she had revealed nothing. It seemed she could do this after all.

'Lady Emily,' that familiar deep voice called out, just as the footman was about to help her into her carriage.

She turned around and saw the Viscount approaching. Her ordeal was not yet over. Despite her pounding heart, she adopted what she hoped was a nonchalant expression.

'What is it?' In her determination to prove this man meant nothing to her, it came out perhaps more sternly than intended.

'At some time in the near future it would be a good idea if we met to discuss securing future patronage for the on-going funding of the school.'

'But I thought Mr Greaves said we had—'

His eyebrows arched, halting her words.

'Oh, yes, of course. That would be an excellent idea. When do you have in mind?'

'Tomorrow afternoon, if that suits you.'

'Yes, I believe it does.'

It suits me more than you could possibly imagine.

Jackson held out his hand to help her into the carriage. As he did so he passed her a note, which she quickly closed her hand around.

'Until then, Lady Emily,' he said with a formal bow.

'Yes, goodbye.' She took her seat and Jackson closed

the door. The moment the carriage drove off she opened the letter, then stared at it in disappointment. It was an address. What had she expected? A declaration of love? He had merely given her instructions on where they were to meet. And that was as it should be. She did not need a declaration of love, nor did she want such a thing, and she'd be horrified if she actually received one. This was not about love. This was merely an adventure, an exciting adventure, but nothing more than that.

She looked back down at his handwriting. Her disappointment was chased away as a delicious thrill coursed through her. Tomorrow that adventure would continue. He wanted to see her again. He had written this note before he came to the meeting, ensuring he would see her again as soon as possible. While he was talking to the board members, pretending there was nothing between them, this note had been in his pocket and he had been waiting for an opportunity to pass it to her.

Did that mean he was thinking of her throughout the meeting, just as she was thinking about him?

A frivolous side of her nature, which she hadn't known existed, hoped this was the case, while her more sensible side knew it was unlikely. This would not be affecting him the way it was affecting her. If she was to keep that frivolous side of herself in check, her sensible nature needed to never, ever forget that.

She placed the note in her reticule and reminded herself to stop being so flighty and emotional. This was an arrangement that suited them both. It was a chance to have some fun, to experience something wonderful and forbidden, but it meant no more than that. To think anything else was an absurdity.

Chapter Twelve

The next day at the arranged time Emily found herself wandering around the Tanner Street Shopping Arcade, pretending to admire the hats, gloves and ribbons on display in the shop windows. As if admiring the ornate fixtures and fittings, she looked around, taking in the high arched-glassed ceiling, the faux marble columns, and the brown and white tiled floor. In reality, rather than admiring the modern shopping area designed to attract discerning women with plenty of money to spend, she was looking for the small passageway that led to the door of the Viscount's private rooms.

She spotted it between a glove shop and a hat shop, exactly as his note had described, and made her way along the arcade acting as innocently as every other woman out for a day's shopping. A pretence that would be easier to achieve if every nerve in her body was not alive, her stomach wasn't rolling, her heart beating so loudly in her chest it was hard to think above its pounding.

As surreptitiously as possible, she looked around to see if anyone was observing her. No one was paying her the slightest bit of attention. Instead, elegant women, moving in groups, pairs or alone, were looking in shop windows, chatting, entering and leaving shops to the sound of tinkling bells.

With as much boldness as she possessed, she walked down the short alleyway to the black door at the end. Unable to stop herself, she took a quick, furtive look over her shoulder before she opened the door and slipped inside. When the door closed behind her, she leant against it and released her held breath.

She had met no one she knew, and was sure if anyone did see her, they would never suspect that well-behaved Lady Emily Beaumont would be up to anything other than a bit of shopping.

No one would ever suspect she, of all women, was about to make love to one of London's most notorious philanderers. Still leaning against the door, that guilty thought sent a delightful shiver coursing through her.

She was Viscount Wickford's mistress and would soon be making love to him. It was unbelievable, even to her, so it was sure to be unbelievable to anyone who did happen to see her at the shopping arcade.

She entered the living area, to find him waiting for her while holding two champagne flutes, the bubbly liquid resembling her own fizzing emotions.

Her heart pounded faster in her chest as she took the glass from his outstretched hand. 'I see you were confident I would come,' she said and took a sip, the bubbles tickling her nose.

'If you hadn't, I would have drunk all the champagne myself to drown my sorrows.'

Or shared it with one of your other women, a killjoy voice murmured.

But Emily would not think like that. She would not be possessive. She would not be jealous. That was not what this was about.

'I'm afraid I don't have that much time. I told Mother I needed to shop for some gloves.'

He removed the champagne flute from her hand and placed it on the small table beside the settee. 'You're going to have to tell your mother it took a long time to decide on the perfect gloves, because I don't intend to rush this.'

'Oh,' she gasped, loving that idea.

'Last time was somewhat hurried. This time I want to enjoy you fully. Last time I was so desperate to have you we didn't even disrobe properly. This time I want to undress you, entirely.' He smiled at her, that slow, sensual smile that made her legs turn to jelly. 'Will you let me do that?'

Emily could only nod, excitement and nerves jangling within her, making her almost weak. He was desperate for her. He wanted to take her slowly. She definitely liked the sound of both those concepts.

'We best get started,' he said, his smile becoming decidedly devilish, driving her longing for his touch to fever pitch.

He reached up and removed the clips holding her hair in place. Her hair tumbled around her shoulders. He ran his hands through the locks, combing it out so it curled freely and naturally.

It was a small gesture, but it sent Emily's pulse racing in expectation of what was to come.

That wicked smile still curving his full lips, he slowly undid the buttons at the front of her blouse, then frowned. 'I believe these tiny buttons are designed to drive a man insane, or perhaps they're a devious way to increase my expectation and make my desire for you even more fierce than it already is.' He smiled at her. 'If that was the intent, it's working.'

Emily silently cursed herself. Why had she not chosen a blouse that could be removed more easily? She had taken so much time selecting her clothing, picking the pale lemon blouse because she thought it flattered her complexion.

But he *was* right. As each button was slowly undone, her desire for him did grow increasingly fierce. His hands lightly swept across her hard nipples and she moaned lightly, wishing he would just be done with it and rip the cursed thing off her.

The buttons finally undone, he slipped the blouse off her shoulders, pausing to kiss each shoulder. She closed her eyes and all but purred at the touch of his lips on her skin. This was what she wanted. This was what she was risking her reputation for.

He dropped the blouse onto a nearby armchair, and undid the buttons of her matching skirt, pushing it down over her hips. She was standing before him dressed only in her underwear. She should be feeling awkward, nervous, embarrassed, something she would expect a well brought-up young lady to feel, but all she felt was deliciously wanton and burning with expectation.

'Turn around,' he commanded, his voice thick with desire for her. She did as he asked and released a sigh of pleasure when he lifted her hair and kissed her neck. His hands moved to her corset, unhooking it with more expertise than her lady's maid had ever shown.

He's probably had more experience in doing so, Emily thought, then pushed it out of her mind.

It mattered not how many other women he had stripped naked. He was with her now. Now was all that mattered, and now was wonderful, exciting, intoxicating.

He placed her corset on the chair on top of her blouse

and skirt, reached up under her chemise and pulled down her drawers. When they reached the ground, she stepped out of them.

With his hands on her shoulders, he turned her around.

'Raise your arms above your head,' he ordered, his voice thick and husky. She did as asked and her chemise was quickly skimmed off her body, leaving her standing in front of him wearing only her silk stockings, held up by garter belts. The cool air caressed her naked skin but could do nothing to relieve the soaring heat of her body.

He stepped back. His gaze swept over her, slowly, appreciatively.

'My God, you are perfect, Lady Emily.' His gaze slowly moved up and down her naked body, his eyes dark and hooded.

She bit her bottom lip, her teeth running across the sensitive skin, her body throbbing for his touch.

'Emily. Call me Emily,' she said, her husky voice unrecognisable.

'Emily,' he repeated, his voice soft and soothing. 'My beautiful Emily. And you of course must call me Jackson.'

'Jackson,' she repeated, loving the sound of his name on her lips.

He stepped towards her, his gaze returning to her face, and cupped both breasts, his thumbs rubbing over the hard nubs as he watched her reaction, his eyes sparking with desire. She clasped the material of his shirt, holding onto it to steady herself as her body became a deep throbbing want.

Her lips parted and her eyes closed as she surrendered to his touch. When he kissed her—deep, hard and slow— she sank into his arms, her sensitive skin rubbing against the fabric of his shirt and trousers. His kisses moved slowly down her neck and traced a line over the top of her breasts.

Was he teasing her, playing with her? If he was, it was a delicious cruelty. His kisses inched closer to her waiting nipples. When he took a tight bud in his mouth, she released a deep sigh of gratitude, which soon turned to gasps of ecstasy as his tongue moved in circles while his lips suckled, driving her wild with need.

With each stroke of his tongue that need grew fiercer, more demanding. Her heart beating faster, pounding through her entire body, she moaned her mounting desire for him so loudly a small part of her worried she might be heard over the noise of the shoppers.

Taking his hand, she placed it between her legs. No longer thinking, just reacting, her body moved against his rubbing hand, her back arching back and forth, needing the release only he could give her. Her gasps growing louder, the pounding between her legs mounting, she took hold of his shoulders, her fingers gripping the material of his shirt.

'Jackson,' she cried out as the cresting wave took her up to a peak and crashed over her, leaving her gasping in its wake.

He stood back and gazed down at her, desire radiating from his face.

'You are even more beautiful when you climax. And I want to see that sight again and again.'

She gasped in a few breaths, that insistent pounding once again resuming in response to his words.

'First, I want to see you naked as well,' she said, surprised her voice sounded so in control given the torrent of desire raging inside her. But she did want to see his body, and to feel his naked skin under her fingers and lips.

He smiled at her and spread his arms wide as if his body was hers for the taking. With surprisingly steady fingers she undid the buttons of his shirt. Unlike him, she was not able to go slowly, but quickly undid each button and pushed the garment off his shoulders so she could feast her eyes. His chest was just as she remembered it when she had bathed him in hospital, minus the bruises and cuts. The muscles were as sculptured, the stomach as hard and firm, and that line of hair was just where she remembered it.

Unable to resist the temptation to do so, she kissed his chest, his skin warm under her lips. Her fingers moved down to the buttons of his trousers. She could feel him hard inside, telling her just how much he wanted her. In the same way that his hands had lightly brushed against her breasts under the guise of undoing her buttons, she lightly brushed her fingers over his arousal. He gasped, grabbed her hands and took them up to his lips.

'If you want me to be good for what is to come, I would advise against that,' he said, taking her hand and lightly kissing her fingers. 'I want you so much, Emily,' he said, looking down into her eyes. 'But I want to take things slowly, so I better call a halt to this before I lose the ability to do so.' With that, he scooped her up into his arms and kissed her, his lips hot and insistent.

Still kissing her, he carried her through to the adjoining room and placed her down gently on the large bed. His eyes never leaving her, he quickly discarded his trousers and boots.

'Stop,' she called out as he was about to join her on the bed. The surprised look on his face under any other circumstances might have made her laugh, but instead she couldn't take his eyes off him.

'You took your time to look at me, you can at least allow me the same enjoyment.'

The surprised look turned to one of amusement as he stood in front of her completely naked. Her gaze moved slowly up and down his body, taking in every glorious inch of his masculinity. He really was magnificent. Like a statue of an athletic Greek god, each muscle was sculptured and delineated and packed with explosive power. Her eyes moved down his slim hips, to those long lean legs and back up again, pausing at his arousal, loving the knowledge that it was a reaction she had caused.

'Turn around,' she commanded. And he did so, giving her a glorious view of his round, tight buttocks. She had felt them under her fingers when they had last made love. She knew they were hard and muscular, and the sight of them sent a delicious thrill ripping through her. Soon she would be feeling them again as he moved between her thighs, bringing her to that delicious state of abandonment.

'Now you can join me,' she said, loving the way she was in charge.

'Thank you, my lady,' he said, that seductive smile once again returning.

His hard body stretched out beside her, warm naked skin against warm naked skin. He took one curl of her hair and wrapped it around his fingers, his blue eyes gazing into hers with something that resembled love but she knew to be lust—wonderful, marvellous lust.

'What do you want me to do now, my lady?' he asked with that slow, cheeky smile that promised delightfully wicked things to come.

'Kiss me,' she ordered. The words had barely left her lips and she was in his arms. His lips were hard against hers, taking her with a force that would have been overwhelming if her desire had not been as strong as his. She melted against him, seemingly turning to liquid in his arms, as his tongue entered her mouth. Her need for him was almost painful. She had to feel him inside her. Now. She needed him to relieve her deep, pulsating desire for him.

Unable to speak, she wrapped her legs around him, telling him with her body what she needed.

'God, I want you, Emily, but I wanted this time to take you slowly.'

'I don't want slow,' she gasped out. 'I want you inside me. Now.'

Responding immediately to her command, he placed himself between her legs, hips against hips, thighs against thighs. She lifted her legs and wrapped them around his waist, opening herself up for him, showing him what she wanted, what she had to have, what only he could give her.

'Emily, you really are ready for me, aren't you?' he murmured close to her ear as he pushed himself deep inside her. She released a long sigh, finally getting what she wanted so badly, what she had been constantly thinking about since she was last with him.

She cupped his buttocks, loving the feel of those taut muscles under her hands, flexing as he pulled out of her and pushed in again, harder and deeper. With each thrust her pounding need intensified, her moans coming louder and louder in time with his rhythm.

'I want to watch you,' he whispered in her ear. His chest lifted off hers. She opened her eyes and looked up at him. He was staring down at her with such adoration, such passion. Her gasps still matched his thrusting as they held each other's eyes. Emily felt so beautiful as he gazed down at her with such intensity—beautiful, wanton and desired.

As the fire within her burned more fiercely, she reached up to him, wrapping her hands around the back of his neck. His eyes holding hers, he thrust into her, again and again, until the fire became an inferno, flashing through her body, and she cried out his name then collapsed back onto the bed, exhausted and fulfilled.

Kissing her panting lips, she felt him pull out of her and release his own pleasure, then he lay on top of her, his heart pounding furiously against her chest, his body slick with perspiration.

Through the fog of her desire, Emily knew she must not see this for anything more than what it was. It was just a physical act, a glorious, sensational physical act, but nothing more. Despite knowing that, right now it did feel like so much more than just physical. She felt so close to him, felt adored by him, even loved by him.

It was all so confusing. But, right now, Emily refused to let that confusion undo this wonderful sensation. She would just lie here, with this magnificent man still so close, and enjoy the feeling of his weight on her and his arms holding her. All thinking, all reasoning, all introspection could be left for another time.

His pounding heartbeat slowed. He lifted himself off her and laid down by her side. 'I didn't take it slowly the way I had planned, but at least we managed to get our clothes off this time,' he said, amusement in his voice. 'But next time we must make sure we have even more time. There is so much more we could do.'

More? Emily liked the sound of that.

He brushed a lock of hair back from her cheek. 'Do you

think you can get away again soon? Maybe you could tell your mother you need to visit your dressmaker, or something that will take all afternoon and we can spend hours and hours in bed together.'

'Oh, no, my mother.' She sat up suddenly. 'Mother thinks I'm shopping for gloves. She'll be wondering where I am. Especially as I told her it was merely a quick visit to a shopping arcade and I would not need a chaperone.'

'Quick,' he said with a laugh. 'You know how to wound a man, don't you?'

Emily had no time to ask him what he meant by that— she had to leave, immediately.

She jumped out of bed and rushed back to the adjoining room, followed by Jackson. In a rapid reversal to her slow undressing, Jackson quickly helped her into her chemise, laced up her corset and, with two sets of fingers working together, they buttoned up her skirt and blouse.

'Here, let me fix your hair,' he said, turning her around and lifting up her locks. To her immense amazement, he brushed out her hair with his fingers, expertly twirled it into a bun at the nape of her neck and secured it with clips.

How had he learnt to do that?

Perhaps she'd rather not know.

Once he was finished, he quickly turned her around, did a quick inspection and kissed her lightly on the lips. 'You're the very picture of innocence and propriety,' he said. 'No one will have the slightest inkling that you haven't been out on an innocent shopping expedition.'

Emily hoped so.

'Until next time,' he said.

Next time? Could she actually wait until next time? Her eyes raked over his still naked body. It was a wonderful body, one capable of making her feel things, want things, need things that a few days ago she had not even known it was possible to feel.

Could she stay? Just a bit longer? No, of course she couldn't. She had to go.

'Yes, until next time,' she said and rushed out of the door.

She entered the shopping arcade where women continued to wander from shop to shop. It was difficult to believe the world had carried on as normal outside his flat, while inside she was being transported to a place of ecstasy. But there was no time to dwell on that. She raced into the shop that sold gloves. Grabbing the first pair she saw, she thrust some money into the shopkeeper's hand.

'Don't bother to wrap them and keep the change,' she called out as she raced towards the door.

'Thank you, miss. Thank you very much indeed,' the man said as the door closed behind her.

As quickly as she could without drawing attention to herself, she rushed out the arcade and climbed into a waiting hansom cab. Then she drew in and slowly released a deep breath. She looked down at the new gloves clasped in her hands.

She closed her eyes as if to block out the shocking sight, then opened them and looked again at the gloves she was holding. The second glance was no better.

They were red, fingerless and lacy. It was a brazen style she would never be seen dead wearing. This peculiar purchase was going to take some explaining when she got home.

Emily was far from being the first woman Jackson had entertained in his private flat, nor was she the first woman who had been forced to rush away due to commitments in her other life. Even though he had not acknowledged it before, it had always been a relief when that happened. They had both got what they wanted, gone their separate ways, and he could move onto the next source of fun without a backwards glance.

It should be the same with Emily. But it wasn't.

He pulled on his trousers, contemplating this strange reaction, which almost felt like loss. Could it be because making love to her once again was so unexpectedly passionate it had left him wanting so much more of her? But that would not fully explain these odd sensations gripping him.

It wasn't just that he wanted to make love to her again, although he certainly wanted that. He wanted her, here, with him.

After they had made love, he'd wanted to continue to lie in bed with her in his arms, talking and discovering all there was to discover about this complex, unusual and delightful woman.

He huffed out a laugh of disbelief and pulled on his shirt. That too was a first and something he struggled to understand. His ethos when it came to women was always: keep it light, keep it fun, keep it uncomplicated. Any other approach was far too dangerous. That could lead to women expecting more from him than he was prepared to give, more than he was capable of giving.

And yet, somehow, this time it was different. He slowly buttoned up his shirt. Perhaps it was simply that she was his first virgin. He exhaled a long breath. Had it given him some strange sense of responsibility? He hoped not. Responsibility had never been something that sat easily with him.

He also hoped it was not something he was going to live to regret. Emily had been his first virgin and he had been her first lover.

He stared at his reflection in the looking glass as he tied his cravat. Didn't virgins become attached to their first? Hadn't he heard that somewhere? Hopefully, it was a fallacy. He did not need any woman becoming attached to him, nor would it be wise for Emily to waste time and emotion on a man such as him.

To avoid such a possibility, perhaps the kindest thing to do was end it now.

He sat on the still warm bed and pulled on his boots. Yes, that was what he should do, end it now. Their love making was already far too intense. While that was immeasurably pleasurable, it was causing him to react in an unfamiliar manner and that was something he did not like.

He turned and looked at the tousled sheets and inhaled deeply. Her unadorned scent still lingered on the linen.

Yes, he should end this now. He should not have taken her virginity and he should not have compounded that wrong by inviting her to his rooms, further corrupting that innocent woman by making her his mistress.

He closed his eyes and inhaled her scent, taking it deeply into himself. And yet, while he knew what he had done was wrong, he was also completely aware of what a weak man he was. He would not be ending this. Not yet. He would go against everything he knew to be right so he could indulge himself in something he knew to be wrong, at least one more time.

He shook his head and stood up. Once again, his father had proven himself to be correct. He was a no-good scoundrel who thought only of his own selfish needs. A better man would have resisted. A better man would not have taken her virginity. And if a better man did transgress, he would immediately be down on bended knee proposing marriage to make right his appalling behaviour. But as everyone knew, including himself, he was not a better man.

Yes, he definitely was a no-good scoundrel. Even though he knew this to be wrong, all he could think about now was the next time he would have her in his arms, in his bed, her glorious, curvaceous body beneath his. He groaned as the memory of how she looked when they made love consumed him—her eyes closed, her lips panting and calling out his name. God, that image was going to haunt him until he did have her back in his bed. Yes, he was indeed a weak man. A man who would not be able to resist her until he was completely sated. And he suspected, given the strength of his desire for her, that was going to take longer than it had with most of his mistresses.

Hopefully, by the time he did finally satisfy his lust for her, she wouldn't have done something silly like think she had fallen in love with him.

He sighed loudly, stood up and moved away from the bed. Without her scent distracting him, he might be able to think more clearly.

If he had stuck to his type of woman, he would not be facing this dilemma. He would have just made love to a woman and would not be wracked with all these conflicting emotions and arguments.

Why hadn't he just stuck to his type of woman? The ones who lived outside of Society, who could weather the ignominy if the affair became public, or were well-versed in burying scandal before it did become public.

Emily was not that type of woman and he knew the

price of getting involved with a woman such as she. If they were discovered, to avoid a scandal, to stop her from being ruined, he would have to marry her. Neither wanted that. For both their sakes he should stop thinking of his carnal desires and end this now.

He looked back at the bed, still bearing the imprint of her body, and released another deep moan. But perhaps not quite yet. One more time would surely not be too much of a risk. One more time and maybe, just maybe, he'd have got her out of his system. One more time and he could inform her that the most sensible thing for both of them would be to never meet again and forget it had ever happened.

He snorted a laugh. Or, in his case, *pretend* it had never happened, because he doubted he would ever forget what had happened this afternoon.

He pulled his fob watch out of his jacket pocket and flicked it open. By now Emily would be far away from the shopping area and it would be safe for him to leave. But what was he to do with his time until he saw her again?

That too should not be a problem. It had never been so before. One thing he never lacked for was entertaining ways to fritter away his time, but right now he could not think of a single way to occupy himself until Emily was once again his.

Chapter Thirteen

Days, weeks, months passed, and Jackson was no closer to ending his involvement with Emily. He was seemingly caught up in a never-ending circle of lust, regret, determination to end it, then lust consuming him yet again the moment he saw her.

He had hoped he would soon tire of her, as he had with every other mistress, making ending things so much easier. But instead of his desire waning, it increased with each meeting. It was as if he was in her thrall, under some sort of spell she had innocently cast over him and he was powerless to break free.

This was a situation he had hitherto never encountered. As was his difficulty in faking his indifference to her each time he saw her in public.

That too had never been a problem with any of his previous mistresses. He was well practised at living a double life. Making polite conversation with a woman he had just bedded, acting as if they were merely passing acquaintances, it was all second nature to him. But every time he saw Emily, no matter where they were, he wanted to touch her, to kiss her, to let the world know they were lovers.

He had to constantly remind himself to be on his guard when in public. No one could ever know of their involvement. If anyone found out it would cause such a scandal she might never recover and it would send deep shame crushing down on her parents. A shame that could only be mitigated by a proposal of marriage.

It was with that in mind he stood at the entrance of The Women's Education Institute, composing himself before he attended yet another meeting. One where Emily would be present, one where he would have to watch everything he said, every gesture he made, every look he gave her so no one would ever suspect the truth of their relationship.

He could do this. He had done it before over the preceding months, many times. He had held in his inclinations through all those other meetings, when they'd been called to inspect the renovations of the school, and through the official opening. Now he could do the same for this meeting, to show off the school to a group of local dignitaries and an assortment of other interested worthies.

Mr Greaves had been so excited about this tour, which would provide an opportunity to display the accomplishments the school was already achieving. Mr Greaves expected Emily and Jackson to be equally as proud and enthusiastic. And Jackson was. It would just be a lot easier to concentrate on being enthusiastic if he wasn't constantly thinking about Emily and how much he wanted to be alone with her so he could drop all this pretence.

He entered the now bustling school. Local tradesmen had placed dividers to create classrooms in the previously cavernous building, and it all now looked highly professional. Even before the official opening, a large number of girls and women of all ages had signed up for the courses. The school had a lively energy about it, with students and tutors buzzing about, laughing and chatting.

He joined Emily and the board members in the reception area, where a tour group had assembled. He nodded his greetings to each man and made certain his eyes did not linger on Emily. A command made especially difficult as she was looking particularly pretty today, in a cream and gold striped dress and wearing a simple straw hat adorned with a few roses perched on her lustrous chestnut hair. Thick hair that was held back with a few clips. The temptation to remove those clips so her locks flowed over her shoulders was all but overwhelming, so he placed his itching hands in his pockets.

'Welcome to The Women's Education Institute,' Mr Greaves said to those assembled, and sent a smile in Emily's direction.

The board had wanted to call the school The Women's Reform School or The Refuge for Fallen Women, but Emily had insisted they avoid anything that sounded judgemental. She had convinced the board it was essential the school be open to all women, and they should not have to feel they had to have fallen or were in need of reform in order to take advantage of the opportunities offered.

'The school has been a great success,' Mr Greaves continued. 'Already most of our classes are full. Many of our students come from desperate circumstances and have had little opportunity to improve their unfortunate lot in life.'

With a sweep of his hand, Mr Greaves indicated Jackson, standing at the back of the group. 'And we have to thank Viscount Wickford for spreading the word among some of London's more unfortunate women, so they would know that the education institute is open to all, no matter how far they have fallen from grace.'

As one, the members of the tour party turned to face

him, some, but by no means all, were smiling at him with approval.

'Kitty, I mean Miss Kathryn Trotter, one of the inaugural students, played a large part in publicising the school,' Emily said quickly. She'd have realised that anyone who read the scandal sheets would see no advantage in having a known reprobate involved in a school for fallen women. 'She recruited her friends and asked them to tell everyone they knew. She is already one of the highest achieving pupils and has provided an invaluable service to the school.'

Most of the tour party had turned to Emily and were smiling, although those who had been scowling at Jackson continued to look at him as if their delicate sensibilities had been offended by his mere presence.

Jackson shrugged it off. Yes, he was a man with a reputation that shocked the sanctimonious, but he was proud of the work he had achieved at the school. It was possibly— probably, well, definitely—the first time he had been proud of any achievement, and he would not let a few judgemental old fogies dampen his spirits. If they wanted to upset him, they'd have to do more than just turn up their noses. He'd had enough experience ignoring his father's disparaging looks to be disturbed by a few scowls.

'Now, if you'd all please follow me, you'll be able to see first-hand the good that we are achieving and meet some of our students,' Mr Greaves said, and led the worthies into a classroom where a group of women were being instructed in dressmaking, Pretty Kitty sitting among them. She beamed at Jackson, filling his heart with joy and driving out the sour taste left by those few disagreeable visitors.

'And this is the student Lady Emily mentioned,' Mr Greaves said, indicating Kitty. 'Miss Kathryn Trotter was the first student to join the school and has made sterling progress already.'

Kitty stood up and made a small curtsey to the group. 'I'm pleased to meet you,' she said in a demure voice. She had also signed up for the speech and deportment classes and was apparently a star pupil, although Jackson hoped that didn't mean she would lose her delightfully cheeky spirit.

While the party moved around the room, Emily and Jackson stood at Kitty's desk, admiring her work.

'This is really lovely needlework,' Emily said, running her fingers along the stitches.

'Thank you, my lady,' Kitty said, beaming fit to burst.

'I'm sure it won't be long before you are able to get work as a seamstress,' she added.

Kitty's large smile grew wider, something Jackson would not have thought possible if he hadn't witnessed it himself.

'I already have,' Kitty said. 'The broker I used to pawn me clothes to—I mean, my clothes to when I was really down on my luck has given me a job doing repairs. But I don't want to be stuck there repairing all those old rags. I hope to get a job with a real dressmaker and make lovely outfits like the one you're wearing.'

They both looked at Emily's gown, and under the circumstances Jackson could see no reason why he couldn't sweep his gaze over her luscious figure. After all, he was doing nothing more than admiring the work of her seamstress.

'That's wonderful news, Kitty,' Emily said, picking up her embroidery sampler.

'Yes, wonderful,' Jackson added, returning his gaze to the material in Emily's hands. 'What do you call these stitches,' he said, running his finger along the embroidery and lightly stroking the tips of Emily's fingers. He smiled to himself as she gave a little gasp, which she covered up with a cough.

'That's back stitch and those little ones there are French knots,' Kitty said proudly, her smile moving between Jackson and Emily. 'Who would have thought when I met His Lordship in that dirty alleyway that I'd be soon learning how to do all these fancy stitches.'

One of the women on the tour group turned and sent Jackson her most accusatory glare, causing Kitty to give a small harumph, hold up her sampler and wave it in the disapproving woman's direction.

'It's French knots and back stitch,' she called out. 'It makes a nice change from French letters in back alleys.'

'Kitty,' Emily gasped out while Jackson laughed at the look of horror that crossed the old shrew's face. Kitty hadn't lost her fighting spirit. Thank God for that.

'As you can see,' Emily said, with a conciliatory smile directed at the outraged woman, 'the school plays an important role in providing young women such as Miss Trotter with alternative sources of employment.'

The woman merely sniffed and walked away to join the group, which was moving off to another schoolroom.

'Sorry about that,' Kitty said, not looking particularly sorry. 'But old cows like that really get my goat.'

Jackson laughed at the bizarre animal imagery.

'I'd like to see her find herself without a penny to her name, debts mounting up, kids to feed and no decent jobs available and see what she has to do to try and make ends meet,' Kitty said, her fists firmly on her hips.

'But that life is now in your past,' Emily said, causing Kitty to smile again.

'Yes, and I'm ever so grateful to the two of you. I've told everyone I know that they must join up. In no time at all there's bound to be a long waiting list of girls wanting to get into the school. You're going to have to have another one of those fancy balls and raise more money for a string of schools.'

Jackson and Emily exchanged a smile. Another one of those fancy balls didn't sound like a bad idea. Then there would be no reason why he couldn't dance with Emily, holding her in public instead of constantly having to hide away, as if they were doing something shameful.

'Yes,' Emily said. 'And why stop at one more school or restrict ourselves to London? Why not schools of this sort all over England?'

'I'm up for it if you are.'

They continued smiling at each other until Kitty coughed, drawing their attention back to her. 'Um, I think you've lost your friends and I need to get back to perfecting these French knots.'

'Yes, yes, of course,' Jackson said. 'Goodbye, Kitty,' he added then placed his hand on the small of Emily's back to escort her out the room. It was perhaps a bit overfamiliar, but the desire to touch her again was more than he could bear. And surely it would only be interpreted as a polite gesture.

'I have to see you again,' he whispered in her ear as soon as they left the classroom. 'Can you meet me this afternoon?'

She nodded and an erotic charge of lust rushed through him. All he had to do now was get through the rest of this tour, act normally for another hour or so, and he would have her back in his bed. He swallowed and dropped his hand, which had unaccountably moved from the small of her back to her rounded buttocks.

He was surely capable of acting normally and keeping his desire under control until this interminable tour was over. Forcing a smile onto his face he joined the group and commenced nodding at everything Mr Greaves said. He also took the sensible course of not looking at Emily again so his act of normality would not slip, and his thoughts would not drift off to the exquisite pleasure to come.

The moment he was free, Jackson rushed back to his private rooms to ready them for Emily's visit. He wanted to make sure the flat looked inviting. That too was something he had never worried about before. A servant regularly visited and did whatever servants did, but Jackson always felt the need to inspect the rooms before she arrived. He had also instructed his staff to make sure there were always fresh flowers in each room.

Another first, and sometimes he wondered why he made such an effort. Their time together was always far too short and they certainly did not waste a second of it admiring the large bouquets the servants arranged. But he wanted it to be perfect for her, because in so many ways *she* was perfect.

He moved the vase of flowers onto the main table, then moved it back to its original position, then laughed to himself at his odd behaviour. He took yet another look around the room, flicked open his pocket watch and frowned. What was keeping her?

He looked at the champagne bottle sitting in the melting ice. That was something else he insisted on, although more often than not the bottle remained unopened as they had no time to waste on drinking anything other than each other.

He paced around in circles, his agitation growing with each passing second. The door opened. She entered and rushed into his waiting arms.

'I am so sorry. I don't have much time,' she said, pulling at the buttons of his shirt. 'Mother says she wants to discuss my wardrobe for next Season. She's curious about all these visits I'm making to the shops and to my dressmaker. She wants to know when she's going to see some of these new gowns and dresses I'm having made.'

'What are you going to say?' he asked, his own fingers frantically undoing the line of buttons down the front of her dress.

'I don't know, but I'll think of something.'

Freeing her of her interminable clothing he took her hand and they rushed through to the bedroom. He so wished this did not have to be so hurried. It would be wonderful if they could spend entire days together, nights together, entire weeks, an entire life.

An entire life?

He paused. His lips withdrew from hers.

'What's wrong?' she asked, lightly stroking his jawline.

'Nothing, absolutely nothing,' he replied, scooping her up into his arms as he tried to digest what he had just thought. Would it be so bad to spend an entire life with this glorious woman? He placed her on the bed and joined her, his lips exploring her glorious body.

No, it would not be bad at all, he thought as he kissed, licked and nuzzled every inch of her. Then he could take all the time he needed to really get to know everything about her.

Each time they made love they learnt new things about each other's bodies, but Jackson was sure there was so much more to learn it could take a lifetime, and he was a more than willing student.

When she reached another shuddering climax and he found his own relief, he encased her in his arms and held her tightly against him. This too was what he lived for, this closeness, this feeling that they were one.

'Well, that was a nice way to end a frightful day,' she said.

'Nice?' he asked with mock offence. 'Is that how you describe what we just did?'

She playfully poked him in the ribs. 'Very nice, then.'

'I think my performance is being damned by faint praise.'

'And I think you're fishing for compliments. You know how good it was for me, how good it always is. And you were right, it does get better and better the more we know each other.'

He stroked back a damp lock of hair from her forehead. 'That's better. As long as it was more than just nice. So why was your day so frightful?'

'That woman at the school, the one that kept giving you those terrible looks. She was so rude and it was so unfair.'

'Oh, that. I'd forgotten all about her. I'm used to disparaging looks. I don't believe my father has looked at me any other way from the moment I was born.'

She turned onto her side, lifted herself up onto one elbow and looked down at him. He wrapped a lock of her hair around his finger then released it, watching it drop down and curl around her glorious full breasts.

'You never talk about your father or your family.'

'What? That's because there's not much to say.'

She raised her eyebrows and he knew she wanted more.

And whatever she wanted, he was prepared to give, especially after what they had just exchanged.

'What can I say? My parents were like so many other couples. Their marriage was arranged by their parents. They were completely unsuited to each other. My mother did her duty and produced the required heir, then they barely spoke to each other again.' He paused briefly, pain starting to push through his flippant manner. 'My mother died when I was thirteen. I was away at school at the time and my father didn't bother to inform me until I came home for the holidays.'

Her eyes grew enormous and she lightly stroked his cheek. 'That's terrible. You must have been devastated.'

The memory of that day crashed in on him, causing his chest to tighten, his stomach to clench. It was a reaction that talking of his mother always caused, a reaction he had learnt to push away with fun and frivolity. But for some reason he wanted to talk about her with Emily.

'I was devastated, unlike my father who remained unaffected by her passing. After telling me of her death he said we were better off without her.'

'The brute,' she gasped. 'Did you miss her terribly?'

'Yes,' he said, that one word holding a wealth of distress. 'She was so lively, kind and loving, or at least she was when I was a small child. I remember the two of us running together around the estate, playing games in the maze, picking apples, having picnics.'

He smiled at the memory. 'But eventually being married to my father seemed to sap the life out of her and she became a shadow of her former self. He was such a misery and expected everyone around him to be just as miserable.'

'I'm so sorry,' she said, her hand running gently over his chest and helping to relieve the tightness.

'He ruined my mother's life and he tried to ruin mine. That's why I'm determined to never let him, or people like him, affect me, including that old bag in the tour group.'

'Your father can't possibly disapprove of you now? You've founded a school for disadvantaged women. That is surely something that has made him see what a good man you really are.'

Jackson huffed out a mirthless laugh. 'I believe when he found out he said something along the lines of, *"I see you've found a way to corral all your whores in one place so you can have your pick."*'

'That's appalling.'

'That's to be expected. He would never think I'd done something for altruistic purposes.' Guilt surged through him, and he wondered if his father might be right. Had his intentions been entirely altruistic, or had he made the proposal to start the school because he was looking for a way to spend more time with Emily?

'Well, he's wrong about you, and that woman in the tour group was wrong about you as well,' she stated emphatically.

Jackson chose not to answer, suspecting that those two had a more realistic understanding of his true character than the lovely, forgiving Emily did.

She sunk back onto the bed and stared up at the ceiling. 'I'm surprised your brute of a father hasn't insisted you marry. After all, you will be the Duke one day. You are expected to produce your own heir.'

He gave another laugh containing no humour. 'That's one of the reasons I avoid him as much as possible. He never stops going on about it being time I married and produced an heir. That and ranting on about what he's read about me in the scandal sheets. One of his favourite speeches is that I'll never find a decent wife if I continue to carry on the way I am, which of course only encourages me to do everything I can to prove him right.'

'I see,' she said quietly.

He cringed at what he had just said. Right now, he was holding a young lady who was eminently respectable, exactly the sort of woman any man would be happy to take as his wife. At least she would have been until he ruined her. *That* was precisely the sort of debased behaviour his father would expect from him.

'I'm sorry, Emily,' he whispered.

'Sorry for what?' She lifted herself back up onto one elbow and gazed down at him.

'For this.' He waved his hand around, encompassing their naked bodies, the tousled sheets and the flat where they had to meet in secret. 'I have never wished to marry, if for no other reason than to spite my father, but I'm sure, despite what you said, one day, when you meet the right man, you will want to wed. If any of this gets out it will—'

'Oh, that.' She dropped back down onto her side. 'I told you I have no wish to marry. Gideon finally opened my eyes to that realisation.'

'But won't your parents insist you do so, eventually? Isn't that what parents always do? It's what my grandparents did with my parents, and what my father wishes he could do with me. I'm surprised they haven't already found a suitable man for their lovely, well-connected, clever, delightful daughter. One certainly more suitable for you than Gideon Pratt.'

'My parents married for love and they want me to do the same. They have always said I should make my own choice. They encourage me, and they live in hope, but that's all. They have never put any pressure on me the way some parents do with their daughters.' She sighed lightly. 'And yes, I did once hope to marry, but unfortunately I have a terrible habit of falling for completely unsuitable men.'

'Like me?'

She sat up quickly, a hand on her chest, covering her heart, while her eyes grew enormous. 'No, I didn't mean that. Not that I mean you're unsuitable. I mean, you are suitable, and I'm not intending to marry you. And I haven't fallen for you, so I suppose you are unsuitable.'

She collapsed back onto the bed. 'It's different with you. It's not serious. We're not going to marry.'

Jackson refused to let that hurt. After all, she was saying nothing he didn't already know.

They remained silent for a few breaths.

'Well, you did make a rather unfortunate choice with Pratt,' he said, moving the subject away from him. 'But you said men. Were there more unsuitable men, other than me and Pratt?'

She sighed deeply. 'Yes, Gideon was my latest mistake, but not my first.'

He rolled over to look at her. 'I thought I was your first.'

She pushed him playfully in the chest. 'I mean the first man I thought I was in love with. The first man I wanted to marry.'

Love? Marriage? Neither of which applied to Jackson. Again, he would not let that affect him.

'So, who was your first love then?'

Why was he asking this? Did he want to torment himself?

'Randall Cochran.'

He collapsed onto his back beside her and stared at the ceiling. 'I see what you mean. They don't come much less suitable than Cocky Cochran.' *That is if you exclude Jackson from the list of potentially unsuitable husbands.*

She gave a small laugh and rolled onto her side to look at him. 'Is that what you call him? If I'd known that was his nickname, I wouldn't have fallen for his tricks.'

'That man almost makes me look like a saint.' *Almost.*

'I know. My parents didn't approve of him either, which, being an eighteen-year-old girl, made him seem even more attractive, as if he was a bit wild and exciting. Fortunately, I found out before it was too late that he was merely a cruel man who treated women like they were commodities, things he could play with for his own amusement.'

She sighed lightly as Jackson's chest tightened with guilt. *No, he was not that bad. He had always been honest with the women he was involved with. He had never used any woman and never deceived them. That had to count for something. Didn't it?*

'That was why I was so keen to marry Gideon,' she continued. 'He was everything Randall was not, except he was deceiving me just as much as Randall was. Or at least, I'd been deceiving myself as to the sort of man he was, trying to make him fit into an image of my perfect husband. On the night he proposed, when I couldn't delude myself any longer, I realised that despite thinking of myself as an intelligent woman, when it comes to men I am completely gullible.'

She shook her head and gave another sigh. 'Mother didn't appear to approve of Gideon either. At the time I thought it was just snobbery, but perhaps she could see something I couldn't.'

'Or perhaps he tried to solicit her into becoming his private patient, as he'd done with me and every other titled person he came into contact with.'

'Yes, perhaps.'

'Well, at least you'll never have to see him again.'

'Thank goodness. It's strange how he suddenly resigned, but I must say I'm very pleased that he did.'

Jackson wondered whether he should inform Emily that there was nothing strange about it at all. It had merely taken a quiet word with Mr Greaves. Once the board chairman had been informed that the good doctor had chosen to treat a member of the aristocracy with minor injuries ahead of men who had been seriously burned in a foundry explosion, Mr Greaves had lost all confidence in the doctor and had suggested he tender his resignation before he was dismissed.

Jackson had said nothing that wasn't the truth, but had done so to ensure Emily never again had to be in that odious man's presence.

'Mother said it was good to see the last of him. I suspect she knew I was hoping to marry him.' She rolled over onto her stomach, and ran her finger gently along his jawline. 'Strangely enough, my mother thoroughly approves of you.'

'Well, that just shows she has no insight into a man's true nature. If she could see us now, I don't think she'd be approving of me one little bit.'

'I suppose not,' she softened this with a smile. 'But unlike those other men, you have never tried to pretend you are anyone other than exactly who you are.'

Jackson doubted that was a compliment and chose to

laugh it off. 'No, with me, what you see is exactly what you get.'

She ran a finger down his neck, and across his chest, her gaze following her finger. 'And what I see I like. Rather a lot.'

He took that as a signal that their conversation had now come to an end, slid his arm underneath her and rolled her on top of him.

'Do you have enough time?' he asked, looking up at the glorious body straddling his and praying she would say yes.

'I suppose I could tell Mother the seamstress made a complete mess of my dress and I insisted she start all over again, right back to taking my measurements.'

His prayers were answered.

She leant down and kissed his lips, her breasts skimming his chest. He groaned with expectation as her kisses moved down his neck, across his chest and trailed a line down his stomach.

All thoughts of the future and the past, all questions about what others would think about what they were doing, all of it left his head. Right now, he was exactly where he wanted to be, with the woman he wanted to be with, doing what felt so right it could not possibly be wrong.

Chapter Fourteen

A few days after her last meeting with Jackson a letter arrived for Emily in the morning post that sent shivers of anxiety charging through her. She had been summoned to a meeting with Mr Greaves to discuss a very serious matter. Emily folded up the letter, pushed it back into the envelope and placed it beside her plate.

'Is something wrong, dear?' her mother asked, pausing in the buttering of her toast.

'No, not at all,' Emily said with a forced smile, and poured herself another cup of tea, the tremor in her hands causing her mother's eyebrows to raise further up her forehead in question.

'The board have asked me to attend a meeting. I'm just a bit worried that it might be bad news,' she said. 'About the school I mean.'

'Oh, I see,' her mother said, her voice suggesting that she had no real interest in the goings on at the school. 'Will Viscount Wickford be there?' she asked, her voice perking up with interest.

'I have no idea.' Emily took a sip of tea, wanting this discussion to come to an end. She could only hope the meeting was to be about the school and that it would be a problem that could easily be put to rights. If word had got back to

Mr Greaves about her clandestine meetings with Jackson then the outcome for her could be catastrophic. She would no longer be welcome at the school or in the hospital. Mr Greaves might feel honour-bound to inform her parents what she had been up to. They would be deeply ashamed of their daughter. Exposure had always been a danger, and yet she had willingly put herself in peril, had even, dare she admit it, enjoyed taking such a risk, seeing it as wickedly exciting. She had also enjoyed having such a salacious secret that she'd not even shared it with her closest friends.

And now she was to pay the price for throwing good sense to the wind and going against how Society demanded a respectable young woman conduct herself.

Breakfast over, Emily took the family carriage to the school. Her heart a dull thud in her chest, her stomach a tight, churning knot, she entered the school and took the curved wrought iron stairs up to the board room to find only Mr Greaves and Jackson waiting.

Both men stood as she took her seat, Mr Greaves's face was mournful, while Jackson sent her a small, supportive smile, although he couldn't disguise the anxiety gripping his usually relaxed body, or those two lines that appeared between his eyes whenever he was worried.

'Thank you for coming, Lady Emily,' Mr Greaves said. 'I'm afraid I have received some rather disturbing news.'

Emily took her seat, gripped her hands tightly in her lap and prepared for the worst as the two men also took their seats.

'I've received a rather disturbing letter from a Mrs Turnbull,' Mr Greaves said, holding a letter in his hand. 'She is the chairwoman of a group called the Ladies for the Promotion of High Moral Standards.'

'Oh,' Emily said, her voice coming out as a small squeak. Jackson placed his hand lightly on her knee under the table and patted it in reassurance.

'Rather disturbing, indeed,' Mr Greaves said, looking back down at the letter. 'They're calling for the closure of the school as they believe it is encouraging moral laxity. Unfortunately, it mentions you, Lady Emily, and you, Viscount Wickford, by name as encouraging such abominable vices.'

Mr Greaves coughed lightly, placed his spectacles on the end of his nose and held the letter close to his face as he read.

"A student encountered by one of our members while inspecting the school was undeniably a woman of ill repute. This student made a lascivious and repugnant comment that shocked the esteemed gentlewoman, leaving her shaken and insulted. Rather than rebuke the offender and expel her from the school immediately, Lady Emily Beaumont and Viscount Wickford encouraged her disrespectful and offensive behaviour by laughing."

Emily placed her hand on her stomach as relief swept through her. They were objecting to Kitty's joke about French letters and back alleys. Thank goodness for that.

'I believe I was the only one to laugh,' Jackson said. 'Lady Emily was not amused.'

'It goes on,' Mr Greaves said frowning. *"This incident proved to our members that there is no moral guidance being provided by the organisers of The Women's Education Institute. Unless it is closed immediately our group will be forced to mount a sustained campaign until we bring an end to this debased institution."*

Jackson gave a dismissive snort of laughter.

'I'm afraid this is no laughing matter,' Mr Greaves said,

placing the letter down on the table and removing his spectacles. 'The school does not need such bad publicity. There is a danger that our patrons will withdraw their support, not only from the school but possibly from the hospital as well.'

'They wouldn't do that, surely,' Emily gasped out, suddenly aware of the full impact of the letter. 'These women wouldn't ruin all those people's lives just because Kitty made a silly joke and upset one woman?'

'I have no doubt that they will. We need to do something before this gets out of hand,' Mr Greaves said, tapping the letter. 'That is why I called you here today.'

'Do we know who is in this group?' Jackson asked, his slow drawl suggesting he could see an easy solution to the problem.

'Yes, I had my assistant make some inquiries and he has compiled a list. They are mainly middle-class women whose husbands are businessmen, lawyers, bankers and so forth.'

Mr Greaves rustled through the papers in front of him, found the one he was looking for and handed it to Jackson.

Jackson scanned down the list and scoffed. 'I know several of these men, including John Turnbull, the husband of the esteemed and outraged leader of the moral guardians. They are members of some of the somewhat less than reputable gentlemen's clubs I have also been known to frequent.'

Mr Greaves frowned, as did Emily. They both knew what sort of clubs he was referring to, and neither wished to be reminded that Jackson visited such places. Although Emily suspected Mr Greaves had a different reason to object than Emily did, thinking only of the reputation of the school. But she had always known what sort of man Jackson was. That was why she had chosen him. There was no point being upset about it now.

'Or, should I say, places I used to frequent.' He handed back the list to Mr Greaves. 'So I believe that is your answer.'

Mr Greaves and Emily both shook their heads, waiting for him to explain.

'It means, shall we say, they are men who use the services of women such as Kitty.'

Mr Greaves looked in Emily's direction, his face pained. 'I don't think it is appropriate to—'

'It is all right,' she reassured him. 'Let's just hear what Jack...what the Viscount has to say.'

'They're threatening us, so why not threaten them?'

'I don't think—'

Jackson held up his hand, interrupting Mr Greaves. 'If I make it clear to those men that their less than moral behaviours will be exposed to their morally upright wives if they don't nip this immediately in the bud, or if I inform a few of the more influential women, such as this Mrs Turnbull, that their husband's less than virtuous behaviour will be made public, I am confident this campaign will die an immediate death.'

'You want to blackmail them?' Emily was hardly able to believe what he had said. Randall Cochran had told his friends he intended to take Emily's virginity then blackmail her parents under the threat of making it public. Such behaviour was beneath contempt.

'Yes, all in a good cause.'

'Good cause or not, I cannot countenance that,' Emily said.

'I'm afraid I must agree with Lady Emily,' Mr Greaves

said. 'It would do the school's reputation no good if such an action became public.'

'Then we make sure it doesn't become public,' Jackson said, his nonchalant manner making it clear he could see no moral dilemma in such an action. 'And the ladies and their husbands would have a vested interest in making sure no one ever does find out. That is the beauty of blackmail.'

'No,' Emily repeated. 'That's wrong. Perhaps if Kitty apologises?'

'I did write to Mrs Turnbull and suggest that,' Mr Greaves said. 'She replied that under no circumstances did she want to come into contact with a woman such as Miss Kathryn Trotter.'

Jackson sent Emily a wide-eyed look as if to say, *'See, that is the sort of person we're dealing with.'*

'Perhaps if the Viscount and I apologised and explained that it was merely a joke, a bad joke at that, the likes of which will never happen again,' Emily suggested to Mr Greaves.

'That is a kind offer, but I doubt if even that would assuage this woman. I even suggested in my letter that we expel Miss Trotter to make an example of her.'

'No,' Jackson and Emily said at the same time.

'But even that would not satisfy Mrs Turnbull,' Mr Greaves continued with a shake of his head. 'She said all she would countenance was the expulsion of every woman of lax morals.'

Which would include me, Emily thought dolefully.

'That would effectively cause the demise of the school and everything it is trying to do,' she said instead.

'Well, if they want lax morals exposed,' Jackson said, raising his hands, palm upwards, as if he had won the argument, 'then threatening to expose the lax morals of their husbands should do the trick.'

'No,' Emily shot back. That was a level of hypocrisy she would not countenance. While she did not approve of men who used the services of women like Kitty, she would not stoop to the level of blackmail. And if she was being completely honest, her own secrets would make her a good target for a blackmailer. It was a dangerous path to go down, one over which they could easily lose control.

'I have another idea,' she said, looking from one man to the other. 'Let me invite the Ladies for the Promotion of High Moral Standards to an afternoon tea and try and persuade them the school is committed to reforming women and taking them off the street. I am confident I can make them see the school is a force for moral good and something that all upstanding women should support.'

Both men looked at her dubiously, Jackson in particular.

'If you think that will work,' Mr Greaves said uncertainly.

'I'm sure it will,' Emily said, not sure in the slightest, but determined to try.

'Well, I suppose we have nothing to lose by you attempting to change their minds,' Mr Greaves added.

'And if scones and jam don't work, I can always blackmail them,' Jackson said. Emily sent him a stern look, which merely caused him to smile back at her.

Mr Greaves stood up to signal the end of the meeting. They exchanged their goodbyes and Jackson escorted her out of the office, down the staircase and towards her waiting carriage.

'So do we have enough time for a bit of outrageous, immoral and lascivious behaviour of our own? Before you mount your campaign to convince the Ladies for the Promotion of High Moral Standards just how moral and high standing you are,' Jackson said as he took her hand to help her into her carriage.

'Yes, I believe we need a further meeting to discuss our strategy,' Emily replied, the pleasure of anticipation erupting inside her.

'Charles,' she called out to the driver, 'I wish to do a spot of shopping before I return home.'

'Very good, my lady. Would you like to go to the usual shopping arcade?'

'Yes, thank you. I always find their service so satisfying.'

As the door closed she heard Jackson's low chuckle and smiled to herself.

Driving through the busy streets, she reminded herself that this time she really must buy something other than gloves as evidence that she had been on another impromptu shopping excursion. The pile of multi-coloured gloves taking over several shelves in her bedroom cupboard was starting to look a tad questionable. And, after this morning's scare, the last thing she wanted was anyone, including her mother, to start asking questions.

Chapter Fifteen

⁓⁓⁓⁓

It was just an afternoon tea, but so much was riding on its success and that was making Emily nervous. She had gathered her friends together, hoping the members of the Ladies for the Promotion of High Moral Standards would be snobs, and the presence of the Duchess of Ravenswood, the Duchess of Redwood and Lady Amelia would impress them and make them forget all about their campaign.

Gilded invitations on the stationer's most expensive card had been sent out, informing each lady by name that Lady Emily Beaumont invited her to afternoon tea at the Belgrave residence of the Duke and Duchess of Fernwood.

When the women started to arrive Emily could see immediately that such a ploy was having the desired effect. The women were all dressed in their finery of silk, satin and chenille gowns in a bright array of colours. Elaborate hats bedecked with ostrich feathers, lace and ribbons sat proudly on their heads, and Emily could only wonder at the expertise of the milliners who had created these fantastical concoctions.

The women entered the drawing room and were conspicuously on their best behaviour. Tea was sipped with pinkies extended as far as it was possible for fingers to go, backs remained ramrod straight, noses were held firmly in the air and pretentious smiles adorned every lip.

Emily was sure some had even adopted contrived aristocratic accents for the occasion.

Irene, Georgina and Amelia were also on their best behaviour, taking their role of gracious aristocrats seriously, and chatting and laughing with each and every woman. Emily was heartened to see the women were finding this attention flattering.

It was perfect, and she was determined to prove Jackson wrong. When they'd been lying in each other's arms he had still maintained that blackmail could achieve so much more and a lot faster than fancy cakes and cucumber sandwiches ever could. She had responded that the diplomatic approach might take longer but it resulted in everyone being pleased with the outcome, and no one got hurt.

He had wished her good luck but had remained unconvinced.

Now all she had to do was prove that she was indeed capable of diplomacy.

Several maids circled the room, making sure each woman had everything she needed, that her cup was filled and her plate overflowing with an array of delicious treats.

'You are so lucky to have such attentive and polite staff,' Mrs Turnbull said to Emily as she smothered more cream on her scone. 'The servant problem is really becoming something of a trial.'

This elicited nods of agreement from the assembled ladies.

'And your cook is simply marvellous,' another woman added. 'My cook makes scones that would be better used as door stops.'

The women all tittered their agreement.

'Yes, I had heard there was a servant shortage,' Emily said, shaking her head in sympathy. She could have added that if the women were prepared to pay decent wages and provide good working conditions they might not struggle to find staff, but this afternoon was about diplomacy, not lecturing.

'Oh, indeed there is,' Mrs Turnbull added, shaking her head mournfully. 'A terrible shortage. Something really needs to be done about it.'

'That is why The Women's Education Institute includes lessons on an array of domestic skills,' Emily said, pleased that Mrs Turnbull had provided her with the perfect opportunity to discuss the reason for the afternoon tea.

Mrs Turnbull's lips grew thin, but before she could speak Emily rushed on.

'I'm sure you'll be interested to know the afternoon tea you have just enjoyed was prepared by young ladies from our cooking, baking and pastry courses.'

The women all looked at the scones, pastries and sandwiches they were eating and frowned, their looks suggesting they were wondering whether eating such light and fluffy delicacies meant they were now morally contaminated.

Emily forced herself to keep smiling in her most benign manner. 'I know what you are all thinking,' she said, knowing no such thing. 'You're all wishing you could hire the pastry cook and have her create such impressive fare when you host your own afternoon teas.'

No one agreed with her, but no one disagreed either, which had to be a good sign.

'But I'm afraid I have to disappoint you. The young

woman who made the pastries has been offered a job at the estate of the Duchess of Redcliff, so you won't be able to poach her for your own staff,' Emily added with a small laugh as if she had made a joke.

'I'm so sorry, ladies,' Irene said. 'I'm afraid I have a terrible sweet tooth and once I tasted the cook's Victoria sponge I just had to hire her.'

This caused renewed twittering from the ladies. Emily nodded to the maid, to indicate she should serve each woman more cakes and pastries. They immediately commenced eating, presumably under the assumption that if a duchess could trust the cook, then the cakes were probably safe to eat.

'And the maids who are doing such a marvellous job today are all students in our domestic science classes at the training school.'

The women looked at the young ladies moving unobtrusively among the guests, dressed in black gowns and perfectly starched white aprons and caps. There was not a hair out of place among them and certainly not a painted face to be seen anywhere.

'You have done an admirable job,' Mrs Turnbull said to Emily, but her tight-lipped expression contradicted her compliment and indicated a threat to come. 'But I for one would not give house room to a woman who had proven herself to be of low moral character.'

Taking their lead from Mrs Turnbull, the other women nodded their agreement and several placed their now empty plates on a side table, as if in protest.

Emily forced herself not to react but to continue smiling, all the while wondering whether Jackson might be correct.

Perhaps now might be a good time to drop a hint or two regarding Mr Turnbull's night-time excursions.

'I agree,' another of the moral guardians said. 'Men can be led astray so easily by a wanton woman. Such women should be punished for the harm they cause to men who would otherwise not fall from the path of morality, and for the harm those women cause to their families.'

Emily swallowed her annoyance and tilted her head as if listening to the woman's outrage with interest.

'Yes,' another moral lady added. 'Such women need to be made to see the error of their ways, not rewarded for their moral turpitude with training and jobs in fancy country estates.' This was greeted by another round of nodding from the women.

Mrs Turnbull sent Emily a condescending smile. 'I know you mean well, but it is essential that such women are provided with strict moral guidance. They need to be taught the difference between right and wrong, and need to be made aware it is essential they repent and pay the wages of their sins.'

The nodding continued.

'I agree entirely,' Emily said, causing her friends to send her surprised looks. 'That is why we have several clergymen on the board of directors for the school. They also provide religious instructions and guidance for the students.'

Emily saw no need to add that all these clergymen were compassionate and non-judgemental. Like Emily, they saw no need to punish women who had already suffered so much, and they only had the students' well-being at heart.

'I am pleased to hear that,' Mrs Turnbull said. 'And that is no less than I would expect. Someone needs to address these women's lack of moral rectitude and ensure they are redressing their sinful pasts.'

She looked down at the fluffy scone on her plate, and her expression softened slightly, before once again becoming stern. 'Lady Emily, your promises that the school will take a high moral stance at all times and that any straying from the path of righteousness will in future be severely dealt with has provided me with some reassurance.'

Emily hadn't quite given that assurance, but now was no time to quibble over details, not when victory appeared to be at hand.

'Therefore, I believe the Ladies for the Promotion of High Moral Standards can find other areas in this sinful city on which to focus our good and essential work.'

Emily released a held breath and smiled at Mrs Turnbull.

'But rest assured,' Mrs Turnbull continued, raising one finger and pointing it at Emily, 'I personally will be monitoring the school. At the first sign of any moral lapses, my ladies and I will resume our campaign to have the school closed with renewed vigour.'

'Thank you. That of course is to be expected,' Emily said.

'So, now that that is settled,' one of the moral guardians said, 'are any of these young women looking for work?' She eyed the young maids lined up against the serving table, who all stared straight ahead, their bodies rigid, as if to say, *Please do not pick me.*

'Unfortunately, these young women are still receiving training,' Emily said and could see the young maids' shoulders relax as they drew in relieved breaths. 'But if you wish you can make inquiries at the school.'

Inquiries that will be ignored, as none of the students

deserve to be subjected to such intolerance and harsh judgement from their future employers.

The woman smiled at Emily, thinking all her servant problems had been solved.

The afternoon tea continued in a congenial manner, with the moral guardians taking every opportunity to inform Emily and her friends just how sinful London was, and how easy it was to slip off the pathway of righteousness. Emily continued to nod and smile, and resisted the temptation to mention the decidedly unrighteous gentlemen's clubs that their husbands were reputed to frequent.

When the afternoon tea came to an end, and the footman finally showed the ladies out and into their waiting carriages, Emily and her friends slumped back into their chairs, exhausted from so much false smiling and forced civility.

'You were all marvellous,' Emily said to her friends and the maids. 'I believe we've just saved the school.'

Maids and friends joined in a rousing cheer.

'And after all your hard work, I believe you deserve your own afternoon tea,' she said to the maids. 'I've asked the cook to make sure there are plenty of treats left over and they're waiting for you down in the kitchen.'

The maids wasted no time clearing away the tea service and departing. As the door closed behind them, giggling erupted along with much joking and teasing about which one of them was the biggest sinner and who was destined for the worst type of damnation.

'I don't know about you ladies, but I for one need a stiff drink after that,' Georgina said, rising from her chair and pouring four glasses of brandy before anyone had answered.

She handed the glasses to her friends, then raised hers above her head. 'Here's to slipping off the path of righteousness and falling into a world of vice and sin.' She took a deep swig of her brandy, sighed, then refilled her glass. 'Long may it continue.'

'Speaking of sin and vice, how is Jackson Wilde?' Irene asked.

Emily almost spluttered on her brandy. 'Jackson Wilde?' she asked, as if unsure who they were talking about.

'We've seen so little of you recently and we've all been dying to ask,' Georgina added. 'We had been hoping you would reveal all before now, but you've been playing your cards rather close to your chest.'

Emily stared at her friends, who were smiling back at her as if all party to the same secret.

'You all know?'

'Well, we don't know the details,' Amelia said. 'But we all saw the two of you together at the fundraising ball. And you have been decidedly conspicuous in your absence over the last—what would it be since the ball, six months?'

The other women nodded.

'I've called at your house a number of times over the last few months and your mother always says you're in a meeting with the Viscount, either that or shopping for gloves,' Amelia added.

'Gloves,' Georgina said with a laugh. 'That's an interesting name for it.'

'And you bounced back remarkably quickly from the end of your involvement with Gideon Pratt,' Amelia added. 'To my mind that usually means there's another man involved.'

As one, her three friends leant forward, all looking at Emily in expectation.

'So, are you going to tell us what's happening, or are we going to have to drag it out of you?' Georgina said, looking as if that was exactly what she wanted to do.

'Oh, all right, I'll tell you the whole story, and thank goodness the Ladies for the Promotion of High Moral Standards have left, otherwise they would be scandalised.'

'Oh, goody,' Georgina said, topping up everyone's brandy glasses. 'There's nothing I enjoy more than a good scandal, so don't leave out a single detail.'

Chapter Sixteen

Jackson waited in his carriage, discreetly parked up the street from Emily's parents' home, anxious to hear how the meeting went. He watched those self-righteous old dragons leave the house, smiling and simpering as they chatted on the doorstep, their extravagant hats perched like exotic birds on the top of their heads, bobbing along with the conversation. Then, with repeated calls of goodbye and much waving of gloved hands, they climbed into their carriages and drove away.

He was unsure whether smiling and simpering was a good or bad thing when it came to dragons. Did that mean they were joyfully preparing for battle and the destruction of the school? Or did it mean Emily had managed to negotiate a diplomatic solution and they had happily driven away never to be seen again?

As much as he liked the thought of indulging in a bit of well-placed blackmail and threatening to expose the level of their hypocrisy, he hoped it was the latter, and Emily's scones and cream had worked their magic.

Once the street was clear of carriages, he waited a few moments longer in case there was a straggler or two. No one else emerged from the house, so he knocked on the door and informed the footman he wished to see Lady

Emily. It was his first visit to her parents' house since the ball, which did go against his strict rule of never ever meeting his mistresses outside of his rooms, but today he would make an exception. This was about the school, and he knew he wouldn't rest until he heard the outcome of her meeting.

'Lady Emily is in the drawing room,' the footman said. 'Please wait here and I will announce you.'

'No need to trouble yourself,' Jackson said. 'I'll find my own way.' He looked up the black and white tiled entranceway with its array of doors and frowned.

'It is the fourth door on the right,' the footman said, seeing his predicament. 'The one that has been left ajar.'

Jackson nodded his thanks and approached the door. His progress was stopped by the sound of female voices. Damn, not all the moralistic viragos had left. A few must have found some remaining fire and brimstone that they still had to cast far and wide.

It was time for Jackson to make a quick and tactical retreat before his presence reinforced for the remaining harridans that the school was a den of vice, and only they could save the world from its corrupting influence.

His shoes squeaked on the highly polished tiles and he froze, his breath held. No incensed crones came rushing out armed with pitchforks and burning torches, so he released his held breath and took another quieter step forward.

'We just knew there was something going on between you and Jackson Wilde,' an unfamiliar woman's voice said, halting his progress and causing his breath to once more catch in his throat. 'But we didn't know things had gone quite so far.'

This was a disaster. It would take a lot more than a few

diplomatic scones to save the school now. He waited for the remaining vipers to start convulsing with paroxysms of moral outrage over their relationship, then threaten to burn down the school, with Emily and Jackson in it.

'You really are a dark horse, aren't you?' another woman said, the amusement in her voice sounding anything but outraged. 'And I must admit, Jackson Wilde is, how shall we say?'

Jackson quietly moved closer to the door, wondering what Jackson Wilde was.

'A bit more exciting than Dr Gideon Pratt,' the woman added.

This caused the other women to laugh. It was a compliment, but not much of one. You didn't have to be particularly exciting to be more exciting than Pratt. Nor was it a conversation that Emily was likely to have with the moralising women. It was evident she was chatting to her friends. About him. He should leave. Even though he was the one under discussion, it was a private conversation and to eavesdrop would be an invasion of her privacy, the height of bad manners.

He leant in closer towards the open door.

'I must admit, I had my doubts about you marrying Dr Pratt,' a woman said. Jackson nodded at the astute woman's comment. 'I know you thought him upstanding, dedicated and all that, but well.' She paused. Jackson could have added, *'But the man was a social climbing bore and his treatment of Emily was beneath contempt.'*

'He was a little *too* upstanding,' she added. It seemed Emily wasn't the only one dedicated to diplomacy.

'So how is, you know, with Jackson Wilde?' another female voice asked. This was a question to which Jackson would also be interested in hearing the answer, assuming he and the woman speaking meant the same thing by 'you know'.

'It's good.'

Then again, perhaps he'd rather not hear Emily's answer.

'Oh, all right, it's very good.'

That was better he supposed, but still, not exactly a ringing endorsement.

'Oh, all right, yes, it's wonderful. He makes me feel things I did not know it was possible to feel. Sometimes I just have to think about him and my body starts to react as if I can feel his touch. It's as if I can't get enough of him. He really is the most magnificent lover.'

A chorus of female voices sighed.

That was more like it. Jackson would like to believe his pleasure in hearing those words was because it was further confirmation that he was satisfying Emily, but he knew his smugness was simply due to his prowess in the bedroom being admired.

'So where to now with Jackson Wilde?' another voice asked.

That too was a question Jackson was also interested in having answered.

'Nowhere,' Emily stated emphatically. 'It's just some harmless fun. It means nothing to either of us.'

Those words should have held no surprise for Jackson. Emily was saying nothing he didn't already know. That had been the agreement when they first became involved. She had promised to make no demands on him, to have no expectations. So why did hearing her repeat it now in such a dispassionate manner make him feel like he had just been punched in the stomach?

'Are you sure?' the interrogator asked. 'It's not like you to be so cavalier. You've always been, shall we say, somewhat intense.'

'Well, people can change,' Emily stated. 'I've changed. Haven't I? No one, including the three of you, who know me so well, would have thought I could ever become the lover of a man like Jackson Wilde.'

This drew murmurs of agreement, and Jackson was hoping they would ask what she meant by 'a man like Jackson Wilde', even though he suspected he already knew what the answer would be. No one asked that question.

'After I realised what Gideon was really like, how he was using me, and how he was more interested in my connections than he ever was in me, I decided I was done with men and marriage,' Emily continued. 'No more looking for the right man. That was why I became involved with Jackson.'

Because he was not the right man? So if he wasn't right what was he? Wrong?

'Was it because Dr Pratt hurt you so badly?' a woman asked quietly. 'Did you take up with Jackson Wilde so you could get over him?'

Jackson's mood sunk even lower. Surely he was not merely a sop for her to recover from Pratt. His previously puffed-up masculine pride could not have deflated further if Emily had taken to it with a hat pin.

'No, not really,' Emily said, giving him some hope. 'My feelings for Gideon were deluded. It was such a shock to discover I had done it again. I had once again been deluded into thinking a man was the person he pretended to be, just as I did with Randall Cochran, only this time it was worse. The signs were all there showing me what Gideon was really like, but I'd convinced myself they weren't, because I wanted him to be the perfect husband for me. He wasn't lying to me. I was lying to myself. What happened with Gideon merely reinforced the lesson I should have learnt with Randall. I am a terrible judge of character when it comes to men. But at least with Jackson I know exactly what he is like.'

Jackson held his breath, sure that what he was about to hear would not be something he would like.

'He's a philanderer, a man incapable of committing to one woman,' Emily said, confirming his suspicions. 'He's the sort of man no sensible woman would ever think of marrying.'

'But if you changed, can't he change as well?' a woman asked.

Emily laughed as if someone had made a joke. 'Not Jackson Wilde. That man will never change.'

The room went quiet, then a woman asked. 'Emily, are you sure about this? Isn't there a danger that you might fall in love with him, despite what you say?'

'No, never,' she stated, her voice loud. 'That is why I picked him, because I knew I could never fall in love with such a man. In choosing Jackson I could, well, to not put too fine a point on it, I could enjoy all the pleasures a woman can experience with a man without risking my heart.'

Jackson slumped back against the wall. Everything she was saying was the truth. He was the sort of man no sensible woman should fall in love with, and women didn't get much more sensible than Emily. But that did not make the words any less painful to hear.

'But do be careful,' the same woman added, her voice

full of concern. 'We all know how easy it is to fall hopelessly for a man you think is wrong for you.'

This caused a murmur of agreement from all present. All, he assumed, except Emily.

'We all saw how upset you were over Randall Cochran,' the woman continued. 'We'd hate to see you have your heart broken again.'

Emily laughed dismissively. 'I had hoped to marry Randall, and yes I was hurt when I discovered he had no feelings for me. But I have no such aspirations with Jackson.'

'But that doesn't mean you can't have your heart broken. We're pleased that you're having fun, but we just don't want Jackson Wilde to hurt you.'

Jackson wanted to burst into the room and inform these women that he would move heaven and earth to ensure Emily was never hurt. How could he possibly hurt the woman he loved?

He placed his hands against the wall to steady himself as the full implication of that thought crashed down on him.

Love?

He was in love with Emily Beaumont.

That was what he was feeling. That was why he thought about her constantly. That was why he missed her so intensely, even when they were only apart for a short time. That was why everything about her delighted and entranced him.

He loved her.

And that was why her words cut through him like a rapier.

He was in love and suspected he had always been in love with her. For him, what had happened between them had never been just fun. From the first time he had made love to her it had been something much deeper, much more profound. It had been love. He just hadn't realised it.

He had fallen in love with a woman who saw him as a man not worth loving, a man no sensible woman marries, a man who was only good for having fun with. Once that was how he would have described himself as well. Once he would have hoped that any woman he took as his mistress would see him that way. But not now. Not when it came to Emily.

'Jackson won't hurt me,' Emily stated, and Jackson was relieved that at least she saw him as possessing one virtue. 'Nor will he break my heart,' she added. 'For the simple reason that I am not in love with Jackson Wilde and never will be. As soon as this relationship has run its course I will leave it in my past where it belongs. As I said, it's just nothing more than a bit of fun that means nothing.'

With as much dignity as he possessed, Jackson quietly retraced his steps back down the hallway and out into the street where his carriage was waiting. Hardly aware of anything around him, he told the carriage driver to go, not caring where it took him, just knowing he had to escape.

Emily was unsure who she was trying to convince more, herself or her friends. Whichever it was, it wasn't working. Her friends' concerned expressions made it clear they didn't believe a word she was saying, and her aching heart made it abundantly clear *she* did not believe a word she was saying either.

'None of that is true,' she whispered, pleased to be finally speaking the truth despite the pain gripping her heart.

'Oh, Emily,' her friends said as one and quickly gathered around her on the settee.

'My relationship with Jackson means more to me than just some harmless fun, so much more. I am such a fool. I've done it again. I've fallen for a completely inappropriate man and this time I knew he was inappropriate, but I fell in love with him anyway.'

Arms wrapped around her as her friends tried to reassure her that she was not a fool.

'I promised myself, and I promised him, that this would mean nothing,' she said, taking a handkerchief from Georgina's outstretched hand and wiping her eyes. 'I said all it would be was fun, and it *has* been fun, but it has also been so much more than that. For me at least.'

'You can't help what your heart does,' Irene said. 'Is that why you fell in love with him, because being with him was so much fun?'

Emily smiled and nodded through her tears. 'When we're together he makes me laugh so much. It's wonderful. Never before have I felt so carefree and joyful as when I'm with him.' She swallowed a sob that was neither joyful nor carefree. 'But that's not why I fell in love with him.'

The three women tilted their heads, as if asking the same question.

'He's so surprisingly kind. I hadn't thought a man with his reputation could be so kind to everyone he meets, no matter who they are. He was so popular with the other patients in the hospital, and he never treats anyone as if they're beneath him. And he's so brave. Look how he saved Kitty.'

She placed her hand over her heart and looked from one friend to another, each of whom was nodding in agreement.

'And he respects me and what I do.' She shook her head in wonderment. 'That too was a surprise. The school was really his idea, but he involved me right from its inception.' She looked at her friends in question and continued to slowly shake her head. 'How did he know that I would find establishing the school so fulfilling? It's as if he knows me better than I know myself. He could see that I wasn't really needed at the hospital, and was searching for something that would fully engage me. How did he know that?'

She looked from friend to friend, who were all bearing the same knowing look.

'Perhaps he feels the same way about you,' Amelia said. 'Have you asked Jackson how he feels?'

'No,' Emily responded immediately, 'I haven't said anything to him. He knows nothing of any of this, and that is the way I'm going to have to keep it.'

'Is that wise?' Amelia asked, her voice gentle.

Emily nodded, wiped her eyes again, then crumpled the damp handkerchief into a small ball. 'Yes. I don't want to look like a complete idiot in front of him. I've already done that in front of two men and I never want to do that again.' She squeezed the ball tighter. 'I decided to become involved with Jackson because I thought there was no danger of falling in love with him and no danger of making an ass of myself again, because I knew exactly what sort of man he was, and that he was a man I would never want to marry.'

'But things change, people change, feelings change,' Irene said, handing her another dry handkerchief. 'Your feelings for Jackson Wilde have changed. Perhaps his feelings for you have also changed.'

Emily looked at Irene through her damp eyes and wondered whether this could be true.

'And you're never going to know unless you ask him,' Irene added.

'It will take courage,' Georgina said. 'But you've always had plenty of courage.'

Emily was not entirely convinced by that.

'It took a lot of courage to suggest to him that you become lovers, didn't it?' Georgina asked in a soothing voice.

Emily could only nod. It *had* taken an enormous amount of courage, more than she thought she possessed, but that was nothing compared to the amount of courage it would take to expose her feelings to a man who had the power to break her heart.

'And you can be courageous again and find out how he is really feeling,' Georgina added, as if it was all that easy.

'And you're not going to know for certain how he does feel until you do ask,' Irene said, stroking Emily's hand. 'All you're going to do is assume he wants nothing more from your relationship.'

'But if I do tell him how I'm feeling and he's horrified by me wanting more, I might lose him completely.' The thought of that caused the tears to once again well up in her eyes, but she blinked them away. 'Although, I suppose if he doesn't want anything more from me, then I'm going to lose him eventually anyway, when he finally loses interest in me and moves on to the next woman.'

Emily gripped the sodden handkerchiefs tighter, her nails digging into her palms at the thought of Jackson with another woman.

Irene continued to gently stroke her hands until she released their tight clench, while Georgina and Irene once again wrapped their arms around her shoulders. As sad as she felt, she was grateful to have such close friends to share this with.

'I do want to know how he feels,' she confessed. 'But I don't want the pain of finding out he cares nothing for me.' She gave a small, humourless laugh at her predicament. 'I want to know but only if he tells me exactly what I want to hear.'

She looked down at her hands. 'But I supposed one way or another I'm going to find out eventually. By not asking him then I'm only delaying the inevitable. If he leaves it will be heartbreaking, but I've got over heartbreak before, I can do it again. And perhaps it will be better to find out now rather than wait until I'm even more hopelessly in love with him.'

Emily was unsure whether any of that was really true. Yes, she had recovered from finding out that Randall Cochran was not the man she thought he was, but her heartbreak had been over a man who did not really exist, and a disappointment that she would not have a successful first Season that would end in her becoming a bride. With Jackson she knew exactly what he was like. She was in love with the real Jackson Wilde, with all his faults and flaws. And was it really possible to be even more in love with him than she was now? She doubted that.

'Or you might discover that he is in love with you as well,' Georgina said, always the optimist.

She smiled at her well-meaning friend. 'Perhaps. But you're right. I'm never going to know until I ask him. So I'll do it. I will ask him how he feels about me, whether we have a future together and what that future will entail.'

Her smile started to quiver as her friends held her closely, and she wondered whether she would actually be able to be true to those brave words.

Chapter Seventeen

The letter from Mr Greaves requesting Jackson's presence at a meeting at the school could only be about one thing; the outcome of Emily's attempt to cajole the Ladies for the Promotion of High Moral Standards into dropping their ridiculous campaign. He still didn't know whether she had succeeded or not, and he wanted to find out what, if anything, the ladies had planned. He just wished he did not need to see Emily again in order to do so.

It was ironic that only a day ago he lived to be with her again, but one day could change everything. One day ago, he didn't realise what he was feeling was love. One day ago, he did not know that the woman he was in love with did not feel the same way about him. He did not know that he was of so little importance to her. He did not know he was nothing more than a passing diversion.

If he'd heard any of his previous mistresses talking in such a manner he would have been relieved that they wanted no more from the relationship than he did.

But Emily was different. How he felt about her was different.

Now he was going to see her again, knowing the truth about how she felt about him and aware of the depth of his feelings for her. Feelings that were not reciprocated.

This was going to require a level of fortitude he was unsure he possessed.

He arrived at the board room slightly later than the time Mr Greaves had arranged, finding endless reasons to delay his arrival. He entered to find Emily and Mr Greaves waiting for him. Mr Greaves was smiling, fit to burst, making it obvious what he was going to say. Emily's expression was less easy to read. Nothing should have changed for her, and yet her expression was, what? Tentative? Shy? Whatever it was, it was not his place to try and analyse what was going through her mind about the meeting with the moral ladies. He knew her mind when it came to him, and that was all that concerned him.

He made his greetings and sat down.

'I was just telling Lady Emily the wonderful news,' Mr Greaves said, holding up a letter and waving it in the air triumphantly. 'We had another note from Mrs Turnbull, this time singing the praises of the school.'

'That's excellent news,' he said with as much enthusiasm as he could muster. And it *was* excellent news. The school was safe. Kitty and all the other girls and women attending the school could continue to pursue new lives. They wouldn't be stuck in the dire circumstances that had been forced on them by lack of opportunity.

'Congratulations, Lady Emily,' Jackson said with a polite nod. 'Your approach has proven to be the correct one and you are to be commended.'

'Hear, hear,' Mr Greaves added, smiling at Emily, before his expression turned more serious. 'But we're not entirely out of the woods,' he continued. 'Mrs Turnbull does say that she and her ladies will be monitoring the school and, should they detect any sign of scandal, inappropriate or immoral behaviour from anyone at the school—students, teachers and board members included—they will not hesitate to mount a campaign to have the school closed.'

Jackson made a point of not looking in Emily's direction and hoped she was doing the same. If those moralistic ladies got even a hint of what had been occurring between them it would be the end of the school, not to mention the destruction of Emily's reputation. They were risking so much, and all for what she described as meaningless fun.

'I believe in that case it might be wisest if I tender my resignation from the fundraising committee,' Jackson said, surprising himself.

'Why?' Emily said, rising slightly from her chair.

'That is most unfortunate,' Mr Greaves said with a frown. 'And I don't believe it is necessary.'

Mr Greaves obviously did not read the scandal sheets, or perhaps he did and had noticed Jackson's absence from them over the last six or so months and erroneously thought him a reformed man.

'Be that as it may, I still wish to resign.'

'I am so disappointed to hear that,' Mr Greaves said, shaking his head. 'You have been a marvellous asset to the school, simply marvellous. The school owes its very existence to you. It was your idea and you and Lady Emily have been the driving force to get it started.'

Jackson smoothed down a non-existent wrinkle in his trousers, being unfamiliar with such adulation and not sure how one was supposed to react.

'Is there anything I can do or say to make you change your mind?' Mr Greaves continued. 'You will be such a great loss to the school.'

It was kind of the elderly gentleman, but if he knew

Jackson's real character he would not be so quick to praise him, and would be enthusiastically welcoming Jackson's resignation.

'No, I'm afraid my mind is made up,' Jackson said.

'Lady Emily, perhaps you can change his mind,' Mr Greaves said, looking at Emily in appeal.

'Nothing can change my mind,' he interjected before she could say anything. 'I am afraid there are things in my past that the ladies could use to damage the school's reputation.'

'But that's all in the past,' Emily said. 'They can hardly fault anyone for what they did in the past. And isn't that what this school is all about, giving people a fresh start, letting them put past mistakes behind them?' She looked from him to Mr Greaves, who nodded his agreement.

'I doubt if the moralising ladies would see it that way.' Jackson countered.

And it's not exactly in the past, is it? he could have added.

'So you're going to let *them* blackmail *you*?' Emily said, looking somewhat irate.

'I'm going to make sure they're not in a position to blackmail the school,' he said, not wishing to argue about this, particularly here in this office. 'My mind is made up,' he said, turning back to Mr Greaves.

'As you wish,' the older man said. 'It is very disappointing, of course, but I can see you have done so for the highest motives.'

Jackson winced. He had done so because he did not wish to spend time with a woman he loved, a woman who saw him as nothing more than someone to pass the occasional enjoyable afternoon with, not a man she could ever take seriously.

The meeting over, he escorted Emily out to her carriage,

knowing he not only had to cut ties with the school, but also with her, if he was to ever shake off the despondency that had possessed him since he overheard that conversation.

'I believe we should have our own meeting so we can further discuss your resignation,' she said, as he helped her into her carriage.

Instead of giving his usual enthusiastic response, he climbed into the carriage beside her. 'We can have that discussion here and now,' he said.

'Oh, yes, well, I suppose we could,' she said, looking around at the interior of the carriage, her brow furrowed.

Jackson drew in a deep breath and tried to compose the words he planned to say to her, words he both wanted and didn't want to say.

She waited. He prevaricated. If he said nothing, if he pretended he had not overheard what she had said to her friends, would that be so bad?

If he ignored what he'd heard, if he ignored how he felt, they could go straight to his rooms. He could have her naked, in his bed, writhing under him, giving him the exquisite pleasure only she could provide. But then she would leave, and he would have to continue dealing with the truth. He would not be able to ignore that the woman he loved would never see the time they were together as anything more than an enjoyable past-time. And every time he thought of that, the pain he would feel would only intensify. No, he had to be strong and end this. Now.

'I also believe it would be best if we no longer see each other.'

Her eyes grew enormous and her mouth opened in an unspoken *'oh'*. He was tempted to retract that statement, to tell her he did not mean it, that he wanted her, wanted her desperately. But he would not be a coward.

'It has been fun, Emily,' he said, cringing at that word, a word that had wounded him so deeply. A word that summed up all that their relationship had ever been for her. 'But I believe it has run its course.'

Wasn't that what she had said to her friends, that it would eventually run its course and it would be over?

'Oh, I see,' she said, staring straight ahead.

'We both knew this would happen eventually, didn't we?'

'Yes, we did.'

'And we've had our fun, haven't we?'

'Yes,' she responded, not looking at him.

'So, what with everything that has happened at the school, and the moralistic women's threats, now is probably a good time to end things.'

'Yes.'

'We both agreed this would only ever be a dalliance and that neither of us would take it seriously.' *An agreement I broke.* 'So I believe it is time we gave each other the freedom to pursue other relationships.'

She took a quick look in his direction, then resumed staring straight ahead. 'Is there another relationship you wish to pursue?' she asked.

'What? No, not at the moment. No.'

'I see,' she said, looking down at her hands clasped tightly in her lap. 'Not at the moment, but you hope to pursue another relationship sometime soon?'

'I haven't really thought about it.'

And doubt I ever will.

'But you too will be free to pursue other relationships.'

One that is more than just fun…one where you love the man as much as he loves you.

'I will never have another relationship with a man,' she said quietly, looking down at her hands, still clenched tightly together.

'You don't have to worry,' he said, wishing he could take her in his arms and reassure her. 'No one knows about us. No one will ever know. As far as all of Society is concerned you are still a chaste young woman who is above reproach. There is no reason why you can't enter into another relationship, one that could lead to marriage.'

To a man you consider worthy of marriage, a condition that excludes me.

'I don't wish to marry anyone else,' she murmured. 'I told you that when we first—well, when we first became lovers.'

Jackson closed his eyes briefly and drew in a deep breath. She still wanted to be his lover, but that was no longer enough for him. He could not weaken now. He had to be strong.

'That might change,' he said, pleased his controlled voice revealed nothing of his inner turmoil. 'Situations change. People change.'

God knows I've changed since I met you.

'Yes, I suppose I have changed. Knowing you has changed me,' she said, still staring down at her hands.

Her response mirrored his own feelings and he was curious to know what she meant, but he would not allow himself to get sidetracked. He needed to end this as quickly as possible before he waivered.

'And with those moralising ladies still on the rampage

we need to exercise more caution,' he continued. 'If our relationship became public it would destroy your reputation.'

'I don't care what they or anyone else thinks of me.'

'Well, if you don't care about it for your own sake, you should care about it for the sake of the school.' He really was a pompous ass. Who was he to sound so superior and judgemental? He had not resigned purely to save the school. It was so he did not have to see her again. And he was not calling off their relationship because he was worried the moralising ladies would find out. He was doing it for his own selfish reasons. It was all to protect himself, so he would not have to continue to feel this crushing pain every time he looked at her.

'You do understand, don't you, Emily?' he continued, sounding even more high and mighty. 'It would be best for the school. We don't want our behaviour to place the school in jeopardy.'

'Yes, I suppose you're right.'

Jackson hated himself for the way he was speaking to her. This was the woman he loved, the woman he had shared countless blissful afternoons with, the woman he had made love to, who he had held in his arms and shared his private innermost thoughts and feelings. Now he was ending their relationship as if it was something he cared little about, when he cared deeply. Too deeply. But it had to be done. And there was no point letting Emily know just how miserable he was.

She was a kind woman. That was one of the many reasons he loved her so. If Emily knew how much pain he was in he knew he would have her pity, but he did not want her pity. He wanted her love, and that was something he could never have.

He looked over at her as he made ready to leave, wondering how he was to say goodbye. Did he kiss her? No. Apart from the fact he was unsure how he would react if he once more felt the touch of her lips, they were in a public place. Anyone walking by could see them. A kiss on the hand? Surely that would not be misconstrued. But he did not trust himself. Even the touch of her skin might undermine his resolve.

Did he merely bow his head and wish her well? It was so formal and faintly ridiculous after all that they had shared. But he had to leave. He could not remain sitting here, staring at her for an eternity.

'Goodbye, then, Jackson,' she said, once again staring straight ahead.

He remained sitting still for a second or so, then climbed out and watched as the carriage drove out the gates, down the road and out of sight. He turned and walked towards his own carriage.

It was over. It was now time to get back to the life he had lived before he had met Lady Emily Beaumont, although right now he could no longer remember what that life had entailed.

Emily's mind and body remained numb as she drove home. She saw nothing of the chaotic traffic outside her carriage window. The passing houses, the shouts of drivers, the whinnies of horses were all a blur. All her mind was focused on was trying to digest what had just happened. She desperately tried to remember all that he had said, but the words kept whirling round in her head and refused to settle.

The only thing she knew for certain was that it was

over. Jackson didn't want her. He didn't want her in his life any more.

The carriage pulled up in front of her home. As if in a trance, she climbed out and looked up at the house, hardly recognising it. What did she do now? She had been expecting to attend a meeting, bathe in the praise of Mr Greaves and Jackson for saving the school and then celebrate that victory in private with Jackson. Then she would return home to her parents, her mind and body singing after an afternoon of bliss. She had even intended, if the time was right, to confess to him her true feelings and bare her soul. That was some consolation, she supposed. He had broken things off before she had completely humiliated herself and told a man who was now tired of her that she had done what she promised she would never do—she'd fallen in love with him.

She took a step up the path and stopped. If she went inside now, feeling as she did, her mother would know something was wrong. She was bound to ask, and Emily was incapable of thinking of a credible, yet false, reason to explain why she was so distressed.

'Please take me to Lady Amelia's home,' she told the carriage driver and climbed back inside the cab. As the editor of a successful women's magazine, Amelia was often at her business premises during the day, but Emily hoped she would be at home. If she wasn't, she would wait for her, she'd hide away until she had a chance to come to terms with this shocking news and was able to face the world, and her mother, again.

She was greeted by the footman who informed her that Lady Amelia was indeed at home today. Not waiting for

the footman to announce her, she rushed down the hallway to the drawing room.

'What is it? What's wrong? Is it the school?' Amelia
asked, standing up from her desk and rushing towards
Emily, her arms outstretched.

All Emily was capable of doing was shake her head.

'Is it Jackson?' she added, quietly.

Emily nodded. Just as Amelia encased her in her arms
the tears she had been holding back flooded from her eyes.
No longer numb, the full force of her feelings crashed down
on her, making her weak as her friend led her to the nearest
chair and held her as she cried herself out.

Her tears finally drying, she sat up and wiped her eyes.

'I'm so sorry,' Amelia said. 'Do you want to tell me
what happened?'

Emily took in a few slow breaths, her hand on her heart
as if that could reduce the intensity of the pain. 'He's finished with me.'

'Oh, no. I'm so sorry,' Amelia repeated.

'I don't know why I'm so upset. I knew it would happen one day.'

Amelia said nothing, but Emily was sure she knew what
she was thinking.

'Yes, I know. I've been shown up as naïve and gullible,
yet again. I've again set my sights on the wrong man. And
this time I've been even more of an imbecile. I've actually fallen in love with a man I knew from the very start
was wrong for me.'

Amelia continued to say nothing, merely lightly rubbed
Emily's back.

'I, of all people, should have known better. I had thought
Randall and Gideon were right for me, but I'd been wrong.

That had hurt, but I suspect it was more my pride being damaged that caused my pain. But this is different.' She placed her hand on her stomach to ease the pain. 'This is unbearable.'

Amelia wrapped an arm around her and Emily placed her head on her shoulder.

'And worse than that, I knew he was the wrong man for me, right from the start,' she continued. 'He never tried to deceive me about his true nature. That's the very reason why I set my sights on him. Because he was so wrong for me. I knew, or at least thought, I could never fall in love with such a man. I am such a fool.'

'You're not a fool, Emily, and you're certainly not the only woman who has fallen in love with the wrong man. The heart doesn't always do what the head commands.'

'But I really thought my head was in control,' Emily said, sitting up straighter and trying to make sense of how this had happened to her. 'Until it wasn't. Somehow, somewhere my heart took over and I stopped thinking rationally. I forgot who Jackson really was. I forgot what our relationship was really all about. It was all so illogical. Did I imagine it would go on for ever, even though I always knew it wouldn't? That to my mind is the very definition of a fool, someone who knows what is real but refuses to believe it.'

'No, that's the definition of someone who has fallen in love only to have their heart broken.'

'Well, I don't want to be a fool. I won't be a fool.'

Amelia held her top lip with her teeth, as if holding back the words she wanted to say. But there were no words that would convince Emily she was wrong. She had fallen for the wrong man, again, but she would get over that disappointment. Again.

She was a sensible woman, more than capable of over-coming hardships and putting them behind her. And that was exactly what she would do now. She would triumph over this adversity and become all the stronger for it.

'Well, thank you for our talk and all your good advice,' Emily said, making ready to leave. 'I will just have to get on with my life. It's not as if this is unexpected. It had to happen eventually. It's all a bit silly of me to take it so badly. I suppose it was because I wasn't expecting it to hap-pen today. But I knew it had to happen one day and that's what I'd hoped for really. As Jackson said, we've had our fun. Now it's over and it's time to return to our real lives.'

She shrugged as if it were all that easy. 'I thought I was in love, but, well, I'm not the first woman to think she's in love. I'll get over it. Other women have got over heartache, and I will do the same.'

She nodded, determined that her statement would be true. 'And one thing I can say about Jackson, he might be a man who moves from one woman to another without a backward glance, but at least he is discreet. I suppose he's had to learn how to be.' She swallowed down those pesky tears that were threatening to fall. 'No one will ever know about what happened between us.'

Amelia looked at her with sad eyes, as if not convinced by her confident words.

'Don't worry, Amelia,' she said, patting her friend's hand in reassurance. 'I'm perfectly fine now. It was just the shock of it happening so suddenly when I was looking forward to spending more time with him. In fact, it's all for the best that it has finally happened. I really haven't been dedicating nearly as much time to the school as I would like. I can now throw myself into that worthy cause, heart and soul.'

She stood up, stuffed her sodden handkerchief back into her reticule and lifted her chin. 'Thank you so much for listening to all my prattling.'

'Perhaps you would like to come to afternoon tea tomorrow,' Amelia said gently, also standing and taking hold of both her hands. 'I'll invite Georgina and Irene.'

'Yes, that will be lovely. It will be so good to catch up with them and find out what they've been up to. We didn't have much time to really chat last time. I rather monopolised the conversation, I'm afraid.' She gave a small dismissive laugh, as if her confession that she had fallen in love with Jackson was a mere folly. 'Yes, I've been far too preoccupied lately and have neglected my friends.' Emily pulled her watch out of her reticule and frowned at it. 'But I really must be going. I have so much to do.'

Amelia escorted her to the door and out to her waiting carriage. 'If you want to talk, anytime, please don't hesitate,' Amelia said and kissed her lightly on the cheek. It was kind of her, but Emily could see no point in talking further about what had happened between her and Jackson. It was over. It was time to put all this behind her and focus on what was important in her life.

Chapter Eighteen

Jackson had never been one to look back and he was determined not to start now. It was over, as he knew it one day would be. It was time to get back to enjoying his life in the manner he had done for all his adult life. Wine, women and song would replace worthy causes, one woman and sensual afternoons. No, forget the last one. He would not think about those afternoons he spent with Emily. He would forget all about her, as he was sure she would forget all about him, if she hadn't done so already.

Yes, it was definitely time to get back to those women, that wine and perhaps a bit of that tuneless singing, which sometimes followed when sufficient wine had been consumed.

To that end he headed to his club where a group of his friends appeared to still be where he left them, six or so months ago, propping up the bar, contemplating the night to come or reliving the previous night's revelries.

'Jacko,' came the jubilant cry from the assembled men.

'Long time no see,' Giles Winthrop said, pulling over a stool for Jackson. 'A little bird told me that you've been involved in some charity or other, something to do with fallen women.'

This elicited much raucous laughter from the men, back-slapping and the expected jokes about Jackson and women of ill repute. Jackson took it with as much good humour as he could, all the while thinking of Pretty Kitty and knowing she did not deserve to be the butt of these privileged men's humour.

'What have you got planned for tonight?' he asked once they'd exhausted all their jokes.

'First we're off to the Gaiety Theatre,' Giles said. 'The latest play finishes tonight so there should be a high old party afterwards. And plenty of chorus girls who will just be dying to show an earl, baron or viscount or two how to really have a good time.'

Once again this was followed by raucous laughter and jokes about chorus girls, most of which bore a similar theme to the jokes about fallen women. Were his friends always this predictable? Or was it because, unlike them, he was completely sober?

That was something easily remedied. He signalled to the steward, who picked up a brandy balloon and poured a generous amount, knowing exactly what Jackson's tipple was.

He downed it in one and signalled for a refill, hoping the ennui possessing him could be washed away in a tide of alcohol. That soon he'd develop his familiar enthusiasm for parties, chorus girls and women who wanted to show a viscount how to have a good time.

Once sufficient liquor had been consumed, the men climbed into a series of hansom cabs. Encouraging their drivers into a competition with promises of generous tips for the winner, they raced across town to the Gaiety Theatre, where the performance was coming to an end.

With much noise, a few men tripping over their chairs and guffaws of laughter as if this was a hilarious comedy act, the group took their seats in a reserved box. Once they'd settled, they looked down at the chorus girls dancing on the stage below.

'Look at how high those chits can get their legs,' one man said, causing more guffawing from the others and a few smutty jokes about the party to come.

Jackson sighed at the lack of respect for women who were merely doing the job they were paid to do, while his friends continued to laugh heartily around him. He really was becoming the sort of man he once despised, a judgemental bore who doesn't know how to enjoy himself. That really had to stop.

The performance finished, the men made their way round to the backstage, where they were welcomed by the same young ladies they'd seen dancing. Before long Jackson found himself at a raucous party in the back rooms of a nearby tavern, where there was indeed plenty of wine and women, with the singing provided by the performers, thank goodness, and not by Jackson and his friends.

'This really is a high old time,' a chorus girl said to him, sliding her hand around his waist and pressing her comely body into his. 'Isn't it?'

She was such a pretty young thing, with big blue eyes, a cheeky smile and the lithesome, strong body you'd expect from someone who made their living through dance. In other words, exactly the sort of young woman that always attracted him. And that look in her eye made it clear that she intended to celebrate the final performance by letting her hair down and going delightfully wild.

Yes, she was exactly his sort of woman. He placed his arm around her shoulder, and that cheeky smile became ever the more encouraging.

'Indeed it is,' he said, introducing himself.

'Pleased to meet you, Jackson,' she said. 'I'm Maggy.'

'A delightful name for a delightful young lady,' he said, surprised at how easily this all came back to him. 'And perhaps you and I could make tonight even more of a high old time, in private of course.'

'I imagine that could be arranged,' Maggy said with a quick, saucy wink.

With his arm draped over her shoulder they made their way towards the door. 'Are you in the chorus?' he asked, even though he knew the answer, but a smattering of polite conversation was surely required.

'Yes, but I'd love to be an actress. Unfortunately…' She shrugged then smiled up at him.

'Unfortunately what? What's stopping you? I think you'd make a fine actress. You're certainly pretty enough.'

She simpered slightly at the compliment. 'But I never did learn my letters and it's a bit hard to remember all them lines if you can't read.'

He stopped walking just as they reached the door. 'No, don't let that stop you—' His words were cut off by Giles, who crashed into him, his arms around two smiling chorus girls.

'Watch out for that one,' Giles said to Maggy, laughing at his own joke. 'We used to call him the three-minute man, because he could get most women out of their drawers in less than three minutes.'

Jackson rolled his eyes at his friend's attempt at bawdy humour, took Maggy's hand and led her back into the room towards a quieter area of the chaotic tavern.

'It's true,' Giles called out from across the noisy room. 'We timed him once.'

'That's quite some achievement,' she said, that saucy smile returning. 'I might not be able to read and write but I can tell time, so maybe we can put you to the test.' She frowned as she took in the small nook. 'Just not here, if you don't mind, you promised me somewhere private.'

'No, that's not why I brought you back here. I wanted to tell you about The Women's Education Institute in the East End. They provide lessons in reading and writing skills. Its free and the tutors are extremely kind and encouraging. If you learnt to read, I'm sure in no time at all you'd be out of the chorus line and a star in your own right.'

The young woman's cheeky smile disappeared and her face became serious. 'Honestly? Do you really think I could learn to read?'

'I know so. And I know that if you really put your mind to it, you could become the fine actress you want to be.'

She smiled at him, her eyes sparkling. 'Right. I'll go along tomorrow. Ta ever so much. I better get going so I can get a good night's sleep and get down there first thing in the morning.' With that she rushed out the door.

Jackson watched her go, a sense of satisfaction and achievement washing through him.

'What on earth did you say to scare that one off?' Giles said as he staggered over, his own companions also having disappeared. 'The way that one was looking at you I was sure she was in the bag.'

Jackson slapped his friend on the back. 'I have hopefully helped her achieve her dreams, and I must say it feels rather good.'

Giles frowned at him briefly then laughed. 'Well, there's plenty of others whose dreams you can also answer. These two girls said that they'd be happy to…' He looked around as if suddenly discovering he'd lost his companions. 'Where did they go?' Spotting them in the corner talking to a group of men he staggered off, a champagne bottle raised above his head, and burst into off-key singing.

The two young women joined in with his singing and some impromptu high-kick dancing, which Giles in his inebriated state unsuccessfully tried to replicate, much to the hilarity from everyone else in the heaving room.

This was exactly Jackson's type of place. These were exactly his type of people. So why was he staring at the large clock behind the bar and wondering when it would be all right for him to depart?

It was gone three o'clock. Surely that was enough mayhem for tonight. He'd made an effort. He'd indulged in the activities he used to enjoy. It hadn't been quite as much fun as he remembered, but perhaps he was just out of practice.

Tomorrow night he'd make even more of an effort to once again restore his reputation as a reveller, a man for whom no party was too wild, no indulgence too excessive.

After all, if he didn't do that, what else did he have?

Despite the confident words she had said to Amelia, and then repeated to Georgina and Irene at their afternoon tea, Emily had stayed away from the school for several days, nursing her wounds. But she could put it off no longer and today was the day she would take back her old life.

'Will you be shopping again this afternoon?' her mother asked as Emily stood at the front door while the maid helped her into her coat.

That simple question hit Emily so hard in the chest it took her breath away. She closed her eyes briefly then smiled at her mother. 'No, not today. I'll be visiting the school in the morning and I should be home for luncheon.'

'Oh, do you finally have enough gloves?'

Emily felt her eyes grow wide as her mother continued to smile at her. Was there a hidden meaning behind that innocent question? Did her mother really know how Emily was spending her afternoons? Was guilt making her overly suspicious?'

'Yes, I have sufficient gloves now.' Enough gloves to last me a lifetime, and each pair of gloves will be a painful reminder of where and why I bought them. Emily breathed in deeply and exhaled slowly. She would dispose of those gloves at the first opportunity. She most certainly did not want their presence undermining her determination to remain stoic, or her ability to put her time with Jackson firmly where it belonged, in the past.

'Perhaps there is something else you could shop for. Hats perhaps,' her mother added.

'I do not need to shop for anything,' she said louder than she meant, causing her mother to widen her eyes in surprise.

'Will Viscount Wickford be at the school today?'

'No,' Emily replied, suddenly wishing her mother would go back to discussing shopping. 'He is no longer involved with the school.' She swallowed down the lump that had formed in her throat.

'Such a shame. Men like the Viscount are a rare breed.'

Emily stared at her mother. Was she serious? 'Well, all I can say about that is thank goodness. The fewer rakes there are in the world the better.'

'There's nothing wrong with a man who knows how to enjoy himself,' her mother said, causing Emily to wonder if she had ever really known her mother. She had despised Randall Cochran for being a rake, now she was praising Jackson for the same behaviour.

'And I've never seen you happier than when the two of you were working together to make that school of yours a success,' her mother added, smiling at Emily. A rather self-satisfied smile that made Emily wary of what was to come next. 'It made you almost as happy as all those shopping expeditions did.'

Emily swallowed again. Her mother knew. Or at least she suspected her involvement with Jackson. Emily could only hope she did not know just how involved she had really become. If she did, she certainly would not be smiling.

'My dear,' her mother continued, dismissing the maid with a wave of her hand. 'Happiness is a rare commodity. Whatever has happened to make you stop shopping so regularly, I believe you should try and find a way to rekindle the desire to do so.' With that her mother patted her on the arm and walked up the hallway, leaving a stunned Emily staring at her retreating back.

With as much composure as she could muster following that bizarre conversation, she left the house and took the carriage to the school. Her new life was to start again, today. It was time to put all her troubles away, and bury herself in what she loved doing most; working hard for the benefit of others.

With that in mind, with her head held high and her shoulders firmly back, she walked from classroom to classroom to see where she was best needed. Each classroom was fully occupied in the task at hand, whether it was reading and writing lessons, classes training young women to become maids, kitchen staff, dressmakers or an array of other areas of employment. There was even a new class teaching young women how to use modern typewriters, the loud clacking of keys filling the air. And there was Kitty, sitting among the dexterous women. Was there no skill she was determined not to master?

She looked around the busy room and at the tutor, providing instruction to one struggling student.

No one needed Emily's help. That was all for the good, even if it did not satisfy Emily's need to be busy. She scanned the classroom one more time to see if there was something, anything, she could do. Kitty waved to her from the back of the class and signalled her over.

'What are you working on now, Kitty?' she asked, looking down at the confusing metal contraption with all its levers, rollers and ribbons.

'I'm typing out a business letter. This is actually rather fun. I think I prefer it to embroidery and sewing. I can see myself working in a nice warm office.' She smiled up at Emily.

'I'm very pleased to hear that,' she said, looking over Kitty's shoulder at the piece of paper poking out from the typewriter's roller. It was a letter from a fictitious lawyer to a client and looked rather professional.

'So, is everything all right with you, my lady?' Kitty asked.

'Why, yes, of course it is,' Emily responded, surprised that Kitty should enquire after her health.

'Well, you don't seem your usual self, and you have been looking ever so happy lately.'

'What? No, everything is fine.' Emily attempted to cover her surprise with a large smile. A reaction that only caused Kitty to glance at her sideways, eyebrows raised.

'Will the Viscount be gracing us with his presence today?'

Emily was sure she detected some hidden meaning in Kitty's words, but perhaps she was just being overly sensitive to the mention of Jackson's name. Just as she had with her mother's comments about shopping.

'I very much doubt it,' she said, keeping her voice as even as possible. 'He has informed Mr Greaves he will no longer be involved in the running of the school.' Good, her voice betrayed nothing of what she was feeling.

'That's a shame,' Kitty said, still giving her that strange sideways look. 'He's such a fine, upstanding gentleman, that one.'

Emily gritted her teeth together. She did not need a lecture from Kitty on Jackson's character.

'You'll meet none better,' Kitty continued. 'A real hero to my way of thinking.'

Emily gave a tight smile and nodded, while looking down at Kitty's typed letter as if fascinated by the legal terminology. 'Well, yes, I suppose he did act rather heroic on that evening he saved you.'

'I reckon he's not the only one he's saved.'

She turned her attention to Kitty, trying to decipher the meaning of her words. Everyone appeared to be making obscure, cryptic references today that she couldn't quite grasp. Kitty with her claims that Jackson is a saviour, and her mother's reference to her need to find happiness through shopping. Or was she reading more into their words than actually existed? Emily deemed it sensible to assume the latter.

'I wouldn't know,' she said, looking around the room at the other busy typists, as if intrigued by all the activity.

'I reckon any woman who had a man like him in her life would be silly to let him go,' Kitty said. 'She should fight tooth and nail to keep him.'

She did know.

Emily grasped the edge of the desk, her legs suddenly weak.

'Don't worry,' Kitty whispered. 'Your secret is safe with me, but I've been around long enough to know that look in a woman's eye when she's enamoured with a man, and a gentleman's eye to that matter, when he fancies a lady.'

Emily knew she should admonish Kitty and tell her that she had gone too far. Instead, she stared at Kitty, unable to talk, words flying around in her head and refusing to settle into sensible sentences.

'I also know what a woman looks like when she thinks she's lost her man. All I'm saying is, that one is definitely worth fighting for and you shouldn't just give up until you've won him.'

'It's not as easy as that,' Emily finally choked out.

'It never is, but if something is worth fighting for, it doesn't matter how hard it is, you just have to fight even harder and never give up.'

Emily looked around at the other students, who were engrossed in their work and paying them no heed.

'All I can say,' Kitty continued, 'is you deserve a good man in your life. One who makes you laugh and smile. You need a man who makes you happy. That musty old doctor never did it.'

Emily raised her eyebrows. Was there nothing this young woman missed?

'I saw the way that doctor looked at you when I visited the hospital, like you were a meal ticket. And I saw the way you looked at him.' She shook her head. 'It was nothing like the way you looked at the Viscount.' She sighed and smiled contentedly. 'I could tell you were in love.'

'It doesn't matter whether I was or I wasn't,' Emily said, lowering her voice. Kitty leant forward so she could hear. 'The Viscount was the one to end things, not me.'

'Well, sometimes men don't know what they want and it's up to us women to let them know. You need to show him that he is in love with you, even if he doesn't yet realise it.'

For Kitty it all seemed so simple, but she did not understand. Jackson did not want her. By now he had probably moved onto the next woman. Some other woman was making discreet visits to his flat at the Tanner Street Shopping Arcade. Some other woman was in his arms, in his bed, some other woman was experiencing what she so briefly experienced and would never experience again.

'I have to go,' she muttered to Kitty, rushing out the room before the tears started to fall and she made herself look ridiculous in front of the tutor and all these industrious students.

Chapter Nineteen

Jackson was trying, really trying, but his nights were not going to plan. Each evening he set out with a renewed determination to enjoy himself to the full, and each morning he came home feeling as if it was all somehow pointless.

Every night followed the same pattern. There was gambling, there was plenty of wine and brandy, there were willing young women, everything a man could possibly want to ensure he had a memorable night. And yet his good humour was forced from the moment he arrived at his club, and each night had ended the same, with him returning to his bed in the small hours of the morning, alone and dispirited.

'You're losing your touch,' Giles informed him last night, or was it early this morning? 'All those good works have ruined you for having a good time,' he'd added, laughing uproariously as if he had made a hilarious joke.

It wasn't particularly funny, but was it right? He *would* rather spend his time helping to improve the lives of people like Pretty Kitty than carousing night after night with his old friends. And, damn it all, he'd much rather be doing so with Emily.

He'd asked Giles's chorus girlfriends about Maggy and was pleased to hear she had indeed signed up for reading lessons. She was reportedly so excited about what she was learning that she had convinced several other girls in the chorus to join as well. This caused Giles to roll his eyes, but it gave Jackson more satisfaction than anything else that had happened since he had ended his relationship with Emily.

He picked at the plate of food in front of him. It was closer to lunchtime than breakfast, but after a night on the tiles his first meal of the day was always a hearty breakfast. Cook claimed it was the best way for Jackson to get over the excesses of the night before and prepare himself for the night ahead. Usually, Jackson would agree, but unfortunately, once again he had no appetite. No appetite for food or for anything else it would seem.

He speared the bacon with his fork. Perhaps tonight would be different. Perhaps tonight his spirit would be revitalised. Perhaps tonight he might not have to push himself so hard to have the good time that used to come to him so naturally.

He'd arranged to meet Giles and the others at his club in the early evening, yet again, for another night of carousing. This time they planned to attend a party hosted by the Prince of Wales's latest mistress. Such parties had always been a highlight for any man determined to enjoy life to the full. Not only were they wild and raucous but they were often featured in the scandal sheets, which provided the added enjoyment of shocking his father.

He sighed deeply. What was wrong with him? Even the thought of shocking his father held no real appeal. Giles was right. All that good work had ruined him for having a good time. Or was it Lady Emily Beaumont who had ruined him for having a good time? Was it the memory of her face, her smile, not to mention her gorgeous body, that had changed him on such a fundamental level he no longer knew how to enjoy himself?

No, that wasn't right. He'd enjoyed himself when he'd been with Emily, more than he had realised was possible. There was a certain irony in what had happened, which he could find funny, if he didn't find it so tragic. He'd been horrified when he'd woken in the Hope Charity Hospital to find the do-gooding Lady Emily looking down at him. He'd worried he'd be subjected to moralising sermons about his wayward lifestyle. Never for a moment did he think she would destroy his ability to live a wayward lifestyle, not by sermons, but because he fell in love with her.

But he would not let her change him for ever. Nor would he let his unrequited love destroy the life he had lived before he met her. He was not the first man to experience a heart-break, although this was the first time this particular man had experienced that particular affliction. But it would pass. It had to pass. Didn't it? All he had to do was try harder, live it up more recklessly and indulge himself even more excessively. Easy.

He quickly sliced up his bacon into small pieces as if to underline the strength of his feelings. From this moment on he would stop thinking about Emily and what they had shared. Yes, they'd had their fun, just as he'd had fun with numerous other women before her and would do the same with countless women in the future. She'd made it clear the extent of her feelings for him, which did not extend very far, and he would waste not a minute longer ruminating on what was or could have been.

He *would* go out again tonight. He *would* have a good time. He would drink, carouse and lose himself in the arms of some delightful young woman and he most certainly would not spend even a second pining over her.

Keeping that in mind through the day, and crushing down any thoughts of Emily every time they surfaced, he entered his club that night and plastered on his most joyful smile. He was determined to show the world that bonhomie he was famous for.

'So, are we up for painting the town red before we join His Majesty and his friends?' he asked, slapping Giles on the back with a hearty thump.

'That we are,' his friend replied with genuine happiness at seeing him. 'I've promised to take those two chorus girls along. They're so excited about meeting a member of the royal family, and I'm sure they'll be more than willing to show their gratitude.' He winked at Jackson then called out to the steward for more bottles of champagne to be opened. 'But first, let's celebrate the night to come.'

Corks were popped. As the stewards quickly poured the bubbling wine into glasses before it frothed down the sides of bottles, the assembled men let out a resounding cheer, as if it was an unexpected event, instead of what they did every night, night after night.

But Jackson would not think about that now. In fact, from this moment on, he would not be thinking. He would misbehave, he would frolic, he would revel, romp and roister.

And, hopefully, his antics would make it into the scandal sheets. Then he would have the satisfaction of not only shocking his father, but with any luck Lady Emily as well. Then she would know that he was well and truly over her and had not given the end of their time together a second thought.

* * *

Jackson had achieved everything he set out to achieve, at least the pounding in his head and his ferocious thirst suggested he had. Of the night before he had little recollection, which had to be a good sign, didn't it?

Just after midday he stumbled downstairs and slumped into a chair at the breakfast table, still dressed in his robe.

'The morning and the midday mail,' the footman said, removing a small pile of letters from his silver tray and placing them beside Jackson's plate. One bore his father's familiar handwriting. With a resigned sigh he picked up a knife and cut it open. It contained the usual information on the estate, but surprisingly no admonition on Jackson's behaviour. That was presumably because Jackson's antics had not made it into the scandal sheets recently. Hopefully whatever he got up to last night would be covered in salacious detail and that odd state of affairs would be put to rights.

The next bore the elegant handwriting of his solicitor. He quickly perused the legal jargon, only to be reassured that the state of his finances was predictably healthy.

He turned over the typewritten letter. It bore no address of the sender, so he cut it open and quickly perused its contents as he buttered his toast.

His knife clattered onto the plate as the full force of the vile words hit him.

I am writing to inform you that I am disgusted to learn that Lady Emily Beaumont has been party to immoral practices involving yourself.

For an unmarried woman to indulge in such vices with a man who has no intention of making an hon-

est woman of her is the very definition of moral tur-
pitude.

Jackson gripped the letter tightly, his thudding head-ache gone, his raging thirst forgotten.

I also wish to inform you of my intention of alert-
ing the board members of The Women's Education
Institute, who I am sure will immediately dismiss a
woman of such low character. I also intend to write
to her parents, who no doubt will deal with her im-
moral behaviour as they deem fit.

Jackson shoved the offensive letter into the pocket of his robe and rushed upstairs, yelling for his valet to help him dress, immediately. Without bothering to shave, or wait for his cravat to be tied properly, he rushed out of the house, ignoring the footman attempting to hand him his hat and gloves.

With no time to arrange for his own carriage he waved down a passing hansom cab and gave him instructions to take him to the Beaumonts' townhouse. As the cab drove through the busy streets, far too slowly and cautiously in Jackson's opinion, he tried to think what he would say to Emily and her parents.

Nothing came to mind, apart from how sorry he was, something that was less than useless under the circum-stances.

The cab pulled up in front of her house. He jumped down before it had come to a complete stop and threw some money in the driver's direction.

'Thank you, guv,' the driver said. 'You'll be wanting

some change,' he called out as Jackson raced up the pathway and pounded on the door.

A footman opened the door and, before he could speak, Jackson pushed passed him, ran down the hallway into the drawing room and found Emily seated by the window, drinking a cup of tea and perusing a magazine.

He stood in the doorway, gasping to catch his breath, and stared at her. Had she always been this divinely beautiful? With the light streaming through the large sash windows, she was bathed in golden sunshine, giving her a radiance that was breathtaking. Everything about her seemed to glow—her chestnut hair, that soft, dewlike skin, those big brown eyes.

How could he not have fallen hopelessly in love with such a woman. He was only a man after all, a particularly weak man, and she was like a goddess. It was so obvious now that a woman like her could never love him the way he loved her. And it just went to show how intelligent she was that she had seen straight through him to his true character, and knew he was not for her.

'Jackson—I mean, Viscount Wickford, this is a surprise,' she said, standing up, her eyes large, suggesting this was more than a surprise. She was shocked.

Jackson remembered why he was here. It was not to admire Emily. It was not to wallow in self-pity over what he'd had and what he'd lost. It was to deal with the letter, its incendiary contents burning a hole in his pocket.

'I am so sorry, Emily,' he said, rushing over to her chair. He was about to take her hands to comfort her, then stopped abruptly, remembering he had no right to do so.

Instead, he stood before her, crushed under the weight of guilt and shame.

'I will of course inform the board that you were completely innocent. I shall tell them that I forced myself on you and then once I'd had my way with you, I blackmailed you into continuing to meet with me against your will. I'll say I threatened to blacken your name in Society unless you gave me what I wanted, but at all times you were completely innocent and completely unwilling. If that results in your parents prosecuting me, then so be it, but believe me, I will do everything in my power to make sure you are not punished for what I have done, what I should never have done.'

She frowned and shook her head as if trying to make sense of what he was saying.

'I am so, so sorry,' he repeated, knowing his words were ineffective, and there was nothing he could really do or say to undo this travesty.

'And I'm sorry too because I have no idea what you are talking about,' she said.

'The board, the threats, the accusations.' He fumbled into his pocket to pull out the letter. 'Here, this arrived this morning. I had assumed a similar one had been sent to you as well.'

She smoothed out the crumpled paper, read its contents and her hand flew to her mouth to cover a gasp.

'I'm so sorry,' he repeated ineffectively.

'Who? How? Why?' She gasped out. 'We were so careful. No one knew. I'm sure of it.'

'It hardly matters who, how or why. Someone saw us. Someone is planning on telling the board and now I have to make things right.'

She stared up at him, the offensive letter clasped in her hands.

'By telling everyone you forced me? By telling a lie?'
Jackson shrugged. 'Yes, of course.'

'But you didn't force me.'

'But I should not have let it happen. I know the consequences for women such as yourself who stray off the strict path laid down by Society.'

'As did I.'

'But, Emily, you don't understand. You'll be ruined. Society will shun you. You'll, well, you'll never be able to find a husband.'

She rolled her eyes, causing him to wonder if she realised just how serious this was.

'They're threatening to tell your parents. They will be scandalised,' he continued, desperate to make her understand. 'They're threatening to tell the board members. You'll never be able to do charity work again. Your life will be ruined and it's all my fault.'

'No, it's the fault of whoever wrote this appalling letter.' She turned it over. 'They don't even have the decency to sign it.'

He threw his hands up in the air. 'That hardly matters. It was probably one of those women from the Ladies for the Promotion of High Moral Standards.'

She frowned. 'Yes, except they wouldn't hesitate to sign it, and would not warn us of their intentions. They'd go straight to the board, and they wouldn't just want my resignation. They'd use this knowledge to have the school shut down.'

'I don't know, perhaps one of them is planning to blackmail us first.'

She turned the letter over, looking remarkably calm under the circumstances. 'If it was a blackmail letter surely it would say what they expect from you, so they don't reveal this information.' She shrugged. 'They'd ask for a large amount of money or something. And it's strange that a blackmailer would send it to you when it is my good name they are threatening. Surely they'd try and extort money out of me.'

He threw up his hands again in exasperation. None of that surely mattered. 'All that is as it may be, but we need to end this. So, I shall tell your parents immediately what I have done. Are they home?' He looked towards the door.

'No. And I believe we should think this through before you take any hasty action.'

She reread the letter. 'The writer hasn't told either my parents or the board members yet. I met with Mr Greaves earlier this morning and he made no comment about anything that is mentioned in this letter. He did, however, mention you.'

Jackson's stomach clenched tighter. 'Mr Greaves is a decent man. If he had been told, he would no doubt see this would all be my fault, not yours, and presumably did not wish to distress you, but the sooner I confess and put an end to this the better.'

'I don't believe that to be the case. Mr Greaves continued to sing your praises. He said, not for the first time, it was such a shame you had resigned from the school. He said he even intends to contact you to see if he could encourage you to change your mind.'

'He what? Well, he won't be thinking that once he hears about this.' He pointed at the offensive letter.

'Did you know that the school has invested in several typewriters and is teaching secretarial skills?'

'What? No.' And surely under the circumstances it would be of no interest to him.

She read the letter again and smiled.

Smiled? She actually smiled.

Had the shock of the letter caused her to lose her mind?

'There's only one person I'm acquainted with who knows how to use a typewriter.' She looked up at him, still with that incongruous smile. 'I think what we have here is the work of one Miss Kathryn Trotter.'

'What? Who?' he all but shouted.

'Also known as Pretty Kitty.'

'What? Who?' he repeated, his confusion growing with every word she said. 'Why on earth would Kitty want to threaten us, blackmail us and try and ruin your life?'

He looked to Emily, imploring her to make sense of something so senseless.

'Because she knew exactly how you would react. She is trying to prove a point to me. And it looks like she succeeded.'

Chapter Twenty

'Point, what point?' Jackson said, pacing backwards and forwards as if trying to control his explosive energy.

Emily looked down at the letter in her hand, unsure how to answer that question without revealing too much.

'All I can say is I am confident she had no intention of threatening us or of blackmailing us, or even of going through with anything she said in the letter.'

He shook his head, his eyebrows drawn so close together they were almost touching. 'None of this is making any sense.'

Emily lightly scratched her forehead. She was going to have to tell him of her conversation with Kitty. She wished she did not have to, but given Jackson's obvious agitation, what choice did she have other than to put him out of his misery? 'What I suspect she is doing is a bit of match-making.'

'She's what?' He stopped his pacing and looked over at the letter in her hand. His confusion was justified. If you want to get two people back together it certainly was a strange way to go about it. But then, it had succeeded in a way, hadn't it?

She drew in a strength-giving breath, determined to get this over as quickly as possible so he could be on his way.

'I was talking to Kitty the other day and she is under the impression that you and I are more than just colleagues, that there has been, shall we say, a dalliance between us.'

'It seems Kitty is rather perceptive. Let's hope she's the only one,' he said, staggering over to the divan and sitting down. 'But why on earth would she send me such a letter? What on earth is she hoping to achieve? And what's all this about matchmaking?'

'She believes you to be a hero. She would know that if you believed me to be under threat you would immediately try and rescue me, just as you did with her.'

He continued frowning as if he could not understand Kitty's reasoning. But Emily knew Kitty was right. Jackson *was* an honourable man. He was a man who would do whatever it took to save a woman in distress, but that did not mean he loved her. He had taken a beating to save Kitty and she had been a complete stranger to him. Of course he would save a woman in distress, any woman.

'If that's true, then it means your reputation is safe,' he said slowly.

'Yes.'

'That's good then, I suppose. It means no one knows about what happened between us.'

'No one knows except Kitty, it would seem.'

'Yes, but if what you suspect is true, then she means you no harm.' He exhaled a low, loud sigh, looked up at her, then quickly stood, as if suddenly realising he was seated in the company of a woman who was still standing. That was a formality they had hitherto abandoned but it seemed such behaviour was no longer acceptable.

'So what exactly did Kitty say to you that made you realise the letter had to be from her?'

She took a seat, and indicated for him to sit, giving herself time to formulate how she was going to phrase this. 'As I said, she has a very high opinion of you and thinks you are a hero.'

He laughed dismissively. 'You save one street walker and suddenly your sullied reputation is redeemed and you're a hero.'

'You did save her from a terrible fate.'

He shrugged as if it were of no account.

'And you did just offer to confess to a crime you didn't commit, one that would surely have had dire consequences for you, all to save my reputation.'

He shrugged again.

'If my parents had decided to prosecute you could have been sent to jail. *Your* reputation would be sullied for ever.'

He gave another shrug as if that sacrifice was also of no account.

'I believe you have heroic qualities you prefer not to acknowledge.'

'I'm just relieved this will go no further, although I still can't for the life of me understand Kitty's thinking.'

'I suppose she didn't just want to prove to me what a hero you are, she also wanted to get us back together so we would talk and, perhaps, well, you know.' It was her turn to shrug, suddenly feeling shy in front of a man with whom she had shared so many intimacies, both physical and emotional.

'That we would become lovers again,' he added for her.

'Yes, I suppose so. Although I think she even believes that we could be more than that.' She gave a false laugh as if dismissing Kitty's romantic delusions. 'Perhaps she thought that you'd offer to make an honest woman of me, rather than offer to go to jail.'

He huffed out a dismissive laugh. 'Then Kitty doesn't know as much as she think she does. Did you not tell her you had no intention of marrying, and certainly a man such as me?'

'I may have alluded to that, but I don't think she believed me.'

'You should have spelt it out for her then and told her you didn't want any more from me than you'd already had. That all you'd ever wanted was some fun with a man you could never have any real feelings for. Then she would never have written that letter and caused us such distress.'

'Why would I say that?' Emily asked quietly.

He looked down at his hands, clasping his knees. 'I'm sorry. I have a somewhat embarrassing confession to make. I arrived at your house on the day you hosted the afternoon tea to save the school, after the moralising ladies had left, and overheard your conversation with your friends. So I know how you really feel about our relationship.'

Heat burst onto Emily's face. He had overheard her tell her friends she was in love with him and then he had immediately ended things.

'Is that why you said we should not see each other again?' she choked out.

'Yes.'

Emily's heart shattered into even smaller pieces.

'I suppose then it is me that should apologise to you,' she said, unable to control the small tremor in her voice. 'I know it was not what we agreed when we became lovers.' She looked down at her hands, gripped tightly together to stop them from shaking. 'I know I told you there would be no emotional involvement, but I promise you, I never had any intentions of not abiding by our agreement. I would never have made demands on you.'

He leant forward in his seat and stared at her, his forehead once again furrowed. 'Demands on me? Abiding by our agreement? What are you talking about?'

Did he really want her to spell it out? Could he not see that she was already humiliated enough? So much for being a hero. 'What I said to my friends. You know.'

'About me being someone with whom you just want to have fun? Someone who could never mean anything more to you than that? That you were just waiting for it to run its course and end?'

'No, the rest of it.'

'What rest of it? There was more? What you had said was hurtful enough, even if I did have to agree with the sentiment.'

He didn't know. He hadn't heard her tell her friends she had fallen in love with him. Relief swept through her. She had not completely humiliated herself in front of the man she loved, the man who had no feelings for her.

'So you might as well tell me the whole story. What else did you tell your friends? That you were better off without me in your life? That it had been a big mistake getting involved with a lowlife like me in the first place?'

'I said none of those things because none of them are true.'

'Perhaps you should have.'

'No, and you shouldn't think like that about yourself either. You are a good man even if you refuse to admit it. You saved Kitty. You wanted to save me. You started up a school that is helping a lot of women and will help countless more. And you've done all that without once wanting to take any credit, like so many other men would.'

Kitty's words came back to her. *'That one is definitely worth fighting for.'* She was right. But how do you fight for a man who doesn't want you? Perhaps she could start by being truthful. What was the worst that could happen? She had already been rejected by him. He was already lost to her. There was nothing worse that could happen.

'You only overheard the first part of what I was saying to my friends. When I was trying to convince them and myself that you meant nothing to me.'

His furrowed brow smoothed out as he raised his eyebrows in question.

'If you had stayed a bit longer you would have heard me tell them what I really felt,' she rushed on before she risked losing her nerve. 'You would have heard me confess that I had fallen in love with you.'

The words seemed to hang in the air as she held her breath and waited for his response.

'Did I just hear you correctly? Did you say you told your friends you were in love with me?'

She stared at the ground as if there was something fascinating on the carpet. 'Yes, but you were never supposed to hear. I know I promised you I would not fall in love with you, but, well, I failed.'

She looked up at him. 'But don't worry. I don't expect anything from you. Don't start acting all heroic and thinking you have to marry me or anything.'

'Oh, Emily, my love, my darling,' he said, smiling and slowly shaking his head. 'When I heard you telling your friends that you could never love me, I had to end our relationship because I could not bear to continue to see a woman I had fallen hopelessly in love with, all the while knowing she did not feel the same about me and never would.'

'What?' Emily spluttered. 'Love? You? Me?'

'Yes, love, you, me,' he said, crossing the room, taking her hands and lifting her to her feet.

'I love you, Emily Beaumont,' he said, and kissed her.

Was this really happening? Emily could hardly believe it to be true. But could her imagination really conjure up that familiar heady scent, the touch of his rough skin against her cheek, the feel of his muscles against her? No, this was reality, and it was so much better than any dream.

When he withdrew from her lips, he lightly kissed her on the forehead. She closed her eyes and sighed.

'You can't possibly know how happy you have made me,' he said.

'You're wrong.' She opened her eyes and looked up at him. 'I think I know exactly how happy you feel.'

'Emily, my love,' he said, gently stroking her forehead and pushing a stray lock of hair behind her ear. 'I never thought I'd have you in my arms again, and that thought was torture.'

'Yes, torture, for me too,' she said, amazed at how inarticulate his kisses had made her. 'So kiss me again and end this torture.'

He laughed lightly, but did as she commanded, his urgent lips finding hers.

Fire burned within her as his kiss deepened. He loved her, that had to mean he still wanted her for his lover. She kissed him back, releasing the fervid desire for him that she'd been denied over the painful days and nights of their separation.

He broke from her kiss and she wondered if he was thinking what she was; that they should lock the door so no one would enter, and fully satisfy their need for each other.

'As we have so much to thank Pretty Kitty for, perhaps we should invite her to our wedding,' he said, smiling down at her, the smile that always made her weak with desire.

'Yes, of course,' Emily said, sure she would agree to anything that would stop his talking, so those lips could return to hers.

'What?' she said, withdrawing from him as the intent of his words hit her.

'That is if you would do me the honour of becoming my wife.'

She looked into his eyes. Was he teasing her?

'Will you, Emily? Will you marry me?' he repeated.

Emily could only nod, seemingly incapable of forming words.

'I promise I will do everything in my power to make you happy, every single day of your life,' he continued as if she hadn't already given her agreement. 'I love you so much it is hard to believe that one man could possess so much love, and I need to share that love with you.'

She nodded again.

'If you will be my wife, I promise I will try to be a man worthy of you, worthy of a woman who is so good, so kind, so beautiful, so wonderful in every way.'

She nodded faster. 'Yes, I will marry you,' she said, finally finding her words. 'And you don't have to prove you are worthy of me, you have already proven that, again and again.' She smiled up at him. 'Although, if you really do want to prove your worth to me, you can kiss me again, right now.'

'With pleasure,' he said, his arms holding her closer as he kissed her long and deep. A kiss that expressed more eloquently than words ever could how much they loved each other.

Epilogue

'I knew eventually you'd find the perfect man,' her mother said when she told her she was to wed Jackson, while her father merely smiled at them both benevolently.

'And now my little girl is going to marry for love, just as your father and I did,' she patted the corner of her eyes with her lace handkerchief.

Once again her mother had seen what it had taken Emily so long to see, that Jackson *was* perfect for her. The man she had once thought wrong in so many ways, but in the end he was exactly the right man for her. Her mother had been correct about Randall and Gideon and she had been right about Jackson.

'Thank you, Mother,' she said, squeezing her hand. 'And thank you for seeing Jackson's fine qualities even before I did.'

'I hope that means you're going to listen to me in the future.'

Emily shrugged, then smiled. 'Of course I will. Especially when you encourage me to do things like go shopping.'

Her mother arched her eyebrows, smiled slightly, but said nothing.

While her parents couldn't be happier, Jackson's father did not greet the news with such joyousness.

'Wonders will never cease,' he said, frowning at them over his newspaper. 'You've actually found a decent woman prepared to marry you.' He directed his frown at Emily as if unable to understand how she could possibly want to spend the rest of her life with his son.

'Yes, I found my hero and I'm never going to let him go,' she said, smiling up at Jackson while the old Duke looked on in disbelief.

'Seems she's a bit addled in the head,' he muttered before returning to his newspaper. 'You're made for each other.'

Jackson's expression turned dark at what had been intended as an insult, but Emily placed a restraining hand on his arm. She would not let that bitter man ruin their happiness.

'Yes, you're quite right, Your Grace,' Emily said, causing Jackson to look at her as if she was indeed addled in the head. 'We are made for each other, and if this is what addle-headed feels like then I hope I remain this way for the rest of my life.'

This caused Jackson to laugh, and the old Duke to huff and shake his newspaper as if wishing to be rid of them.

'You're right,' Jackson said, when they left the old man's presence. 'His constant criticisms used to annoy me, and even provoke me into acting in ever more outrageous ways, just to horrify him further, but now I can see he is merely an unhappy old man and I feel sorry for him. Perhaps if my parents had been able to marry for love, if they had found the happiness I have...' He paused and kissed her on the top of her head. 'Then he would not be so angry all the time.'

Emily smiled at her husband-to-be, admiring his compassion for someone who had treated him so unfairly. But he was right. Without love, his father had become bitter and angry, and she was ever more grateful she had found a man she could love with all her heart and who loved her in return.

Just as Emily had been a bridesmaid for her three friends, Amelia, Irene and Georgina accompanied her up the aisle on her happy day. Emily could hardly contain her excitement throughout the wedding ceremony. She was about to become Jackson's wife. They would be spending the rest of their lives together. There would be no more subterfuge, no more hiding, they could love each other openly whenever and wherever they wanted.

And, as agreed, they invited Kitty to the wedding. Jackson even mentioned her in his speech at the wedding breakfast, and thanked her for bringing them together in the first place, and for her somewhat unusual way of bringing them back together when a terrible misunderstanding had nearly driven them apart.

They also had Kitty to thank for suggesting they hold some more of those fancy balls so they could open more schools. That was exactly what they intended to do. The success of The Women's Education Institute had shown them just how great the need was for such places for young women. Plans were already in place for another school in London, and Jackson and Emily could see no reason why this model could not be reproduced throughout England. All it took was dedication and hard work, something the two of them were eagerly anticipating.

The board members of the school and hospital, and many of the staff, also attended. Everyone was universally overjoyed by the union, although Jackson's friends still found it hard to believe that two people who had seemed so wrong for each other made such a happy couple.

'Being in love is the best feeling in the world,' she over-heard Jackson telling his disbelieving friend Giles during the ball following the wedding breakfast. 'When you fall in love yourself, you'll understand what I'm talking about. Emily has changed me and made me the man that deep down I always wanted to be. She has made me see what's important in life.'

The friend merely shook his head, presumably agreeing with the old Duke that love made you addle-headed.

'It changes a woman as well,' she said, sliding her arm around his waist. 'It makes her see what is important.'

'And what is really important is you and me, and our future together,' he said, leaning down and kissing his wife.

* * * * *

A Deal With The
Rebellious Marquess

Bronwyn Scott

MILLS & BOON

Bronwyn Scott is a communications instructor at Pierce College and the proud mother of three wonderful children—one boy and two girls. When she's not teaching or writing, she enjoys playing the piano, travelling—especially to Florence, Italy—and studying history and foreign languages. Readers can stay in touch via Facebook at Facebook.com/Bronwyn.scott.399 or on her blog, bronwynswriting.blogspot.com. She loves to hear from readers.

Author Note

This series has centered on the Holmfirth flood of 1852, and I've tried to be faithful to the history of the event. The names of the people involved, like coroner Dyson, are historical figures. Captain R.C. Moody, whom Fleur meets with in chapter one, is real, as is his role in investigating the flood. The butcher store market that Fleur visits is real, as is the reference to the Water Street houses not being rebuilt. Those Easter eggs make for interesting reading. Also true, no legislation was ever passed regarding an improvement to dam oversight. In 1864, another dam accident took place at the Dale Dyke Reservoir that was even more deadly.

The collapse of the dam could not be pinned on any one person because it was indeed a case of collective error. Many things went wrong at many parts of the process. The Holmfirth Reservoir Committee was financially mismanaged among other things and the Huddersfield Bank did loan them money (as noted later in the story). (The banker who helps Jasper and Fleur was a real historical figure and truly did write the essay referenced.) So, Orion's disaster is not too far-fetched, although Orion is fictional, as is his involvement in the dam.

For more about the details of the Holmfirth flood, I highly recommend Ian Harlow's book *The Holmfirth Floods: The Story of the Floods in Holmfirth*, which I heavily relied on for details.

DEDICATION

For the puppies: The first book without Huckleberry sitting beneath my desk, but also the first book with Stevie beside me, because for every ending there are new beginnings. And always for Bennie, who is celebrating his twentieth book with me.

Prologue

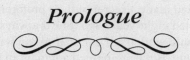

Fleur Griffiths loved her friends more than she hated whist, which explained why she was up an hour past midnight, playing poorly at cards in Mrs Parnaby's lace-curtained parlour and being positively trounced by Emma Luce, who was on her way to navigating a grand slam. Normally, by one in the morning, she would be asleep beside her husband. They all would. Except *this* evening they'd sent their men home without them. Fleur sighed and tossed out a useless card—Emma was unstoppable tonight—and reassessed her reasoning for the late night. It wasn't all due to her affections for her friends. It was about the quarrel, too. She was here because she didn't want to be *there*, in their temporary lodgings with Adam, not yet. Her temper was still too hot.

She and Adam had fought—hard—tonight right before all three couples had left their lodgings on Water Street in the nearby village of Hinchliffe Mill for supper at Mrs Parnaby's in Holmfirth proper. Beneath the table she pressed a hand to the flat of her stomach. They'd fought about the baby, or rather the potential of a baby. Nothing was certain yet. She wanted children, Adam did not.

Neither had made a secret of their preferences when they'd married eight years ago. She'd always assumed the issue would work itself out, that Adam would come around in time. But he remained adamant in his stance that a man should not start a family in his late fifties. Now, though, it seemed possible that nature disagreed with him. Her courses were late and with each passing day, her hopes rose that there would be a son who would grow up and take over Adam's news syndicate, a collection of newspapers that stretched from London to York in the north and all the way to Bristol in the west.

Surely, with such a legacy on the line, Adam would see the merit of having a son, someone to carry it all on. What was the point of all this work and sacrifice to build the newspaper empire if there was no one to leave it to when she and Adam were gone? But Adam had been grim tonight when she'd floated the idea. 'Let's hope it's just stress causing the lateness,' he'd said. She should have left it alone. After all, nothing was decided. But she'd pushed the issue. She'd gone to him, helping him with his neckcloth, pressing up against him, flirting as she fussed with his clothes. 'Would it really be so bad?' she'd cajoled, hoping for a smile. She did not get one.

'Yes, yes, it would,' was the terse response she'd got instead and, because there was a real possibility the child was no longer the hypothetical subject of an old argument, she'd not let the discussion go. Hot words had been exchanged along with blunt opinions that had sustained hurt on both sides.

She tossed another card. Would this hand ever end? It wasn't she and Adam's first fight. They were a rather volatile couple in private, something that would surprise Emma and Antonia with their perfect marriages and doting husbands. *They* didn't have disagreements. They had discussions. Not so with her and Adam. Fleur prided herself on having a 'real' marriage where there were quarrels and hard truths and imperfections but where there were also apologies, commitment from them both to do better and sex—the glorious, heated sex that reminded her that, beneath it all, Adam loved her and she loved him, desperately, completely. Together they could conquer anything.

Tonight had felt different, as if here at last was something they'd not get past. When Emma had suggested an impromptu round robin of whist after supper, Fleur had let Adam go without a kiss or whispered, 'I love you.' She'd stood apart from him in the hall while the others had said goodnight to their husbands and the three men had headed back to the Water Street lodgings. No doubt, the men would stay up a while, have a drink together and discuss the business of the mill that had brought them all to Holmfirth. Then they'd retire.

She knew Adam would retire first. He didn't like late nights. In London, he preferred to rise early and get into the office while it was still quiet. She knew his routine, his preferences, intimately. She'd spent eight years adapting her schedule to fit his. If not, she might never have seen him. Adam loved his work as much as he loved his wife. On nights like tonight, nights where they fought, she wondered if he didn't love it more. Or perhaps she was just selfish in wanting all of his attention.

Emma was just about to claim the last trick when Fleur heard it—a sound in the street: running feet, a shout. She froze and looked up from her hand. She could not hear the words, but she knew what panic sounded like. The shout came again, closer now. 'The embankment's breached, the river's in Water Street!'

Oh, God, the men! Adam, asleep in his bed. Would he even have a chance? Similar thoughts were mirrored on the faces of Emma and Antonia. Fear galvanised them. The four women raced to the lace curtains to peer out into the night. They could see nothing but darkness, but they could *hear*. Even at their safe distance, they could hear the river ravaging, hear its heavy churning as it rushed through Holmfirth, hungry to devour the next village in its path.

'We'll be safe here,' Mrs Parnaby tried to assure them, but Emma was inconsolable in her panic. She raced for the door.

Fleur grabbed for her. 'Help me, Antonia! Help me hold her!' The silly fool meant to go out after them. With Antonia's help, she wrestled Emma from the door. 'What do you think it will accomplish, you running out there? You can't see a thing,' Fleur scolded her friend too harshly in her own panic. 'It's too late to warn them.' She forced Emma to sit.

Antonia took Emma's hand and knelt beside her. 'They're strong men, they can take care of themselves.' That was Antonia, always the optimist. Fleur could do with a little of that optimism herself right now.

Mrs Parnaby was all bustling practicality, ordering a

tea tray. 'We'll go help when the water has settled and there's less chance of us being another set of people in need of rescue ourselves.' Fleur knew what that meant. It meant there was nothing to be done until daylight. Fleur noted the grimness around the woman's mouth. Despite her hopeful words, Mrs Parnaby already feared the worst and, in truth, Fleur did, too.

It was the longest night Fleur could remember, especially given that their vigil hadn't started until half-past one, the night already well advanced. But the five hours until there was enough light to be abroad dragged at a snail's pace, the hall clock seemingly frozen in time. None of them could sleep. They spent the night wide awake in the parlour, ears craning for the sound of footsteps, for a knock on the door. None came.

The moment it was light, they donned cloaks and followed Mrs Parnaby to the Rose and Crown Inn, but morning did not bring relief, only reality, and what a grim reality it was to see the result of what they'd heard last night. Fleur noted it all with a reporter's eye as they picked their way through mud and debris: the dead cow mired in the muck, the various parts of metal machinery deposited willy-nilly wherever the river tired of carrying them, the heavy oak furniture reduced to sharp, dangerous splinters, the timbers and stones that had once been houses, torn asunder, the sheer amount of ruined home goods, and the oddness of the things that had survived intact.

They passed a credenza still whole and a set of uncracked blue dishes. Fleur wondered if their owner would find them. How many miles had that credenza travelled down the river? There was hope in that. Some things in the river's wake had survived the night. Perhaps that meant their husbands had, too.

Others were at the Rose and Crown. It was fast becoming a gathering point, a place where families could find each other, where people could exchange news and where those in need could get help, medical care, a blanket and a hot meal.

Fleur tied on an apron and went to work immediately. There were children who'd come in alone, bedraggled and looking for parents, armed with horrifying stories of having spent the night clinging to the roof timbers of their homes and praying the water wouldn't reach them. Those were the *least* horrifying tales. Others told terrible stories of watching their families being swept away in the raging current.

She spent the morning washing faces, spooning broth, the journalist in her avidly listening to stories and asking questions. She offered reassurance where she could. Across the room, she saw Antonia do the same, quite often with a small child on her hip. Antonia had always been good with children. Fleur tried to keep her eyes from the door, to keep her attentions on those she could help. She tried not to think of Adam. He would come. If he was with Antonia's husband, Keir, he'd be out there helping those in need first before helping himself. He would come when he could.

There *was* good news. James Mettrick, one of the men they'd come to do business with who also lived on Water Street and had been in his residence at the time of the flood, straggled in mid-morning, bruised but alive.

This was tempered with the reality that his family had not survived. Fleur clung to the knowledge that survival was possible. If James Mettrick had survived, perhaps Adam had, too. Perhaps Adam was still out helping others. Perhaps he'd been pushed downstream and needed transport back, or perhaps, heaven forbid, he was hurt and even now some kind stranger was caring for him as she was caring for others. It gave her own hope a much-needed second wind.

That second wind was short-lived. At ten o'clock, George Dyson, the town coroner, arrived. Fleur tracked him with her eyes as he sought out Emma. Fleur watched Emma nod before Emma turned her direction with a gesture that indicated the three of them should adjourn to the Rose and Crown's private parlour.

In the parlour, Antonia stood between her and Emma, gripping their hands as Mr Dyson cleared his throat and addressed them, using Emma's title, Lady Luce. The formality lent an ominous quality to his tone and Fleur braced herself against words that never prefaced the positive. 'I wish I had better news.' Oh, God. Fleur felt her stomach sink. 'I will be blunt; Water Street didn't stand a chance. The river hit it from the front and the side, absolutely obliterating the buildings.' He paused and swallowed hard.

How many times today had he needed to deliver bad news? Fleur wondered. But the wondering didn't make his next words any easier to hear. 'James Mettrick's family and the Earnshaws, with whom you had business dealings, are all gone. Their homes are entirely destroyed.' Homes that had been next to the ones Fleur and her friends had rented.

The world became muffled to Fleur. She was vaguely aware of Emma arguing something about James Mettrick, the son, surviving. Dyson was shaking his head, delivering the death blow as gently as possible. 'Lady Luce, the bodies of your husband and his friends have been recovered.' There was more. Fleur didn't care. She'd get the details later. For now, all that mattered was knowing they were gone. Garret was dead. Keir was dead. *Adam* was dead.

No, it had to be a mistake. Adam couldn't be dead. Not when there was unresolved anger between them. Not when there might be a child to raise. Her world reeled. She staggered forward, catching herself on the fireplace mantel lined with blue ware pieces like the set they'd seen in the mud, unbroken and whole. Rage surged. Damn it all! Why should the universe choose to save dishes over the life of one good man, *her* man? It wasn't right. But she could make it right. She picked up the blue ware piece nearest her and threw it hard against the wall, watching it shatter into a thousand pieces. Like her heart. Her life. Her very soul.

Anger began to burn, a source of fuel against her grief. This was what Adam had feared—that the dam was insufficient to its task. It was the reason Garrett had asked him to come, to bring his investigative journalistic talents to bear on determining the quality of not only the mill, but the river that mill depended on. Now the very worst had happened. Naturally? Or as the result of human error? If it were the latter, she could make sure someone paid for all they'd taken from her.

* * *

Apparently, one could live on anger, at least for four days. While Emma and Antonia had stayed in with their grief at Mrs Parnaby's, Fleur had gone out, channelling her rage into walking the muddy, ruined streets of Holmfirth. She helped with the recovery effort from daybreak to sunset. She helped rehome those who'd lost everything. She sat on the committee charged with collecting funds to distribute to those in need—of which there were many when the realisation set in that the river had destroyed homes *and* jobs. There was no work to go back to, no income to earn. In the evenings, she wrote copious articles to the newspapers Adam owned, sharing first-hand testimonies of survivors and reports of the developing situation. She instructed the editors to send artists to draw pictures. She wanted lithographs printed, she wanted word spread far and wide about the depth of tragedy in Holmfirth.

Anger could only go so far, though. It kept her fuelled and busy. But it could not change the fact that Adam was gone. 'We're widows now. Widows before the age of thirty,' Fleur ground out, pacing before Mrs Parnaby's fireplace. The woman had been a generous hostess, taking in three women who were only supposed to have been dinner guests.

Emma spoke up as if reading her thoughts from across the room. 'I think it's time to go. There's nothing more we can do here.'

Fleur raised an eyebrow in challenge. Nothing more to do here? There was plenty to do here. She couldn't possibly leave now. But of course, Emma would be thinking about concerns with Garrett's estate and his investments. She would need to be in London. Antonia nodded agreement, citing the need to take over the reins of Keir's department store project. That was a bold move on Antonia's part. Fleur was aware of Antonia's gaze on her as her friend asked, 'Shall we all travel together as far as London?'

Fleur shook her head, not daring to look at her two closest friends. They would argue with her. They'd not been out in the streets and seen what she had seen. 'No. I think I'll stay and finish Adam's investigation. There are people to help and justice to serve.' She would take rooms at an inn if Mrs Parnaby needed her privacy back.

Emma's face showed disagreement. 'Do you think that's wise, Fleur? If this disaster was man-made, there will be people who won't appreciate the prying, particularly if there's a woman doing it. You should think twice about putting yourself in danger.'

'I don't care,' Fleur snapped. She loved Emma, but they often butted heads, both of them stubborn. 'If Adam died because of carelessness or greed, someone will pay for that. I will see to it and I will see to it that such recklessness doesn't happen again.'

Emma's gaze dropped to her waist and Fleur snatched her hand away from her stomach. She'd been unaware she'd put it there. But it was too late for Emma's sharp eyes. 'And Adam's babe? Would you be reckless with his child?'

Fleur reined in her anger, softening her voice. 'I do not know if there is a child. It is too soon.'

Emma relented with a nod. 'Just be careful, dear friend. I do not want anything to happen to you.' Emma rose and came to her, Antonia joining them. They encircled each other with their arms, their heads bent together. This would be their private farewell. 'We're widows now,' Emma echoed her words.

'We have lost much,' Fleur murmured, 'but we are still friends. Whatever else changes, that will not, no matter where we go, no matter what happens.' She looked at the pale faces of her friends, her resolve doubling. For Garrett, for Keir, for Adam, for Antonia, for Emma, and for herself, there would be justice for them all.

Chapter One

❧

London—
May 1853, fifteen months later

There'd been no justice, just a vituperative, albeit sincere, outpouring of extreme dismay from the Government Inspector over the negligence surrounding the construction, maintenance, and oversight of the doomed Bilberry Dam. If one thing had been made clear in the investigation, it was that the dam had been plagued with misadventures from the start on all levels.

Sympathy and outrage were not enough for Fleur. It had not been enough last February when the inquiry concluded with a call for increased legislative oversight to prevent future disasters and it was not enough now, fifteen months later, which was why Fleur had scheduled a morning meeting with Government Inspector Captain R.C. Moody at the *Newcastle Forge*, one of the Northumberland papers owned by the Griffiths news syndicate. Owned by *her*.

It was one of the myriad changes that had occurred in the past year. Adam's empire was hers now, hers to look after in his place, although it was not a role she would have chosen for herself. Being a newspaper magnate had been Adam's dream, not hers. She'd wanted to be a storyteller, nothing more. Running the syndicate was a daunting task, but one that offered her the leverage to continue to pursue justice for the dam accident.

If the truth wouldn't come to her, she would go to the truth. So, here she was, in Newcastle upon Tyne, sitting in Adam's regional office, surrounded by Adam's things, sitting behind the desk in the chair Adam used to occupy when he was in town. The company might be hers, but the office was still very definitely his. She took strength from that, from feeling his presence. Before her on the desk were the documents regarding the dam accident. How many times had she read them in the hopes that she might uncover something new? She tapped her fingers, impatient for Captain Moody to arrive. A glance at the small desktop clock encased in masculine walnut indicated her impatience was not warranted. Moody wasn't even late yet. There was no basis for it except her own eagerness.

She'd met Moody before during the inquest. He'd been a perfect gentleman, considerate and well spoken, aware that his task as the Government Inspector was not only to investigate the cause of failure, but also to ensure the region recovered. He'd been sensitive to the rawness and depth of loss the people had experienced. In those days, she'd been just another widow, angry and grieving. Today, she was a businesswoman at the helm of a newspaper empire. She could not be handled with platitudes and consolation. Today, she wanted accountability and truth.

A knock on her closed door was followed by the paper's receptionist announcing Captain Moody's arrival. Fleur rose and ran a smoothing hand down her bodice and her green tartan skirts before straightening her shoulders. She would be politely charming, personally enquiring and, above all, professional. The past months had taught her the merits of such decorum when dealing with Adam's testy board of directors who hadn't liked change when it came in the form of a woman. 'Send him in, Miss Grant.'

She could hear Miss Grant in the outer office. 'Mrs Griffiths will see you now, Captain.'

That was her cue to come around the desk and extend a hand in greeting as the Captain entered the room, *her domain*. This was her space; she was in charge here, despite it being marked with Adam's effects. 'Captain, it's so good of you to come. I know you're a busy man these days overseeing the Royal Engineers in Newcastle.' She smiled. 'And somewhat recently married, too, I hear. Congratulations.'

He smiled the smile of the newlywed bridegroom, part-blissful enchantment, and part-bashful humility as if he couldn't quite believe his good fortune. 'Yes, Mrs Griffiths, you've heard correctly. Mary and I were wed last July.' Quite the marriage it was, too. Fleur had done her research. The Captain's wife was the daughter of an extremely wealthy industrialist and, rumour had it, already expecting their first child—not that she would bring that up.

'Please, have a seat.' She gestured to the leather club chair set on the guest side of the big, polished desk. She crossed to the matching console where Adam's Baccarat decanters and a silver coffee urn were displayed. 'It is probably too early to offer you a drink, Captain, but I have hot coffee and fresh rolls.'

'Coffee, thank you, Mrs Griffiths.' He took the seat, sitting with evident military bearing. 'How have you been?' he asked as she passed him a warm mug of coffee and a pastry plate, his question a reminder of how differently the year had treated them. Her marriage, her hopes for a family, had ended while his had begun.

She took her own seat behind the desk, a hand slipping surreptitiously to the flat of her stomach. There'd been no child. Perhaps there never had been. Perhaps all that had ever been in her belly was hope: hope for a child, for the type of family she'd been denied growing up, hope to redirect a marriage she'd sensed was coming to a volatile head between two strong-willed people who wanted different things. Instead of new life, she'd got death.

'I've been well, thank you.' It wasn't quite a lie. She'd been busy and she supposed that was as close to well as she'd get these days. Busy enough to not miss Adam every waking minute. Busy enough to not be entirely eaten up with the regret and the guilt that surrounded that fateful night in Holmfirth. Busy enough to convince herself she was indeed moving on, that she was making progress in a man's world with a board of directors who'd sooner oust her than support her. Some days she actually believed in that progress.

She took a sip of her own coffee and got straight to business. 'I've asked for this meeting because it's been over a year since the inquest delivered its verdict on the dam and nothing has been done. There has been no preventative legislation introduced and now I fear that momentum has been lost. The public has forgotten the urgency behind the issue.' But she had not. She would never forget the horror of Holmfirth and the terrible days that followed when she'd roamed the streets helping survivors, grappling with the loss of Adam and all it meant.

Captain Moody gave a slight nod, but it was a nod of empathy, not agreement. She hoped he would not condescend to her with pity, which seemed to be a man's default when dealing with a widow. 'Mrs Griffiths, you were there when the verdict was read, and prior to that, when my own conclusions were presented. Even now, I will still stand by every word of my statement. While there was proof of gross negligence and ineptitude of such capacity that it turns my stomach to think of it, there was no one person or firm who could be charged with the irresponsibility that led to the dam's demise. This made it impossible to render the charge of manslaughter,' he explained patiently. 'Truly, I understand how disappointing such a finding must be for you.'

Disappointment did not encapsulate the entirety of her feelings in that regard. She knew the words of those findings by heart. She'd heard them spoken out loud at the original presentation of the jury's verdict. She'd read them over and over when the report had been published.

We regret that the reservoir being under the management of a corporation prevents us bringing in a verdict of manslaughter, as we are convinced that the gross and culpable negligence of the commissioners would have subjected them to such a

verdict had they been in the position of an indi-
vidual or firm.

Regret was a mild word compared to the *devastating*
guilt she felt. Regret was what one felt when one had
to decline an invitation to afternoon tea. It was a polite
word. Politeness had no place when discussing the loss
of eighty-one lives, or the deaths of people swept from
their homes in their sleep. Mildness was an inappropriate response when listening to the tales, as she had
in the early days of the flood's aftermath, of those who
watched, helpless, as loved ones were carried away by
the angry torrent. There was no room for complacency
when people realised the river had stolen lives and livelihoods, that the flood had devastated their economic
well-being.

She wanted to give in to the rage the issue deserved,
but she remembered in time the promise she'd made herself earlier. She would be professional. No one respected
hysterics. A man was entitled to an angry outburst, but
a woman, never. 'You are right, Captain Moody. It is
extraordinarily disappointing.' Fleur cultivated careful
neutrality, letting him see only the steady steel in her
gaze instead of the rage in her heart. 'Especially when
you acquired an impressive record of names. Your enquiry clearly stated that if there was an individual or
firm on which blame could be fixed, prosecution would
be possible.' Justice would be possible.

His gaze narrowed. 'What are you suggesting,
ma'am?'

'That your enquiry, while timely and thorough,
should be viewed only as the beginning, not the end of

the interrogation on the dam.' The government *had* acted with surprising alacrity. The inquest had opened immediately on the sixth, the day after the flood. By the eighteenth of February, Moody had given his report to the jury and by the twenty-seventh, the jury had come back with their final conclusions. The amount of paperwork he'd amassed in those two weeks had been impressive and detailed, as was the list of names, both of individuals and companies who'd been involved with the dam at any point in its construction and maintenance. 'The inquest should be reopened and individuals investigated more thoroughly.'

To his credit, Moody took the suggestion seriously. 'On what grounds? It is not the custom to try a man or a firm twice for the same crime unless there is new evidence come to light that reshapes our understanding.'

Fleur reached for a folder lying beneath the papers on her desk. 'There is this.' She slid it across the desk to him and gave him a moment to peruse the single sheet inside. She steadied her own breathing. Everything hinged on this. Some might say her case hung by a thread, but she thought it wasn't so much a thread but a rope—a strong rope made of hardy hemp, the kind that didn't unravel at a first picking.

She'd spent the last fifteen months reviewing every detail, retracing every step that had led up to the dam disaster, starting seven years prior. She'd had the time to dig deeply that Captain Moody had not. And she'd found something. *Someone.* A singular person whose actions had caused the disaster. The singular person needed who could be prosecuted and held accountable.

'Lord Orion Bexley?' Moody quirked a brow and

set the folder down. 'You want to go after *him*?' It was not a challenge, but an opportunity to make her case.

She gave a sharp nod. 'He's the only one who was a consistent presence at the dam. The others—Mr Sharpe, Mr Leather, Mr Littlewood—they're contractors, inspectors, and masons. All of them are people who temporarily intersected with the dam at various points in its development. None of them was singularly responsible for the accident, although,' she added a stern pause, 'all of them do *share* in the blame, all are responsible in part.'

'But you feel Lord Orion is somehow more responsible?' Moody asked.

'Yes, he was on the board of commissioners and didn't sign off on certain reports. It's all there. Much of the mismanagement can be traced directly to him. Particularly this order, which was initiated by him, but, even after funds were delivered, the repairs were never executed.' Follow the money. Adam had been fond of claiming that as one of the top rules of good investigative reporting. Money and blood always told.

Captain Moody was silent for a long while. 'I admire your tenacity and your zeal to see justice done, Mrs Griffiths,' he said at last in quiet tones. 'However, I do not think you are aware of what or who you're up against. It will be legally difficult to get to Lord Orion Bexley even if you had an ironclad case against him, which you do not. You have some interesting leads and conclusions, but be honest—they are not airtight.' He was right. She had strong leads, but it was entirely possible they might go nowhere. Still, she wouldn't know until she tried and she simply couldn't give up.

'What do you mean that I cannot get to him legally?'

That had grabbed her attention. 'No man is above the law. Just because he has a title does not mean he is automatically blameless.'

Moody chuckled. 'Unless that man is the brother of a marquess. Then it's a bit trickier. You know that, Mrs Griffiths. No *common* man is above the law. Lord Orion Bexley is far from the common man.'

She sighed. She knew first-hand that the peerage played by its own rules when it suited them. She'd learned that lesson the hard way through her uncle. She hadn't realised Bexley ran quite that high in the instep, though. 'A marquess?'

'Yes, the Marquess of Meltham, an old and venerable title. The family seat is near Holmfirth,' Moody supplied, discreetly filling in her gaps. She'd not looked up Bexley's title specifically because she preferred to let a man's actions speak for him rather than a title he had not earned beyond the accident of his birth.

She refused to be daunted. 'Well, if I can't get to him legally, perhaps I can get to Lord Orion Bexley socially.' An idea was already taking shape in her mind—a publicity blitz. 'I would think some articles suggesting Lord Orion's culpability would bring him under social censure.'

The Griffiths news syndicate owned seven papers in the north that spanned the distance between Newcastle-upon-Tyne and Sheffield. Those papers could expose the role played by Lord Orion Bexley and apply pressure by making regular appearances. The more often the public saw an issue in print, the more likely they were to view that issue as important and give it their attention.

'The peerage may not have to answer to the law, but

it does answer to society and popular opinion. No one cares to be disliked. Society has its own unwritten rules. Blacken a person's name enough, throw enough aspersion in one's direction and there will be socially unpleasant consequences.'

'Unpleasant consequences for both parties, ma'am, if you don't mind me saying so. If you were wrong, for instance, it would go poorly for the papers and for you. I do not know the Marquess personally, but I would guess he'd not take kindly to his brother, his family, being slandered.' It was only slander if she was wrong. And she knew in her gut she wasn't.

'Truth is indeed a double-edged sword, Captain.' She gave a polite smile. 'I have lost my husband, sir, due to carelessness and cavalier neglect. His death and the death of others were senseless, purposeless. That loss will not go unavenged while I have the ability to see justice done.' She rose to signal the meeting was concluded. 'Thank you for your time, Captain.'

Moody stood. 'I wish you luck and I urge you to take care. Tweaking noses can be dangerous work, Mrs Griffiths.' Especially when those noses belonged to powerful marquesses, but such was the price of justice, and she would pay it if need be. She might not be able to get to Lord Orion Bexley legally, but often, what the law couldn't do, the press could, and it would start today.

Meltham House, London—
Three weeks later

Jasper Bexley, Marquess of Meltham, liked to start his day with quiet and coffee in the morning room, a bun drizzled with icing for his sweet tooth at his elbow, a plate of fluffy scrambled eggs before him and the latest newspapers at the ready. But if he had to choose between the food or the quiet, he'd choose the quiet. He preferred quiet above all else.

Quiet was a sign of order, of steadiness, of readiness. Most of all it was a sign that all was right in his world and Jasper Bexley was a man who valued that rightness in all its forms. It allowed a man to think rationally, plan methodically, engage with his world logically. For him, silence was indeed the golden currency of quietude, especially during the Season when the demands on a marquess's time were extreme.

So, when his brother's strident tones, accompanied by the loud *thwack!* of a newspaper on the polished surface of the breakfast table set Jasper's cup to jangling and his coffee to sloshing in its saucer, much more than the pristine silence of the room was broken. His train of thought was broken, the peace of his morning was broken, and such things were not easily mended or restored.

Jasper sighed and dragged his gaze from *The Times*. The morning was giving every sign of going downhill from here. He took off his wire-rimmed spectacles and set them aside. He suspected it would be a while before he got back to his reading. With Orion it was never just a single interruption, but the beginning of a long line of other disturbances.

'Don't you have rooms at the Albany?' he queried coolly, fixing his younger brother with a freezing stare, both of which were meant to remind him that this was to be the Season of his living independently and embracing his adulthood. It was beyond time. Orion was thirty, eight years older than Jasper had been when he'd become the Marquess.

'They can't keep saying these things about me! There's been articles up north and now there's one in the *London Tribune*.' Orion abused the table with another swat of the newspaper, slouched into the chair and conveniently ignored the question.

'Conveniently ignoring' was a coping strategy his brother had cultivated as a boy and honed to perfection as an adult. The only other thing Orion cultivated with such care was his appearance—always immaculately groomed and expensively turned out, even, Jasper noted wryly, in the midst of his latest crisis. This morning, Orion wore a grass-green silk waistcoat, a sky-blue silk cravat and a bottle-green jacket of superfine, his jaw clean shaven, his champagne-blond hair—Orion's term for a hue that was not quite gold or brown—neatly trimmed.

Jasper always felt a bit rough around the edges compared to his brother. His own hair was decidedly longer, a collection of unruly nut-brown waves that tangled easily no matter the amount of pomade his valet applied. He was too busy to think about clothes. He left that to his tailor and valet. Between them, they hadn't failed him yet.

Jasper breathed in through his nose and gave a long exhale, preparing to jump into the impending fray. 'What is it this time? Did the society column not care for your latest waistcoat? Or is it money trouble again?' Perhaps a gaming debt that had lingered too long for repayment. It wouldn't be the first time. He hoped that was all it was. He hoped it wasn't worse—a wronged earl's daughter caught kissing Orion in a garden at a ball, perhaps—because Orion would make a terrible husband. He loved his brother, but that didn't mean he wished Orion on an unsuspecting wife.

'Brother, you have to make them stop. It's gone too far. It never should have been allowed to start.'

Jasper did not care for the accusatory tone with which the last part was said. Nor did he like the feeling that he'd entered in the middle of a play and didn't understand the plot. He rubbed the bridge of his nose. 'I am going to need more detail than that, starting with who "they" are in this little drama and what *is* the drama?' Because it was always drama with Orion. Mountains from mole hills were his speciality, usually because they'd been ignored too long before they reached Jasper's attention.

Orion shoved the paper the length of the table. '"They" are the *London Tribune*, the *Leeds Messenger*, the *Sheffield Tribune*, the *Bristol Intelligencer* and a host of smaller papers from here to York.' Orion's chagrin seemed genuine for once and, for a moment, Jasper sensed something else beneath it—authentic concern? Perhaps a sincere sense of worry? But it was gone as quickly as it came. Still, he thought, the observation was worth filing away.

Jasper reached for his glasses and picked up the paper, his brow furrowing as he read the half-page article, which was quite a bit of space devoted to an issue that was over a year old and one that had been settled. 'This is about the dam accident in Holmfirth last February.' More specifically, it was about the enquiry that had occurred afterwards. Orion had been on the Board of Commissioners for the Holmfirth Dam project, a position Jasper had arranged in the hopes of giving Orion a sense of purpose and direction when Orion had finished a brief, disappointing stint in the military with the engineering corps.

He looked up at Orion. 'What does this have to do with you? The verdict was clear: there was no one person or organisation that was accountable for the accident.' The dam had been a tragedy of collective errors, to be sure, and a travesty of bureaucratic nonsense.

'Someone is attempting to reopen the investigation,' Orion groused, reaching for the silver coffee pot and pouring a cup before pulling out a flask to enliven the brew. Jasper frowned. It was barely half past eight. A bit early, in his opinion, to be 'enlivening' beverages.

'Let them search. They are not bound to get far. The law won't retry a case without new evidence and there was no conviction last time due to there being no one or no group *to* bring to trial.' Jasper failed to see what the worry was.

'But that's the point. Someone *is* looking for a person to pin it all on and that person is *me*!' Orion blurted out with dramatic angst. 'The newspaper articles have named *me* in a manner that suggests I am the someone who should be held accountable and whoever is doing it is using the papers to whip up support. You must put a stop to it,' he insisted.

'You want me to use my title to suppress the press?' Jasper surmised bluntly. And when *or* if that failed, Orion would want him to use his title to suppress the individual citizen behind it. Did Orion even see the irony in that, given his voting record in Parliament regarding lowering the stamp tax on newspapers and abolishing the excise tax on printing paper? He championed free press. He didn't censor it.

Orion leaned forward in earnest. 'I want you to use your title to suppress slander, Brother. Someone is trying to ruin me.' It was said with all the aplomb of a Drury Lane thespian—he was giving *quite* the performance.

Jasper nodded. Orion *was* named specifically. That alone required his attention. The family name must be protected from unrighteous scandal. But he also knew that with Orion there was always a nugget of truth involved and many other types of nuggets, too. There was likely more to this than what Orion was letting on. He just had to figure out what that more was. Regardless, the situation would have to be handled delicately.

If the press was indeed slandering Orion, it would indirectly be akin to slandering the marquessate, which Jasper would not tolerate. His father had taught that lesson well and often. The Marquess must protect the family. Of course, that assumed that was indeed happening. Cases were *never* black and white with Orion. He would not let his brother be wronged, but neither would Jasper risk the marquessate's good name by using it to undermine a free press, one of the life bloods of an evolving society, a view that often made him unpopular in the House of Lords. It was a view he'd fought for on more than one occasion because ideas—scientific, philosophical, or otherwise—were critical if a society were to modernise and advance, something the reclusive and often eccentric Marquessate of Meltham had long believed in. It was a legacy he was more than happy to keep alive.

He sighed. This was going to be tricky indeed. 'I'll

look into it right away. Get me a list of all the papers that ran articles about you.' He was already mentally reorganising his morning to move this to the top of his task list as a thousand questions clamoured for his attention, mercilessly drowning out the quiet.

Chapter Two

If the British system of primogeniture had not so mercilessly designated that Jasper Bexley be a marquess's heir simply on the merit of his birth and sex, he would have, by his own choice, been a scientist, a participant in a field of discovery that was rooted in logic and careful, reliable methodology that sought predictability. The scientist's life was a quiet, orderly life of logical experimentation that led to logical outcomes, where everything had explanations and reasons.

Since his first encounter with Francis Bacon's treatise, *Novum Organum*, which he'd ponderously and determinedly waded through in its original Latin at eighteen, the year his father had inexplicably taken ill, the Baconian Method had become the lens through which Jasper processed and understood the world—logical reasoning through classifications instead of syllogisms, and most of all the discovery of truth, of knowledge through an organised process that began with questioning and observation.

Bacon had appealed to him at a time in his life when he'd been desperate for answers. His father, a generally hardy and robust man, had taken ill with pneumonia and had never recovered despite four years of trying. Both the illness and the lack of recovery had seemed random and inexplicable occurrences to Jasper.

How was it that a healthy man like his father could be cut down still in his prime? He'd sought answers and reasons in his craving to rationalise the tragedy playing out before him. His father dead at the age of fifty-four. The title and the responsibility of leading the family his at the young age of twenty-two. Since then, Bacon had become a tool to guide him through managing the title and a tool for managing his life so that he might use the order of logic as a shield against the chaos and pain of emotion.

That tool was serving him well today. Questions were a scientist's stock in trade and there were plenty to ask at present. Jasper dedicated his morning to doing that asking: why was someone seeking to reopen a decisive, thorough investigation? Who might that someone be? Why was his brother the target? Why was his brother worried about being the target if the previous investigation had turned up nothing directed at him? What was different this time?

Questions led to research. To create answers, one had to gather information—*objective* information. He could not resolve the situation if he didn't understand the *whole* situation. Too many people, Orion included, saw the world as *they* were, not as it factually was. Truth, by its very definition, could *not* be subjective. It must remain inviolable.

As long as one asked the right questions, that truth was not so hard to come by and, by the late afternoon,

Jasper had discovered two interesting pieces of information. First, all the papers were owned by the Griffiths News Syndicate. Second—and this was where it got interesting—the *woman* in charge of the syndicate was Fleur Griffiths, who'd lost her husband in the flood. A woman. A widow. Certain conclusions could be drawn.

Jasper drummed his fingers on the surface of his desk as he imagined the scenario the information provided: a grieving widow with a news organisation at her disposal and a proverbial axe to grind. Motive didn't get more obvious than that. She'd lost her husband. She would have been disappointed with a verdict that didn't assign clear blame. Clear blame would have given her closure and the explanation she was no doubt looking for: why had this random, freak accident claimed her husband's life? Without that explanation, her grief remained unassuaged, unable to rest.

He knew those feelings. They were the feelings he'd had when his father had died. He'd taken comfort in his Francis Bacon, searching for that understanding. She was out looking for vengeance and wielding her presses to do it. Perhaps she hoped if she could find a culprit, it would appease her grief, close her wounds. No. Strike that last part. He was extrapolating now about a woman he had never even seen. He would need to rectify that.

One had to be careful not to infer too much. After all, he didn't know anything *factual* about Mrs Griffiths's character, another reason why it was necessary to encounter her. His scenario upon which the 'obvious motive' was based assumed she grieved, which was based on another assumption—that all women grieved. Mrs Griffiths was a woman, therefore she grieved. Wasn't this the very concern of syllogistic reasoning that Bacon had railed against? One must test each step in that dangerous ladder.

He strode to the sideboard against the wall and poured an afternoon brandy, testing those logical rungs in his mind. Perhaps she did not miss her husband? Perhaps she was glad to be free of him, free of matrimony? Especially when she now had a fortune and empire at her disposal. He knew there were such women in the world who aspired to be more than wives and mothers. Perhaps she was one of them? But that brought another set of assumptions to test. *Did* she have a fortune? An empire? Perhaps there were others controlling it? Perhaps she was nothing more than a figurehead? Perhaps someone was controlling her?

By the time his secretary, a tall, slim, serious, dark-haired fellow, appeared for further instruction, two items had become clear. First, Mrs Griffiths was a person of interest to him and he needed to confirm she was the person responsible for these articles both up north and in London. Second, to move along his understanding of the situation he needed to know *her*. A good critical thinker tested not only the content of the argument being made, but the source who made the argument. He could not answer his remaining questions or form a viable hypothesis without that. To know her required meeting her, but not as the Marquess of Meltham. She would never receive Meltham and even if by some miracle she did, she'd be on her guard, wanting to protect herself.

'I need you to ascertain if Mrs Griffiths is in town,'

he told his secretary. He was fairly sure she was. It was the Season, Parliament was in session and all the news was here, after all, as well as the syndicate's headquarters. 'If she is in town, I want to know where she'll be tonight.' And he would miraculously be there, too. Not as the Marquess, of course, but in the guise of one of his lesser titles. Perhaps the Baron, Lord Umberton, would make an appearance this evening. The irony did not elude him that sometimes acquiring the objective truth often required a bit of subterfuge and, according to his secretary when he returned a couple hours later, a ticket to the theatre.

The Adelphi on the Strand was not the type of theatre Jasper was used to. It was not Covent Garden or Drury Lane—the theatres where *he* had boxes—but its façade was imposing despite its less than aristocratic population. Jasper tugged at his white waistcoat, feeling a bit overdressed. To be fair, there were a few aristocratic swells in the crowd—young bucks out for adventure beyond the confines of Mayfair—but most of the attendees were salaried clerks who worked at Gray's Inn or at firms throughout the City writing briefs, tallying ledgers and hoping for eventual promotion. Certainly, it was an educated if bourgeois crowd. Still, these were not *his* people. However, they *were* Mrs Griffith's people and that was interesting, informing.

Jasper purchased a playbill from a young usher and tried to draw a picture in his mind of Mrs Griffiths; perhaps she was a stout, determined older woman. He could imagine the sort: iron grey hair, a double chin from good living, a bosom worthy of a ship's prow and a waistline that corseting had long since failed to define. Perhaps, despite her age, she enjoyed an evening out among the younger set and embraced the novelties of the new modern era, which seemed likely if she had indeed taken over her husband's news syndicate after years of perhaps assisting him from the sidelines.

His own mother would be the first to tell him behind every great man there was usually a strong, tenacious woman and Adam Griffiths had been at least a great businessman to have acquired such a news network. Aristocrats didn't hold the monopoly on greatness as they once did. His father had predicted it, prepared him for it, prepared him to embrace change even as those in his set resisted it with every fibre of their being.

Jasper scanned the crowd as he took a seat on the floor. He'd not sat on the floor amid the masses before. But he didn't plan on being here long. He took out a pair of opera glasses and scanned the boxes. *She'd* be in a box. Griffiths would have been on top of the food chain here, the very sort of man these clerks aspired to be.

Jasper began dismissing boxes as his opera glasses roamed. No, not that box, not that one, not this one...all of them were full of grey-haired businessmen with their wives or perhaps, in some cases, their mistresses. Whoa! His opera glasses came to a full stop on the woman in the second box from the end. A lone woman dressed in a gown of burnished gold silk, cut fashionably low to show off a lovely bosom, auburn hair smooth and well coiffed, her bearing straight-backed and regal amid the heavy red velvet draperies framing the box. *Maybe her?*

Or was that just wishful thinking because she was positively stunning and bore no resemblance to the picture he'd drawn in his mind? His opera glasses would have lingered on her regardless of his errand. But it was her posture that made him consider her as a candidate for being the woman he sought, because goodness knew nothing else about her fit the anticipated mould of what he'd expected Adam Griffiths's widow to look like—a woman who was commensurate in age to Griffiths and well past the first blush of beauty.

This woman was thirty at most and she sat like a queen, her spine straight with authority, her shoulders squared with confidence, her chin tilted up a fraction of an inch as if to say, 'I dare anyone to come to my throne.' And like a queen, she was alone, unapproachable, untouchable. Thoughts of Queen Elizabeth teased the edges of his mind. Perhaps it was the red hair that sparked the comparison.

He checked the remaining box to be sure he wasn't overlooking anyone. No contenders there, just an older man and a woman with white hair—too old for what he was looking for. Jasper returned his opera glasses to the prior box, to his queen. Despite her surprising youth, it had to be her—the expensive gown and the confident bearing of one who was used to being in control. And she was alone, which spoke volumes to him as the house lights flickered, prompting the audience to take their seats. Before the house went dim, he summoned a fruit seller and pressed a coin in the girl's hand. 'At the intermission, tell me which box belongs to Mrs Griffiths.' He needed to be one hundred per cent right on this. He didn't want to make a fool of himself and approach the wrong woman.

The play was a performance of John Morton's *A Des-*

perate Game, a one-act farce which would be followed by other performances after the intermission, but sitting in the dark as those around him were excitedly impatient for the curtain to rise on the stage, Jasper's attentions were engaged inwardly instead, mulling over the woman in the box above him and her defiant aloneness. If he set aside his adherence to Baconian Law and engaged in the luxury of the loose logic of assumptions, things began to make sense now that he was sure he'd sighted her.

Bereft too young of a husband, she wanted justice. No, she wanted more than justice. She wanted rectification. She wanted someone to pay for her husband's death and she thought that someone should be Orion. It was there in the tilt of her chin. She would *hunger* for it perhaps with a vengeance, a passion, that had become misguided despite the purity of its initial intent to see right done.

He knew a bit about good intentions gone wrong. Much of what he tried to do for his brother seemed to end up in that category. He could certainly empathise with the wanting to do good. But he could not sympathise with it when it meant allowing the marquessate to become the whetstone for the brutal knife of her grief.

When the house lights went up, the fruit seller was waiting to confirm his hopes. The woman alone was indeed her. He made his way to the stairs leading to the boxes and fought his way upstream. The Adelphi did brisk business among the middle classes and the house was full tonight. At last, he reached the box tier. It was quieter up here and far less crowded. Ushers were po-

sitioned outside the boxes to see to the needs of the patrons within them and at the entrance to the saloon in
order to prevent interlopers from intruding.

Jasper counted the boxes and approached the one containing his quarry, another coin at the ready, just in case
he needed it, a hum akin to the thrill of the hunt thrumming in his veins. 'I'm here to see Mrs Griffiths.' He
watched the usher's gaze move over his dark evening
clothes and white waistcoat and conclude he was someone of import. But it wasn't enough.

The usher consulted his list. 'Mrs Griffiths is not
expecting anyone in her box tonight.'

'Of course,' Jasper demurred in agreement, ingratiating himself to the usher. 'I did not know if I'd be able
to attend tonight. It was all rather last minute.' Not a
lie. He'd not had a ticket until two hours ago. 'If you
could tell her Lord Umberton is here, it would be appreciated.' He offered the coin. He'd let the usher do
his job and announce him. He had no desire to get the
young man into trouble, but he would follow him in. He
wasn't going to stand outside the box waiting to be refused. It was much harder to evict a man once he was
inside. He did do the usher the courtesy, however, of a
two-step head start.

In the dimness of the box, the usher cleared his throat.
'Mrs Griffiths, Lord Umberton to see you,'

Jasper stepped around the usher as she turned her
head, meaning to take advantage of the moment of surprise only to find the tables entirely turned on him.
Viewing her from a distance had not done her full
credit. Stunning was an inadequate word to describe
this woman. Proximity provided details. Up close, her

eyes were green. Her skin was pearly luminescence and porcelain smoothness from the sweep of her check to the expanse of decolletage. She rose and the susurration of gold silk called attention to the exquisite simplicity of her gown and how it made love to every curve and angle of her, the body within the gown's only ornamentation. She was elegant beauty personified and his body answered to it, roused to it, most dangerously, because this was not logic.

In the heat of the moment with his usually organised thoughts in a riot, he could not recall the last time he'd responded so immediately, so thoroughly to a woman and so inconveniently. Very well, he rationalised. Being aware of the nature of his attraction meant he was forewarned against it. He was here to take her measure— objectively. Her green eyes were on him in cool perusal, his moment of surprise slipping away. He found the words to intercept the refusal before she could evict him. 'Pardon the intrusion. When I saw you were in attendance tonight, I wanted to take the opportunity to share my interest in the articles your paper has been publishing about the Bilberry Dam.' Also not a lie. He was interested but in a way that differed from the interest of her news syndicate.

A slim auburn brow arched. 'I do not come to the theatre, Lord Umberton, to discuss business.' It was meant as a rebuke, a cool scold, but it did not entirely hide the spark of another type of interest. Neither did he miss the subtle sweep of her gaze. She might not approve of the interruption, but something in her gaze said she approved of him.

He pressed his advantage. 'Perhaps I might persuade

you to join me for supper afterwards. I have a private table at Rules. What do you say to oysters and champagne?' He could see the idea tempted her even as they both understood how daring the offer was. In the circles he usually ran in, such an offer would not be made. They'd not been formally introduced. But this was not a pink-wool-wrapped debutante. This was a woman of the world, a woman of a man's world, to put a finer point on it. She ran a newspaper syndicate. One could not do that without getting a little dirty.

Her hand fingered the gold and pearl pendant at her neck, her auburn head tilting in consideration. 'Since I do not know you, Lord Umberton, nor you me, I will take mercy on you and offer you a lesson instead of a set down. I do not come to the theatre to discuss business, or to spend the evening in the company of gentlemen with whom I am not familiar.'

He chuckled. He probably deserved that. He'd behaved audaciously and he couldn't remember the last time he'd done that either. Still, he was no quitter. He might not know her, but neither did she know him. It was his habit to never leave a room until he got what he came for. Her refusal only meant she was careful, not that she wasn't interested. He gave a nod, allowing himself the luxury of a little flirting. 'What *do* you come to the theatre for?'

She snapped open the fan that hung at her wrist, an expensive black and gold creation. 'I come to forget, Lord Umberton, to set aside the world for a bit.' It didn't take much to read between those widely spaced lines as she no doubt intended. The house lights flickered. It was time for him to close the deal.

'I do apologise for my poor timing.' He gave a gracious bow. 'Perhaps tomorrow at your London offices would be more appropriate. I shall call on you at ten o'clock.'

'Will you be up by then?' she queried. He was up right now, to be truthful, but that wasn't the kind of up she was referring to. 'I was unaware lords rose before noon.' There were all sorts of wicked responses he could make to that given the rising action he was experiencing at the moment—nothing outrageous or obvious, he had more self-control than that—but certainly his interest flickered like the house lights, prompting, prodding.

'Rising by ten will be no problem for me, I assure you.' He offered a cool half-smile. 'I'm a different sort of lord, Mrs Griffiths. You'll see.' He exited then, before she could refuse. He'd got what he'd come for and quite a bit more, but it appeared he was up for it in all ways.

Chapter Three

Fleur had been up most of the night. The unexpected visitor to her box had been the perfect—as in perfectly upsetting—ending to an already difficult day: Adam's birthday. He would have been fifty-nine. She'd not been in the mood for people. But the man himself had been upsetting in an entirely different way that transcended the intrusion.

Even now, as she paced her office at the *London Tribune* waiting for the clock to chime ten, her sleepless body was full of restless energy, her mind insisting on recalling every detail of Lord Umberton in vivid colour and imagined tactile texture: the tousled tangle of rich nut-brown waves that tempted a woman to run her fingers through them, to tame them as a woman might wish to tame the man; the topaz depths of his gaze that managed to be both gem-sharp and warmly inviting; an intriguing combination which explained why she'd almost accepted his offer of oysters and champagne at Rules. That, and the fact that she'd been vulnerable last night, missing her friends. Missing Adam.

The box was too lonely without Antonia and Emma to join her. Their husbands had purchased the box together years ago and the six of them had spent count-less evenings there. Now, Antonia was sailing for Tahiti with Lord Cullen Allardyce. Last month, Antonia had literally walked away from her life, her business, her de-partment store in London, with nothing but the clothes on her back to be with him. Emma was in Cumières, France, running champagne vineyards with her hus-band, Julien Archambeau, Comte du Rocroi. Both of her friends had gone on to new lives, new loves, and she'd been left behind with an empty theatre box and an empty bed.

But more than she missed her friends, she missed Adam. She missed the bed and the sex the most. She and Adam had fought hard and fornicated harder... And, oh, how she missed it. Sex had been on her mind all day yesterday, making her ache, making her want as she'd gone through the ritual and the pain of privately mark-ing Adam's birthday. Last year, Antonia had been with her. This year, she'd had to face the day alone.

It wasn't just the physicality of the sex she missed, it was the emotional connection, too. The knowing look they could cast one another across a room that said *I want you. Only you in this whole wide world.* The pre-cious moments afterwards when the world narrowed to only Adam's arms, when there was peace, when the newspaper didn't intrude and it was truly just the two of them. Bed was their safe space. Perhaps that's why she liked it so much. In bed, they could talk about any-thing, say anything. She'd never felt more connected to Adam than when they were in bed together. In bed, she could forget all she'd given up for him and remember the glory of what they had together.

That was what she missed, what she craved, what she envied Emma and Antonia for. They had that again, for a second time. Of course they did. They were both generous and kind. They'd loved their first husbands. They'd been good stewards of the love they'd been given. They'd proven to the fates that they were worthy of having that love again. She wasn't like them. She'd fought with Adam, she'd resented that Adam wouldn't allow them a child, that she'd given up her family, such as it was, and the life she'd thought she have for him. In return, she'd expected some sacrifice on his part. But there'd been none. Adam was uncompromising, unyielding in all aspects of his life and his principles, even when it came to his wife.

She'd not honoured those principles as she should have. She'd lost a good man and that loss posed a dark question that loomed large in the deep hours of the night when ghosts walked hand in hand with regrets: was she worthy of love a second time? She had to prove herself worthy of love, of Adam. Justice for the dam would do that, would prove that she'd been a good and loyal wife who had loved her husband.

Then, *he'd* appeared in her box, Lord Umberton, and made it clear she needn't be alone, at least not physically. Oysters and champagne could easily lead to other things—things she might have taken him up on last night if her common sense hadn't intervened. He could only give her sex. He was a stranger. He couldn't give her the rest.

In the moment, his invitation had made her wonder if the interest in the Bilberry Dam had simply been an excuse, a conversational opener, a reason to meet her. The thought had lasted until he'd manoeuvered the morning appointment out of their interaction. Either he didn't take no for an answer, or he truly did want to discuss the dam. The businesswoman in her hoped for the latter. Perhaps her articles were beginning to bear fruit, perhaps this man might become an ally. The businesswoman also hoped that by morning light with her vulnerability caged, he would not be so handsome and that he'd be late—something that would make him unlikeable. She desperately needed him to be unlikeable, desperately needed to have something with which to temper her reaction to him.

But he wasn't late. Nor was he early, not even by a blameable minute. He had the audacity to be punctual *and* he was still handsome, perhaps even more so than he'd been last night. In the daylight she could make a study of the interesting juxtapositions he presented: the tousled waves contrasting with the immaculate clothes; the razor-sharp nose abutted by the soft gaze of his eyes from behind the round rims of wire frames.

Had spectacles ever looked that sexy on a man before? They were a definite lure, baiting a woman to draw near, to sit on his lap—no, not merely *sit*—to hike her skirts to her knees, straddle him and face him eye to eye as she removed those wire frames so that nothing stood between their mutual gaze while she went on to remove other items: his cravat, the ruby tie pin within its folds...

She refocused her thoughts on the study she was making of him. If it weren't for the obviously advertised expense of his clothing and its excellent cut, one might take him for a new Bohemian—who lived outside of society's restraints. But he was quite the opposite by dint of his title. Anyone bearing the title 'Lord' was *not* outside society's constraints. Her uncle had been keen on reminding her of that. A lord's niece, like herself, had obligations, too. Obligations she'd not upheld. She'd been cast out for those transgressions.

It was a reminder, also, that for all the lap-straddling fantasies running through her head—fantasies in which she was the initiator—that he was not powerless. She had only to look at the body beneath his high-end clothes to know that. The breadth of his shoulders, the leanness of his waist, the long length of his trousered leg all reinforced the message that beyond the inviting depths of his curls and the warmth of his eyes, he was a man confident in his own power, his own appeal.

'I trust I don't disappoint?' Umberton said casually, taking a seat as the door shut behind him. *There* was that confidence she'd noted in him, the confidence to nonchalantly toss off a nuanced phrase with its double meaning and the confidence to correctly attribute her gaze to the interest he raised in her. It was not arrogance that drove him to it. Experience, perhaps? How many women had looked on him and not found him wanting? Perhaps it was the same experience that led her to understand his interest in the box last night had extended beyond their mutual fascination with the Bilberry Dam. This was like recognising like.

'Not in the least, Lord Umberton.' She took her seat behind the desk, noting that his gaze had followed the swish of her skirts. 'Did you enjoy the rest of the performances last night?' She would test him and his authenticity before they went any further. Was he really interested in the dam? How truthful would he be about his motives?

'I did not stay, Mrs Griffiths.' He favoured her with a smile and his topaz eyes teased. 'There didn't seem to be a reason to after you turned down my table at Rules.' Score another point for him. Lord Umberton was punctual *and* truthful. He had indeed departed the theatre straight away when he'd left her box. She knew because she'd spent the rest of the evening scanning the crowd for him and not caught sight of him. Not that she'd admit it, especially not to him. There was a thin line between confidence and conceit, and she would not unnecessarily feed his ego.

He asked the reciprocal question demanded by politeness. 'Did you enjoy the performances, Mrs Griffiths?'

'They did what they were supposed to do.' She offered a polite smile and smoothly moved the conversation to the business at hand. 'What can I help you with regarding the Bilberry Dam?'

He leaned forward, his gaze friendly but intent. 'I am looking to have my curiosity satisfied. The *London Tribune* has run an article this week regarding responsibility for the accident, and other articles about the same have been run earlier in regional papers owned by your corporation. I am curious as to the purpose.'

The response made her prickly. She had real work to do. She did not have time for the mere satisfying of a man's personal curiosity or answering to a private citizen. 'So, like the entitled lord you are, you thought to invade my privacy by approaching my theatre box during non-business hours at a non-business venue and simply ask me why my newspaper publishes what it does? You do see the audacity in that, don't you?'

She certainly saw the fault in it and the fault was all hers. She'd encouraged this when she should have evicted him from her box. In a moment of weakness, a moment of missing Adam on a difficult day, she'd had her head turned by a handsome man. She should have challenged him the moment he'd suggested the appointment. Instead, she'd opted for petty raillery over rising early that contained a hint of bawdry innuendo. 'Do you have appointments at *The Times* today as well? Perhaps you'd like to discuss with them why they didn't run a follow-up story to the newly signed Perpetual Maritime Truce in the Lower Gulf?'

He chuckled at her attempt to shame him with hyperbole. 'The Bilberry Dam is much closer to home and it is an issue which has already been settled. News by its very definition is *new*, something that is as yet unexplored or shared with the masses. What is there new when it comes to the dam?' He paused, a question on his handsome face. 'You *are* aware that a case cannot be reopened and retried without new facts, are you not?'

'I am aware of how the law operates, Lord Umberton.' Her temper rose. He was baiting her on all fronts. She did not care for the condescension veiled as 'politely informing' her about the function of the law.

'Then you *do* have new information?' he said eagerly. 'The articles hint at it, but one wonders what the sources might be and why they weren't brought forward earlier when all of this was considered the first time.'

The man vacillated like a weathervane. What should she pay attention to? The eagerness in his voice because he meant to be her ally and wanted to test the veracity of her claims before he aligned himself? Or should she be wary of the discreet, polite jabs his conversation took at her knowledge of the law and the lateness of presenting this recent angle? Or, a third option reared its head to make the game even more complicated, was he baiting her in the hopes of fishing for information? Did he want her to spill all she knew? If so, for what purpose?

In defence, she took a leaf from his own book. 'I'm not sure how much *you* know about quality journalism, Lord Umberton, but an honourable reporter protects their sources.'

He levelled his gaze at her, the topaz of his eyes sharpening at her tone. 'Let me ask you this, then. Are you instigating this or is the paper reporting on behalf of others?'

'I can't reveal that.' She held her ground, wishing she could dislike his line of questioning as much as she liked his gaze. Any other man would have been evicted from her office by now. 'I don't see how it makes a difference, nor do I see what business it is of yours. Why are you interested?'

'Because I sit in the House of Lords and the dam accident was the product of communal negligence. I would like to see that an accident of that magnitude does not happen again. There are other dams in England, Mrs Griffiths.' He paused before adding sharply, 'Perhaps that makes my curiosity less banal to you.'

That sounded more like an ally despite the rebuke and Fleur felt a trill of excitement race through her. It was beginning! Shortly after the dam accident last year, she'd hoped MPs would introduce legislation on their

own after the call to action from the Holmfirth report
which had been clear that laws were needed. But after a
year, nothing had been forthcoming. Yet here was trac-
tion at last and from higher up the ladder of power than
she'd dared to hope. She might get both justice *and* the
long-elusive legislation passed with a man like Umberton on her side. And his friends. Where he led, surely
others would follow.

'I think you and I may have almost got off on the
wrong foot, Lord Umberton.' She smiled, determined
to seize the opportunity.

'Almost?' He arched a dark brow, but his eyes were
flirting with her. 'You've called me audaciously entitled and accused me of using that title to selfishly satisfy my curiosity.'

She answered his teasing eyes with a lift of her own
brow. 'And you barged into my box, quite disrupting my
night.' In ways he could not imagine. She'd had to seek
self-pleasure after midnight to find any relief.

'Then we are even, the playing field levelled,' he
suggested, the conversation becoming more game than
negotiation.

'Perhaps we can start again, beginning with lunch.
Can I interest you in an early déjeuner at Verrey's on
Regent Street? If we leave now, we can get a head start
on the noon crowd.'

He put on a show of considering the offer, clearly enjoying the transition to the easy by-play between them.
'You turned down my supper invitation. Why should I
accept yours to lunch?'

'Because we are starting over and we are no longer
strangers,' she replied, doing some flirting of her own.

'What sort of woman goes to supper with a man she's just met? I had to decline on principle no matter how tempted I *might* have been.'

He gave an infectious grin. 'You *were* tempted?'

'Maybe a little,' she answered with a smile of her own. 'I am assuming that's a yes for lunch?'

'I am not in the habit of refusing lunch invitations from beautiful women.' Good lord, how he loved an assertive woman. A debutante of the ilk his mother was always throwing his direction would never dream of inviting him to lunch. Jasper stood and held her coat. She shrugged into it and he caught a coy whiff of her scent: notes of vanilla and jasmine mixed with something he couldn't name.

It was enough to make him smile. So that was what confidence smelled like. No delicate roses or sweet lilies for this woman. Of course not. Such delicacy didn't suit a woman who sat alone at the theatre and scolded anyone who dare intrude on her sanctuary even as she flirted with her eyes and considered bold proposals—both his and hers.

It prompted him to wonder what other proposals might be made between them. But such wondering came with a warning. To make this into anything more than what it was intended to be—a fact-finding mission—came with complications. He would need to choose his response wisely. Orion and the family were counting on him, as was his good common sense. Francis Bacon would not approve of being ruled by spontaneity.

Chapter Four

Verrey's Café was an interesting choice. The main floor was long and narrow, dotted with small, square tables draped in white tablecloths that stretched back to a three-quarter wall of mirrored glass in the rear that gave the space an added sense of largeness. It was still early for lunch. Only a smattering of patrons sat at the tables.

The restaurant was quiet and of that Jasper approved as the maître d' led them to a discreet table at the back, partially hidden from common view by potted palms. Jasper approved of that, too. For all her boldness, it seemed Mrs Griffiths had a sense of discretion, as well. This was a nearly invisible table and she was dining in advance of the crowd. The woman liked her privacy.

'I can't decide, Mrs Griffiths, if you're simply circumspect in your social behaviours or if you don't want to be seen with me,' he offered wryly as they took their seats. In truth, he preferred the privacy as well. There was less chance someone would recognise him and call him Meltham.

She fixed him with her green eyes, emeralds when scolding, grass green in her softer moments. They were emeralds at the moment. 'I eat for fuel because my body demands it. I do not eat for the sake of being seen.'

He could not resist. 'And the theatre? Is it fuel or for being seen?'

'Fuel,' she answered without hesitation. 'For my mind, for my soul.'

'And yet your gown last night was made to be seen,' he prompted with a little argument. She might have sat alone, might have claimed she wanted no intrusion, but in that gold gown she had to have known she invited intrusion. She'd not passed the evening unremarked. His were not the only opera glasses that had lingered on her box.

'I like fine clothes. They are a fuel of another sort, a fuel for my eyes, for my fingers. I love the textures, the layers.' The confession carried a sensual quality to it or was his imagination running away with him at the thought of her touch on his sleeve, her fingers stroking the tight weave of his superfine coat? It was an unseemly thought about a woman who was most likely his enemy.

The waiter came and set the first course down in front of them, *oeufs à la Russe* with grey caviar for the discerning gourmet who would not appreciate black carp roe. Verrey's was one of those fine restaurants where menus were not necessary. Regulars knew already what was served or at least knew with confidence that whatever the chef chose to put on the table would be excellent. To have a menu was to mark oneself as an outsider.

'I must be seen, of course,' she added with a touch of ruefulness when the waiter left. 'It inspires confidence in those I do business with to see me out and about, expensively gowned as if I haven't a care in the world. It tells them that the syndicate is solvent, that it is business as usual even if Adam Griffiths is no longer at the helm. To become a recluse would be to inspire panic and concern.'

Her comment struck a note of empathy within him. He understood that need to be seen. If it were up to him, he'd spend his life at Rosefields, puttering with his science experiments. But the title didn't allow for that. The Marquess must be seen, the very sight of him a reassurance that all was well for those who counted on him. He spent his days in service to those people as Mrs Griffiths spent her days in service to her people.

'Did the theatre feed your soul, then, despite the need for a public display?' he asked as they ate. It seemed odd to him that one might find solace in a farce. A Shakespeare tragedy he could understand. But a comedy? They were made for laughing more than soul-searching reflection. But perhaps she'd had no choice if she wanted to be seen. What had she been looking for last night? He might examine later why it mattered so much to him to find out.

'Yes. Last night I was thinking of my friends. Remembering. My husband and I shared the box with Lord Luce and Mr Popplewell and their wives.' There was a shadow in her eyes as the waiter cleared the table and another set down plates of *sole à la Dugléré*. 'I had not been to the theatre since the accident. Last year I was in mourning, of course,' she explained, taking a flaky forkful of the fish.

Jasper felt like a cad. The evening had been of some

significance to her, a private commemoration of sorts, and he'd barged in to disrupt it. He deserved every word of her set down and more. In retrospect, he thought he'd got off rather easily. 'I must apologise again for my intrusion. It could not have been more poorly timed.'

She gave a small smile, but said nothing. What was he expecting? Absolution? Did he want her to say it was all right? She was too astute for that and he admired her for not letting him off for his intrusion. He'd behaved badly.

'Are your friends, the wives, not in town? Could they not have joined you?' Surely she hadn't needed to face the box and its memories alone last night.

She shook her head, her mood lightening slightly. 'They are both living abroad.' She slid him a sly look. 'Both of them have found new husbands.' She raised her wine glass, containing a sharp white wine. 'One of them has married the man who provides the wines to Verrey's and other fine establishments in London. The other has sailed with her true love to Tahiti. They are not married yet, but they soon will be.'

'I do recall now reading about the Popplewell department store fire and the story the *London Tribune* ran about the Popplewell's contributions to the community.' His mother had been devastated. She'd been looking forward to the new shopping experience.

'Well, Antonia has turned tragedy into triumph.'

'Yes, I hear she sold the store and her other business interests to the Duke of Cowden for a tidy sum.' Was that what Fleur Griffiths envied? Did she wish to sell and unburden herself from the enterprises her husband had chosen? After a year in the editor's seat, was it proving too much? Yet here she was, using her papers to renew interest in the Bilberry Dam. That scenario seemed unlikely.

'Do you desire to follow in Mrs Popplewell's footsteps?' He studied her, trying to read her expression. What was hidden there? Regret? Grief? Envy?

'To new lands or new husbands?' she parried, meeting him with a bold gaze. 'What makes you think I want either?'

'You said you were missing your friends. It is not unrealistic to suppose you felt their new husbands have competed for their attentions and won.' Fleur Griffiths struck him as the type of woman who enjoyed competition, but not losing. He toyed with his wine glass, shooting her a strong look at the last. 'Perhaps you miss what they now have?'

Her retort was sharp. 'And what exactly do they have?' The boldness of his question was not lost on her.

'They have love again and they both have a second chance for whatever their former lives failed to give them,' he mused out loud.

'I am happy for my friends, not because they have new husbands but because they have what they need. If that need comes in the form of a man, then so be it.' She took a swallow of her wine. The swallow was manufactured, he'd wager, to cover emotion. He'd turned over a few rocks with his comments. Why not flip another one over?

'What of your need, Mrs Griffiths? What would you do with a second chance?' he enquired.

'Perhaps I don't need a second chance. Perhaps I have all that I require. I have my work. Running a newspaper syndicate is an all-consuming job. It leaves little time for other things,' she replied hotly, outwardly offended by his assumption, but it evidently wasn't the entire truth as something shifted in her eyes, darkening them with another shadow. This woman still grieved, although not only for her husband. She'd lost something more, something beyond Adam Griffiths, something her husband had perhaps been a gateway to.

A family? Children? How ironic that her husband's job pulled him away from such things whereas Jasper's position as a marquess drew him in, binding him and his family ever more tightly together. His fate was their fate, and their fates were his. Something he'd best remember when dealing with Mrs Griffiths. His intrigue with her was slowly leading him from the intended path. The questions that filled his mind weren't about the dam or the information she had linking Orion to the disaster, but about her—what did she want from life? Did she enjoy the newspaper business?

'I have all I need, Lord Umberton.' She was cool again. 'I have my work. There is little time for anything else at present.'

He paused his questions and took a small spoonful of the *crème pistache* that had just been set in front of them—cool and green, like Mrs Griffiths's eyes. At this proximity, the comparison could not be escaped. 'Is that why you've opened the dam investigation again? Your work demands it? Or does something more demand it?' It was time to bring the conversation back to business.

'My work *is* the search for truth. That is why I am bringing the Bilberry Dam to the public's attention again. Is that not your work as well? As a member of the House of Lords?'

'And you feel the truth is that Lord Orion Bexley is at fault for the entire accident? Your articles suggest as much.' He watched her face carefully.

'His name is the one thread that runs through the paperwork documenting the building of the dam, the issues with the dam's structural integrity as well as the lax oversight of the commission. The verdict was clear that in order for a conviction to be made, there must be a singular culprit. I think one has emerged.'

She was so sure, so confident as she said the words. He saw the situation from her perspective: find a culprit, blame him, claim a verdict. And then what? Had she thought beyond that for herself, for all who would be affected? Her confidence did raise some concern for him. What did she think she knew that fuelled that confidence? What did she know that he did not? Because, not for a minute did he think Orion had told him everything. Worry in the form of sweat began to bead beneath his collar and pristine cravat.

He gathered his calm. 'Forgive me for the bluntness, Mrs Griffiths, but what have you discovered that Captain Moody's investigation and the subsequent enquiry did not see at the time? Captain Moody is known for his thoroughness. It is hard to believe something this significant went without his notice.'

'The enquiry was thorough and it was expedient,' she agreed, her tongue flicking over the tiny spoon of *crème pistache* in a manner that spoke to him of other ways that tongue might be employed. 'But while expediency has its merits, it does not allow enough time for deep truth to bubble to the surface, for patterns to be unearthed and understood. But I've had time.' The last rang like a warning in his mind.

'If I am to come alongside your new efforts, I would want to know what those patterns are. You must understand that a man's reputation is a precious commodity. I cannot squander it on conjecture.'

Her eyes flared and her shoulders straightened. 'And a woman's reputation is to be squandered on conjecture?' He'd insulted her. 'Do you think I am in the habit of running a newspaper syndicate on conjecture and rumour? I assure you, when I tell you I have real evidence by which the dots can be connected, that I have it.'

Another frisson of concern snaked down Jasper's back. *What if she did?* What if Orion was indeed involved? Orion and Trouble were fast friends. He immediately felt disloyal to his brother for the traitorous thought. The onus of proof should be on this green-eyed minx who sought to stir up that trouble.

The waiter brought coffee to signal the end of the meal, a meal that had provided Jasper with food for both body and thought. 'I would like to know your goals. What do you hope to accomplish?'

She fixed him with a long incredulous stare as if it wasn't obvious to him. 'Why, justice, Lord Umberton. It has been a year and more and there's been no legislation introduced to improve dam oversight and there's been no attempt to make a conviction.'

He was swift to correct her. 'There *has* been an attempt and it was unsuccessful because a conviction was not possible. I do agree. The lack of forthcoming legislation is immensely disappointing given that the findings at the dam strongly identified a need for it. I can give you help with legislation.' He gave a shrug. Legislation was something they could agree on, something he could help deliver.

On the strength of that common ground, she might entrust him with the information she had regarding Orion's involvement with the dam accident. If he was to test the veracity of her information, he had to have access to it. His conscience stirred a bit at that. He was walking a fine line here. But the pursuit of truth and logic demanded he set aside empathy. How else would he know what he was really up against?

He did care about dam legislation. Meltham wasn't far from Holmfirth. The dam project that serviced the rivers in that area was a constant concern for him. He'd hoped having Orion on the commission would have been a step towards better management. But the reverse had happened instead. It was imperative he know how deep in Orion was.

'Legislation is a start, but it is *not* justice for what happened,' she said in a stern tone. He could not miss the emotion beneath.

Jasper gave a slow stir to his coffee, mixing in the cream and watching it lighten as he carefully chose his words. 'And justice is not the same as vengeance. I wonder if you've confused the two.' He watched her go still and braced himself for an outburst that could very well see his coffee dumped on his lap. No matter how she tried to mask it, Mrs Griffiths had a temper. Emotion was beneath her words, beneath her choices. She wasn't afraid to boldly speak her mind. She was a woman who *felt* things, a stark contrast to his own logic.

'I think you overstep yourself on such brief acquaintance,' she said quietly. Too quietly. 'There are very few people who dare to speak to me that way.'

'Then perhaps there should be more,' Jasper countered. 'Have you thought of what happens if Lord Orion Bexley is legally prosecuted? Or even if he is just socially prosecuted by his peers, which has already begun? Let me remind you that actions have consequences, Mrs Griffiths. For better or worse, a man's life will be ruined, his family's as well simply by association. And all for what? What will that ruination achieve? What will it change?'

She gave him a long look and for a moment he thought perhaps she'd seen through him, that he'd pushed too far and given away his hand. He didn't expect his little ruse to last for ever. All she had to do was look him up in *Debrett's* if she was interested in Baron Umberton. But he did prefer it last a bit longer until he could complete his reconnaissance.

'He is the brother of a marquess. If anything, he ought to be held to a higher standard. He has all the advantages most people lack and his one responsibility is to take care of his people. He couldn't even do that.'

'Spoken like a woman who resents the peerage,' he commented wryly. 'Is that why you've picked him out? Because he's a lord, even if just an honorary one.'

'I don't hate the peerage. I'm having lunch with you, aren't I? I've picked him out because he is guilty,' she snapped. 'I can't decide, Lord Umberton, if you are friend or foe. One moment I think we could be allies in this and the next you're warning me off pursuing a legitimate culprit.'

He thought that, too. One moment he was trying to protect his brother, discover the truth of Orion's association with the dam accident, and the next his mind was running riot with a thousand curiosities about Fleur Griffiths. 'I'm not warning you off, Mrs Griffiths. I would not seek to decide for you or to know your mind.'

He certainly wasn't seeking to obstruct the pursuit of the truth. He wanted to know the truth about Orion's involvement as badly as she did, only for different reasons. 'I am, however, cautioning you to consider the long-reaching ramifications of your choices and to think about your motives for them. I am merely offering counsel since you seem to have none to rely on.'

'You mean I've been left unsupervised to run amok in the world, wreaking havoc.' Her tone was cutting. Fleur Griffiths wasn't afraid to speak her mind.

He inclined his head. 'I would hope not. I would hope you had more decorum and restraint than that. Business is not a place for hot heads. A newspaper is a powerful tool and must be wielded accordingly for the benefit of society.'

'As is a title,' she responded with the sharp heat he'd come to associate with her. He supposed some men would be turned off by her knife-edge sharpness. He was not one of them. Lord help him, but he found it deuced attractive. If it weren't for his brother being involved… Who was he kidding? If it wasn't for his brother, he wouldn't have encountered Mrs Griffiths at all.

Wealthy newspaper widows weren't exactly in his circle of association. She was of the City. He was of the *ton* and seldom did the two meet. There was only one path that would be acceptable for him to pursue with a woman like Fleur Griffiths—a private path that kept to the shadows and ended when he walked a different path to the altar with another woman. He put himself in check. Was he really considering an affair—even in the hypothetical—with the woman who wanted to use his brother as the scapegoat for her grief?

It was perhaps a testimony as to how attracted he was. If only the ladies of the *ton* were half as challenging, half as thrilling. Perhaps it was the danger, the risk that came with her that attracted him, or perhaps it was simply that Fleur Griffith made no secret of the fact that she would bite if provoked.

The bill came to the table and Jasper automatically reached for it, but Fleur Griffiths was faster, her eyes brooking no dispute. '*I* invited *you*,' she said, signing the cheque.

Well, that was an interesting change. A woman had never bought him lunch before. Jasper rose and reached for her coat, holding it for her as she slipped it on. He wasn't sure how he felt about that. It felt disturbingly as if he'd given up a modicum of control. She pulled on her gloves and stepped away from him, their eyes meeting, hers with a message: she who had her own money made her own rules.

He escorted her to the front of the restaurant, the place much fuller than it had been when they'd arrived, his hand light at her back, his body close enough to hers to breathe in the scent of her. 'I shall take a cab from here. I need to return to the office, Lord Umberton.' She made his dismissal clear. Their business was concluded. She would not allow him to drag it out with a cab ride.

He found he didn't like being dismissed any more than he'd liked having his lunch paid for.

'I'll wait until you're safely on your way,' he negotiated smoothly. His honour demanded he not leave even a self-sufficient woman alone on a street corner and his pride demanded he restore the balance of power at least a little before they parted. She needed to know that he would not allow anyone to walk over him.

He hailed her a cab. 'I'll be in touch, Mrs Griffiths, and the next time our meal will be on me,' he said, helping her inside, breathing her in one last time, memorising the scent to decode later.

'I hope our meeting was enlightening.'

'Most enlightening.' He was positively aflame with enlightenment. He could not recall the last time a woman had so tempted him while simultaneously terrifying him. She was indeed trouble. He gave away none of that turmoil. He smiled politely and shut the door, sending the cab off before his town coach pulled to the curb. His own afternoon would be busy indeed, his mind already formulating lists of things he needed to know and answers his brother needed to provide. Orion might have tangled with the wrong person this time. He'd accused her of seeking personal vengeance instead of public justice, but Jasper couldn't shake the nagging question growing in his mind. What if she was right?

Chapter Five

'You think she's right. *You* are taking her side. I cannot believe this.' Orion paused his agitated pacing before the fireplace long enough to push an equally agitated hand through his hair. Jasper wondered if he'd practised the move. Perhaps it had been a mistake to give Orion advance notice of this meeting.

Advance notice had given Orion time to think about how to posture, how to position his arguments and his emotions. Orion was nothing if not the sum of his emotions, all of which he felt entitled to display whenever he felt them. Real adults weren't ruled by their emotions, in Jasper's opinion, or at the very least real adults controlled and contained those emotions.

The thought immediately conjured images of Fleur Griffiths over lunch today. She'd been emotional, heated and then cool in turn, calm at moments, angry in others. But she'd kept those emotions under control. It was fine to feel, just not to feel too much too often, that was Jasper's credo. Too much emotion undermined Baconian law, after all, left a man feeling exposed, vulnerable. He'd had a strong taste of that after his father died. He wasn't willing to drink from that cup again.

'I am not siding with her,' Jasper corrected from the sideboard that held decanters at the ready for a pre-prandial drink. 'I had lunch with her today in order to hear her position.'

'You took her to lunch?' Orion said the words as if he'd indulged in the eighth deadly sin.

'We took lunch together, at Verrey's Café. To be honest, it had not been my intention. She invited me, if you must know.' Jasper crossed the room and handed a tumbler to his brother.

'Why?' Orion swirled the brandy and gave a sorrowful look into its depths. 'You're always asking questions. Did you think of asking that one? *Why* would she invite a man to lunch whom she doesn't know, who is, by the way, related to the man she seeks to pillory? It is not the done thing to dine with one's enemies.'

'Perhaps you should test some of the assumptions undergirding your last statement.' Jasper took a swallow of his drink and waited one beat, then two as dawning came to Orion.

'She doesn't know who you are. You've given her some trumped-up name.'

'Not trumped up, a real name. Baron Umberton. I did not lie to her. I *am* Baron Umberton.' Although he hadn't ever used that title. The Earl of Wincastle had been his honorary title growing up, one of his father's titles bestowed on him at birth.

'You made her believe you were interested in her articles,' Orion went on.

'Also not a lie. I was and continue to remain interested in her articles because they involve you, because you asked me to look into it. I did.' That took a bit of the wind out of Orion's agitated sails. It was time to be serious before Mother arrived in the drawing room. Jasper lowered his voice. 'She has convinced herself you are a person of interest, the one common thread between all the separate pieces that went wrong leading up to the accident.'

Orion merely scoffed. 'I could have told you that from the articles. That's not new. You needn't have gone to lunch to learn that.'

'But I did learn something new, though. I learned that she is the driving force behind it. She's the one who wants to reopen the investigation. She is not merely reporting what someone else has told her.' He waited for the import of that to reveal itself to Orion. When Orion remained blank, he explained, 'She is driven by emotion, by her grief. She has nothing but anger to sustain her. When she realises she has no proof she will have to let the issue drop and face the fact that she was seeking a scapegoat, not justice.'

'But in the meanwhile, I am to bear the brunt of her tirades? The aspersions on my name, on *our* name?' Orion's sense of drama returned. 'How long do you think it will take her to calm down? A week? Maybe two?'

That was a very good question. 'I don't honestly know.' After meeting her today and taking her measure, Jasper wasn't sure she'd calm down quickly or let go of her quest, not on her own at least. This certainly wouldn't be over in a mere set of weeks without some form of iron-fisted intervention. Weeks were like eons to Orion.

'It may take some time before she opens up to me and

shares what she knows. She and I are both interested in proposing legislation for better dam oversight. I hope to build on that connection in order to discover just how strong she thinks her case against you is.'

His conscience gave another kick. He did not like the not entirely honest aspects of the plan, but it was already underway and what else could he do? His father had raised him to be honest, to seek truth, but his father had also imbued him with the importance of responsibility. There was no greater responsibility than caring for the family, protecting the family. What took precedence when the two came into conflict?

'Your plan had better work,' Orion groused ungratefully, oblivious for his dilemma.

'If you don't like it, you can always try cleaning up your own messes for once,' Jasper growled. 'Just tell me this—is there anything legitimate for her to base this new case on? We cannot afford to be ambushed.' He didn't think Fleur Griffiths was someone to make idle claims. If she thought she had something, she truly might. That worried him, especially when Orion hesitated too long to answer, their conversation cut short at the sound of rustling skirts in the hallway.

'Cannot afford to be ambushed about what?' His mother, the Dowager Marchioness of Meltham swept into the room, dressed for a night out. 'I've got the Swintons' ball tonight. Colonel Taggart will call for me after we eat.' She looked between him and Orion. 'Now, what is this about an ambush?'

Orion cleared his throat, a bit of devilry glinting in his eyes. 'Jasper didn't want to be ambushed by anyone on your list of lovely debutantes for him to consider this Season.'

Jasper shot Orion a quelling look. That damnable list was a sore topic because of the subject that always followed the list: when was he going to marry and ensure the succession? 'I don't need a list. I can find my own bride.' He tried to prevent the inevitable production of the list from his mother's pocket or her reticule or wherever she'd happened to stash it at the moment. It was always on her person. But he was too late. She produced it with a flourish. He winced. It seemed longer than the last time he'd seen it.

'Oh, don't look at me like that,' she scolded with affection. 'I assure you every mother in the *ton* has a list. We can go over the list at dinner so that you are not "ambushed". I think you'll see the candidates are all quite reasonable. There's room in the Colonel's carriage for you if you'd like to attend tonight. Many of these girls will be there. It would be very efficient and I know how you like efficiency.'

'No. Thank you for the offer, though, Mother. I have some business that requires my attention this evening. You should take Orion.' He shot his brother an *I-am-getting-even* look followed by a lift of his brow that said *You-owe-me-because-I-worked-all-day-on-your-behalf.*

Orion shot him a resigned glare before smiling at their mother. 'I would love to go.' The butler announced dinner and Orion offered Mother his arm. 'Whose lists am I on?' he asked as if he didn't know the only lists he was on were the naughty ones. 'Do you think *I* should marry soon? Perhaps a wealthy heiress?' Orion was the king of distractions and he could make their mother laugh. For that, Jasper would forgive Orion nearly anything. It had been an invaluable gift in the early days after their father's death when Mother had been inconsolable.

Despite his earlier dissatisfaction with his brother, Jasper couldn't help but chuckle to himself as he watched the two go in ahead of him, their blond heads bent together, Orion charming, his mother laughing as she said, 'Oh, not you, not yet, my dear. You needn't rush to marry.'

Watching them brought fond memories. It had always been this way ever since he and Orion had been allowed down to dine with his parents. He'd been fourteen, Orion seven, and he'd been the one to insist Orion be able to join them, that they should dine as a family when he was home from school. Orion and Mother made a habit of going in together while he and Father, the 'men of the house', had lagged behind, talking business about the estate.

He remembered how his father's gaze would follow his mother in those moments, his eyes soft with contentment, shining with love. Some would argue his parents' marriage had been the best of both worlds—a marriage made on the grounds of mutual respect, but which had blossomed into an abiding love over time. Then his father had died and he'd seen how the loss broke his mother, how she'd cried and wept, how her strength had deserted her for a time. He did not want that for himself. Love hurt; love cut deeply. To him, it was the greatest of illogical ironies that something meant to be beautiful could turn so ugly.

Would Fleur Griffiths agree with him? His thoughts

seemed to drift rather too easily to her. Wasn't she also proof of the damaging capacity of love? She was so wrecked by grief and anger that even a year later she was still looking for a culprit, someone to pin her loss on, even when empirical evidence already suggested she would not find that someone.

If that was what love did to people, he had no use for it. He was the Marquess. He could not afford to be weak. A weak man could not protect his family. He'd promised his father on his deathbed that he would care for Mother and for Orion always, that the family would go on, would continue to thrive. A weak man could not keep that promise.

No, he was quite certain that love was a luxury that was not for him. He had to protect his family, his people, his lands and for that he had to be strong. He glanced towards the family shield that hung over the fireplace as he passed. *Officio et Diligentia Semper.* Duty and diligence always. Love did not factor into it. Such was the life of a marquess.

Burning the midnight oil, toiling over ledgers and adding up unrelenting columns while everyone else had long gone home to families and hot meals. Such was the life of a news syndicate owner. Fleur sat back from the desk and stretched. She'd been working relentlessly since she'd returned from lunch. Her stomach rumbled in reminder that *that* meal had been ten hours ago. That meal had been a delicious feast for the tongue as well as the eyes, which was the very reason she'd assigned herself a punishing list of tasks that needed completing. If she went home she'd have nothing to distract her.

She'd spend her evening reliving lunch with the all too attractive Baron Umberton. He was exactly the sort of man her uncle had wished she'd married. The amount of thought dedicated to Umberton was a sure sign that she'd been alone too long. Not that she needed another sign. Last night had been proof enough. This afternoon's luncheon was merely affirmation of what she already knew: she was lonely.

You ought to take a lover. That would appease your loneliness.

Her inner voice whispered the wicked temptation. It wasn't the first time she'd thought of it. Nor would it be the first time she'd acted on it. She had taken a lover last autumn in the wake of Emma's marriage. It had been an *adequate* experience. There had been comfort, but not much else. But perhaps it had been too soon. Maybe she'd expected too much, been too desperate. Perhaps with the distance of a year, it might be better.

Fleur walked to the sideboard and poured herself a midnight brandy from Adam's favourite decanter of Baccarat cut-crystal. It had been a gift from Emma and Garrett one Christmas. Garrett had been a staunch believer in investing in Baccarat crystal. The memory made her smile. She raised her glass to the ghost in the room. 'I miss you, Adam.' She took a long swallow, letting the brandy burn her throat, wishing it could burn away the pain, too, burn away the sense of loss.

She felt closest to Adam in this space that had been his office in London where they'd spent most of their time. Like the Newcastle office, the room still bore the marks of him: the cherrywood panelling, the green damask wallpaper, the masculine accoutrements—the decanters, the globe, the paperweight, the heavy furniture and draperies—a shrine to a successful man who'd reached the apex of his career.

Yet Adam had not been perfect. The imperfections that had lingered beneath the surface of their life together, both personal and professional, had bubbled *to* the surface. She'd given up her life for him and in exchange he'd left her the burden of a news syndicate in debt. Revenue was down. Confidence in her leadership was down. How long would the board of directors allow her to continue if she couldn't right their course? She didn't know what to do. She'd tried generating more revenue by selling more ads, by offering subscription specials to bring in new readers, all the usual strategies. But still, circulation remained stagnant.

It was a hard pill to swallow in acknowledging that she was the reason for some of the stagnation. People were leery of a woman at the helm. It helped only somewhat that she was Adam's widow. She understood that she borrowed credibility from him. But she was also honest. It wasn't entirely her fault. There'd been debt before his death and he'd hidden it from her. Discovering the debt had felt like a betrayal.

Fleur felt anger flare. For both of them. Her anger had more than one source. How dare Adam leave her with this burden. Newspaper debt was a fact of journalistic life. It went in cycles. She could tolerate that. What she couldn't tolerate was the secrecy. Adam had *kept* this from her and she'd been ambushed with it. She'd appeared unprepared in front of the board of directors. On a personal level, the betrayal went deeper. The secrecy was further proof she and Adam hadn't been partners in the truest sense, that while she'd given him everything, Adam had two separate lives despite the fact that they lived and worked together.

She shook a fist at the empty room. 'You should have told me. Damn it! Why didn't you tell me?' Had he doubted her? Was that why? 'You set me up for failure,' she said to the ghost in the room. She didn't need any help there. She'd become quite good at failing all on her own. She could not fail him in death as she'd failed him in life. She owed him. It was too late to atone for being a selfish wife, for not kissing him goodbye that last night, for pressing him about a child when he'd been clear he didn't want one. How could she atone if she couldn't do this, couldn't hold on to the thing he'd spent his life building? Saving the syndicate was her last chance.

She'd spent the night racking her brain for a solution. The best she could come up with was that she could sell some of the smaller papers, focus her attentions on the papers in the significant regional cities and the *Tribune* in London. That would keep the business stabilised for a while until she could figure out a way to increase growth. But the choice undermined Adam's mission to bring news to all parts of England and with it to bring literacy to rural villages.

To Adam, news was about information, about sharing power with all citizens and that required the ability to read and the ability to have access to something *to* read. When she'd first met him, she'd been as attracted to that vision as she was the man. Here was a man who felt as she felt, believed as she believed. She'd cherished that similarity between them. Together, they had nurtured those ideals. It would positively gut her to sell off those rural papers. But what else could she do?

Even that decision was not risk free. There would be ramifications to either choice. To sell might be akin to signalling blood in the water. Selling might make investors and subscribers all the more hesitant. But to *not* sell meant she had to find another way to generate subscriptions and funds. Perhaps she should consult with the Duke of Cowden who she knew through his wife, the Duchess, and the charity work on the literacy ball. Cowden had a mind for business and investment. He would have advice about the direction she should go. Meanwhile, she needed a good story, something that would sell papers.

She *had* a good story. There'd been a slight uptick in sales in the north when she'd run the Bilberry Dam articles. Of course, the dam accident was still very much on their minds. In the north, by Holmfirth and York, people lived with the residue of the accident daily. They were still recovering fiscally and physically from the ruins. And of course, Meltham was in the north. Lord Orion Bexley was a person of interest to northerners more so than he'd be a person of interest to someone in Bristol in the west. Perhaps it was time to run another article. If she wanted to bring about justice, she had to keep the pressure on.

Umberton had called her justice vengeance today in that quiet but firm tenor of his, those topaz eyes studious and considering. There was no doubting he was a serious man with serious thoughts. Which stirred her anger. What did he know of it? It was only an accident to him, whereas it was a disaster to her. It had changed everything. She simply could not share the same level of detachment he brought to it. But he could still be her ally. He was the one person in London who'd shown direct interest.

An idea came to her as she finished her drink. He could be the first link in the chain she'd forge, the first of the powerful lords and MPs she could rally to her banner if she could gain an introduction through the right kind of person—and Umberton was definitely the right kind of person.

Not just for politics either. Her inner voice was active tonight. *Perhaps you might have a dual purpose for him? There was more than business between you last night and again this afternoon.*

Perhaps. Perhaps it would be all right to mix a little pleasure with business just this once, especially since there would be no expectations beyond the moment.

Fleur returned to her desk and drew out a piece of stationery with the *Tribune's* letterhead on it and drafted two notes, one to Cowden and one to Umberton, realising as an afterthought she had no idea where to reach Umberton. She stifled a yawn. She'd tackle that in the morning. For now, weariness had found her at last. Thank goodness. Sleep was all too rare for her. The downside was that she was too tired to make her way home. She would sleep on the long leather sofa in the office. After all, what did it matter if she slept at home or here? Either way, she'd be sleeping alone. Nothing awaited her but her dreams. That was her penance. It was no less than what she deserved.

Chapter Six

The letter was waiting for him at White's when Jasper arrived the next afternoon, looking for peace and quiet, none of which was to be had at Meltham House. Today was his mother's at-home, the one afternoon a week when she invited every worthy matron and their eligible daughters to flood her drawing room in the hopes he'd make an appearance. He'd done his duty today, mostly to appease his mother and to make up for not having gone to the Swintons' ball with her last night. He'd spent twenty minutes in the drawing room meeting some of his mother's favourites from the list before he'd made his escape.

Jasper took his usual seat in a club chair at the back of the room. He turned the letter over, studying the crisp, strong hand in which the address had been written: *Lord Umberton, White's*.

A rather simple address that offered not a lot of information other than that it was from *her*. Only Mrs Griffiths would call him that. She'd written, so soon after their lunch. The thought of seeing her again made his blood hum, like a soldier preparing for battle. But that humming was quickly tempered, two thoughts occurring to him before he even broke the seal.

First, she'd been rather ingenious to send it here in her deduction that the odds were decent he was a member—many lords were. He saw, too, that this message was an attempt to balance the power between them. If she could find him, she could level the playing field. Right now, he was the only one with a way to contact or reach her. He knew where she worked. He could contact her at any time. But she could not contact him. Not without some guesswork, which was what this was.

That led to the second realisation. The staff at White's had known he was Umberton. If they knew, did she know? Was his element of surprise up already?

The waiter came with his brandy and the newspapers. 'Stay a moment.' Jasper halted him when he would have slipped away with customary unobtrusiveness. Jasper waved the note. 'How did you know I was Umberton?' It was not a title he'd ever publicly used. It was simply one more thing that had come with the entailment. The waiter looked nervous. 'I am only curious, I mean nothing more by it,' he coaxed the man to relax.

'We didn't know, my lord,' the waiter confessed. 'We weren't sure who to give the letter to, so the manager looked it up in *Debrett's*. We keep a copy downstairs for membership purposes.'

'Very good, I like that. Taking initiative to solve a little mystery,' Jasper complimented to assure him he'd done nothing wrong. 'Thank you.' He dismissed the waiter with a smile, but he was already making a mental note to find a better way, a less *public* way, for Mrs Griffiths to contact him.

He slipped a finger beneath the sealing wafer and read. It was good news and bad. The good news was that she was eager to meet again to start working on a legislative proposal. The bad news was that in her boldness, she'd already concocted a plan. She wanted him to take her to a ball or two for the sake of making introductions to others in Parliament who might be of help. She even had a list enclosed. Jasper sighed. What was it with ladies and lists? Perhaps it was something they were born with.

He scanned the balls she'd chosen. He couldn't possibly comply. People would know him there. He'd be Meltham to them. There were solutions to that, though. He took a swallow of brandy for thinking. One option was to come clean with her. Telling her was inevitable anyway, it was just a matter of when. Timing was important because there *would* be repercussions. Most likely, he would be cut off from further participation in her investigation. She would be furious for what she would perceive as duplicity.

Originally, that hadn't mattered to him. He'd thought to see her once, determine what she knew and what she meant to do with it. That would be it. He'd not planned on there being more to learn, more to do. He wasn't ready to let the association go.

Be fair, his conscience nudged, *you are not ready to let her go. You're attracted to her and her saucy tongue.*

The other option was that he knew where she'd be. He could make sure he wasn't in the same place. Of course, he'd have to persuade her that splitting their attendance at events was in their better interest, that they could cover twice as much ground. He would attend events she could not get invited to and she could continue to cultivate her circles. But to persuade her, he'd have to see her. A letter would not suffice.

He gestured for the waiter. 'Can you send an errand boy to Fortnum and Mason for a tea basket? I need it delivered to the *London Tribune* to Mrs Fleur Griffiths.' He pulled out his pocket watch. 'By three o'clock.' Two hours from now. That should be plenty enough time to gather his thoughts and prepare for a battle of wits, a prospect that was more thrilling than it ought to be.

A thrill ran through Fleur at the sight of the tea basket delivered to her desk by a wide-eyed clerk. *He was coming.* With his topaz eyes, tousled curls and argumentative nature. Her pulse raced. She didn't need a note to tell her that. He'd warned her as much yesterday at the curb. *Next time our meal will be on me.* He'd not liked the idea of 'owing' her. Well, *she'd* not liked the idea that by not giving her a way to contact him, he had seized control of determining when they might meet again. Clearly, her shot in the dark—or at least in the semi-darkness...many lords did belong to White's, after all—had paid off. Her letter had reached him and this was his response: a basket brimming with every possible delicacy and utensil needed for a proper tea right down to a stone bottle of hot water and a pot to pour it in.

How much time did she have? She glanced at her clock. Fifteen until the hour. With hot water on the line, she'd guess he'd be here at three. She set about laying out the tea on the low table by the sofa where she'd slept last night. She unpacked white pastry boxes containing iced lemon scones, ginger nut biscuits and violet crèmes, boxes that contained triangular-shaped finger sandwiches of ham and chicken. There were two hand-painted teacups with matching saucers, linen napkins and two small plates meant for cakes and biscuits, all of which matched the teapot. She wondered if he meant to make a gift of the tea set afterwards? And if he did, what did it signify? Their relationship was still in a nebulous phase where they were neither business partners nor personal acquaintances. A gift at this point would make things...interesting, if not escalated.

Umberton arrived at three, dressed in a jacket of blue superfine and a top hat, a walking stick of blackthorn finished with a brass knob in his hand. He looked like a gentleman out for an afternoon stroll rather than someone making a business call. Is that what she saw because that was what she wished? That this was more than a business call? Fleur smoothed her skirts, suddenly conscious that she was wearing the spare dress she left here for occasions like last night when she didn't go home. It was a nice dress of bright blue cambric patterned with pink and yellow flowers, the short sleeves and scooped neck trimmed in the palest of ivory lace, but it was not a fancy dress, something that had not bothered her until now.

'Your tea has arrived.' She gestured to the table as he took off his hat and made himself at home. 'It is quite lavish, more like a meal than a snack.' She led the way to the sofa, acutely aware that there would be little separating them beyond the voluminous layers of her skirts. Every fibre of her being seemed to be intensely aware of his presence today in new ways. Perhaps that was due to the new thoughts that had plagued her last night.

'I remembered what you said about meals being merely fuel. I guessed you might not be in the habit of fuelling up as regularly as you ought.' His eyes twinkled. 'Am I right? Did you skip breakfast this morning? Perhaps even lunch?' He sat, crossing a long leg over one knee. If their closeness on the sofa was of particular note to him, he gave no sign of it.

'You are very intuitive, Lord Umberton.' She settled her skirts. 'You are close. I skipped dinner last night after our lunch together. I woke up ravenous, but I only had time for a sweet bun and coffee and I skipped lunch.' She waved a hand towards her messy desk in explanation. 'Too much to do. So, yes, I am hungry.' She gave him a considering look. 'I do not know if I find your intuition endearing or downright intrusive.'

'That makes two of us, then. *Your* intuition sent a letter to hunt me down at my club.' He smiled, eyes warm. 'We are two people who value their privacy and yet we've invaded each other's on multiple occasions now.'

'The letter was more deduction than intuition,' she corrected, reaching to pour the tea. 'This is a pretty teapot, by the way. What do you intend to do with it after today?' No time like the present to address that particular elephant in the room. There were others, of course, a veritable herd of them, but she'd start with this one.

He took the cup and added his own cream. Ah, so he liked cream in his tea *and* his coffee. 'I mean to leave it here in case we have tea again.' His eyes were on her over the rim of his teacup as he took a small sip.

'Do you think we will have tea again?' Fleur queried

carefully, understanding full well that after two meetings, today was a watershed of sorts, determining how they would go forward.

'We'll see. I like to be prepared for eventualities.' That was no answer at all. He took another sip of his tea and filled his plate with items from the tray. 'I wasn't sure what you liked so I ordered a bit of everything.' He gave a boyish wink as the food piled up on his plate. 'I'll tell you a secret. I skipped lunch, too. Today is the day my mother hosts at-homes at the town house and I wanted to make my bow and get out of there as fast as possible. Eating would only have delayed my departure.'

'What's wrong with your mother's at-homes?' The reporter in her immediately sensed a story, a point of interest, or was that the woman in her who wanted to know more about this man with the quiet manners and powerful personality? Where was the line between the two roles?

'They're full of women with daughters who want to marry me.' It was clear he said it without thinking and they both laughed. 'I'm sorry, that came out a bit arrogant and unfeeling.' He gave an abashed smile that was all too endearing.

'It was honest.' Fleur reached for a violet crème. '*Do you expect to marry this year?* If it is not too personal to ask,' she added, but she suspected it wasn't and that he would answer since he'd brought it up. Perhaps because it weighed on his mind and he wanted to talk about it— he just needed an opening and perhaps a stranger to tell.

'Do I expect to marry this year?' He shook his head. 'If only it were that simple. I just have to put it on the calendar as if it were another appointment, as if it were as easy as going to Tattersall's and selecting a horse for this year's hunt season.' He gave a self-deprecating chuckle that communicated the opposite—that this was no laughing matter. 'I can't seem to bring myself to reduce it to such a common denominator. Perhaps it would all be easier if I did. My mother has a list, you see.' The spark was back in his eyes.

'Tell me about the list,' she prompted out of some type of morbid curiosity. Was she trying to convince herself this fellow was off limits?

'Well, there's Lady Claudia Shipman, daughter of the Earl of Coventry. She has a horsey face and fortune and nothing in common with me.' He devoured a ham triangle in a single bite. 'Then there's Aurelia Dunston…' The list went on with him regaling her with a brief biography of each of his mother's candidates. He'd make a good news writer, she thought. He had a knack for picking out salient details without going off on a tangent.

He was an entertaining storyteller, too. It had been a long time since she'd enjoyed a conversation this much. Too many of her conversations in the past year had been exercises in verbal fencing, protecting herself against probes into the business and the situation Adam had left her with. She could not afford to give too much away.

She poured the last of the tea, dividing it between their cups. The tea tray was down to a few lavender crèmes and ginger nut crumbs. 'It seems as though your mother has a certain type of woman in mind for you.' Obedient, pretty, young, a blank slate for him to write on, to fill with his opinions and purposes. 'But what do you prefer for yourself?' It was clear from his tone that those things did not appeal to him. They'd not appealed to Adam either, although she knew very well that those traits were greatly desired by most men.

He reached for one of the remaining lavender crèmes and popped it into his mouth. He made a sour grimace. 'Yuck.' He turned aside and spat the morsel into his napkin, taking a swallow of tea to wash away the taste. 'Do you like these? Truly? They taste like…soap.'

She laughed. 'I like them. They're…airy…sweet… floral.'

'I prefer floral in my flowers, not my sweets,' he countered, mischief in his eye.

'Some say if clouds had a taste, lavender crèmes would be it.'

'No, absolutely not,' he argued with a laugh. 'Clouds do *not* taste like soap.' He smiled and retrieved the last crème. 'I guess that means this last one is for you.' He leaned forward, offering the crème. Her pulse quickened at the realisation. He meant to feed it to her. She answered his smile with a coy smile of her own, leaning towards him to allow the liberty, the flirting, the lingering of his fingers at her lips, sending a jolt of awareness down her spine, his own topaz gaze meltingly warm, less teasing now and more tempting. The atmosphere in the room changing with the electricity conjured at his touch.

She should not have pressed, knowing full well the question served a dual purpose. 'You haven't answered me yet. What sort of woman do you prefer?' In the interim since the asking it had become a loaded question and he pulled the trigger.

'A woman who knows her own mind, who has her own opinions—well-formed opinions, of course. Anyone can have opinions. Not all are worthy of consideration.' His voice was quiet with an unmistakable husk to it, proof that he felt it, too, the current of awareness connecting them.

'Those kinds of women can be difficult. Demanding. Determined. Are you sure you wouldn't want an easier woman?' Her own voice was also quiet as if they were exchanging secrets. They were weaving intimacy between them with their words.

'Your husband didn't mind such a challenge, why should I want any less?' It was a bold question with a bold implication—that *she* was the sort of woman he sought. An intimate compliment indeed, with intimate opportunity. He filched a remaining ginger nut hidden among the crumbs and broke it in two, feeding her half.

'Will you tell me about him?' He brushed a crumb from her lip with his thumb. 'We've talked about the women who seek to capture me. But what of you? What sort of man was man enough to win you?' The last was said with a chuckle, but it was asked in earnest. This was no joke.

'A bold man.' She smiled, in part because he'd asked. Perhaps he'd sensed that she needed an opportunity to talk about this as much as she'd sensed his need to give voice to his mother's matchmaking efforts. In part she smiled from memory, recalling Adam's courtship over eight years ago.

'We met at Lady Brixton's first ever literacy fundraiser, which she holds during the Season. Adam was very passionate about literacy and early education for children. He believed no one was too young to learn to read and he was appalled at the conditions of the poor, which prevent any opportunity for education.' She paused. 'Lord Brixton is the Duke of Cowden's son—do you know him?' Her uncle had once hoped for an alliance there—Brixton for his niece. But Brixton had eyes only for Helena Merrifield and Fleur had been swept off her feet by Adam.

'I know Cowden, not so much his son, though. I know Brixton only by name as he won a seat in the Commons recently. Our paths have not had a chance to cross yet.'

'Then we should make a chance. Brixton should be on our list for the dam legislation,' she digressed from the personal, offering them an opportunity to bring the conversation back to business. But he didn't allow her to take it. The second half of the ginger nut popped into her mouth.

'I believe we were talking about you, not Brixton,' he scolded with a tease, his voice a low, intimate tenor. 'So, you met your husband at a fundraiser. Then what?' Was it wrong that she wanted his fingers to stay on her lips? To want those fingers elsewhere—on her neck, in her hair, on her body. God, she was lonelier than she'd ever been.

She gave a small smile, their eyes holding. 'Then he kissed me and that was it.' She wet her lips, wanting to stay in the present, not wanting to be dragged into the past. 'You can tell a lot about a man by the way he kisses.' She made the conversation an invitation. This was not as much about Adam any more as it was about her loneliness. If Umberton kissed as well as he looked, maybe she could drive away the loneliness for a while. She'd be willing to try.

His fingers stroked her cheek and lingered, cupping

her jaw. '*I* would like to kiss you.' His lips hovered beneath her ear, his words quiet but bold, turning her blood from warm to hot.

She turned into his touch, catching his wrist with her hand and pressing a kiss to his palm. 'Not if I kiss you first,' she whispered, reaching for him, her hands in the luxurious dark mop of his hair, pulling him to her.

Chapter Seven

{decorative divider}

At the first touch of his lips she knew what this kiss was: mutual madness. His mouth was ready for her and the kiss *she'd* initiated was instantaneously not hers any longer, but *theirs*, the product of an afternoon spent building towards this moment when curiosity and want could no longer be contained by an exchange of stories or pacified by the faintest brush of fingers as he fed her sweets. Combustion was the only outlet left.

Yet even in the meeting of mutual want there was also the mutual need to duel, to dominate, to claim control. Neither of them wanted to be weak, to be subdued. It was there in the press of his mouth, the probe of his tongue, the nip of her teeth as they sank into his lower lip.

Fleur gave a breathless moan that was part-pant, part-gasp, sucking hard on his earlobe as his mouth found her neck. The heat within her escalated with the kiss. The kiss was no longer about mouths meeting mouths, but bodies meeting bodies. He was all tastes beneath her tongue and textures where her hands slid beneath his coat, palms running over the silk of his waistcoat, feeling the plane of muscle beneath.

It wasn't enough. It wasn't enough to taste the tannins left behind by the tea, or to feel the muscle of him beneath his clothes and to know it was there. The more she had of him, the more she wanted of him, this man she barely knew, and in fact had not known forty-eight hours ago, this man who had sought her out and now had her nearly writhing for him in her office. That was unacceptable.

Fleur fisted her hands in the lapels of his coat and broke away with no small effort. Her body did not thank her for it. The only consolation was that he seemed to feel the loss of the contact, too. His topaz eyes were darker now, the colour of a tawny port, his breathing jagged as he gathered himself in the aftermath. But his wits had not deserted him. He gave a slow smile, overtly seductive. 'Well? What does my kiss say about me?'

Fleur took the opportunity to create distance. Goodness knew she desperately needed some. She rose from the sofa, smoothing her skirts and donning the exaggerated pose of a professor delivering a lecture. 'Your kiss suggests you are a man who is used to being in control. When you don't naturally have control, you will find ways to seize it. It also suggests you are a bold man, unafraid to kiss a stranger on the briefest of acquaintance.'

He smiled and leaned back against the sofa, looking entirely too at ease for what had just taken place. 'I won't say you're wrong. I am used to being in control. I was raised to it, it's part of my job. My family, my social position, expects it of me.' There was a twinkle in his eye. 'But I must disagree on the last. I am bold, but are we truly strangers?'

'We've only known each other for two days.' She

was aware he was stalking her with his eyes, recording every swish of her skirt, every movement of her hands.

'Is there a required amount of meetings before we are no longer strangers?' he asked with feigned innocuousness. He was baiting her. 'Three meetings? Four? If we go to lunch tomorrow, will we suddenly be friends? I know married couples who have been together for a lifetime and are still strangers to each other. Yet, I feel as if you and I know each other better than you think even on short acquaintance,' he drawled in a quiet tone.

It was always the quiet ones one had to be on guard for. Who would have thought Lord Umberton with his untamed hair, wire-rimmed glasses and quietly stern tone would be so wild underneath? She smiled and shook her head, his words making her feel warm and pleasant because they matched how she felt and there was relief in knowing he felt it, too, that she wasn't alone. There was some indefinable quality about being with him that spoke to her. The French would call it *je ne sais quoi*.

'Is that all my kiss says to you?'

'Are you fishing for a compliment?' She busied herself picking up the remnants of their tea. It was best he leave now. She wasn't sure where they went from here. Kisses were like that. Watersheds that divided a relationship into two time periods. B.C.—before curiosity was satisfied, or 'before combustion' if one preferred—and A.D.—after detonation. It was like eating from the Tree of Knowledge. Now they knew what it felt like to act on the chemistry between them and in the knowing, they would have to decide what to do next. Choose exile? Never meet again? Pursue the knowledge? Or perhaps try to ignore their knowledge by stuffing it back into the Pandora's box they'd opened. Was that even possible?

'If you don't want to talk about my kiss, shall we talk about yours and what it says about you?' His sibilant tenor was utterly inviting and dangerous. Part of her wanted to return to the sofa, sit down beside him and play the little flirtation game he was initiating, to let it go where it would. But that was an easy out. She knew where it would go with the current climate of the room being what it was. The heat of seduction, the desire for more, the craving, was still here.

If she sat down beside him, she knew where this would lead. She knew, too, that she would regret this. He was the one lord she'd connected with so far who supported her work on the dam. Conflating business with pleasure might jeopardise that connection and, if word got out, it might jeopardise the project's credibility and hers. This was not a decision to be made in the afterglow of a passionate moment. If she was going to sleep with him, she needed to give it some thought and if he wasn't going to leave, she'd have to make him.

'I don't need you to tell me about my kiss. I already know,' she said briskly, piling the linen back into the basket to be returned to Fortnum and Mason. 'My kiss is the product of desperation, of a woman who occasionally suffers bouts of loneliness because she misses her husband and the intimacies of their marriage, both physical and emotional.' She shut the lid of the basket and held it up. 'The basket is ready to be returned. Thank you for the tea.'

He stood slowly, the heat of his eyes cooling as he

registered the dismissal. But by no means was he willing to cede the field. 'Are you saying you used me for sex, Mrs Griffiths?'

'Not sex, Lord Umberton. It was just a kiss,' she corrected, but his words had done their damage, creating images of what might have been—a floor covered in abandoned clothes, bodies entwined on the sofa seeking completion, seeking distraction from the real world, from their individual worlds. They'd not been far from taking that step and perhaps they would have if she'd not called a halt to it.

'And was the kiss successful?' he asked, taking the basket from her, fingers brushing hers where they met at the handle, perhaps on purpose, knowing full well the jolt such contact would send up her arm, a reminder that she could banish him from the room, but not from her thoughts or from her body.

She gave him a cool smile. 'Tut, tut, Umberton. You know better than to ask. A lady never kisses and tells.' Especially when he already knew the answer. He was not oblivious to how she'd roused to him. 'Good day.'

Good lord, what had she done? She watched him exit on to the street and step into his coach, her thoughts in a riot over what had happened and how she felt about it. She'd kissed a man in Adam's office and it hadn't been just a kiss, a physical connection of mouths. She'd *enjoyed* it. It had electrified her because it had electrified *him*. They had been falling *together* on the sofa, their bodies answering one another. It had not been like that before when she'd sought comfort. This had been different. Did she dare pursue it? Did she *deserve* to pursue it while Adam's newspaper foundered and her leadership along with it? Or was this just another way she'd fail Adam?

She'd have her chance to find out. She'd have to see Umberton again. They hadn't done the one thing that they should have. They hadn't discussed business or next steps. At least not next steps with the dam legislation. Which meant two things: she'd have to see him again, and it looked as though she'd be attending the Harefield ball on her own. Lord Harefield was an avid politico with an eye to a cabinet position. He'd be sure to invite guests who could grease the wheels of his own political advancement and she meant to make use of it.

'Mrs Griffiths?' A clerk poked his head in. 'This note came for you. A man in the Duke of Cowden's livery brought it.'

Ah, yes, the other letter she'd sent. It took a moment to bring her thoughts fully back to business. She crossed the room and took the note, smiling as she read the contents. Cowden would see her tomorrow. At least that was one thing that was going right today. She looked up at the clerk. 'Thank you. I have to pick up my gown for the ball, so I'm going to step out and then head home.' He nodded as if he and the staff weren't aware she'd slept here last night. At least they couldn't doubt her dedication. No one could say the paper failed while she danced the night away.

He knew where she'd be tonight. Dancing at the Harefield ball. It had been at the top of the list she'd given him. Jasper stared idly at the pages before him, unable to concentrate on the latest report from his steward at Rosefields, the estate in Meltham. He'd gone back to the town house after tea, confident that his mother's at-home would be finished, the premises safe for unmarried bachelors once more.

He'd had every intention of doing a couple of hours' worth of work before supper, but other than sitting behind the desk in his study, he'd not made any progress. Instead of crop yields, his mind wanted to think about the yield of her lips beneath his, only Fleur Griffiths hadn't yielded for long. It had been a mere strategy before she'd launched her own attack on his senses. Even now, the echoes of her touch reverberated through his body: the caress of her fingers in his hair, the tug of her teeth at his ear, her hands, palms flat, pressed hard against his chest as if they'd prefer to rip the shirt from his body and press against the heat of his skin. His mind and body liked the image of that. He wouldn't mind removing a few of her clothes either. He did, however, mind her motives for it, though.

Jasper played with a pen. The thrill of the kiss, of their interlude, had been tempered by the ending. Reality had a way of dousing even the most heated of passions. She'd been feeling lonely, and he'd been a handy substitute. It was a bit lowering to realise that he'd been nothing more than a tool, a means to an end, an external end, one that had nothing to do with him specifically if she was to be believed. It raised the question of whether or not she'd assuage that need with just anyone?

Jealousy pricked at the idea of Fleur Griffiths kissing another. Perhaps that was just him being proprietary, or, in her words, controlling. He didn't like to share. Or perhaps that was his ego being bruised over the idea he might merely be an interchangeable part for her. *He* certainly did not feel that way about her. He knew that she roused him especially, uniquely.

He couldn't deny that he'd not been roused like this for ages, not since his one early and foolish foray into the realm of amour, his single lapse in Baconian-driven good judgement when he'd let emotions lead the way— nearly to disaster. Between that disaster and his father's death, he had good reason not to indulge again and he hadn't up until he'd met her. He'd had occasional affairs, yes. He wasn't a rake, but he wasn't a monk either. Passionate indulgences though, no. But he *had* indulged today with that kiss.

Truth be told, he'd been indulging since he'd met her—the flirting at the theatre, the lunch that had veered far afield from a discussion of shared business. She'd tempted him from his usual path and he'd allowed it. That bore examination. Why her? Why now? It made little sense. She was not a logical choice for attraction.

You do see the contradiction, don't you? His conscience laughed at him. *You want to logically select a compatible wife and yet you can't bring yourself to select a carefully curated girl from your mother's list and be done with it.*

But just picking a wife from a list wasn't necessarily a good application of Baconian logic either. That damned list assumed his mother knew what he needed and that was a dangerous assumption to make.

Who knew better than he what he wanted in a wife? A partner, a strong woman with strong opinions unafraid to gainsay him when required. A woman who would help him with Rosefields, who would raise his children with him instead of consigning them to the nursery until they were 'interesting'. A woman who saw more than a title and power when she looked at him. A woman who saw *him*.

It wasn't the fault of the girls on his mother's list that they fell short in his categories. Debutantes weren't raised to view a man in that way. How could he expect something of them they weren't able to give? To see? The more powerful the man, the harder it was to see those things.

And so instead you rouse for Fleur Griffiths, who wakes your primal man, and you answer to it. You like it even though it flies in the face of your precious Baconian code. The attraction makes no sense. She's the enemy, but you cannot get enough of her. Why?

Fleur Griffiths had not been daunted by his power or position. Perhaps because she was aware of her own. *She'd* bought *him* lunch, she'd initiated correspondence with him, she'd initiated their kiss and there'd been a few moments on the divan when he'd thought she'd might initiate more than that. She'd asked meaningful questions this afternoon about him. She'd listened when he talked about his mother's list. It was no wonder he didn't feel she was a stranger even after so few meetings. When they were together they spoke their minds. They argued as freely and fiercely as they kissed.

An interesting conjecture began to take shape: had she really meant it today when she'd claimed to have simply used him to assuage her loneliness? It was certainly plausible. He did not doubt that she was lonely. She was not made for loneliness, for a passionless life.

Was that *all* today had been? Was there no part of her that had kissed him just because she wanted to for herself? For the sake of satisfying the curiosity of exploring the spark between them? Because their attraction to one another was unique, despite her claims to the contrary?

It was a hypothesis that would be interesting to test. Testing it would require more research, more observation, more gathering of data. All of which could be done at the Harefield ball. Could he do it without giving himself away? It wouldn't do now to be exposed as Meltham, not when there was so much yet to learn about her.

And learn for Orion, came the sharp reminder.

What was he thinking? This was what happened when one gave passions free rein and forgot logic. This was not all for pleasure, it couldn't be. He needed to remember his original purpose, the only purpose that mattered. No matter how intriguing Fleur Griffiths was, her newspapers were putting his brother in jeopardy with their claims. He could not lose sight of that. Going to the Harefield ball was first and foremost for Orion. For the family. He needed to plan carefully.

His sluggish mind, which hadn't been able to focus on crop yields, was suddenly vibrant and alive with planning. If he arrived late, no one would pay attention to his arrival. Even if he was announced, it would be too crowded for anyone to put a face with his name if anyone noticed at all. Arriving late also meant he could take advantage of others being already involved in their own evening contretemps to pay attention.

She would be none the wiser if he was introduced as Umberton or Meltham. Harefield's would be a crush. The crowd would allow him to be anonymous among them, to have total control of when she saw him and when he approached her. He could waltz with her, take her out to the garden. They would definitely skip supper. That was too risky. He could suggest they have that discussion about business which had eluded them today. What had happened to that discussion anyway? She'd produced her list, and, oh, yes, then he'd produced his and they'd ended up talking about his mother and marriage. They'd never got back on track after that.

He hummed as he headed upstairs to change into evening attire. It was amazing what the prospect of the unusual, a little derring-do, could accomplish in livening up a normal *ton*nish evening. His inner voice wasn't done with pricking, though, as it whispered the dangerous thought, *Maybe it wasn't the derring-do. Maybe it was a woman.*

Chapter Eight

A woman unescorted in a ballroom had to be careful
to cultivate just the right amount of attention: enough
to be noticed, but not enough to become too interesting,
especially when it was that woman's first ball in over a
year. But not her first public appearance, Fleur reminded
herself as she steadied her nerves, moving through the
receiving line leading into the Harefield ballroom. There
were other reminders she gave herself as well: being out
alone was not new to her. She was used to being on her
own in boardrooms and business offices, at the theatre.
She was used to managing the precarious balancing act
of attention. Tonight would be no different.

In the year since Adam's death, Fleur had mastered
the art of attraction. Her position as the head of the
newspaper syndicate had left her no choice. She didn't
have the luxury of becoming invisible. She was expected to lead. The syndicate would never have survived
if she hadn't. And yet there were other expectations for
her as well. Society expected her to mourn, to behave as
a decorous, circumspect widow for the entirety of a year.

Business and society hadn't stopped to wonder how
those differing expectations might co-exist, how she

might manage to straddle those obligations, or even unite them. Yet she'd found a way. Her theatre box had remained empty for a year, but not the chair at the head of the long table in the *London Tribune's* conference room. When board members had questioned her decision, she'd reminded them that it was perfectly acceptable for the public head of a household—she did not dare use the term 'man' here—to discreetly carry on business affairs while in mourning. Her case was no different.

Fleur pressed a hand to her stomach in a quiet, steadying gesture. She had mastered boardrooms, but ballrooms were a different matter. Ballrooms held different memories—personal memories—and it was those memories that were with her now: intimate memories of dancing with Adam, of waltzing with him while he whispered interesting titbits about the guests in her ear that made her laugh and promises about later that made her burn, made her forgive whatever difficulties the day had held.

She reached the front of the reception line and offered her hand to her host. 'Mrs Griffiths, it is a delight to see you this evening.' Lord Harefield bowed over her gloved knuckles.

'I thank you for the invitation. It is time I started circulating in society again. My husband would have wanted me to be abreast of all the political happenings first hand.' She gave the little speech she'd rehearsed in front of her vanity mirror this evening. Two sentences were all she'd have time for with her host and she wanted those sentences to convey a strong message that she was firmly at the helm, carrying out business in a way Adam would approve of, and that she was personally involved in cultivating the high-quality news coverage people had come to associate with the *London Tribune*. She was fully back in circulation and it was business as usual.

'I am working on a piece about dam infrastructure. I was hoping you could point me in the direction of a few members of Parliament who might be interested in commenting.'

'Mr Elliott from Somerset.' Lord Harefield nodded in the direction of a tall, blond-haired gentleman. 'He'll be eager. It's his first term in Parliament,' he explained in a low voice. 'I'll walk over with you and make the introduction.'

It was the beginning of a long evening. Fleur smiled, she chatted, she asked pertinent questions, she let the blond Viscount from Somerset lead her out on to the floor for a dance and then introduce her to a circle of his friends. More dances followed, more chances to make polite conversation. It helped to think of the evening as business. She was dancing as a means of building her support base, of establishing a network of those who might be called on to promote legislation regarding dam oversight. But all the reasoning in the world could not stop the hunger that was unfurling inside her.

These dances, these touches, meant nothing. They were empty and perfunctory, required for the activity of the dance and nothing else. It had never been that way with Adam and the absence of that heat only emphasised her loneliness all the more. *There'd been heat with Umberton*, came the reminder. Their kiss was proof that heat, that passion, with another was indeed possible for her.

It was something she'd wondered about after the disappointment of taking that first lover. She'd thought perhaps she was doomed to never feel such things again. But she'd felt something with Umberton, something wild and reckless and wonderful. But Umberton was not here. Maybe that was for the best. Adam's empire was on tenuous ground. The last thing she needed to invest her time in was a personal affair. It was Adam's empire that required her attentions. But quelling her need was easier said than done.

By eleven o'clock she was feeling worn out from the effort of useful conversation and she was feeling keenly vulnerable in her craving for meaningful interaction, something, *anything* that would fill her. It wasn't the first time since Adam's death she realised how empty she felt. Until now, she'd attributed that emptiness to the isolation that came with her position at the paper and being in mourning. She'd assumed once she re-entered society social interactions would fill that emptiness. She'd been wrong. She could fill her days with work and her nights with entertainments, but quantity was no substitute for quality.

Fleur detached herself from the group she was currently with and made her way to the garden. The cool air felt good on her cheeks and helped to settle the riot of her thoughts. She found a quiet bench near a fountain and idly fanned herself. She missed Adam, imperfections and all. At least with Adam she'd never been lonely. If Adam were here…

'Shouldn't you be inside dancing?' Pleasant, familiar tenor tones teased from behind her and she felt the tension in her shoulders ease.

She turned, taking in the welcome sight of a familiar face, her thoughts tripping over just how welcome Umberton was. How was it that he'd come to claim such a coveted spot in such a short time? Hadn't they just been arguing over that exact thing today and here she was feeling as if she had a partner now, someone to face the evening with. 'Umberton, this is a surprise.'

He came around the bench to take the spot beside her, looking well turned out in his dark evening clothes, not unlike the way he'd looked the night at the theatre. 'A pleasant surprise, I hope?' he asked with a smile that managed to communicate a little humility on his part, as if he wasn't sure of what his reception might be after their afternoon developments. She liked a man who knew the limits of his arrogance.

'Yes, a pleasant surprise,' she assured him. She would have to explore later exactly why she found his presence so pleasant. 'I didn't expect you. Why have you come?'

'Because we have unfinished business.'

Literally, figuratively. He'd not been able to stop thinking about her. Jasper let his gaze linger, taking in the loveliness of her as his mind continued the unspoken answer to her question.

Because you're here. Because I didn't want to wait to see you again. Because I may not have you to myself much longer due to our circumstances. Because I wanted one night with you before things got complicated.

That last was debatable. It was already complicated.

She gave a soft laugh in the darkness. 'I realised after you left that we never got around to making any plans.'

'Perhaps if you walk with me, we could make those plans now. The Harefield garden is quite pretty for a town garden.' He'd love to show her the gardens at Rosefields in full summer bloom, to walk the gravel paths while trying to match the scent of her to one of the many flowers there. But that was a fantasy. In all likelihood she would not be speaking to him by then. He wasn't supposed to care about that when his charade had begun. He was to care only for his brother's reputation. But now he cared for both and wasn't sure how to reconcile the two, or even if they could be reconciled.

He rose and held out his arm for her to take. 'May I say you look lovely tonight? Green becomes you.' The deep summer-green gown brought out the jade of her eyes, the auburn of her hair, the cream of her skin. She'd looked like a painting when he'd spied her in the garden. He'd stood back a few moments when he'd arrived to simply take her in: the curve of her jaw in profile, framed gently by the soft length of an auburn curl draped over her shoulder. He'd taken in more than her beauty. He'd noted a sense of resignation.

Something in the evening had saddened her. Was it that she was alone? Or was it that she *wasn't* alone? Had being among people brought it all back? His mother had once told him after his father died that it had been difficult to go out and do the things she'd once done with his father. Those activities seemed empty without him.

The poignancy of Fleur Griffiths's sadness mixed with her beauty had stolen his thought, his very breath. He'd needed the moment to gather himself, to remember why he was here. Reconnaissance. His brother was counting on him, the family's reputation was counting on him and she was a threat to that. Although it was hard to believe it when he saw her as she was now, alone, sad, fragile. Perhaps because he didn't *want* to believe it.

'I appreciate the compliment.' She smiled and took his arm. 'I admit that I was out here feeling sorry for myself. It was harder than I thought to go to a ball alone.'

'You're missing him?' he said quietly, digesting her confession and what it meant. 'It's your first ball?' He should have realised based on what she'd shared about her outing to the theatre. For all the external toughness Fleur Griffiths displayed with her sharp wit and quick temper, there was a softness, a vulnerability beneath that she kept well hidden. Did he dare believe he was the only one allowed to see it? Best not to be taken in by it, though. Empathy was an emotional response.

She gave a sigh. 'Yes, to both questions.' They stopped beside one of the small fountains in the garden and she trailed a hand in the basin. 'As long as I think about tonight as work, it's not so bad. I have made some connections. We will make more tomorrow night. I thought we could attend the Langston rout. It attracts the political crowd.'

'You should go.' He headed the suggestion in a different direction. The sooner she was disabused of the idea that they would go places together, the better. He could sustain his ruse a while longer. 'I'll go to Lady Elmore's.'

'Divide and conquer?' She slid him a considering look, but he heard a hint of disappointment in her voice.

He liked to think she would miss his company. He would miss hers.

'I think it's our best hope of moving quickly and of avoiding any speculation that we might be conflating business and pleasure. I would hate for legislation to suffer because someone misunderstands our association.'

She arched a slim auburn brow. 'Or perhaps you're worried about your reputation suffering? Perhaps you've realised that you should not be too closely linked with me. I am hardly of your set and, as you say, people will talk, especially when unattached men and women are together no matter what the reason.'

It sounded awful when she put it that way. 'You make me out to be a snob.' It also sounded like something his mother would say. That Fleur Griffith was wealthy because her husband had *worked* for his money. 'I am not embarrassed to be seen with you, if that's what you mean,' he replied. If she knew who he was, it would be she who would be embarrassed to be seen with him.

'It's just a fact. It's how the world is. I know it first-hand.' She gave a rueful smile. 'I was raised by my aunt and uncle. My uncle is an earl's second son and they had no children of their own. They had aspirations for me, primarily that I marry a title of my own. Brixton, in fact, was their grand hope. If not Brixton, then the young heir to the Taunton viscountcy. Taunton hadn't any money, but he had a title and that was all that mattered.'

She sighed and gave a shake of her head. 'But I fell in love with Adam and I refused to be swayed. My aunt and uncle were all the family I had, but they couldn't get past their disappointment in me. I'd failed them by choosing my heart. They didn't come to the wedding and I haven't seen or heard from them since.'

'I'm sorry.' Jasper reached for her hand in an offer of comfort. The confession had saddened her. He'd not intended for that. He *was* sorry. Sorry that her family had disowned her, sorry that she still felt she'd failed them because she'd made her own choices instead of following theirs. 'Do you have regrets?' he asked softly. Had losing her family for what amounted to eight years of marriage been worth it? Had Adam Griffiths, kisser extraordinaire, been worth it?

'Regret not marrying Brixton or Taunton?' She gave a little laugh. 'Brixton never looked my way and I hear Taunton is trying to put funds together for a risky venture to import alpacas.' She shook her head. 'I don't think I would have suited either of them.'

Thank goodness, Jasper thought, because she suited him quite well. 'You gave up more than your family, though. You gave up a lifestyle. You could have been a duchess or a viscountess.' Marrying Adam Griffiths had taken her out of the peerage, out of the life she'd been raised in: the Season in spring, grouse-hunting in the autumn, Christmas at country houses and back to town when the roads cleared to do it all over again. Adam Griffiths was a businessman, a man who worked every day on Fleet Street, who was wealthier than many, but still carried ink stains on his fingers.

'It might surprise you to know that all I ever wanted was to be a storyteller. In a way, I got to be that with Adam. I wrote features for the papers. After the flood, I collected stories from the survivors and had them printed. I never aspired to a title.' She gave him a strong look. 'I like to decide for myself who a person is. Titles are not people and people are not titles.'

Jasper hoped she'd believe that once she knew who *he* was. Inside, a waltz began, its strains drifting out to the garden through the open doors. He held out his hand in an uncharacteristic burst of spontaneity. 'Dance with me.'

'Why? What has brought this on?' She laughed, something flashing in her eyes that alerted him to danger. He needed to tread carefully. She was vulnerable tonight and he was intoxicated by her, by her stories, the glimpse into her life. He already knew how want and need could flare between them, how it tasted, how it begged for more.

He flashed a smile as she gave him her hand. 'I want to prove to you I don't mind being seen with you.' He was playing with fire as he swung her into position, his hand at her waist, her hand at his shoulder. 'We're as proper as Almack's. See, nothing to worry about.' An absolute lie although he wanted to believe it. There was *everything* to worry about. This woman was magic. He could have listened to her stories all night, asked a thousand questions, so immersed had he been sitting beside her at the fountain. Had Adam Griffiths known what a wife he'd had? Had he guessed the depths of all she'd given up for him? He'd like to think he wasn't envious of a dead man, but he wasn't sure he wasn't.

Fleur looked up at him with a bit of mischief in her eye. 'I'm not sure a waltz in the garden proves that. We're virtually alone out here. There's little chance of us being noticed.'

He gave a low chuckle as he turned them about the fountain. 'It's all the more scandalous then, isn't it? If someone notices, it's a much bigger deal than if everyone is watching in the ballroom.' Never mind that he couldn't afford either type of notice at present. 'This proves I am willing to take the risk.' He was getting caught up in the moment, the heat of the afternoon's kiss flaring within him. She was worth the risk. This moment was worth the risk. Perhaps it was worth it to her, too. Perhaps, while the music lasted, they could both find what they were looking for.

She was easy in his arms as if she was made for them, her movements fluid as they glided over the stone pavers of the garden, their steps as light and sure as if they danced across a polished floor. The Harefield fountains burbled against the strains of the music as he turned her at the top of the garden, taking the opportunity to hold her closer than he might have otherwise in a ballroom full of watchful eyes. It gave him an excuse to breathe in the exquisite scent of her. 'What is it that you wear for perfume? I smell jasmine and vanilla, but there's something else, too.'

She laughed up at him, giving a toss of her hair. Some of the sadness she'd admitted to had dissipated as they'd danced and that pleased him. 'Ylang-ylang. It's a flower grown in the South Pacific.' Provided no doubt by Popplewell and Allardyce Enterprises, her connection to the South Pacific, he thought, recalling her friend Antonia, and then marvelling that he could make such a connection, that he could have such an understanding of her in such a short time.

'It suits you.' He smiled down at her. 'Dancing suits you.'

'Dancing with *you* suits me,' she amended, a daring

wickedness flaring in her eyes. His own body surged in response to it, forgetting this was to be only a dance. He'd had a taste of that wickedness this afternoon for better or worse and his body was hungry for more despite the contentious words they'd exchanged at the end. They were waltzing in shadow now, far from the shafts of light coming from the ballroom, the music barely audible.

They did not need the music. Their bodies were as close as clothes allowed. If anyone saw them, it would be a scandal, her hips against his, the fullness of her skirts flattened where they met his trousers, her breasts pressed to his chest so that every inch of him could not help but be aware of her. Her arms had moved to his shoulders, his neck, so that both of his hands rested at her waist, their dancing nothing more than a slow swaying in the shadows, away from moonlight and prying eyes.

Her gaze was green-flame-hot as it looked up at him, her tongue flicking over her lips. 'Do you know what else would suit me? This.' Her last word feathered over his lips a fleeting moment before her mouth took his in a slow, lingering kiss that struck him like a match to a length of fuse, his body left roused in its wake. Her hand dropped to the front of his trousers, hidden between his coat and her skirt, moving over the length of him, moulding him to her touch until he groaned.

'What do you want?' he whispered. He knew what he wanted—he wanted to wash away her sadness, wanted to bring her to life, bring her to happiness. He wanted to wash away the hardship of her year. Whatever she wanted, he would give her. He was already dancing her backwards to the garden wall, some part of him aware that their bodies had reached an answer to what their minds had yet to decide.

'You. I want you,' she whispered into his mouth. 'I want obliteration.'

Chapter Nine

Obliteration was neither a safe request nor a flattering one, if he thought too much about it, which he didn't. He knew very well as he pressed her to the garden wall that she was using him. He would have to grapple with that later. Yet he did not think she'd made the request lightly. Still, good sense argued he ought not to grant it. But he was too far beyond what he ought to do. He was here, wasn't he? If 'ought to dos' held any sway he wouldn't have braved Harefield's to begin with. He was very much the Montague at the Capulet ball.

If she knew who he was...well, that was all the more reason to put an end to her hand on his cock, his mouth at her neck, his own hand at her breast. But for once, he was not listening to any of that logic. In the grips of intense passion, he was content to deal with the aftermath.

She had got his trousers open and her hand wrapped about the hot length of him, no more fabric between them, no more pretence. He knew exactly what she wanted, what she needed and what he needed to achieve the obliteration she asked for. She raised a leg to hook at his hip, skirts quashed between them, as he brought his hand up to skim the silken skin of her thigh, then higher to skim the damp curls that guarded her womanly gate, their dampness a prelude to the wetness he'd find within. Such readiness nearly undid him.

What a treasure she was, a woman confident enough to own her need and claim her passion. Her teeth gave a fierce nip at his ear as if scolding him for being too slow, for lingering and he laughed against her neck.

'Patience, my dear.'

'Patience is a virtue. I think we're well past virtue here.' Her voice was a smoky rasp, low and throaty.

He could not argue with that even if he had been capable of thought. At the moment he was capable only of responding to the primal urges of his body and of hers, his only thoughts revolved around giving her what she needed. He lifted her and thrust hard to their great mutual satisfaction. Her head went back against the fence, her neck arching, the heat of her gaze meeting his for the briefest, most beautiful of seconds when the intensity of connection rocketed through them before her eyes left him, fixing instead on the dark night sky above. He thrust again, more deeply this time, as if he could *make* her look at him. He wanted her eyes back, wanted those green flames on him when the critical moment came.

His own body tightened even as the truth of obliteration came to him too late. Climax would find them shortly; his body was already gathering for it as was hers. When it came it would be explosive, shattering, and for a few precious moments there would be blessed nothingness. Only, she would not be there for it. Oh, her body would be there for it, but *she* would not, not the part of her that mattered. Her mind and soul were already somewhere else. With someone else.

Her hands tangled in his hair, her hips moved against his, pushing him, pushing them both to grand heights, gasps of encouragement purling from her throat. Her eyes were shut now as she rocked against him, her expression fierce and unguarded. Her breathing came hard and fast as release swept her, her body giving a visible, violent tremble. Sure of her pleasure, Jasper claimed his own release outside her body, his physical satisfaction diminished by the knowledge that he'd been a stand-in—quite literally given their current location— for the man she couldn't have.

He held her steady against the fence, giving her time to savour the obliteration she'd so desperately sought. Her eyes were still closed, but her breathing slowed and the fierceness ebbed from her face. There was a satisfying softness to her features in these moments, a softness he'd seen hinted at in unguarded moments. A stab of envy pricked at him. Her husband had seen her like this. Damned, dead Adam, who'd stolen Jasper's pleasure from beyond the grave. Jasper didn't even know the man and he was jealous. It was a ridiculous reaction for a man who prided himself on being logical. There was nothing logical about jealousy. Envy was a weakness. Covetousness a sin.

But I was the one she wanted tonight. I was the one she chose for obliteration.

At last, she opened her eyes and he set her down. 'Welcome back.' He smiled, reaching in his coat pocket for a handkerchief for her.

'Thank you.' She took the handkerchief and Jasper turned away to give her privacy. Was that a thank-you for the handkerchief alone or for everything else? Not just for being the provider of the act, but for something more? He knew he hoped for the latter. Did she understand that *he* understood what she'd been looking for? He tucked his shirt into his trousers and straightened his clothes along with his expression before turning back to her.

'I think I will leave.' She smiled gently at him and gave a low, throaty laugh that had him rousing once more. 'I'm not sure I could pass muster if I went back in now.'

He reached for a loose curl and tucked it back behind her ear. 'You're probably right.' She looked beautiful, peaceful. The sadness was gone. That was something at least. Perhaps his own disappointment was worth that. Her lips were puffy. They'd lost their elegant colour just as her hair had lost its perfect curl. But it was her eyes that betrayed the most. They were dreamy, far away. One close look at her would give it all away. 'This gate will take you around to the front,' Jasper suggested. 'I will go through the house to fetch your cloak and make your farewells to the hostess. I will see you at the curb in ten minutes.'

Some of her softness faded. 'I intend to go home alone.'

He inclined his head respectfully. 'I understand that.' Too well, in fact. It was further proof he'd been a stand-in for another. 'I mean only to facilitate your departure in a discreet manner. I do not mean to accompany you.' The last thing he wanted was a *ménage à trois* with a dead man. There were limits to what he'd do even for a beautiful woman.

She reached for his hand and gave a sincere squeeze. 'Thank you.'

He cleared his throat. 'At any rate, I need to go back in and dance a few times.' The comment bordered on caddish. He wondered if subconsciously he was trying to stoke her jealousy.

She lifted an eyebrow. 'With girls on your mother's list?'

'Yes, exactly so.' Girls he'd never dream of making love to against a garden wall, never dream of seeking obliteration with. That woman was going home with her husband's ghost.

The wry ghost of a smile played at Fleur's lips as she set down the morning papers. How ironic. If only she'd stayed a little longer. The Marquess of Meltham had made a late appearance at the Harefield ball and the society pages had jumped all over it. Everyone was sure this would be the year he married and the match-making mamas were lining up their daughters. If she'd walked through the ballroom on her way out, she might have met him coming in, assuming she'd recognise him. Perhaps it was best she hadn't seen him. It would have ruined a perfectly good night.

She reached for her coffee mug and took a hot swallow. Despite the late night, she was back at her desk this morning at the *Tribune*, writing letters and following up on last night's conversations while they were fresh. She had a busy day, including a meeting with the Duke of Cowden. There was too much to do to lie abed spending time staring at the ceiling and thinking of last night. Of Umberton. Of what had transpired in the garden. And yet, every few minutes, her mind went back there, unable to stay entirely focused on the work at hand.

Perhaps she should write to him this morning, too? What would she say? *Thank you for sex against the fence?* No, that sounded too much as though he'd done her a favour. Or something more conciliatory? *I am not in the habit of such actions.* No, that made it sound like an excuse for acting outrageously or, worse, that she now regretted her decision.

Regret would be a lie. She did not regret the fence in the least, although she did wonder if he did. There'd been something in his eyes afterward she'd not been quick enough to decode. Misgiving? Pity? Understanding? She wasn't comfortable with any of them. She didn't want him to see too much. She'd just wanted sex, obliteration. She'd not wanted any of the other things that came with it: concern, caring, connection.

She did not want Umberton's concern or Umberton thinking there was a connection between them that went beyond the business of legislation. If he thought there was more, he'd want more. She could not reciprocate. Her heart, her soul, were off limits. She could not give them again. She'd given them to Adam and now Adam was dead. Dead before she'd had a chance to make amends. Did she even deserve a second chance at love since she'd failed at it so spectacularly the first time?

Was I worth it, Adam? Do you regret marriage to me? Was I too difficult? Too headstrong? Would you have been happier with a biddable wife?

These were the dark questions that had followed her guilt over that last night in Holmfirth. That fight had been one of many. Too many? She could not regret that fight without thinking of other fights. How much time had they wasted arguing? And yet she could not be the sort of woman who agreed to everything just for the sake of peace. Compliance wasn't peace, it was conformity, and conformity bred all nature of illusions: agreement, accord, co-operation, uniformity where there was none. Newspapers protected against such illusions. It was one of the many things Adam liked about them.

Perhaps that was why she'd chosen Umberton last night. He was no risk to her. He needed to marry a girl who met his mother's specifications. She met none of them. She'd be a walking scandal for a man such as he and they both knew it. The only risk she posed was to his honour. Bold women didn't fit comfortably into the code gentlemen were raised by. For them to be gentlemen, women had to be helpless, had to require their protection. Such women didn't run newspapers or seek justice for murders. Neither did they boldly take lovers.

Umberton had been very good at his job. Much better than her previous lover. It had almost been embarrassing how much better. She'd nearly lost herself with him, in him, shattering *for* him, which was very different than using him to seek obliteration, blankness. She'd been acutely aware of him, of gripping him as if he were an anchor amid a stormy sea, of riding him hard in order to have all of him within her. With each thrust, she'd wanted. She'd panted and writhed for him. A nearly inexplicable reaction on her part and a dangerous one, too.

If this were to happen again—and that in itself was still an if—she'd have to proceed with more detachment before she ended up investing too much of herself and risking real hurt when it ended, because it would end. That was the beauty and the curse of choosing Umberton.

There was the business aspect, too. If an affair between them came to light, their plans for legislation might be compromised as well as her reputation in the eyes of the board of directors. There were plenty of reasons not to engage with him again as they had last night, yet parts of her felt those might not be reasons enough.

The little clock on her desk chimed. Time to stop wool-gathering. Time to stop fantasising about Umberton. Time to go meet with Cowden and figure out how to save the syndicate without reducing it.

'My dear, you seem distracted today. Forgive me for saying so. It's not like you.' The Duke of Cowden sat back in his red Moroccan leather chair and laced his hands over the slight paunch of his stomach. Approaching his upper years, Cowden was silver haired and sharp eyed, father of three sons, had four grandsons and was the head of the Prometheus Club, a group of investors who'd generated spectacular wealth for themselves and for England. Nothing got past him, Fleur realised belatedly.

'It was a late night last night. I attended the Harefield ball. The first one,' she confessed, 'since Adam passed.' Then she smiled brightly. 'But business must go on and there were people to meet.'

Cowden nodded and she felt encouraged. Best to keep the conversation steered towards business lest Cowden ask anything too personal. He was known to pry lovingly into the lives of those he cared about and he'd cared about Adam and Keir and Garrett. By extension, he now felt a need to watch over their widows. He'd been one of the first to help Antonia when the department store had burned.

'I am making progress with the dam legislation. I think there will be a law to put before the House perhaps before this session is even out.'

Cowden gave another nod, his eyes keen. 'I will look forward to supporting it when it's ready. And the investigation? You've hardly mentioned it.'

Guilt twinged. She'd not given it the usual lion's share of her attention since lunch at Verrey's with Umberton. It was much more pleasant to think about the baron and the baron did not favour re-opening the investigation. 'I've been busy and I've met someone.' She blushed at the admission. 'No one I care to share about at present,' she added rapidly to stave off Cowden's inevitable inquiry. 'But it's definitely still at the top of my agenda.'

Cowden grinned. 'Well, don't let him, whoever he is, distract you.'

'I won't,' she assured him but Cowden's playful teasing stirred a concern. Is that what Umberton was doing? Distracting her? The dam investigation wasn't at the top of his agenda. Every time she meant to discuss it with him, another topic took its place. Was that a coincidence or something more? A seed of suspicion took root. Had Umberton used their attraction and their agreement upon legislation as a means of distracting her? Refocusing her attentions? Other than his philosophical objections, which he'd voiced eloquently at Verrey's, what would his motive for that distraction be? What purpose could he have? Or what did he stand to gain? These were worrisome questions she'd be wise not to put off any longer.

'I hope you're not too busy to re-join my daughter-in-law's committee for the literacy ball? And my wife would love your help for her Christmas charity ball as well.'

Fleur rose, understanding this was the end to the interview. 'I will look forward to returning to their committees. Tell them thank you for me and thank you also for your support of the legislation. It means a great deal.'

She left Cowden house with mixed feelings. On one hand, she was thrilled to have recruited a second ally for the legislation and possibly a third given that if Cowden was on board his son, Lord Brixton, would be, too. On the other hand, she was becoming concerned about the wisdom of Umberton as an ally.

'Where to, Ma'am?' her coachman asked as she settled into her seat.

She opened her mouth, intending to give instructions to go to Lord Umberton and then realised she couldn't. She didn't know where to find him. She couldn't go to White's herself without drawing undo attention, the very last thing she needed. 'To the office.' Concern escalated. She'd have to wait for him to come to her on all accounts. She did not like that he held a certain power in being the one who chose to call and that he could keep her waiting. She wasn't very good at waiting.

Waiting called up fragments of last night's conversation. 'Patience,' he'd whispered when she'd reached for him. Patience was a virtue, she'd replied, something she'd been beyond in the garden and she definitely remained beyond it today.

Chapter Ten

Apparently, Cicero was right. Virtue was its own reward. Umberton was waiting for her at the office. She would have missed him if she'd gone to White's. He was lounging on the divan and dangling a tumbler from his hand with the casual nonchalance of one who felt at home in his surroundings. He rose when she entered.

'How was your meeting with Cowden?'

'Cowden has offered support for our legislation when it's ready. That's good news.' But her original excitement over that was diminished by practicalities. Mainly, she wasn't sure how she felt about him being here as if he could come and go at will when she had no way to find him on her own. 'How did you know that's where I was?'

'Your clerk told me. He let me in.' Umberton looked well rested for one who'd danced the night away. 'It's good news about Cowden. He'll be a formidable ally.' He waved his tumbler to indicate the room at large. 'I hope you don't mind me waiting in here?' he enquired with such sincerity she nearly forgave him for the inconvenience of his lack of address.

'I don't mind too much, but I do mind the inability to

reach you. I realised this afternoon that I couldn't even send you a note to tell you about Cowden.' She slid him a meaningful look. 'I do not think I like *you* having all the power to guide when and how often we interact.'

She went to her desk, her point made, and gathered together all the loose sheets she'd left out, wondering if he'd looked at them and if it mattered. What would he have seen? Would it have meant anything to him? She hated the suspicion that had taken root since her meeting with Cowden. She looked across the room at him. He wore a blue jacket and buff trousers today, with a striped-blue waistcoat beneath, his jaw clean shaven, eyes clear, wavy hair in its usual state of tousled decadence. He looked handsome and harmless.

No, not harmless. He would never be harmless. Inviting was the word she was looking for. Those eyes, that smile, invited a woman to reveal her secrets, to lay those secrets and perhaps her head on those broad shoulders. He was a safe place for a woman to land. She'd taken advantage of that last night. She hoped she hadn't been wrong. Well, the only way she'd know was if she voiced her concerns. She'd never shied away from difficult conversations. She wasn't going to start now.

'I want to talk to you.' She sat behind her desk, letting the big piece of furniture be her source of power and protection. She needed distance for this conversation. She could not have it sitting side by side on the sofa where'd they kissed yesterday, where she'd be reminded of his touch, of the clean scent of him, of all the things that had led her to seduce him last night. She would not mince words with herself. She *had* seduced him.

'Is this about last night? If so—' he said, but she interrupted.

'No, it's not about last night. It's about the enquiry on the dam.' She drew a breath and counted to three. She wanted to deliver this next sentence with even tones, with no hint of anger. 'I want the truth from you.' She fixed him with a hard stare and watched him stiffen in alertness.

'Of course, always.' But he was wary.

'Have you deliberately refocused my attention away from it by pushing the legislative end of things and by…' it was hard to say the last bit '…by conflating business with pleasure?'

His eyes went wide. 'You mean by seducing you?' He gave loud chuckle. 'I believe you were seducing me last night. And our kiss yesterday afternoon seemed fairly mutual to me. So, I think you'll have some difficulty selling that argument.'

'I think you are having difficulty answering the question,' Fleur said firmly. She would not let him distract her with talk of romance and who had seduced whom.

'Why are you asking? Are you having trouble coming to grips with last night? Perhaps you're looking for a scapegoat and would like to blame me?' He rose from the sofa, pacing his corner of the room. 'What is this about, Fleur?' His use of her given name threw her for a moment. 'I would think after last night we could at least call each other by our given names,' he said, reading her hesitation, 'My name is Jasper, by the way.'

Like the stone, she thought. The name suited him. Jasper, the stone of protection, of strength. She tried not to think about other things his comment pointed out, like the fact that she'd engaged with him so intimately without knowing his name, only his title. After her protest to Cowden this morning, there was some irony in that.

'Did you use our attraction to manipulate my agenda? You made no secret at Verrey's as to how much you disliked the idea of re-opening the investigation.' The idea that he had prevaricated in the past and was prevaricating now seemed to affirm her alarm was not unwarranted.

'Do you think I am that sort of man?' he shot back. 'This conversation does not paint me in a favourable light. But I'd be very careful about what I was asking if I were you, Fleur. If you think to pillory me for using sex as a tool, you'd best look in the mirror first.'

'What exactly are you suggesting?' She'd not wanted to talk about last night, but somehow the conversation had gone that direction anyway.

'If anyone was using anyone for sex, it was *you* using *me*.'

She met his gaze evenly. Was that a reprimand she heard in his voice? 'You were not unaware. I told you exactly what I wanted.' She'd wanted him and an escape from the loneliness that had driven her from the ballroom. He'd managed to give her both. 'It seemed to me that you enjoyed it last night. So, I am mystified as to the source of your irritation today.'

He broke from his pacing and approached the desk, leaning over it, palms flat on its polished surface. His eyes glittered with dangerous warning. She should *not* find that arousing. But she did. Or maybe it was the fight she found arousing. She hadn't had a good fight for a long time. Not since… No. She put a full stop to her thoughts. 'You talk about the mutuality of our "activity" last night, but you were not there with me in the end. That's not fair.'

Oh. So that's what this was about. She was surprised he had even noticed. She doubted many men would care enough at that point, too lost in reaching for their own release to note their partner's. 'I told you I wanted obliteration. It's not a state of togetherness. You gave me exactly what I asked for.' But he'd wanted something else, been searching for something else and he'd not found it. It was something of a revelation.

'You were lonely, too,' she said softly, the tension between them gentling with the realisation. But they'd used different means to assuage that loneliness. She'd sought obliteration and he'd sought togetherness. Both of them temporary variations for the real thing.

He fingered the heavy glass paperweight on the desk. 'A lord is always lonely, especially when he's expected to marry. Perhaps that is when he's at his loneliest, knowing that everyone is circling, waiting for him to commit, to give in and choose someone.'

Something in his voice touched her and she reached for his hand out of an innate need to offer comfort. 'You make it sound like surrender, capitulation. A defeat.' Those were not characteristics she'd come to associate with this man.

His gaze held hers, sharp and all-seeing but his voice was soft in its reflectiveness. 'My father once took me to Scotland for hunting. We tracked a herd of elk for miles. There was an older stag with them and our hounds culled him from the herd, separated him from the others until he was alone. The first shot missed and, by missed, I mean it wasn't fatal. It merely slowed him down. We followed him until our hounds surrounded him. He was on his knees in a clearing when we took him.'

He sighed and gave a shake of his head. 'I didn't like it. I suppose it's not manly to admit such a thing. My father assured me it was all part of the circle of life.'

'You were close to your father?' She ventured the personal question. 'Whenever you talk of him or your mother, it sounds as if your family was close.' Was that quite the right word? 'I mean, "is" close. Your mother is still alive.'

'My father was a good man. He taught me about honour and what it means to be a good man. I try to live up to his standards. I loved him and I miss him every day.' He smiled and something warm fluttered in her stomach. 'I love my mother, too, despite her list.' He gave a wry laugh. 'But I think of that story every time my mother drags the list out.'

He chuckled, but it wasn't an entirely happy sound. 'I'm like that bull elk. Each year, all the matchmaking mamas separate those of us who should marry from the herd and do their best to bring us to our knees.' There was another sigh. 'It is an illusion that a man goes courting, that he somehow is in pursuit. I think it's the mamas who are in pursuit. We poor bachelors are all stags on the run.'

She completed the thought for him. 'While the mamas circle and wait to pounce and bring your carcass home for their daughters.'

'Yes. Am I terrible to think that? Nobody puts that in their love poems.'

'No, they don't. It's all roses and blushes. Virgins and unicorns. No one seems to understand that the unicorn horn in the virgin's lap is a symbolic penis.'

'Is it?' He looked astonished. 'I didn't realise...' He cleared his throat. 'Well, that certainly puts a different take on things.' He furrowed his brow. 'I studied Classics at Oxford and I don't think that's quite right. The unicorn is a symbol of purity in Raphael's *The Virgin and the Unicorn* and I am sure the unicorn was used in the Renaissance to depict chastity.' He paused. 'Are you laughing at me?'

'Laughing *with* you. I was quite enjoying the lecture, Professor.' Fleur came around the desk. 'I like my version better. It took your mind off things, didn't it?'

'Yes. My apologies. I was being maudlin.' They made their way to the divan and sat, but Fleur had not entirely forgotten the roots of their quarrel.

She hesitated to revisit the topic of that disagreement after such a nice moment. It had been quietly intoxicating to listen to his story, to know he was sharing something deeply personal and simultaneously troubling to him. But she needed her answers. Perhaps she'd do better with sugar than vinegar. She'd been bold and confrontational earlier and that had resulted in a quarrel. Maybe if she was less direct she'd get a better response. Part of her was very much aware that on at least two occasions they'd meant to talk business and had ended up not discussing anything resembling business. She could not keep letting those opportunities slip away or it would be August and another summer would have come and gone with nothing done.

'If I ring for tea, will you let me show you something?

And will you listen with an open mind? I want to share with you the case I have against Lord Orion Bexley.' It would be the ultimate litmus test for him. It was time for him to prove his worthiness.

He did not want to hear it. His damned brother had messed up a lot in his life and now he was going to mess this up, too, whatever 'this' was that sparked between him and Fleur Griffiths.

'Fleur, you know how I feel about that,' he reminded her in an attempt to dissuade her from showing him.

'Yes, I know exactly how you feel and because of that, is it any wonder I *feel* derailed any time the subject comes up? I want legislation but I also want this: justice for those who died.'

Coward! His inner voice snapped. *Let her show you. This was your whole plan all along, to earn her trust enough to learn what she has on Orion. This is what you came for, what you'd started this whole association for. You ought to be thrilled. You will finally have your answers, finally know how to protect Orion.*

Yet, the only thought that came to the fore as Fleur called for tea and retrieved a file was that he ought to stand up and walk out of the office, that he didn't want to know. Didn't want her to tell him. He didn't want to be reminded that this was business, and she was the enemy. That he'd shielded his identity from her in order to gain access to her world, that he'd misled her about the motives for his interest in her project.

If she knew, she would hate him for it. From her perspective, these were not the behaviours of a man of honour. Yet he could argue from his perspective—the perspective of a man who must protect his family and name—these behaviours were warranted. They were omissions only, none of them outright lies. He could hear his father in his head alongside his own inner voice.

Family first. Your mother, your brother, will need you when I'm gone. You will have hard choices to make.

She spread the papers from the file out on the low table. 'The troubles begin in 1846 when the Holmes Reservoir Commissioners were found to be in a state of insolvency, having spent Parliament's allotment for the reservoir project, but also owing several outstanding debts.' She passed him a sheaf of papers. 'This is the testimony of Charles Batty, who was the drawer for the commissioners, and these are copies of outstanding bills the commission owed. The Huddersfield Banking Company was owed two thousand pounds, money was owed to clerks who worked for the commission and monies were owed to companies who worked on the dam. These are no small sums and the fact that one of these bills ended up in Chancery speaks to the depth of dysfunction in the commission.'

Jasper fished his eyeglasses out of his inner coat pocket and studied the papers. 'If I may play the devil's advocate?' he said after a careful perusal. 'I feel as if this only affirms the original findings that no one person was culpable. There was unfortunate disarray up and down the line when it came to the Holmfirth Reservoirs Act. This notes only that Lord Orion Bexley was on the commission at the time.'

'The debt is curious, is it not? Where did all the money go if the dam was never repaired? What this establishes is the insolvency and that the money set aside for repairs was gone. It allows us to ask—where did the money go? I propose it went into Lord Orion Bexley's pockets by way of a very careful, very expert sleight of hand.' She handed him another sheet of paper.

'What is this?'

'This was issued by the commission on August 26, 1846. It's an order to improve the waste pit so that water could be safely processed and filtered through the dam.' She summarised as he scanned the paper.

An opening should be made in the waste pit of the Bilberry Dam reservoir at the height of eighteen feet above the clough or shuttle and Mr Little-wood authorised to see the same forthwith carried into effect.

He looked up to meet her gaze, waiting for the blow to fall.

'That repair was never made. In fact, although it was authorised, Mr Littlewood testified that he did not know about the request and, in fact, no engineer or construction manager on the project after that date reported knowing about the request or any later requests to carry out that work.' She reached for another stack of papers. 'This is the testimony of those men: Mr Littlewood, Mr Leather, Jonathon Crowther...the list goes on.'

Jasper scrubbed a hand over his face. 'Why would the blame for this, the pocketing of the money, be laid at Lord Orion's feet? Why not one of the other commission members?'

'Two reasons. Because he was one of three men assigned specifically to the Bilberry Dam Reservoir. It was the commission's practice that those members residing nearest a dam took over supervision of that dam. He was one of three who submitted the order.' She paused and said with emphasis, 'It was Bexley's job to ensure that order was carried out.'

'His job and that of the other two men with a particular interest in the Bilberry Dam.' Jasper racked his brain to remember who those other two might have been.

She shook her head. 'Those positions are reappointed every year. Those men left and new men took their places. Bexley is the only returning figure, the only one who could provide continuity. The only one who had knowledge of the order to work on the waste pit and he *never* acknowledges that it wasn't acted on. He never calls attention to the fact that the work order—*his work order*—was placed and nothing occurred.

'That waste pit and its inefficiencies were the cause of the fatal accident. Listen to Mr Leather's testimony.' She proceeded to read slowly and carefully aloud. *'"My opinion as to the cause of the breaking of the embankment on the fifth of February is that it arose from overflowing and washing away the outer slope...if the waste pit had been seven or eight feet below the embankment, the inference is that the embankment would have stood...if the order of the Commissioners in 1846 had been carried out and a hole made... I think it very likely it would have prevented the accident. Had I been consulted I should have recommended such a course of action."'*

Jasper listened intently. He saw the argument she was making in his mind. Orion had submitted an order for repairs, pocketed the money for himself and the repair had never materialised. The lack of that particular repair bore full responsibility for the accident. Had Orion seen the work carried out, the accident would have been prevented despite all the other mismanagement by the commissioners. Fleur's was not an implausible argument, and his worries began to rise. What had Orion done?

Fleur set aside her folder. 'I know what you're going to say—that I don't have proof he siphoned the money. If I had access to his bank accounts, it would be the proof I need.' She gave a little lift of her shoulders, a smile playing at her lips. 'Adam always said to follow the money. Money never lies.'

Jasper was very much afraid of that.

Chapter Eleven

Money never lies. Those words drove real fear into his heart. There was a knock and a clerk entered with tea. She cleared the coffee table, making a space for the tray. 'It's not Fortnum and Mason's...' she smiled '...but it will do. The bakery down the street makes delicious lemon scones.'

How odd, he thought, watching her fix his tea, that everything was still right-side-up in her world when his had been turned upside down. She was calmly stirring cream into his tea while his mind was running riot. What if she was right? What if Orion had pocketed the money? His brother could be tried for manslaughter, eighty-one deaths laid at his door. But Orion was not a murderer. He was a wayward young man with no sense of direction, struggling to find purpose in a world that gave him few options as a second son.

If anything went to trial, his title couldn't protect Orion then. But it could protect his brother now. It could prevent this enquiry of hers from ever getting that far. Would he use his title, though, to obstruct justice? Would he suddenly turn away from his voting record championing free press? To do either of these things would paint him as a traitor to his own beliefs and positions. But perhaps that was the sacrifice required: trading his reputation for Orion's.

She passed him the tea and the warm liquid seeping through the cup settled his thoughts and soothed his nerves. His mind began to work. She had information, she had a hypothesis, but she'd not yet tested it and she didn't have all the research she required to support it. He needed to remember that instead of allowing himself to jump to dire conclusions.

'How would you get a gentleman's accounts? That's very private information.' He hated himself for asking, knowing full well he was not asking honestly, but asking in order to plan his next move, to decide what he needed to do to protect Orion.

Should he need to.

Yes, he couldn't forget that most basic premise. A man was innocent until proven guilty. It was just that in Orion's case, he held out little hope of that. Innocence and Orion weren't the closest of companions.

'A warrant, of course. If the accounts are evidence for a proceeding, they can be acquired.' She took a bite of scone, a crumb lingering on her lips.

'But you'd have to prove that first. I can't imagine banks go turning over gentlemen's personal accounts on just anyone's request.' It might take her a while to get that approval. She'd have to win the argument that Orion's bank accounts mattered in order to have access to them. If her arguments weren't compelling, it would all be over before it began. A good barrister could surely punch enough holes to call her argument into question. It only had to be enough to deny the procurement of those accounts. There was hope in that.

But there was no honour. No ethic. It would be using the arbitrary nature of the courts and his own privilege to prevent an action that might lead to the truth. Or to scandal. There was already scandal enough to upset Orion. The longer this went on, perhaps the more validity it gained in the public eye, the more teeth it had, teeth like a saw blade that cut both ways. He'd not considered that.

He set his teacup aside. 'I think this is a dangerous game you play. If you are wrong, the newspaper could face charges of slander. I think it's been a good idea to scale back publicising this. I know there'd been several articles published in your papers before we met'—for it was thanks to them they *had* met—'but there hasn't been any lately and that is to the good until you are certain of the claims you're making.'

'The board of directors would not agree with you. Safe news isn't interesting. It doesn't sell newspapers,' she said sharply, some of her calm leaving her. This was apparently a sore subject.

'They certainly wouldn't welcome being sued for slander either.' He watched her carefully, a thought coming to him. 'Are you being pressured to pursue this?'

'No, I want to pursue this, but the board would like to pursue it more flagrantly despite the missing pieces.' She crumbled the remainder of her lemon scone on her plate. 'The story sells newspapers, especially up north where people are more concerned with the accident.'

He reached for a scone. 'Do you *need* to sell more newspapers?' This was an additional angle he'd not con-

sidered. Francis Bacon would call it a variable. This was
not merely a question of his brother's waywardness col-
liding with Fleur Griffith's grief-driven search for justice as he'd originally thought.

'Quite a few more.' She gave a wry smile. 'It's really not a surprise, is it? There's a woman now at the
helm of one of Britain's largest news syndicates and no
one knows what to make of it. It's not normal. It raises
questions of competence and capability. Subscriptions
have declined. As a result, advertisers have pulled back,
choosing to advertise elsewhere in other papers where
they perceive there is a larger readership. It makes for
a vicious cycle. The *London Tribune* needs to prove itself. I need to show everyone—readers, advertisers,
the board of directors—that I am personally capable
of delivering the kind of news the paper has always
delivered.'

She leaned forward in earnest. 'If I can break this
story about Lord Orion Bexley, I can do all of that. Ad-
ditionally, the story will serve as a way to restore interest for our legislation on dam oversight.'

Jasper saw all that she imagined and more. She could
vindicate herself and her husband's death in one fell
swoop while getting the board of directors off her back.
It was a potent vision and it was no wonder she was
compelled by it. No doubt, she felt as if her whole world
hung by this one thread.

Against his will, his heart went out to her. The in-
domitable Fleur Griffiths looked quite vulnerable at the
moment, her hands clutched about her teacup, frustration vying for defiance in the green sparks of her eyes
as she waited for his approval, *wanted* his approval.

Every manly attribute he'd been raised with to protect surged to the fore, urging him to take her in his arms, to offer her comfort, to offer assurances that everything would be all right. But such actions would ignore other aspects in their relationship—that she had used him for sex, made him a stand-in for her dead husband and he had not been entirely forthcoming with her about who he was.

These were not small things. Their relationship was established on the rockiest of foundations, assuming that what they had between them was a relationship at all. It ignored the pivotal reality that for things to be all right for her, things would not end well for him, and vice versa. For him to have the things he wanted— his brother's safety and the family name cleared of scandal—he would have to give up his fascination with Fleur Griffiths and his reputation for equality and re- form.

'I see,' he said solemnly. Perhaps for the first time he did see. He saw the complexities of what it meant to be Fleur Griffiths. It was as complicated to be her as it was to be him. Too bad. He rather liked her, rough edges, silk gowns and all. She was unlike any woman he'd ever spent time with. He would have liked to have spent more time with her, but to what end? To what purpose but hurt? This afternoon had shown him how impossible that would be.

Soon, he would have to act on his brother's behalf and she would know who he was and what he'd kept from her. She'd think her suspicions were right, that he'd tried to seduce her to distract her. It would set her against him entirely. She had a newspaper to save and he had a family to protect. There was no option. He had to end this now.

He set aside his teacup and reached a hand to her cheek, cupping her jaw. He wanted to remember her like this—the way she looked at him *before* she hated him—her auburn hair parted and smooth, gathered in a chignon at the base of her neck, her face smiling back at him, a bit of coquetry lighting her eyes. Beautiful, intelligent. A one-of-a-kind woman but not the woman for him, unfortunately. He would go home and throw himself into protecting his brother, and wife hunting, letting the attention on him distract the *ton* from attention on his brother. But first, he'd have one last moment. He drew her close, taking her mouth in a sweet kiss that tasted of lemon and sugar to mark a short interlude that had come to an end.

Fleur knew a goodbye kiss when she saw it—metaphorically speaking. One didn't *see* a kiss as much as *felt* one. She'd definitely felt goodbye in Jasper's kiss.

The days that followed his departure had confirmed her gut instinct as she'd sat on the divan and let him walk out the door, intuitively knowing that he would not walk back through it.

She told herself it didn't matter. She had too much work at present between the Bexley story and arranging to sell a few of the smaller papers to devote time to cultivating a relationship or simply taking a lover. A lover required time as well, which was something she convinced herself she didn't have. But as the last weeks in May blended into early June, he was never far from her thoughts and those thoughts had questions.

He'd simply left. Why? Mixed messages abounded in answer. Their one night in the Harefield's garden had been explosive, both of them matching the other in need and ferocity. As lovers, they'd been a good fit. The kiss he'd given her that last afternoon had been tender, sincere. It was not the kiss of a man who *wanted* to leave. And yet he had. There'd been no note, no attempt to contact her, to explain.

Perhaps he thought she'd know the reasons he'd left. There was no future for them. Class stratification made it an unlikely pairing. A peer with a businesswoman, special emphasis on the woman. Her position was controversial within her own circles. It would be a scandal in itself among his ranks. Titled ladies didn't run newspapers, didn't hold down jobs that required they put in long hours away from home. But she wasn't looking to marry him.

Of course, he needed to marry and that added its own complications. She would not settle for being a married man's mistress. She would not be the wedge between another woman and that woman's husband. Neither did she think he was the sort of man who would have such an arrangement, although she knew many peers did. Such arrangements seemed sure pathways to disappointment and failure.

Perhaps he'd left because he'd realised the relationship was impossible not only romantically but practically. He'd not been comfortable with her case against Lord Orion Bexley. He'd been clear about that from the start and when she'd brought it up again that last afternoon, he'd not been enthusiastic. Her line of reasoning and proof should have excited someone who claimed to be interested in the dam situation.

To his credit, he'd listened as she'd requested. He'd asked pertinent questions and he'd pressed for explanations, but he'd not been imbued with the eagerness she'd hoped solid proof would engender from him. There were even points where she'd sensed he was horrified. At her? At her discoveries? It was hard to tell, further fuelling her suspicion that something was off.

He had softened though, at the end, when she'd shared the situation at the newspaper and how the Bexley story fit into her predicament. But he'd still walked out of her office as suddenly as he'd walked into her theatre box, without warning, without reason.

Fleur paced her office, looking down on to Fleet Street, home to many of London's great newspapers and publishers. It was early evening. Clerks were starting to go home, vendors were working hard to make a few final sales before the day was done. She wondered what Jasper was doing. Was he preparing for an evening out? Had he, perhaps, resigned himself to his fate? Would he spend the night waltzing with girls off his mother's list? Those broad shoulders and tousled hair would be wasted on a debutante. She'd been attending balls in order to carry on discussions and encourage interest in legislation. She spent a large part of those evenings looking over her shoulder hoping to see him. She had not.

Fleur turned from the window at the sound of a knock on her door. 'Mrs Griffiths, this has come in.' The clerk left a large envelope on her desk. In her experience, large envelopes were usually promising. She opened it and sat down to read. It was an offer for a couple of the smaller newspapers Cowden had recommended she sell up north. This was good. The board would be pleased to have such rapid results. It was a sign that their presses were coveted, valued. She looked at the offering price. Yes, definitely valued. The buyer was willing to pay the asking price. No negotiation involved. Was that cause for celebration or for alarm? Who didn't negotiate?

She knew the answer to that: someone who wanted something urgently, no questions asked. But she *would* ask questions. Mainly the question of who? Fleur scanned the document for the name of the party or parties involved, her gaze landing on the name at the bottom of the proposal: the Earl of Wincastle. She could not recall him from personal acquaintance. Perhaps he was an acquaintance of the Duke of Cowden's? How like him it would be to send a buyer in her direction. She glanced at the copy of *Debrett's* sitting on the bookshelf. This was one of those times when looking someone up would be necessary. She could not take this offer to the board of directors uninformed.

Fleur retrieved the tome from the shelf and set it on her desk, flipping to the section on earls and then towards the back to the 'W's.

'Wincastle… Wincastle,' she murmured, her finger running over the columns. There it was.

Wincastle, also a title currently held by the Marquess of Meltham.

Her gaze froze. Her mind raced. Wincastle was Meltham? She knew what this was, an attempt to silence the stories about Lord Orion Bexley, his brother. How convenient for him that he could do just that so close to home by purchasing those presses.

She very nearly did not check the cross-reference. It was enough to know that Wincastle was a guise for Meltham and that Meltham was her sworn enemy. It was nefarious enough, this idea that the Marquess would attempt to covertly silence her, but some inner voice urged her to do it, perhaps out of habit to leave no piece of information unclaimed.

Fleur found the listing for Meltham. It was large and contained a detailed family tree going back several generations. The Marquess of Meltham was a well-established title. Her finger scrolled down to the most recent limb of the tree.

David Harold Arthur Bexley, b. March 2nd, 1782,
d. Aug. 19th, 1840. Married to Mathilda...

She hurried past that to their 'issue'. Two sons. Jasper Bexley and Orion Bexley. Jasper... Hmm... A somewhat uncommon name and now she'd encountered it twice in a short time. She read further.

Titles associated with the marquessate: Earl of
Wincastle, Baron of Umberton.

She sat down hard on the desk chair, letting the shock sink in. *Jasper* was Umberton. And if Jasper was Umberton, he was also *Meltham*. The realisation of what that meant was stunning, overwhelming on so many levels. That made her lover, her confidant, a man whom she'd understood to be her ally her *enemy* because at the core of it all, he was Lord Orion Bexley's brother.

Common sense argued that it couldn't be otherwise. Brothers would support one another, like Adam and Keir and Garrett had supported one another, though they had been a brotherhood of businessmen, rather than blood relations. Cross one of them and you crossed all three. Hadn't Captain Moody warned her that morning in Newcastle that to tangle with Lord Orion Bexley was to tangle with the Marquess? That was to be expected. But she'd made a miscalculation. She'd also expected everyone would play fair, that the Marquess would approach her directly, that she would see him coming and, when he did, that it would be an approach through an open confrontation, *not* through stealth and seduction.

Oh. *Seduction.* Oh, God.

She moaned, recalling the Harefield ball. She cringed. Shuddered. In hindsight she'd been stupid and careless in her loneliness. She'd slept with him. Well, sort of. A romp against a fence wall didn't necessarily constitute 'sleeping'. He'd been eager to accommodate. Now she understood why. It was a first step towards working his way into her confidence, the first step in binding them together.

And it had worked. She *liked* him. He was handsome and intelligent and intuitive. As a result, she'd been attracted to him and she'd trusted him with her body, with her secrets. She hadn't talked to anyone in depth about what she knew about Lord Orion Bexley, preferring to keep her own counsel. But with Jasper, she'd laid it all out voluntarily. What a fool she'd been!

Now she knew why he'd left. He'd had no reason to

stay. He'd got what he came for. Was he even now laughing at her? Thinking what a prank he'd pulled? Flirt with a lonely widow, listen to her stories, give her a little fun against a fence and she'll tell you anything? Had he taken her information and bolstered his defences so that she'd never get past them? Never get to his brother as Captain Moody had predicted?

Recriminations came hard and fast. Somehow, she *ought* to have known. If it had just been the sex, she might not feel so badly. But it was everything that was attached to it. It hadn't *just* been sex. Beneath the self-recrimination simmered another logic. She might have trusted too soon. But he had betrayed. And betrayal was a far bigger crime than trusting. One ought to be able to trust by default. People ought to be honest as a basic, expected practice. That he'd not been spoke more poorly of him than it did of her.

Later, when her anger had passed, she'd take solace in that. This was the very crime she'd railed at Adam's ghost for. He'd betrayed her, too.

Fury simmered. Her words had no effect. Adam was not here to be scolded. But Jasper was and she would *not* tolerate *his* betrayal. Not when she was so close to justice. Not when she had so much personally on the line—all of which she'd sat here in this very room and outlined for him as if he were a trusted friend. She stood up and grabbed her coat. At least now she knew where to find him: Meltham House on Portland Square. There was going to be a reckoning. No one played Fleur Griffiths for a fool and got away with it.

Chapter Twelve

There needed to be a reckoning. Orion *had* to account for his time on the Bilberry Dam commission, yet, despite knowing how desperately that accounting was needed, Jasper was loath to have the conversation. It was why he hadn't gone straight to Orion's favourite club off St James's and dragged him out immediately after he'd left Fleur's office for the last time.

That reckoning was also why he'd decided to leave Fleur. This was war, this was shame. Neither were conditions upon which a relationship could be built. How could he face her if she was right? That was the shame—that he'd been ignorant of his brother's role in the dam's demise. And if she was wrong, there would be shame on her side, too, or resentment. The scandal would always be between them as a competition one of them had lost.

He hoped it would not be him. He was the Marquess. He was supposed to protect his family and his people. But people had died and possibly because of a position he'd put his brother in by arranging for a spot on the commission. Beyond the shame of what he perceived as his own culpability, how could he possibly consort with the enemy? Whether she was right or wrong, he had an obligation to protect his brother and by extension the family. But as much as he didn't want her to be right, he also didn't want her to be wrong. She had much at stake and he appreciated how difficult her position was.

In the weeks since he'd left her, he'd done what he could for both Fleur and for Orion. He'd had his solicitors prepare an offer for the northern newspapers in an attempt to mitigate publicising the suspicions being raised against Orion. It would help them both; she needed the sale, and he needed the silence.

However, in the interim, Orion had slipped through his fingers. His brother was gone, leaving only a note that said he was lying low until the scandal blew over. Which meant Orion was avoiding not only the scandal, but also him and the reckoning. That was concerning. Jasper felt compelled to see his brother's action as a sign that Orion had something to hide, something he did not want to confess any more than Jasper wanted to hear that confession. Once he knew, he'd have to act one way or the other. But what kind of action could he justify? Baconian logic was of no help here.

He scanned the shelves of Meltham House's well-stocked library until he found what he was looking for, his worn copy of Bentham's collected works. It was easy to spot with its faded red cover amid the sleek, smooth spines of lesser read books. Perhaps he'd find comfort in the familiar pages outlining utilitarianism as a political moral compass. If not comfort, perhaps direction, a prompt for what he ought to do when the reckoning came not only for Orion, but himself as well. He did not delude himself in thinking the scandal would not touch them all if it picked up enough momentum.

Jasper poured himself a brandy and settled in his favourite chair beside the empty fire. He took a moment to appreciate the quiet of the house. It seemed he hadn't had quiet for days between putting together the offer to buy the papers and evenings out escorting his mother to balls, sometimes two or three a night. But tonight, he'd been firm. He was staying in. No balls, no visits to his clubs to talk politics. Tonight was for him, to settle his thoughts and perhaps to come to grips with them.

He was halfway through his glass of brandy and Chapter One when the commotion reached him. He sighed. Perhaps an evening of peace and quiet had been too much to hope for. He set aside his book, listening to the brisk clack of heels and the rustle of skirts in the corridor. If his mother thought to cajole him into going out, she was going to be disappointed.

Strident tones sounded in the hallway. 'I will not be kept waiting so that you can come back with an excuse as to why he will not receive me.' *That* was not his mother. That was… Fleur. His reckoning was *here* in Meltham House. Which meant… She knew *everything*. Umberton. Wincastle. Meltham. He had nowhere left to shelter. Like the old elk of his childhood, he was flushed into the open.

He barely had time to rise and brace for battle before Fleur Griffiths blew into the library, disrupting his calm with the force of a spring storm. 'You are a bastard of the first order!' Her eyes blazed with green fire as she made the accusation.

His butler stumbled in her wake. 'My lord, I am sorry. I asked her to wait.'

Jasper waved a hand. 'It's all right, Phillips. I will see her.' He would face his reckoning like a man. It's what he deserved, but he would also face her with the hope that from argument arises a new truth. That was what Aristotle believed anyway. He wasn't sure Fleur Griffiths shared those beliefs. The higher truth was that, despite their differences, they needed each other in order to get to the bottom of this business with Orion. Tonight would test that hypothesis.

Phillips left them and Jasper took a moment before speaking to drink her in: the flashing eyes, the flush of her cheeks, the heave of her breasts, her breath coming fast in her anger. She wore a plain blue skirt and a high-necked white blouse trimmed in lace, her hair done in her usual sensible chignon. She'd come straight from work. His offer must have arrived and all else had un-ravelled from there. It had always been a risk. Perhaps he'd wanted her to find out, wanted to end the pretence between them.

'Please, come and sit and you can tell me why I'm a bastard.' He used his coolness to calm her storm. He'd learned many things about her during their short time together. One of them was that she liked to fight, liked the heat of argument. Undermining that heat was his best chance of having a logical conversation with her.

'I prefer to stand,' she snapped, taking up a position near the sideboard with the decanters, dangerously near breakable items. He hoped it wouldn't come to that. He resumed his seat, wanting to juxtapose his outer calm with her obvious turmoil. In truth, he had his own turmoil to contend with. In spite of their contentious circumstances, she was the loveliest woman he'd ever seen. His body roused to her anger as much as it had roused to her passion. Challenge was a heady aphrodisiac to a man with power.

'This is not a social call, Lord Meltham.' She nearly growled when she said his title.

'I did not think it was. You are angry because you feel lied to.' Validating anger often took away the fuel for that anger. Fleur's anger thrived on opposition. Just as fire thrived on oxygen. He would take her anger's oxygen from her.

Her eyes blazed. 'Don't do that. Do *not* pander to me by explaining my anger to me. I know damn well why I am mad. You misrepresented yourself in order to inveigle yourself into my good graces.' He didn't usually hold with women using profanity, but it was *damned* sexy on her. It stirred him, made him want to get up from his chair and fight fire with fire. He held on to his composure a little longer. Perhaps she was counting on that. Perhaps she was trying to melt his ice even as he tried to cool her heat.

'I *am* Lord Umberton. I did not lie about my identity. I will own that it is not my highest-ranking title. But it's right there in *Debrett's* for anyone to find. You could have looked it up.'

Her eyes narrowed. 'That's ironic advice from a man who claims he wants to be known for himself. *Now*, you want your titles to speak for you. As it happens, I prefer to let people prove themselves. I did not look you up because I wanted to form my own impressions.'

'You liked those impressions. You liked the man you

saw,' he reminded her, even as his body reminded him that he liked her, too, differences aside.

'I did,' she confessed bluntly. 'My instincts are not usually so wrong.'

There was condemnation in her eyes. Not all of it was for him. There was plenty for her as well. She blamed him for misleading her, but she also blamed herself for being taken in and he hated that. He also disliked, that she saw this as a personal failure at a time when she shouldered so many other burdens. He had inadvertently added to those burdens and he'd put a chink in the armour of her confidence when she could not afford it. That was not an intended consequence. He wished he could erase that. Since he could not, he could perhaps explain it.

'I am all those things. I *am* interested in dam legislation. I *am* interested in preventing accidents like the Bilberry Dam in the future. I am also interested in you—just you—although I am not sure how we separate that interest from our circumstances.' He softened his tone and allowed himself the luxury of letting his eyes rest on her. 'Nothing I did with you, nothing I *felt* about being with you, was a lie.' Those few days were some of the most vibrant he could recall in recent history.

'That does not change the fact that you betrayed me!' Fleur railed. His attempt to steal the fuel for her fire was failing. 'You used how I felt about you, you manipulated my trust and then—' she reached for one of the crystal tumblers next to the decanters '—you broke it!' Glass shattered against the hardwood floor. Her eyes blazed.

'Fleur!' He was out of his seat, but she was faster. She grabbed another tumbler and smashed it.

'How do you like that? How does it feel to have something broken?' she raged, smashing another. 'You lied to me, you had sex with me, you pretended to care about me! You are a cad of the highest order. You betrayed me on all levels.'

The hell he had. His self-control was gone now. He gripped her by the forearms, wresting the last tumbler from her and dancing her back to the wall, out of reach of shattered glass and things that could be converted into shattered glass. 'Stop it, Fleur!'

'You didn't betray me?'

'Be fair, you betrayed me that night at Harefield's,' he growled. '*You* used *me*, *you* pretended I was Adam.' The gloves were off now. 'No man likes being a stand-in for a dead husband.'

'Maybe I did use you,' she sneered. 'It doesn't mean I deserved to have you lie to me.'

They were pressed against one another, his body trapping her, keeping her from the rest of his glassware, their chests heaving with the exertion of their anger.

He seized her mouth in a hard, bruising kiss, to stop her words, to stop the anger, to make a different argument, to prove to her…something. He shouldn't have done it, but he wasn't thinking clearly.

She bit down hard on his lip. 'Ouch!' He drew back, wiping his hand across his mouth and coming away with blood. 'What the hell?'

'What the hell is right! How *dare* you kiss me, when you know damn well what it's like with us, how we spark, how we burn and look what that's got us!' She pushed him and stepped around him. It had got him a virago in his arms and a shattered crystal tumbler set on the floor. 'There are weighty considerations between us that we cannot shove aside or solve with a kiss. There is the issue of *your* duplicity and there is the issue of your *brother's* culpability.'

No, she didn't get to do that. The issues of fault weren't entirely all his. 'Don't forget there is also the issue of your newspaper's marketability and your voracious tenacity for justice, which may be misplaced,' he said quietly, his own calm reasserting itself. 'Not all of the issues are on my side of the equation.' She could have her anger, but he wanted to make sure she understood it accurately, truthfully.

He gestured to the chairs beside the cold fire. 'Will you come and sit now and sort through it all with me, see what can be salvaged?' He picked up the last remaining tumbler and poured her a drink to match the one he'd left beside his chair.

She scowled, but she took a seat and the drink. If it wasn't exactly peace it was at least *détente*. They sat in silence for a short while, each one assessing, measuring the other. He braved the silence. 'Have you thought about why I would introduce myself as Umberton?'

She slid him a disapproving look. 'To get close to me, to earn my trust so that I might share with you what I have on your brother. You would be able to thwart me. Perhaps even try to talk me out of it with arguments about doing what was right, about considering the consequences and the purity of my own motives even while you sat there knowing full well the impurity of *your* own motives. You did not seek to guide me with good counsel, but to protect your brother.'

That last stung. She was referring to the arguments

he'd made at Verrey's and she wasn't entirely wrong. He'd made those arguments in the hopes of forestalling more articles naming Orion as the guilty party as much as he'd made them out of common sense. 'They were and are still valid arguments,' he said.

'Arguments that you have vested interest in and you hid that,' she replied.

'Careful, Fleur. Can you say *you* have no vested interest in pushing this story, this investigation out into the public?' he queried.

'I am doing it honestly. I am not hiding behind any pretence. I am not fabricating evidence to fit my own needs. If your brother is innocent, I'll admit that. At least I will have got to the bottom of it. Either way there will be closure for myself and for others who lost loved ones and are still searching for some reason, some understanding behind it,' Fleur said earnestly.

'Even if the board of directors would prefer another outcome?' Jasper nudged the argument a little further along. She might believe she was merely on a quest for the truth, but sometimes the truth didn't sell newspapers.

'Of course,' she snapped. 'I am insulted that you would think otherwise.'

'Just as I am insulted you would think me a charlatan,' he scolded. 'Have you stopped to think how you would have responded if I'd entered your box that night at the theatre and announced myself as the Marquess of Meltham? Would you have listened to me? Would you have allowed me to meet with you at your offices? Would you have shared your information with me? Or allowed me to help with the dam legislation?'

He studied her profile as he waited for an answer, watching the first hint of a smile curve her cheek as she stared into the empty fireplace. In those moments he wished it were autumn so that they might have reason to sit beside a warm fire together. It was a potent domestic fantasy he needed to handle with care.

'You know I would not have,' she admitted.

'Correct, because you were at war with Meltham. But you were not at war with Umberton. He had a clean slate, from which real discussion took place. Is it any mystery I took that option?' He leaned towards her. 'Are we not the better for it? Instead of sworn enemies, we are now friends who can decide how they want to handle these circumstances.' At least that was what he hoped.

For once in her life, Fleur didn't know what to say or even to think. She ought to find the suggestion that they were friends ludicrous in the extreme. It was an extraordinary idea, one that was matched only by the extraordinary circumstances she found herself in— sitting in the Marquess of Meltham's library rationally discussing his brother's culpability in her husband's death.

This was not the encounter she'd expected when she'd stormed out of the office and into his town house. She'd expected a fight, expected to throw things—hot words, a glass or two, to give full vent to her spleen, to her sense of betrayal. And she had. But as a result, she'd expected to be bodily removed from the town house. She would have written about that and painted Jasper Bexley, Marquess of Meltham, with the blackest of brushes, an obstructor of justice, a man who was above the law, who threw his title around to protect a guilty brother.

Instead, he'd asked her to sit, to voice her grievances and he'd answered them, explaining his perspective while holding himself and her accountable. It definitely had her off-kilter but not so far off that she'd forgotten what she'd came for.

'I will not let it be that easy.' She gave him a strong stare, although it was difficult to look at him and not see Umberton, not see her lover, a man she'd trusted with her body and her mind. 'You cannot justify your deception because you feel the consequences were worthy. One cannot say bad behaviour is suddenly good because something good came from it.'

She'd had enough of men making that argument. Adam had kept the state of the newspaper from her, no doubt thinking to protect her from worry. And now, Jasper Bexley had deceived her, too. 'Besides,' she added, 'you did not deceive me with the intent of friendship in mind. That was an accident.'

'A *happy* accident,' he countered. 'As I said, we get to decide how we go on. What shall it be, Fleur? Shall we go forward with forgiveness and friendship or with fear and mistrust?' There was no true 'we' about it. He was leaving the decision up to her and she thought it rather unfair that he made it her responsibility to end things when he'd been the one to walk out.

'There is no decision because there are no choices.' Which was probably for the best. The way he was looking at her now, those eyes of his steady on her, his interest, his want, naked in them, there for her to see, made her wish it could be otherwise. But 'otherwise' was not practical. 'The issues between us are too large, they divide us too thoroughly. And even if they didn't, our association would undermine our individual credibility.' Even without the issue of his brother between them, she knew better than to think they could be friends.

He took a swallow from his glass for the first time since she'd sat down. 'I think I'll need you to explain all of that to me. You must excuse my denseness. I'm not a man used to being without options.' He was half teasing, half serious.

'You will be inclined to protect your brother. I can understand that even if I can't support it. On the other hand, I cannot let the truth go unpublished for the sake of...' She groped for the words. She'd been about to say for the sake of a lover. 'For the sake of someone I care for. I cannot be driven by my emotions, or the truth becomes subjective.'

She sighed. 'The chasm is too wide. Either I will be right, or you will be right. Either way, there will be consequences. Which leads me to your idea of friendship. I do not think friendship can survive such pressures. Aside from that, us associating together—the Marquess of Meltham, brother of the maligned Lord Orion Bexley, and the widow of a prominent man killed at the dam Lord Orion Bexley oversaw, will not build credibility for legislation. People will suspect a conflict of interest and neither of us will look well. Perhaps me most of all, since it impacts my ability to be taken seriously at the newspaper.'

Especially if they were found to be friends and Lord Orion Bexley turned out to be innocent. People would wonder what had driven that conclusion and if she'd arrived at it honestly or if it had been kissed out of her. It was a double standard that one always asked such things of a woman, but never asked them of a man.

He nodded, his hand cradling his glass. 'A man you care for? I am honoured by the description. It gives me hope,' he said in a soft tenor. 'I care for you, too, Fleur, despite our differences.' He reached for her hand and the warmth of his touch sent a delicious shudder through her as he lifted her hand to his lips, his eyes intent on her.

'I must disagree with you, though. This difference needn't keep us apart as I once thought. The day I left you in the office, I meant that kiss to be goodbye. I thought there was no way through it. But that's not true. Lately, I've come to believe that we need each other to see this done. Where you see a chasm I see commonality, something that brings us together instead of setting us apart. We are both searching for the truth about my brother's involvement in the dam accident. We both claim honest intentions to see right done, whatever the outcome. Why not work together?'

He gave a small sigh and she saw how much the proposal cost him. Despite his usual confidence there was worry she might refuse. It was a refusal he would take personally.

'If Orion is guilty, I want to make reparations. I want to see that the families are taken of. It can never bring loved ones back, but it can bring practical ease, a way for them to move forward.' His brow furrowed and she felt his grip on her hand tighten. 'Discovering the truth scares me, Fleur. Part of me doesn't want to know.

'For the past year, I've not questioned the original report's verdict that this was a comedy of errors, all conspiring to create the circumstances of the accident. But you've shown me it could be different, that one man could be at fault. Now that I know that's a possibility, I can't ignore it. If I did ignore it at this point, I'd be guilty, too. I could not live with my conscience. Although, I hope it doesn't come to that. It's a damnably awkward position to be in to choose what is right—protecting one's family or protecting the truth.'

She nodded. She felt for him, she really did. His stance on the issue was admirable in the extreme. Not all people would face such a dilemma head on with such integrity. She found that integrity appealing. Adam had been such a man, always standing up for what was right, standing up in print for those who couldn't stand up for themselves even when it was unpopular with those who funded newspapers.

There was no doubting the sincerity of Jasper's confession or her response to it. She wanted to believe him, wanted to join forces with him. His argument was persuasive. It made sense that they work together. Too much sense. She should not accept it at face value.

When an answer sounded too good to be true, it probably deserved more consideration. Was working together simply the 'easy' answer? The answer that allowed them to pursue not only the truth of Orion's involvement, but also the chance to explore the truth of their personal attraction? More time together meant they could continue what they'd started in Harefield's garden.

That posed its own delight and its own danger. To continue their affair would personalise the context of their interaction—there was the risk of emotions and growing attachment forming, emotions that could po-

tentially colour their quest. She could get hurt if that
was the case. Jasper was a hard man not to like with his
integrity, sincerity and tousled good looks.

Was he counting on that? The woman in her who
fully understood how the world worked was wide awake
now. Did he think to use her emotions against her if
Lord Orion was as guilty as she thought he was? Did
he think she would give up her quest for him?

'I want to be clear. I will print what I find, feelings
for you notwithstanding.' Best to air that right now before things went further even if it meant 'things' didn't
go further. After all, a man who manipulated a woman
with sex was a man for whom integrity was merely a
façade. *That* was not the man for her. That was not her
idea of working together. It still stung that Adam had
not told her about the debt. That had been a betrayal of
their partnership. She would not set herself up for another betrayal.

Anger flickered in Jasper's eyes. She'd attacked the
bastion of his honour. But she had to know. 'Do you
think that is the sort of man I am? To use a woman
for sex? To manipulate a person's feelings for personal
gain?' There was no denying that he'd been honestly
engaged in Harefield's garden, present in their pleasure
body and mind as far it went, while she had not. She
didn't like the idea that she'd dealt him some hurt that
evening, even if unintentional.

'Can you blame me for thinking it when you've offered to buy the northern newspapers? If you were
looking to protect your brother, it's not a bad strategy.
Buying them ensures stories of your brother's perfidy
won't be printed. The populace may never hear of it.

Then, seducing the head of the *London Tribune* could be a means by which to silence the printing of her findings in the largest city in England. Out of devotion to you, perhaps you think she'd forgo the story,' Fleur described the scheme bluntly.

'You do know how to wound a man, Fleur. It's a plausible plan except for one thing: the head of the *London Tribune* would never allow herself to be swayed by such sentiment.' He favoured her with a smile that warmed and complimented. 'I am as sure of that as I am of the sun rising in the east tomorrow. I know such a strategy would never work with you. Integrity will be the saving of us, both yours and mine.'

'And trust,' Fleur added. 'We're trusting each other to know our boundaries, to know the cost of the kind of relationship we want to pursue, to accept limitations, and most of all, to keep our promises when circumstances might tempt us to rethink them.' There was no might about it. Circumstances would evolve that would put that temptation right in front of them. 'So, I ask you again. If not to protect your brother, why did you offer to buy the northern newspapers?' There was no time like the present to test their promises of integrity and trust. This partnership might be over before it began.

Chapter Thirteen

Fleur wanted to stop time. She didn't want to hear his answer. Earlier he'd said he was frightened of the truth and what it might force him to face. He was not alone. She was scared of the truth, too. She didn't want to believe this tawny-eyed man, who could heat her blood with a touch, was guilty of deliberate censorship, that he would seek to buy out her newspapers in order to protect his brother. She sat on the edge of her chair, braced to face one more betrayal.

'I wanted to help you.' She'd not expected that. For a moment she was speechless in his presence, yet again. When she said nothing, he gave an elegant shrug of his shoulders. 'You were selling the papers anyway. I thought a quick sale would be helpful to you, to show the board of directors the papers had value.'

She nodded. She'd initially thought the same thing. 'But you if owned the papers, you could also choose to not print any news about the investigation.' She voiced the concern with a certain amount of tentativeness. Here was another answer she didn't want to hear.

He answered slowly, thoughtfully. 'I could and, to be honest, I would probably not print any stories that continued to make my brother appear to be the lone villain until the links were ironclad. I know you would find that disappointing. However, if he were indeed guilty of taking money and not making the repairs, I would not stop the story from running. In my mind, *that* would be undue and intentional censorship.' She felt she could breathe again. It might not be the way she would do things, but it was a tenable compromise, one that was honest and fair.

'Thank you. I appreciate your candour. But I must offer some candour of my own. I do not know how open the board of directors will be to an offer from Meltham, given the...um...circumstances with your brother.' Perhaps that had been another guiding reason for him offering as Wincastle. Now that she had time to think, it was possible that choice hadn't been all about tricking her. He'd been trying to help her as best he could.

'Well, I tried.' He gave a wry smile before sobering. 'He's gone, you know. Orion left a note saying town was too hot for him at the moment.'

That was news. Not that it mattered if he was in town or not. The stories could run with or without him. But she could see his brother's absence bothered Jasper. 'I suppose you blame me for that.'

He gave a short nod. 'I do. The stories in the *Tribune* have called him out as a prime suspect in the "new" investigation the *Tribune* is single-handedly running. It's called enough attention to him that he feels it is difficult to go about in society.' He shook his head. 'He can't go home to Meltham because the story has run in your regional papers up there and it's called him out in front of our people. I don't know where he's gone. I hope he'll resurface. He left before I could talk with him.'

Fleur slipped her hand from his grasp. 'I'm sorry.' She sincerely was. Sorry that he was hurting. Sorry that his brother was gone. Sorry that she was part of it. Through her choices, she'd hurt him, this man she cared for.

He fixed her with a firm stare. 'I did not tell you so that you'd be sorry. I told you so that you would be aware. Your quest has real, concrete consequences, not just for a single individual, or for yourself, but consequences that will spread like ripples on a pond. When you act, you are not choosing those consequences just for yourself, but also for others.'

There was much left unsaid there—that she would be choosing for him. Choosing for his mother. Choosing for Lord Orion. Choosing for all the families affected by the accident. Lord Orion Bexley's leaving was a tangible consequence, no doubt, the first of many that she would be responsible for.

She gave him a solemn nod. 'This quest is indeed dangerous for both of our reputations. I admit that I've printed a story that has caused your brother to flee the town to escape social persecution. But you must also admit that fleeing certainly lends itself to believing he has something to hide, that he is indeed guilty.'

She was silent for a while, letting them both digest that. Neither side of that coin was particularly pleasant for either of them to contemplate.

'You may have the right of it. With so much at stake, this is best undertaken together.' At least for as long as an alliance could last. She did not delude herself in thinking that it would be an indefinite association. If his brother was guilty, Jasper's loyalty would be sorely tested no matter what he said tonight. How would he truly feel when that moment came? Would his integrity and trust withstand that test? It was an enormous leap of faith for her.

'I think to undertake our investigation, we must leave the city,' Jasper said.

She gave him a questioning look. 'What are you suggesting?'

'I am suggesting we go back to the scene of the accident. What we really need to find, we'll find there or not at all. My family seat is not far from Holmfirth. Tomorrow, we leave for Meltham.'

Another woman would have baulked at such a speedy departure for what might appear to be a spontaneous trip to the country in the midst of the Season. But not Fleur. She spent the night packing, writing out instructions for the paper, rescheduling meetings and sending notes of regret cancelling her attendance at a few upcoming events. This trip pre-empted all else because it decided all else. This trip was not as much a spontaneous occurrence as it was an inevitable one. The events of the past year had been leading up to this. This was the way forward.

Fleur closed her travelling trunk shortly after one in the morning, letting the enormity of the trip overwhelm her at last. When she came back from Meltham, it would all be over, the search for justice settled. She was both excited and terrified by the prospect. To have closure, to know for sure, would be a blessing and it ought to bring peace, but she wondered if it would. It couldn't bring Adam back; it couldn't resolve the differences their marriage had ended on. It could not absolve her of the guilt she carried. But it could help the paper, it could solidify her position and her ability to hold on to Adam's empire.

She had slept very little that night, her thoughts in turmoil. She rose early and dressed in a blue travelling ensemble that she liked for its simplicity, then left the house. Better to do her waiting at the station than roaming the house and checking the clock every two minutes. This way she could feel as if she was doing something.

Alone at the station, she had another set of nerves to contend with. She could not ignore the other facet of this trip. She was going away with Jasper. Not the Marquis of Meltham, or Lord Umberton, but with *Jasper*. A man whose touch made her tremble, whose gaze made her warm, made her feel seen. A man who had kissed her, made wild love to her and danced with her beneath the moonlight. A man who made her feel alive, even though he was poised on the opposite side of the business between them.

How might that play out? He'd said they were friends last night. Was that all there was for them? Whatever there could be between them would always be short term, but Meltham offered a certain freedom to explore that potential, away from society's eyes. Away from his mother's list of debutantes, away from politicos and a prickly board of directors who might find their association a conflict of interests.

She caught sight of his tall, broad-shouldered form

cutting through the crowd coming towards her, her pulse quickening at the sight of him in his buff trousers and blue coat. She rather wished her pulse wouldn't do that. It made her mind ask difficult questions like what would happen if they were just Jasper and Fleur, if they could just be themselves? Was that even possible? Or was the business between them too much?

'You're early. I am impressed.' Jasper smiled, his gaze lingering on her longer than needed, and the conversation lagged into an uncomfortable silence. Perhaps he, too, was nervous. What had seemed like a straightforward idea in the quiet of the evening suddenly seemed more complicated by daylight. Or perhaps, like her, it was simply nerves born of their unsettling attraction to one another. He recovered first. 'Are you ready for our adventure? Our train is over here.'

He dropped a hand to the small of her back and ushered her towards the London Northwestern Railway locomotive, already huffing on the track. They let talk of the journey's details fill the empty space and ease the way. 'I have a first-class compartment reserved for us. We might as well enjoy some luxury while we can. I've arranged for breakfast to be served privately.'

She smiled. 'You're spoiling me. Should I be concerned?'

He laughed. 'We'll see if you feel that way at the end of the day. Not all of our trains will be this comfortable.' They'd take this train to Leeds and then a train to Huddersfield. From there it would be a carriage ride to the seat of the marquessate at Rosefields. 'It will be a long day.' He handed her up the steps into the train car, allowing her to precede him down the narrow aisle leading to their compartment, each gesture making her acutely aware of him, of his closeness, of his consideration even though she could very well be the enemy before this was through.

'I don't mind.' She laughed over her shoulder, catching his gaze. 'It is still a marvel to me that we will be in the west Yorkshire Dales tonight when it would have taken three or four days to make the journey by coach just a few years ago.'

'We're right here.' He gestured to the coupe compartment at the far end of the train car. 'The compartment seats three, but I bought the third ticket so that we needn't worry about any intrusions. Ah, look, our breakfast basket has already arrived. Thank goodness, I'm famished.'

She was famished, too, Fleur realised as their day progressed. Famished not for food, but for care. She secretly revelled in the little comforts he'd arranged because *she'd* not had to do the arranging. Along with that secret came another one: part of her liked being cared for, looked after, having someone else to share the burden for once. Not all the decisions had to be hers alone.

She'd had that with Adam. Mostly. At least she'd thought she had. They'd made decisions about which charities to support, which stories to run, which direction to take the newspapers. Of course, she knew now that it hadn't been perfect. Decisions about the debt had not included her. And when it had come to the biggest decision in their marriage, the decision to have a family, Adam alone had made the choice.

With Jasper she would be certain to ensure this was a true sharing of responsibility. She was well aware that control was hard for both of them to surrender. Until last night, Jasper had controlled when they would meet by withholding an address. But she'd paid for lunch. These were small things, but they did hint at the larger need. They were both establishing their boundaries, protecting themselves. And yet the thought tickled: wouldn't it be wonderful if instead of protecting themselves, they could protect each other. She feared circumstances made that an impossibility, a reminder that even this partnership had limitations.

'Fleur, Fleur, wake up, we're nearly there.' A gentle shake roused her as a soft early evening light bathed the interior of the coach. Sweet heavens, she'd fallen asleep. Jasper shifted on the seat beside her and she realised where she'd slept. On the ledge of his broad shoulder, or from the looks of his once perfectly pressed coat, against his chest in that space where shoulder meets torso. She put a quick hand to her face, hoping she hadn't drooled. It was bad enough she'd fallen asleep on him.

'I'm sorry, I didn't mean to...' She stifled a yawn. 'The late night apparently caught up to me,' she apologised.

He gave a soft smile. 'I didn't mind. Although I was worried it might have been my company that had sent you off into the arms of Morpheus.'

'Not at all,' she assured him truthfully. He'd been an excellent travelling companion today, full of interesting small talk about the countryside they were passing. By tacit agreement, they'd discussed nothing too meaningful, or too personal that would lead them back to their business. Yet talking with him had still been enjoyable.

It was no wonder he was one of the most sought-after bachelors this Season. He knew how to put a person at ease, how to engage them even on the most mundane of topics.

He leaned forward to look out the window, then turned to her with a smile that spoke volumes. 'We're coming down the drive now. You can see the house.' There was pride in his voice, she noted, and relief, too. He *liked* it here. Rosefields was not just the seat of the marquessate it was also a homecoming for him.

And he'd invited her here, into his world.

Fleur's hands clenched in her lap as she took in the sandstone façade of the house. The realisation was a bit overwhelming given that it might shortly become the site in which a horrible truth was revealed. How might that taint his associations with the place? 'It's very beautiful,' she acknowledged.

'I'll give you the tour after supper if you'd like. I thought we'd dine on the terrace and enjoy the spring evening.' He paused, reconsidering. 'Unless you are too tired?'

'Not at all. It would be good to stretch my legs. I am not used to so much sitting.' Or so much comfort, so much spoiling. Was that what he was counting on? They'd sworn to be friends, to be on the same side, but he'd deceived her once. She would be foolish not to think about this from a strategic point of view.

Were today's comforts meant to lull her into complacency? Was being here at Rosefields meant as an attempt to soften her desire to pursue his brother? Was their very attraction to each other meant to also be a tool by which her mettle was undone? She didn't want to think of it that way, but she must. Her station in life required it. A woman alone must always be on her guard. Even at the paper she wasn't safe. The board of directors were always looking to question her decisions.

The carriage came to a halt and the step was set. Jasper jumped out first and handed her down, his grip on her fingers warm and sure, yet a cold, warning trill went down her spine as she looked up at the majestic façade of the house. What had she walked into?

She was on the Marquess's ground now and she was alone.

Chapter Fourteen

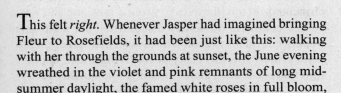

This felt *right*. Whenever Jasper had imagined bringing Fleur to Rosefields, it had been just like this: walking with her through the grounds at sunset, the June evening wreathed in the violet and pink remnants of long midsummer daylight, the famed white roses in full bloom, their scent wafting on the air of the garden.

'The roses are legendary. They date back to the Plantagenets,' he told her as they walked.

'The white rose of York?' She smiled.

'Yes, exactly so. Meltham sided with the House of York. It was in the early days of our title, so I am told. The white roses also symbolise purity and innocence.'

He stopped and plucked a rose from its stem to ensure there were no thorns. 'May I?' He tucked the bloom behind her ear, securing it in the depths of her auburn tresses. She'd changed into a pink gown for supper and the colour looked extraordinary with her hair. 'I didn't think redheads wore pink.' He gave the bloom a last adjustment.

'We can if we're brave enough and our dressmakers are smart enough,' she replied with a laugh. 'I have a gown in a blush pink, too. It's one of my favourite colours to wear. This is the first time I've actually worn this one. I'd bought it before...' Her voice trailed off. They both knew what before signified. 'And then it wasn't exactly something I could wear last year.'

No, he didn't imagine this bright, pure pink would have been appropriate during mourning. He was touched that she'd worn it for him. He was the only man to see her in it. This dress was his alone, something that didn't belong to Dead Adam. 'You match the sunset,' he complimented.

The comment obviously discomfited her a bit, this usually confident woman who always had something to say. Perhaps she was rusty at receiving them, another sign that she'd been alone too long. She quickly recovered, a teasing flare in her green eyes. 'By matching the sunset, surely you mean stunning, fiery, blazing.'

He shook his head and covered her hand where it lay on his arm. She was trying to downplay the compliment and by doing so the sentiment that went with it. 'Those adjectives describe the sun. I am talking about the *sunset*: calm, quiet, serene. You can be those things, too, Fleur. You needn't be fiery all the time.'

'Needn't I? I beg to differ. I think I would be eaten alive.'

'So *you* must be the fire? The consumer?' He gave her a thoughtful look. 'I feel that way, too, when I'm in London. I must protect the family, even myself. There is always business to take care of. I must always be on guard. Everybody wants something from me: money, time, patronage, an introduction, an acknowledgment. But not here. When I'm at Rosefields I am entirely myself. Certainly, there is work. Managing land and people always requires work, but there is also time to be me, to be quiet and still, to lay down my guard and rest.' He gave her a long look. 'I want Rosefields to be that for you as well while you're here.' There was a shadow in her eyes that confused him. Had he not been sincere? Had he not just laid the best gift he could conjure at her feet in a token of his goodwill?

'It is an impossibility, Jasper. Here is the place where I can lay down my guard the least. This is your ground. Not an inch of it is mine. In London there was at least some parity, some neutrality.' Restaurants and ballrooms were neutral territory. Theatre boxes and ballrooms were public. Homes were not.

'Do we need that neutrality?' he asked quietly in the gathering darkness. She did not trust his overture and it stung because it meant that she'd agreed to their alliance last night even though she hadn't fully believed him, trusted him. 'You are safe with me.'

She gave him a long, searching stare. 'But I shouldn't be. You have much to lose and yet you've brought me to your sanctuary.'

Jasper sensed she meant the words to put him off, to remind him of their circumstances. Fleur loved to fight. It was her protection. But the words did not rouse argument within him, only sorrow. This past year had done more damage to this woman than she knew. It was not only grief she carried with her, but suspicion and mistrust of everything and everyone in her world. Was there truly no one she could turn to?

He knew that feeling. A marquess must, by the nature of his position, be somewhat alone. *He* was alone except for his brother, a few close friends and his mother.

Despite her ceaseless matchmaking, his mother was a bellwether for him, a compass. And he had Orion. He relied on them both. Who did Fleur have? Her husband was dead. Her best friends had remarried and left England. Her board of directors seemed more like sharks than supports and her aunt and uncle had deserted her.

'You say I have much to lose and you marvel that I've invited you here. But I say the reverse is true. You also have much to lose and still you have come,' he ran a thumb gently over the back of her hand in a soothing gesture. 'Contrary to your conclusion, I think my invitation and your acceptance of it indicate that there is indeed trust between us, *not* suspicion.' The shadow did not diminish from her gaze. She was wary even now. Good lord, how deep did her hurt go? How did he reach someone that far adrift, that heavily protected by the walls they'd built to hide the damage of loss?

'Are you not afraid of what we might find here?' she asked. It was the first time she'd ever used that word 'afraid'. In the beginning he'd never have associated such a word with her. She was bold, daring, but not afraid. Now, he saw those things as decoys.

'Yes,' he confessed. 'I am concerned about what we might find. However, I am not afraid of how we will respond. I have every confidence that you will handle the information with discretion and professionalism, that you will understand the gravity of how that information might affect people. Likewise, I have every confidence in myself to respond fairly. Our intentions come from a place of goodness. You believe it, too, or you would not have come.'

At least not with him. She might have come alone

eventually, an avenging angel with a flaming sword looking to prove herself. A position of anger was not the way he wanted her to approach this fact-finding mission.

The spring moon had risen above the garden and the night birds had begun to sing. He led her to a low stone bench set amid a bower of white roses. 'You can see the stars from here as they come out. Look, there's the beginning of the Plough.'

He heard her sigh, felt her gaze follow the arc of his hand as he traced the sky, his finger connecting one star to the next. She shifted on the bench as she spoke, her voice soft in the dark, the weight of her head leaning against his shoulder as it had in the carriage this afternoon. 'The country *is* beautiful. It is so quiet out here. A person can hear themselves think. It's not like that in London. London is all busyness and schedules and moving from one activity to the next. It's a good day if I can go to sleep with my list completed. I'm not sure a completed list *should* be the mark of a good day.'

He could feel the rise and fall of her breathing, deep and slow, relaxed. He took comfort from that. She did trust him a little even if she'd not admit to it. He said nothing, waiting and wanting her to speak again. He'd been telling stories all day in the hopes of putting her at ease and in the hopes that she'd share stories of her own. Eventually, she did.

'I haven't spent much time in the country since I made my debut. It's hard to believe that was over ten years ago.' Her hand was idly picking at his sleeve. He liked her touch on him, casual and soft.

'Do you not have a country property?' A man with her husband's wealth could have afforded to buy an estate and many did, thinking it another notch in their belts to show the world they were someone.

Fleur rolled her head on his shoulder. 'No, we lived in London year round. Adam didn't like being too far from the *Tribune* offices. Whenever we left London it was to go to the other papers: Bristol, Leeds, York, Sheffield. We did stay a few times at Antonia and Keir's or Garrett and Emma's places. They had estates not far from each other in Surrey and not far from London. Adam felt he could get back quickly enough if there was trouble.'

Dead Adam was starting to sound like a selfish bastard, Jasper thought, but he knew he *was* biased. The man had had this incredible woman as his wife and his first thoughts had been whether or not he lived close enough to his work. Admittedly, Jasper recognised he knew little about the lives of businessmen. The concept of going to work, of keeping hours, and meeting deadlines was entirely foreign to him in some ways.

'And you worked at the paper as well?' he asked idly, careful not to scare her off with too much prying. This was the most she'd ever spoken of her previous life. His arm had tired of tracing the stars and had gone around her. Lord, this was nice, holding her, talking in the darkness, watching the moon. No London evening could be finer.

'Yes, I did. I wrote feature stories for the *Tribune*. I went in every day.' She gave a little laugh. 'Otherwise, I wouldn't have seen Adam at all.' Aha! Jasper thought. Dead Adam was indeed a selfish bastard. But then her next words deflated his sense of private victory.

'We were very lucky. We enjoyed our work together. We spent our days together. Some couples become strangers with no shared interests, the wife going one way with her charities and ladies' teas and the husband going another with his work and clubs. Soon, they're two different people living in two different worlds.' She gave a light sigh and snuggled closer. 'It's not necessarily their faults. I think the world sets people up to fail when it divides responsibilities, women to the private sector of the home and men to the public. There's not much opportunity for sharing or for paths to cross.'

Jasper ran a hand up and down her bare arm in a languid pattern. 'I suppose that's one way to look at it. Being at work all day doesn't leave a lot of time for family, though.' It was a dangerous question. He knew it the moment he asked it. He felt her tense where his hand ran down her arm.

'Adam did not wish for a family. He felt he was too old. He turned fifty the year we wed and he felt we should have some time to ourselves before we contemplated adding children in the mix. He believed it was important that we get to know each other.' She gave a little laugh against his chest. 'Ours was a whirlwind courtship.'

'Yes, you've mentioned that,' Jasper said wryly. He couldn't forget it. One kiss from Dead Adam and she'd fallen for the much older man. 'But once those years of settling in passed, surely children would be a natural progression to a marriage.' It would be for him. He wanted to be a father, not just for the duty of the marquessate, but for himself. He wanted to give to another what his father had given to him. He yearned for it, but he wanted children with the right woman, not simply any woman.

'By then Adam felt he was too old. He said he didn't want to die and leave behind a half-raised child.' She'd talked a lot about what Dead Adam had wanted. What did she want?

'But you felt differently? Did you want children?' Did she still want children?

'Yes,' she breathed the answer quietly into the night. 'It was a point of contention between us, the one thing we never agreed on.' Ah, so she and Dead Adam had fought. Argued. Had unresolved issues. Children. Time in the country. She'd given up a lot for that marriage. Did she see that? With Griffiths's fortune, she could have spent her days any way she chose: shopping and charity work, decorating and redecorating the town house. Instead, she'd chosen to spend it working at the *Tribune* in order to be close to her husband. Perhaps she'd understood the risk of not doing so—the risk of losing him, the risk of watching her marriage disintegrate.

Something potent, part admiration and part envy, stirred in Jasper. Fleur Griffiths was loyal to the bone. To be the recipient of that loyalty, that devotion, would be the honour of a lifetime. Such dedication should not be given idly to just any man or woman. A person would need to be worthy of it, would need to earn it. Sitting here in the moonlight with her, he realised *he* would like to be worthy of it, even if only for a short time.

'What of you? Have you ever been in love?' she asked. She was deflecting and exacting a little *quid pro quo*. But wasn't this also a sign of trust, proof that she'd meant it last night when she'd said she cared for him?

'I thought I was once. I was young and foolish, though.

It didn't work out, obviously. Hence, my mother's need for a list. I am more cautious these days.' He'd not truly understood how attractive a title could be for ambitious young ladies in those days.

She elbowed him in the ribs playfully. 'And yet you're here with me. That doesn't sound like the cautious choice.' There was nothing cautious about Fleur Griffiths, it was what he liked about her. She was bold but vulnerable, brave but scared. But despite the vulnerability and the fear, she did not hold back, did not let those things stop her.

He felt her draw away from him and some of the magic went out of the evening. He was losing her. 'I should not have said that. It was very leading.' She rose and shook out her skirts.

He rose with her, a hand at her arm. 'It was very *bold*. You know I like that about you. You admit your feelings. You speak your mind. Don't ever change that. Not for me, not for anyone.' Perhaps that had been the appeal of Dead Adam besides his kisses. He'd allowed her to speak her mind. Few men would. Fleur was a lot of woman to handle. No, not to handle. No one handled Fleur Griffiths. He'd do best to remember that. 'You may be as you please here, Fleur. *We* may be as we please.' He let his eyes linger on hers, his gaze conveying the unspoken message of his words. Rosefields could be their sanctuary. Here, they could be Jasper and Fleur until it was time to return to London. Did she understand?

Chapter Fifteen

〰〰〰

Her breath caught. He was asking her to trust him, to be his lover in this place where they could keep the world out, where others wouldn't dictate whether or not they could be seen together. It was a chance to answer the question she'd posed for herself at the station in London just this morning: what could they be if they had a chance to just be Jasper and Fleur, removed from the circumstances of their association? Her body thrummed with the innate recognition that she wanted to know. She wanted to know that answer very much.

'If you dare, I dare,' she breathed, the realisation settling on her that she dared more than trusting him, she dared her heart, she dared a testing of the feelings she'd not yet been willing to name. She was falling for Jasper Bexley, the man. She could not keep shoving that knowledge to the side.

He moved into her, hands at her waist, his mouth hovering inches from hers as he whispered, 'I dare.' He sealed it with a kiss, claiming her mouth with his. This was not like the ravenous kisses they'd shared before in her office or at the Harefields'. This was unhurried, but no less heated for it. The slow burn that spread through her body carried its own brand of intoxication, its warmth searing away opposition in its wake until it was impossible to not want this, to not want him.

All the reasons why this would be a poor idea were obliterated with the stroke of his tongue against her lips, the press of his body against hers, reminding her of the possibilities between them, not the problems. He made her hope—perhaps she did deserve a second chance— it was a wild, reckless hope, full of moonlight's magic and none of daylight's realities.

Her hands reached for his neckcloth, moving to untie it. He chuckled against her mouth, his own hands disengaging to reach for hers. 'Tonight, I want to be with you in a proper bed, without worry of discovery hastening our lovemaking. We have all night; I want to make the most of it.' It was a promise of pleasure, a pledge of protection. He would not take her here, out of doors.

All night.

The prospect sent a delightful tremor through her even as the thought came to her that he'd also want things in exchange—not merely physical passion.

I want to be with you in a proper bed.

She was ready to give that, ready to feel the comfort of being with another. He'd want the things that went with it. He'd not said he wanted to *have her* in a proper bed, bedding her like some archaic medieval lord, but that he wanted *to be with her*. He was asking for her trust, for her presence in a way she'd not given it to him before. This was going to be a deliberate act of lovemaking, not the outcome of spontaneous, riotous emotions, which could be excused in the morning.

And I want it. With him, came the warm thought.

Upstairs, his bedroom was lit with a single lamp that bathed the space in a soft light, a welcoming light. Covers on the tall, carved oak four-posted bed had been pulled back and Jasper's robe had been laid out. The small intimacies sent a shiver of anticipation through her, a reminder that lovemaking was a domestic act, a large intimacy full of smaller ones.

'Shall I play the maid tonight?' Jasper whispered at her ear, his hands already working the laces of her gown, making it a rhetorical question. He pressed a kiss to her neck and she let the warmth of him seep into her skin as he continued his slow seduction. He undressed her with his hands, his mouth dropping kisses to welcome the newly bared skin.

She gave an appreciative sigh as he pressed a kiss to her back. 'You are remarkably good at undressing.'

'Not undressing,' he murmured, his hands unfastening petticoat tapes. 'Unveiling.' The word was punctuated by the soft landing of her petticoat and the silent fall of her crinoline cage shortly after. The last of her undergarments gave way. She was entirely nude, entirely free to feel him against her skin—his chest to her back, his hips to her buttocks, the hard length of him making itself known through the fabric of his trousers as it butted up against her.

His hands cupped her breasts, kneading them gently, thumbs brushing over her nipples in languid strokes, his mouth at her ear. 'Have you ever seen Michelangelo's sculptures *The Slaves*?' he whispered. 'They are statues cut from marble, but they are not entirely finished, on purpose so that it seems as if the marble is a chrysalis the figures are emerging from.'

He nipped at her ear. 'What makes them magical is the sense of effort, of energy one senses when viewing them. It's as though the statues are actively struggling to be free of the marble, the way a baby chick struggles to pierce the membrane of an egg, or a foal struggles to be born.' He blew gently into her ear. 'Unveiling you is like that, Fleur. Each piece of clothing discarded releases you.'

Yes, yes, to all of that, her heart sang. To be free. The clothes were just a metaphor. It was the world she was being freed from. Here in this chamber, naked with this man, she need not worry about the newspaper, about the pressures of being a woman alone in a man's world. She needed only to be herself. She turned in his arms, catching his mouth in a kiss of her own. 'Let me give you that freedom, too. Let me release you from your marble chrysalis,' she whispered, her hands working loose the snowy folds of his cravat, carefully setting aside the gold stickpin.

She undid the buttons of his waistcoat, unfastened the links at his cuffs, liking the domestic feel of helping a man—her man. 'Have you ever considered why it is that a woman must be undressed from the back but a man is always undressed from the front?' She slid him a coy glance as she pulled his shirt tails from the waistband of his trousers.

'Are you going to tell me?' He nuzzled her neck, his mouth teasing her as she worked.

'I have my opinions.' She slid her hands beneath his shirt along the warm planes of his chest, wanting to feel him before she saw him. He *felt* good, warm and solid to the touch. What exquisite musculature he had. She undid his shirt, button by button, outlining her premise. 'I think it's about power, about self-sufficiency. A woman cannot help herself, even in a pinch. In an emergency a gentleman can dress himself. But the wealthier a woman is, the less likely she is able to perform that simple daily function for herself.'

Fleur finished her unbuttoning and pushed the shirt from his shoulders. She'd not been wrong. He was spectacular. 'You look even better than you felt,' she breathed. It was a bold comment, but it pleased him. She watched his eyes darken, his desire growing. He reached for her, but she staved him off with a shake of her head. 'I am not done. You are not free yet. Almost.' She promised, 'Soon.'

'Hurry,' he said in a husky whisper.

Her hands dropped to his waistband. 'Do you think that is how your sculptures felt? Hurry. Free us.' She pushed his trousers over lean hips, her sense of anticipation growing, heightening at the sight of his arousal. He kicked his trousers away and she stared in awe at what she'd unveiled. Such masculine beauty had lain beneath those clothes, a beauty that was at once both rough-hewn and smooth-carved, a body that fulfilled the contradictions she'd perceived in him that first day. She could not help herself. Fleur reached a hand to trace the musculature at his hip where the sinews tapered down towards his groin. She'd not seen such definition before.

'That's the iliac girdle.' He gave a juddering breath as her fingers feathered over his abdomen.

'And this?' She closed her hand over the length of him, feeling the hot pulse of him, his member hard and solid within her touch even as his breath came in shaky gasps. 'I believe we've not been formally introduced.' She loved that this was driving him wild, testing his restraint.

'Phallus.' He murmured the word against her mouth. She could feel him smile as he kissed her.

'You're free now.' She let him dance her back towards the big bed with its inviting turned-down covers. They were both free. The newspaperwoman and the Marquess had been left on the floor, discarded shells from which Jasper and Fleur emerged. She laid back on the bed and pulled him to her, cradling him between her legs. Her body was wet and hot and wanting and his answered. There would be time later for exploration, for lounging in one another's arms. This was not Harefield's garden. There'd been no time then, no unveiling. There'd been only sensation, combustible and bright like a firework and just as fleeting.

He came into her and she let the feel of him fill her, let it purl through her as she gave a slow arch of her back in response, savouring him, welcoming him. The old urge came to close her eyes, to fall into the sensation, but he would not have it. 'Stay with me, watch me as I watch you,' he murmured the instruction, his hips moving against her, setting an easy rhythm. 'Don't leave me. Tonight we are together.' Yes, and for now that was enough. For now that was everything.

She fastened her gaze on his topaz eyes, locked her legs about his hips and took up the rhythm with him. There was wildfire in his gaze, encouragement in his words, adoration in them as his body worshipped hers until restraint broke and they were lost together, gasping and crying, desperately seeking the culmination that waited just beyond them. Then she was there, *they* were there, on the shores of ecstasy, and she was coming apart, eyes wide open as a climax rippled through her body, gaze transfixed on him in his most vulnerable, most complete moments.

Watching him was a mesmerising experience. It left her breathless to see this powerful man wild and undone *with* her, *because* of her, his pleasure a mirror of her own, as was his satisfaction and completion. Yes, despite the undone, deconstructed, bone-shattering quality of their lovemaking, there was also a sense of wholeness, rightness. She wanted to drift in that rightness for ever. Rightness was rare. Nothing had been right or whole for her for a very long time.

She curled into him, fitting her body against the curve of his, her head at his shoulder, her hand at his abdomen. She could feel peace come to him as his breathing settled and slowed. There was a sheen to his skin, testament to their efforts. Their bodies told the truth better than words in those moments and she was content to be quiet, content to let her hands wander idly over his body.

'Clavicle,' he murmured, half asleep.

'And this?'

'Trapezoid.' His body became a litany of words. Pectoralis major, the ticklish spot beneath his arm. Serratus anterior. Rectus abdominus.

'That's amazing.' Her hand came to rest low on his hip on the so-named inguinal ligament. 'How do you know so much anatomy?'

He chuckled, lacing his fingers through hers. 'If I could have been anything I'd have been a scientist.'

'Hmm.' She gave a drowsy, considering sigh. 'That makes sense, I suppose. It explains why you knew about the stars tonight and the anatomy. Why? What do you love about science?'

'Science is precise, dependable. The same efforts get the same results. There are guarantees. Hypotheses are testable. Results can be confirmed. There are sureties not found elsewhere. What about you? If you weren't a journalist, what would you be?'

'I've never given it much thought,' Fleur confessed. 'Perhaps because being a journalist isn't too far from what I might have been. I've always liked writing. I may have fancied being a novelist like Mrs Radcliffe at one time, but writing for the newspaper is close enough and it gave me a chance to...' She didn't finish her sentence, didn't let the words *be with Adam* slip out. She didn't want Adam here tonight in this bed with them, between them. Tonight they were free. Just the two of them.

'To use my writing for good,' she amended hastily. 'News promotes literacy both through reading and information. It also promotes social access, a gateway to participating in the world instead of letting the world happen to you. Wherever there is a newspaper, people have access to information, to reading.'

She gave a little laugh. 'I don't mean to pontificate. The news is off limits tonight.'

Sweet heavens, there were so many things they shouldn't talk about here in bed and she'd nearly broken all those rules. Perhaps it would be best if she stopped talking and turned the conversation back to him.

'How interesting that you are a mar—err...uhm... *man* who likes science. What else do you like? I want to know everything about you.' She snuggled back down beside him, aware that she'd almost made another conversational mistake. He did not want to be the Marquess tonight any more than she wanted to be Adam's widow or a newspaperwoman. Yet for those rules to hold, there were limits to their conversation. It was a sobering reminder amid the pleasure that tonight was a fantasy. They weren't as free as they thought.

He'd been free with her last night, at liberty to be himself and she with him. But now that night was ending. The first tentative fingers of morning were stretching across the floor while Fleur slept in his arms, exhausted at last. Such nights didn't happen often for him. Even with the occasional mistress, he must always be the Marquess, sex was more of a performance than a pleasure. But not last night. Last night with her, he'd been himself. He did not want to waste a moment drowsing even if it was only to stay awake to watch her sleep and to remember, to savour.

It had been exquisite to hold her in his arms, to know that she was with him when they'd found completion. He'd lost himself in the emerald depths of her eyes as assuredly as he'd lost himself in the pleasure of a jointly achieved climax. Even so, lost as he was, he'd been conscious enough to protect her from any repercussions—both times—because talk had led to more lovemaking and then more stories.

He'd told her stories of his boyhood growing up here at Rosefields, stories of his father and the adventures they'd had, fishing in Rosefields's streams, hunting grouse—which he far preferred to hunting elk—in the dales, hiking the hills amid the brilliance of autumn foliage and in the spring amid the purple heather. 'I wish you could see Rosefields in the autumn,' he whispered, knowing she would not hear.

'And at Christmas,' he added, thinking of the evergreen boughs that would drape the mantels and lintels and the Yule log that would crackle in the hearth, the house crowded with villagers and tables groaning beneath Christmas delicacies. She would like that, all the children running around. Fleur was a caretaker. It was what she did with her news stories. She used news as a means of caring for people, of connecting them to their world, of broadening their horizons, and she used it as a tool by which she could advocate for them. He'd rather loved her impassioned impromptu speech earlier about what a newspaper could do. Weren't those the very reasons he championed a free press? It was something they had in common in the real world.

He stretched with a groan, aware that the morning was full upon them. It would be a difficult day for her. They were going into Holmfirth to speak with some people about the dam. It would take her back to the scene of the crime, so to speak, to a place that held only sadness for her. He'd rather stay here at Meltham where there was happiness, where there was this bed and where obligations and memories did not intrude.

She stirred in his arms, her hair a tumbled auburn cloud against the pillow. He thought she was the loveliest woman he'd ever seen. 'Is it morning already?'

She groaned and opened one eye. 'How long have you been awake?'

'A while, sleepyhead.' He gave a lazy smile.

'You should have woken me.'

'You needed the sleep. We have time.' Their eyes met, a bit of the night leaping between them.

'Time for what?' she teased.

'For this.' He rolled her beneath him, his manhood morning ready for her. He might not be able to guarantee how the day played out, but he could make sure it began with a good morning and it could end with a good night.

It did not take long for morning desire to run its course and, though he would have liked to have stayed abed with her all day, duty called for them both. They helped each other dress, taking turns playing valet and maid. He brushed out her hair and sat on the bed watching her braid it into a twist. This was what it would be like with a wife, he thought. He would be privy to these little intimacies, things one could only learn about another by observing them, absorbing them, over time. Osmosis, a scientist might call it. It was another kind of unveiling, the revealing of layer upon layer until all was peeled back.

When she was done, Jasper went to her, putting his hands on her shoulders and pressing a kiss to her neck. He loved kissing that neck, loved breathing in the scent of her where she dabbed her perfume. 'Are you ready?' he asked, meeting her eyes in the mirror over the dressing table.

She reached a hand up to grip his. 'Yes.' She paused and sighed. 'But I hate to leave this. Last night was beyond words. Not just the pleasure, Jasper,' she tried to explain. He nodded. He knew what she meant. He did not think there were words *for* it.

'We will come back. Our room will be here for us, waiting.' He squeezed her hand in assurance. 'We *can* have more.' *If* they were careful. It would be too easy to let the practicalities of the day ruin the magic they'd created last night. With luck, the spell would hold. Magic. Luck. Spell. He laughed at himself. These were not the words of a scientist. But neither was love. He'd best tread carefully here or he'd forget himself entirely.

Chapter Sixteen

She'd forgotten the intensity and extent of the devastation. She'd not thought she would. But somehow, over the course of the year, it had become muted. Not erased, just mitigated perhaps against the grief of her personal loss. Fleur stood in front of Quarmby's Butcher Shop on Victoria Street, staring at the stone that marked the depth of the floodwaters. The water must have been six feet deep at least here.

'Extraordinary,' Jasper murmured beside her. Perhaps it was the very extraordinary quality of it that had indeed caused it to become muted. One could not live with such horror in full force day in and day out. But today, she felt she must. The reminder kept the need for justice fresh. Distance and time dulled the exigence and the pain.

Jasper was her rock as they walked the town. He listened to her recount the night and the days that followed. 'In the dark, we could only hear it and in the morning we could see the wreckage it had left,' she said as they turned towards the river where the damage had been greatest.

The weather was fair, an early summer day with blue sky overhead, but the weather could not disguise the lack of progress that had been made. After a year, the damaged bridge had not been rebuilt and several mills lining the river were still not operational. She understood the recovery effort would take time, that it was no easy task to dredge a river or to haul away machinery that weighed tons, or to bring in new building materials, draw up new plans and all that went with rebuilding. But that didn't change the practical reality that every day a mill didn't operate, people didn't work, didn't eat, didn't provide for their family. Delays cost people money and jobs. Quietly, her heart went out to the families that continued to suffer residual effects of the disaster.

'Whole mills collapsed that night,' she explained as they walked. 'Cottages gave way under the weight of the water flooding them. Mill equipment littered the streets along with livestock and furniture. All the pieces of people's lives gone in a matter of minutes. If I hadn't seen it with my own eyes, I would have thought such destruction impossible.'

She told him about the dish cabinet with the blue set. 'It was indiscriminatory, what was saved, what was lost, who lived, who died. The waters were no respecters of status or money. We learned later that there was a wealthy man, Jonathan Sandford. He had stock in the London Northwestern Railway. He was in the process of buying an estate and there was a rumour he had nearly four thousand pounds in his house the night of the flood, a small fortune. But he lost all of it and his life. His money was never recovered.'

She shook her head. 'There are sadder stories than his, but his stays with me. He was successful, a good steward of his funds, he'd built a comfortable life for himself and his family. He was on the brink of attaining all he'd aspired for and there was no reason he should not have it. It took only thirty minutes for it all to be wiped away. A lifetime destroyed.'

She shot Jasper a strong look. 'Logically, he should have had more. Science might offer sureties, but real life does not.' Perhaps the story of Jonathan Sandford stayed with her because it was so much like Adam's. Adam should have had more, too.

She traced the route of the river that night for him as their walk continued. She stopped every so often to write in a little book, making notes for an anniversary story. To keep interest in Holmfirth alive, it would be good to do a 'where are they now a year later' style story about how the villagers and townspeople had recovered and how they had not. Mills weren't the only things that had been lost. Farmland had been lost, too. When they met people along the river road, she took a moment to interview them about their lives in the past year, their stories affirming the broader conclusions she'd drawn about the effects of the flood.

'This is where Holmfirth gives way to Hinchliffe Mill.' She paused at an unseen border. Water Street lay ahead. The one place she was most loath to go. She'd not even gone there in the days following the disaster. It hadn't been possible. But now there was nothing holding her back except her own choice.

'You don't have to do this,' Jasper said quietly at her side. All day he'd been her strength. He'd walked beside her, reliving the disaster with her and through her. He'd waited patiently as she'd interviewed people, showing empathy and making enquiries of his own. He'd been impressive. People had responded to him.

She had responded, too. Seeing his sincerity in action, directed at people he didn't know, affirmed that Jasper Bexley was a good man. He would go with her to Water Street if she asked it. He'd probably go even if she didn't ask because that's who he was. And he was right. She didn't *need* to go there. She could choose to turn around and go back to the Rose and Crown Inn, have her meetings, and return to Rosefields. Seeing Water Street would not impact her ability to investigate Lord Orion Bexley's involvement.

'I have to go,' she said solemnly. It would bring a different type of closure than the closure she sought with her legislation and her call for justice. This would be a personal closure, maybe a chance to shut the book on her life with Adam, here at the place where they'd last been together.

'Then we'll go together.' Jasper gripped her hand and they made the rest of the walk, slowly and with the dignity of a funeral dirge as if to endow the importance of the event with the respect it deserved.

Fleur did not know what she expected to see on Water Street. Something. Remnants of the place they'd rented, perhaps. It was an unexpected shock to see that there was nothing. Just a gap where the row of houses had been. A woman hurried past with a child. Fleur stopped her. 'Madam, do you know if there's any plan to rebuild these houses?'

Leery of a stranger, the woman shook her head and scurried on. But the impact of that headshake sent Fleur reeling. She'd come to Water Street, treating it as a pilgrimage, a chance to memorialise Adam and the others. But there was nothing she could make into a personal, mental shrine. Adam's part in the tragedy had been entirely washed away, as if he'd never been, as if their stay on Water Street had never happened. There was no stone like the one at Mr Quarmby's Butcher Shop to mark what had happened. A man had died here, a marriage had died here. The life she'd known had died here and there was no marker for it. Rage began to boil. That wasn't right, that couldn't be right. There had to be more.

'Fleur, are you well?' Jasper had a steadying hand at her back. 'You've gone pale, perhaps you should sit down.' Only there was no place to sit. 'Or lean. Lean against me,' he instructed. 'I am worried you might faint.'

She took a shuddering breath. 'I'm f-f-fine', and felt his arm go about her. It took all her willpower not to sag into that embrace, to not simply give up.

'I have seen fine, Fleur, and you most definitely are not,' he scolded. 'You're also a poor liar.'

'I am fine,' she insisted, the need to argue bringing her some resilience. 'It's just the shock of seeing it. Or rather, *not* seeing it.' Then, with his arm about her, concern for her clearly expressed in his eyes, the words began to come, how she'd stayed to play whist at Mrs Parnaby's and the men had gone back early. Then came the words she'd not shared with anyone, not even Antonia and Emma. They'd had their own grief to bear. They hadn't needed her grief and her guilt as well. There'd been no one else to tell. Besides, these were not things anyone wanted to hear.

'I didn't kiss him goodbye. I was angry with him. We'd argued earlier that evening. We argued a lot.'

Guilt jabbed hard. She should not have pushed Adam that night on the issue. Her anger rose. Guilt and anger pushed at her, the pressure of those emotions building. Why hadn't she done better? Chosen better? If she'd only known. The strength of Jasper's chest bore the brunt of her guilt, of her anger, her fists pummelling at an unseen enemy as the dam of her grief broke. 'I should have been a better wife. If I had only known. I squandered our last hours. I should have apologised. I was too stubborn, too selfish.' She sobbed.

'What did you fight over?' Jasper's voice was soft at her ear, calming as his hands ran over her back in a smoothing motion.

'A baby.' She drew a harsh, ragged breath. 'I thought I was pregnant. Adam didn't want the child and I said horrible things to him.' She rocked against him, the horror of those memories sweeping her. 'He told me I was asking the impossible, that it was selfish for me to want a child, to put that burden on him when he didn't want it. I told him he loved himself more than me, that he was cruel and self-centred. That I was sorry I'd ever married him.'

A wail escaped her. What an awful thing to say to someone. She'd never said anything of that magnitude to him before. 'I didn't mean it.' She gulped for air. 'I swear I didn't mean it, but I didn't get to apologise.' Now he was gone, the house where they'd fought was gone. She would never get to make reparations to him directly. The best she could do was to seek justice.

'Breathe, Fleur. Just breathe. It will be all right.' Jasper repeated the mantra over and over, until he felt her body quiet and still against him. He would be calm for her sake. For his, though, he was boiling with rage. He wanted to do harm to Dead Adam. Too bad the man was already beyond his efforts. How dare a man make his wife doubt her place with him?

She lifted a tear-stained face. 'I wonder if he hated me in the end? I can't bear the idea that he died hating me, resenting our life together. It wasn't all bad. We were in love. Most of the time.'

He could give her obliteration, but he could not give her what she really wanted: absolution. He had not known Adam Griffiths, had no guess as to what Adam had thought or felt. He had no insight to offer that wouldn't sound like naive platitudes, that of course Adam loved her. Hell, he had no idea. But his heart broke just a little further. Damn Adam Griffiths and his work-obsessed heart. If he had such a woman as Fleur Griffiths, Jasper would be damned sure he made time for her, that he gave her children, as many as she wanted. 'You've done enough for today. Let me take you home, Fleur.' Home to Rosefields where they could walk in the peace of the garden, talk on the terrace in the still of the evening and make love in the bedroom until the hurt was eased.

'I am sorry I went to pieces,' Fleur said quietly as they took in the garden by starlight, sitting on the stone bench where they'd sat the night before. 'I had not expected to see it all gone. The finality of that was overwhelming. I thought I had come to grips with it, with all of it. I was wrong. Sometimes the grief just comes out of nowhere.' Even now her voice trembled a bit.

'You needn't apologise. When my father died I felt

much the same way. Everyone was looking to me as the new Marquess. They expected me to be strong, to make decisions, to immediately step into my father's shoes. It was, as you say, overwhelming. There was no time for me to grieve privately. I imagine it was much the same for you with the newspapers to run.'

And she would not have given herself a break to adjust. It wasn't her way. In the time he'd known her she was always at work. She'd been 'at work' at the Harefield's ball, garnering Parliamentary support. The only time she'd not been at work had been the night he'd met her at the theatre. She worked because it was what she knew, because it was what she and Adam had done together. Maybe it was part of her grieving, a tribute to him. Jasper wasn't sure Adam deserved such a tribute.

'How did your father die?' She leaned her head against him and he took a quiet pleasure from their closeness and the ease of it.

'He got pneumonia one winter and never recovered. One would not think a cough would bring down such a man as he was, always out riding, exercising. He seemed invincible to me.' Jasper smiled at the remembrance.

'Adam seemed invincible to me, as well.' She sighed. 'I thought there was nothing he couldn't do. But I learned otherwise. He was not so perfect. His newspapers were in debt before I took them over and he didn't tell me. He left me with a struggling newspaper empire, he left me alone and without a family, and there are days when I am furious with him for it. You see, I am truly terrible. I am angry at a dead man who left me behind to sort out his mess. Then I get mad at myself for being mad at Adam.'

He pressed a kiss to the top of her head. 'You are not terrible. You are human, you are honest and something bad happened to you, something unpredictable and unanticipated.' And it had changed the trajectory of her life. He would not have met her if it hadn't happened. But other things wouldn't have happened either. His brother would not be in jeopardy. It was a reminder that while today had been tense with its remembrances, tomorrow would be more so.

'What would you like to do tomorrow?' he asked quietly. They had yet to meet with the regional bank where Orion kept his accounts. The accounts would tell a critical truth about Orion's culpability. In his heart he hoped that they might delay that visit because of what the revelations might do to them. He wanted more time with her before that happened, more time to think about how to survive this because every day he was with her, the more he wanted that: to survive this latest crisis with this relationship intact.

She thought for a moment, perhaps weighing the choices and consequences as he had done, perhaps, he dared hope, she wanted the same thing. After a while she said, 'I want to stay here and write, if that's acceptable? I thought we might also draft that bill for better dam oversight.'

He allowed himself the luxury of relief. He would have her, them, for a while longer. Of course, she would seek refuge in work. After seeing the wreckage, still so visible after a year, it was clear that the region needed help and that something had to be done to prevent other disasters. But there was something else in her eyes that he understood and it warmed him even as he recognised it as a delaying tactic. She, too, wanted more time. With him. Not the Marquess. Just him.

Fair enough. He wanted more time with her, enough time to sort through what happened next, after the accounts revealed a truth that would support one of them and dash the hopes of the other. How could he navigate the outcome without losing her—her sharp wit, her intelligence, her forthright nature, temper and all, without losing her *presence* in his life. There were so many ways to lose her…and, he suspected, his heart. He'd not meant for that to happen.

Jasper lost no time in planning the days they did have together. After all, she wouldn't write the whole day every day. He took her riding in the mornings, something she hadn't done since she'd left her aunt and uncle's, and watched her delight at being on horseback, cantering across Rosefields's meadows. Morning rides turned into afternoon picnics beneath a June sky. There were strawberries to pick and stories to tell, of his childhood and hers. In the evenings there were al fresco dinners for two on the terrace and strolls in the garden, punctuated by stolen kisses and the final stroll upstairs to their bed accompanied by two realisations: the longer he was here with her the more obvious it was to him that he was falling in love and that each day moved them closer to the end. This could not last for ever.

'I wish we could stay here for ever.' Fleur stretched beside him on the picnic blanket one lazy afternoon when the blue sky was greyer than it had been lately.

There were more clouds and they'd been playing the child's game of seeking shapes.

'Well, why not? We have food,' he teased, reaching for the strawberries in a bowl. He popped one into her mouth. 'We have a large blanket between us. We have each other.' He grinned wickedly. There was no chance of being bored with Fleur. 'What more could we want?' He fed her another strawberry from their freshly picked horde. 'I am glad you like it here. I'll say it again, Rose-fields suits you.' And it suited him to have her here, to share this important place with her.

She turned on her side to face him, her auburn braid falling over one shoulder, her expression content. 'It reminds me of my aunt and uncle's home, only Rose-fields is a much grander scale. My uncle had an endless amount of bridle trails. He was the master of the hunt for our bucolic corner of the world and I had a pony from the first day I came to live with them.'

Fleur gave a soft laugh. 'My uncle took me to show me the stables before my aunt had a chance to even show me my room. He had a beautiful white pony waiting for me. I named her Sweetie and I thought she looked like a unicorn minus the horn.' She was silent for a moment. 'Sweetie became my best friend. She was exactly what a lonely little girl needed to start life in a new place.'

Jasper threaded his fingers through hers, taking advantage of the moment. Fleur had never talked before so specifically of her childhood, of life before Adam. 'How old were you?' It was the first of many questions he wanted to ask.

'Eight. Old enough to know that something bad had happened, old enough to remember my life before and old enough to know everything was going to change.' She shook her head. 'I didn't want it to change. I wanted my parents to come home. I wanted to stay at my house. Uncle's house was larger, but I liked our manse with its ivy-covered brick walls, and Papa's messy study and Mama's tiny parlour.'

Jasper could imagine how uncertain the world must have felt for an eight-year-old. His own world had felt unstable when his father died and he'd had the benefit of being twenty-two. Perhaps we're never old enough to lose our parents, he thought. 'How did they die?' he ventured softly.

'It's quite dashing, really. They were in the Mediterranean on one of Papa's explorations—he was a cartographer—and their ship was boarded by pirates. Papa was also quite good with a sword and he stood to fight. It didn't go his way. So, I became a permanent resident at my uncle's.'

'I'm sorry.' Jasper meant it. He gave her a considering look, a new understanding of Fleur Griffiths emerging: a woman who'd first been a girl betrayed by love. She'd lost her parents, then she'd lost her aunt and uncle, then she'd lost her husband.

'I was, too, but I also know I was lucky. It was an entrée into a whole new lifestyle. I went from being raised as a country gentleman's daughter to being raised as a baron's daughter. Life changed, opportunities changed and so did expectations.' She'd mentioned those expectations before. Perhaps it was no wonder she'd been protective of herself in this relationship, less willing to give of herself emotional than physically. Until the day in Holmfirth, she'd kept her emotions—all except anger—on a tight leash.

In that regard, she was not any different than himself. He, too, felt betrayed by love. He, too, tiptoed around embracing sentimental emotions. And yet, here they were on a picnic blanket beneath a summer sky, falling for one another, their worlds turned upside down by the one thing they'd sought to avoid. It made no sense. It lacked all logic. Until one looked beyond social trappings of position and circumstance. In their hearts, they were alike: their hopes, their fears, the things they valued at their core like integrity, honesty and truth. The realisation shook him. It made him reckless.

'I want to be your Sweetie. I want to be like that pony at your uncle's. I want to be the person that makes it possible for you to step into your new life, the safe place you can run to when the world is too much.' In this moment, he wanted that with all his being—to be *hers*, to make up for the disappointments with Adam, for the loss of her aunt and uncle who had stood by her until she chose a different path.

There was a flare of alarm in her eyes; she was rearing back even as he was reaching forward. 'You should not want that,' she warned. 'I lose everyone I love.'

Did she love him?

He knew she meant it as a caution, but his heart sang at the implication. He would not press her on it. She would only retreat, only throw up her guard. He would instead quietly treasure the near-admission and the knowing that he was not in this struggle alone. But her next words tore at his heart. 'I sometimes wonder if I deserve the right to love again. I bungled it so badly with Adam, with my aunt and uncle.'

Anger sparked in him on her behalf. 'Why ever would you think that?'

She sat up and he sat up, too, ready to reach for her, to comfort her. 'My aunt and uncle gave me everything, every advantage, treated me as their own, and I disappointed them by marrying down, by not advancing the family.'

He took her hand. 'Love doesn't work that way. If there is any fault it is theirs. Love is not conditional. If it were, I would have stopped loving Orion a long time ago. He was a difficult brother and I failed him, too. I wasn't ready to be a father and brother to a teenage boy. But we've forgiven each other for our shortcomings.' He paused. Adam was a different matter. 'It is all right your marriage wasn't perfect. How could it have been when people aren't perfect?'

'I was selfish. I wanted more than he could give, and I was not content with that.'

He would not let her get up from this blanket believing that. Jasper pushed a strand of loose hair behind her ear and tipped her face towards his. He wanted her to look at him when he told her the truth he saw. 'He could give less and so you gave more.' Jasper called on everything she'd told him about her years with Adam Griffiths. 'He wanted to work and so you worked alongside him. He went to the paper daily and so did you. You wanted to be a collector of stories, but you made yourself into a reporter to fit his world. You gave up your lifestyle, your ambitions, your family, your dreams for him. That is not selfish.'

If anyone had been selfish it had been Adam Griffiths. The man had either been selfish and arrogant or he'd been entirely oblivious to his wife's sacrifices. 'Worst of all, Fleur, you're *still* doing it. You're running a newspaper syndicate, wearing yourself to a nub trying to overcome his debt. Where is your life in that? What, my darling, do you want? When do you reach out your hands and take it?'

For the second time since they'd arrived at Rosefields, Fleur Griffiths was crying. He had her in his arms, consoling her, but he did not regret sharing the hard truths in an attempt to reshape the narrative she carried in her head. When she told her story he wanted her to tell it right—with herself as the strong, resilient, selfless woman at its core. And he wanted to be there in that story beside her.

'You mustn't say such things, Jasper. I hurt the people I love and I will hurt you, too—you know it's true.' There it was again, that implication that she loved him.

'No, I don't know that,' he argued fiercely. 'You haven't hurt me yet, nothing unrecoverable at least. I have a new set of tumblers on order,' he tried to joke. But he knew what they faced. The trials to date were nothing compared to the last trial that loomed before them. Still, they had a good record of overcoming differences. Just maybe, they'd overcome this one, too. And they were stronger now—surely that worked in their favour as well.

'I don't want this to be over,' she whispered against his shirt.

'Then it won't be.' He hugged her close. He would find a way to prove to her that she deserved a second chance at love, that they deserved each other even as their personal Armageddon loomed.

She drew a shaky breath. 'We can't get over it if we don't go through it.' By 'it' she meant the bank, Orion's records. So the time had come. Their Rubicon called.

He nodded, his grip about her tightening. 'We'll go tomorrow.' Then they'd be on the other side of it. They'd know what their future looked like. He'd not come out on this picnic imagining it to be their last before...the bank. Perhaps it was better this way, to have the decision made without planning and posturing, without argument and formal consideration but instead here in the quiet of the afternoon, after picking strawberries and talking of childhood. The biggest moments of one's life didn't always come with a blare of trumpets but on the whisper of suggestion.

'It will be all right, Fleur. We will find a way to survive it.' He breathed the words into her hair as thunder rumbled in the distance, presaging a summer storm as if the weather understood just how momentous tomorrow would be.

Chapter Seventeen

How would she survive the coming days without losing everything? Without losing herself, without compromising her sense of justice, her task, the newspaper, but most of all, without losing Jasper? And always the answer kept creating the same equation. To save Jasper, she would lose herself, sacrifice justice and perhaps the papers along with it. To keep all she held dear, Jasper would have to be surrendered. There was simply no way to have it all. The realisation of that created a most impossible dilemma, one that had not existed a month ago.

Fleur looked up from her writing at the library table to sneak a glance at him at his desk, wire-rimmed glasses and all, his own gaze intent on his own letter writing. He'd rolled his sleeves up a while ago to spare them from errant ink blots and his forearms with their sprinkling of dark hair were on masculine display. She'd never found rolled-up shirtsleeves and exposed forearms particularly sexy before, but on Jasper they were proving to be quite the aphrodisiac and quite the impediment to the last of her evening work.

She could not give in and set aside her work for another day. She must finish this article tonight. There was no guarantee that tomorrow she'd be back here at Rose-fields enjoying its hospitality. In fact, chances of returning here seemed slim regardless of tomorrow's outcome. Tomorrow morning they would go to the bank and call for Lord Orion's accounts. Tomorrow they would know what they'd come to find out. Tomorrow, their affair would end.

Jasper glanced up, catching her staring. 'Is there something you want?' he drawled. Indeed there was. She wanted him. She wanted this damned quest to be over. She wanted for there to be a way between them that wouldn't cost her everything and he the same. She wanted more of this, of days spent side by side, of evenings in the garden talking of everything from politics to the personal, of nights spent in bed making love. Did he want that, too? Wasn't he worried at all about tomorrow?

Fleur set aside her pen and walked towards the desk. 'There is something I want.' She gave a wicked smile and came around to his side. This might be her last chance. She'd spent the afternoon since they'd returned from the picnic thinking of every 'last': last luncheon in the countryside, last supper, last walk in the garden. Had he spent the time that way, too? She hiked her skirts up to her thighs and straddled his lap.

'What are you doing, Minx?' He was startled, but pleasantly so. She could see the flames of intrigue lighting in his eyes. She'd come to know those eyes so well in the past weeks: how they glowed in interest, darkened with desire, narrowed with disapproval, how they became coals when he was angry, a deep amber when aroused. It would be easy for someone to mistake one for the other.

She wriggled closer. 'It would be cliché to say I've wanted to do this since I first saw you…' she reached for his glasses, removing them gently '…so we'll say I've wanted to do this for a while.'

He slid down slightly in the chair to better accommodate her. 'What is that, exactly?'

'To take off your incredibly sexy glasses and run my fingers through your hair while sitting on your lap.' She moved against him, feeling him rouse beneath her hips.

'Since the first day we met? Really?' Teasing lights glimmered in his eyes. He rested his hands at her hips. 'I thought you didn't like me.'

'I thought you were over-confident. It didn't mean I wasn't interested.' She pressed a kiss to his lips. How was it possible to fall so fast and not realise it? She'd fallen fast before, with Adam. She thought she would have recognised the signs. Or perhaps she *had* recognised the signs—the heat between them, the mental and physical chemistry of being together on her part as well as his—and explained them away as something else—an antidote for loneliness, nothing more, because for them *to* be more was a frightening prospect that brought risk and uncertainty at an already uncertain time.

Was this what it had been like for Emma and Antonia? Only they had happy endings to their stories. She wouldn't be so lucky. There was no happy ending for her. She knew. She'd run the numbers on this. One of them would be right and the other would be very wrong. That would be a chasm too wide for a relationship to overcome even if they managed to survive it on a professional level.

And what do you care? What do you want from Jasper Bexley beyond an affair anyway?

Those were questions she refused to answer.

'You are sad all of a sudden. What is it, Fleur?' His eyes were soft with concern and she felt her heart crack just a tiny bit. She didn't want to hurt him. Why did she always hurt the men she loved? She'd hurt Adam, and she was going to hurt Jasper. Her research was good. There was little chance Lord Orion Bexley was not guilty of negligence on the Bilberry Dam. Jasper loved his brother. Tomorrow would devastate him.

'Aren't you worried about tomorrow?' She smoothed his waves away from his face. It felt domestic and wifely to make such a small, intimate gesture, to have the right to do it, to sit here on his lap, to talk so openly. These were just a handful of the intimate privileges she would lose tomorrow.

'I can't change what we'll find. The reality is already out there. The answer we're looking for already exists.' He reached for her hands and took them in his own. 'And I trust us, Fleur. We have pledged to handle whatever we find with discretion and good faith.' His calmness and logic were soothing. He might be the only man she knew who would draw on the concepts of Plato in the midst of a crisis. She wanted to believe them, but they were incomplete and only addressed half of her worry.

'What does Plato have to say about us? Have *you* thought about what happens to us tomorrow? Do we go back to being business partners?' Or perhaps they went back to being nothing at all. This was her greater worry and that realisation carried its own shock. A month ago, her first worry would have been support for legislation. But tonight, she wondered if she could go back to business-only with him? Every time he was in a room, she'd think about Rosefields, about his big bed, about every consideration he'd shown her, how, for a short while, she'd been cherished for herself. And yet what other choice was there? How did she think this would end?

She pressed a finger to Jasper's lips. 'You don't have to answer my question. Forget that I asked.' She'd known the ending from the start and nothing had happened that would change that. Even if Lord Orion Bexley was miraculously expunged of his guilt, the ending for her and Jasper would not change. He would still be a marquess with expectations to marry a well-titled young gentlewoman.

His fingers curled warmly over hers, gently moving them away from his lips. 'What do *you* want to happen with us? Don't we get to decide? You talk as though the world will happen to us instead of the other way around.'

'It doesn't matter what I want. The facts are indisputable. I'm not on your mother's list.'

'You are on *my* list. Maybe that's more important.' He nipped at her ear, but she had fallen out of a mood for teasing. She moved her head away.

'I will not be a married man's mistress,' she said quietly. 'Nor are you a man who would keep a mistress once he had a wife and family. Don't you see? It's no use. If we do not end now, we will end later. It is inevitable. Marquesses and newspaperwomen have no future together.'

His hands framed her face, warm and confident.

'That is not the sum of who we are. We are people who share the surviving of loss, who know the true value of trust and deep commitment. We are not just our titles.' He kissed her softly. There was more than one Rubicon to cross and this one was definitely more personal, more than the sum of what they found with Orion. 'If we want our relationship to happen, we'll find a way. Not even the findings at the bank will stop us. *That's* the kind of people we are.' He smiled. 'For instance, I want to find a way to get you upstairs.'

'You might start with asking,' she said coyly, sensing that the time had come to accept the inevitable even if Jasper wouldn't. This was likely their last night together. They might as well enjoy it. She could hold tonight as a shield against all the lonely nights to come.

'Asking? Is it as simple as all that? Who would have thought?' Jasper laughed, rising from the chair with her in his arms. It was not a heavily disguised allegory.

'For being a man of science, you're not being very logical, Jasper.' She laughed to cover the severity of her comment.

'Perhaps you've changed me, just a little, or perhaps I don't think my claim illogical to start with.' He juggled her in his arms, passing the library table and her half-finished article.

'Wait, I can't leave it. Put me down. I just need five more minutes,' she protested.

'You can finish it tomorrow. We've done enough work tonight,' Jasper said sternly, never breaking his stride. 'In fact, we've done more in a week than Parliament does in a month. I am very proud of us and you should be, too.'

He turned sideways, manoeuvring them through the door into the hall and began the trek upstairs to their bedroom. 'You're smiling. Are you marvelling at my strength or the amount of work we've accomplished?' They had achieved a lot. One day had turned into a week in which they'd stayed at Rosefields, isolated from the world, drafting a bill, writing letters to potential supporters, and she had written her articles. It had been a productive excuse to forestall their visit to the bank.

'Can I marvel at both?' She *was* marvelling at his muscles. 'I don't think I've ever been carried upstairs before.' She laughed up at him. 'You've done well, you can set me down.'

'No.' He grunted. 'We're not at the top yet and I am no quitter.' There was allegory in that, too, and Fleur duly noted it. He was making this hard on her, on them. Perhaps she should have let him answer her impossible question. Perhaps if he could hear his thoughts out loud he'd realise that their time together had come to an end.

Fleur was afraid. Jasper felt it in her touch and tasted it in her kiss. Jasper held her close, watching her sleep. That fear was a base-note which had underscored their lovemaking. There'd been desperation in that lovemaking, too. Her fingers had traced him as if they wanted to memorise every line and plane and she'd wrapped her legs about him so tightly he'd worried she'd not let him go in time. As delicious as the prospect of spending within her was, Jasper did not want to take the risk. Although that would certainly resolve things. A child would push past the barriers she was so good at erecting, it would strip away all discussion of choice.

A child with Fleur. Perhaps a curly, auburn-haired daughter with her mother's boldness and her father's love of science? He'd build a university just for her. Or maybe a dark-haired son with his mother's green eyes. Or a tall, broad-shouldered son with hair the colour of Rosefields's autumn leaves. He laughed at himself spinning endless possibilities in the dark. Fleur would say they were *impossibilities*.

To be sure, he knew it was a notion born of midnight and madness. Marriage had never come up between them other than that he had to wed. They could not even agree on what happened after tomorrow. It seemed unlikely they could agree on something as big as marriage. And yet, hadn't they implicitly tried it on this week with their prolonged retreat?

They'd made a good team. He'd liked working with her even as he understood the pattern that was enacting itself after her breakdown at Water Street. Work was her answer to grieving. Water Street had hit her hard and she was compensating for that with work, just as she'd once compensated for the loss of Adam. She'd tried to do it again tonight, too, by wanting to work on her last article instead of coming upstairs and facing what she thought would be their last night together. He'd not allowed it. Fear had to be faced if it was to be overcome.

'I'm afraid, too,' he whispered to Fleur's sleeping form. He was afraid of what the bank accounts would show, afraid he would not be equal to the tasks required of him, equal to being the man Fleur would need him to be. If he could not rise to the task, he would lose her.

Tomorrow would just be the beginning of the battle and he wasn't sure his record in battle was all that good.

Look at Orion. For all of his best efforts to be a brother and father to him, Orion was struggling to make the transition to responsible adulthood. He was thirty. It was time, even well past time. Perhaps he shouldn't be so eager to be a father. If he couldn't raise his brother, what made him think he could raise a child? He pushed the thought away. Orion had been spoiled early on. He could not shoulder that blame. Midnight was a cruel mistress, prompting madness on one hand and maudlin reflection on the other. Such introspection was best left to the light of day.

His day started with an empty bed. Jasper rolled over with a groan, his hand meeting a cold pillow. She'd been up for a while and he hadn't even heard her. He must have been deeply asleep. A little smile curved on his face as he thought of the reason for that. They'd worn each other out thoroughly last night. If she was up, she would be in the library finishing her article. His smile broadened. He liked imagining her at Rosefields. Then the smile faded when he looked about the room.

She was gone from his bed and her things were gone from this room. Last night, she'd left a chemise hanging over the chair. The chair was empty now. Jasper got out of bed and padded over to the bureau, pulling open the two drawers she'd claimed as hers. They were empty, too. Gone. No, not gone, he reasoned with himself. She was just downstairs. But she'd packed. Even her gowns were gone from the wardrobe.

A sense of betrayal stabbed at him. She planned to return to London tonight and yet all this time she'd said nothing about it. She was leaving him. After everything that had been said and shared last night, she was *still* leaving him. His immediate reaction was to run downstairs in his banyan and confront her, half-naked and raging. He'd not lied last night. She *had* changed him. Her emotion had rubbed off. It took all the logic within him to realise confronting her *while* he was angry was his worst option. It was, perhaps, even what she preferred. Fleur *wanted* a fight. A fight would make leaving easier. He would not give her one. A fight would allow her to run away...from Rosefields and from them. She would not thank herself for it in the long run.

Jasper shaved and dressed slowly, methodically: grey summer trousers, crisp white shirt, a white waistcoat embroidered with blue forget-me-nots, a grey jacket and neatly tied cravat. The morning rituals helped to restore his equilibrium. Today had to be taken one step at a time even as he kept the larger circumstance in mind.

He took the stairs, recalling how he'd carried her up them just hours before. He found her in the library, breakfast and coffee beside her writing implements, her auburn head bent as she worked, the morning sun catching the highlights of her hair, picking out the rare gold hidden within the red flame. She was ready for the day in a sage-green skirt and a thin, plain white linen blouse trimmed in tiny loops of cotton lace. A matching green bolero-cut jacket lay on the chair beside her with gloves and a straw hat. She was ready to leave on a moment's notice.

'Good morning, Fleur. You're up early.' He entered the room as if he hadn't noticed her jacket and gloves or that she'd left his bed in a manner highly uncustomary of the morning routine they'd established. He dropped a kiss on her cheek as he passed her chair on the way to the coffee urn. 'Did you finish your article?'

'I did. Would you like to read it before I send it in?' She smiled. 'I hope you don't mind that I asked for breakfast to be served up here?'

'You may have breakfast anywhere you like, my dear. Rosefields is at your disposal.' He sat down with his coffee and a roll. 'I'll read your article this afternoon when we get back from the bank.' He arched his brow. 'You let me oversleep. I should have been up long before now.'

'You were tired.' She looked up briefly from organising her papers.

'For good reason,' he teased, but she didn't flirt back.

'I don't want to rush you, but I'd like to be at the bank when it opens.' She fixed him with a straightforward stare. He understood that boldness better now. The bolder she was, the more worried she was. That was how Fleur Griffiths operated. The boldness was real, but it was also a shield.

He set down his coffee cup to meet her eyes without distraction. 'I'll have the coach ready. We'll go as soon as I'm done eating.' The battle was about to be joined.

Chapter Eighteen

The Huddersfield Banking Company was an inauspicious building on Cloth Hall Street, austere and plain fronted with the exception of the tooled double door and its two large discs for knobs. To Fleur, the unexceptional mood of the building seemed at odds with the import of what would happen within its walls this morning. Justice would be satisfied. Her quest fulfilled. By evening she'd be home in London. All of this would be behind her.

She should be pleased. Her tenacity had paid off. Amid struggle and grief, she'd continued to fight. She ought to be proud of herself. But all she could feel as Jasper held the door for her was trepidation. Somehow her quest had become less just, less right.

'My lord, it is good to see you again. How may we be of service?' A neatly groomed man Jasper's age, dressed in a banker's plain dark suit hurried forward, recognising the Marquess of Meltham on sight.

'Mr Sikes, I need to go over the family accounts, particularly my brother's, from 1846,' Jasper said smoothly, recognising the man in turn.

Fleur's sense of trepidation tightened in a knot in her

stomach, her coffee and roll churning. She did not like relying on Jasper for access to information that would betray him. But she could not have hoped to have access to these accounts without him. On her own, she would have had to go through legal channels, made petitions and a fuss to look at anyone's financial records, let alone the relative of a peer. But Jasper had made it easy for her. And private. She shouldn't forget that. This was not a decision entirely without benefit for him.

'Mrs Griffiths.' Jasper turned to her with a formal tone. 'May I introduce Mr Sikes? He's a valued assistant manager at the bank. He's handled the Meltham account since I inherited. One might say we've come up the ranks together. I have no doubt one day he'll make managing director.' He smiled warmly at Sikes. 'Mr Sikes, this is Mrs Griffiths, the head of the Griffiths News Syndicate. She is my guest today.'

Mr Sikes shook her hand. 'It is a pleasure to assist you and to meet you in person. I am sorry about your husband. Allow me to offer belated condolences. One of your papers published an editorial of mine a couple years back about the importance of extending access to banks to the working classes for the purpose of creating savings accounts.'

He cleared his throat. 'I think of all the money people lost in Holmfirth when the dam burst, actual coin that was never recovered, all because money was kept in their homes instead of in a bank. I think, too, how much comfort it would have offered families to know that even in the wake of destruction they had the security of a modest savings to help them start again.'

Fleur managed a smile, knowing the man meant well

and that he couldn't possibly know what was at stake today: truth, justice and a lonely heart that had only just now come back to life. 'Thank you for your kind words and thoughts. I am glad our paper was able to be an outlet for your cause.' Inside, she was sinking, her resolve wavering. She didn't want Lord Orion Bexley's perfidy revealed in front of this man who clearly held Jasper in great esteem. She'd not started this quest to shame the Marquess of Meltham or to ruin a family that was respected in the local eye.

Sikes led them to a small room off the lobby of the bank, which was as austere as the exterior, and left them to fetch the account books. Jasper laughed when she commented on the excess of plainness. 'The board felt the bank would inspire more confidence with local clients if it was less ostentatious. The bank was formed after the panic in 1828. My father was one of the first to invest in it. He admired its mission to focus on local business and to focus on local growth. I was happy to continue banking here when I inherited. I should tell you that the Holmes River Reservoir Commission did much of its banking here.'

'Yes,' Fleur said quietly. She'd noted the bank in Captain Moody's report and in her own documents. There'd been a two-thousand-pound loan the bank had made to the commission for repairs. She drew a deep breath, guilt eating into her. She had to say something before Mr Sikes came back. Her conscience demanded it. 'Jasper, I am sorry.' It was hard to say what she was sorry for. There was so much that required her penitence. She wasn't sorry for the whole situation, certainly. For instance, she was not sorry to have been in his bed, to have had him as a lover. But she was sorry to repay those moments with trouble and scandal. 'I didn't mean it to be like this.'

Jasper held her gaze, his topaz eyes steady. She was feeling penitent. He knew what she wanted to hear, but he wouldn't give her absolution. 'You knew it could be like this, Fleur. You knew this was a risk.' Then he added, 'As did I. Still, I think it is better we face what is in those accounts as friends rather than foes.' He hoped that was the case. This morning had been difficult on them both. They were in the belly of the beast now, forced to face the truth, forced to face their feelings and somehow reconcile them both in a way that didn't leave them broken.

Mr Sikes came back with the records. 'These are the accounts. Let me know if you need anything else,' he offered before leaving them.

Jasper immediately set aside the family accounts, which he'd only requested to divert the bank's attention from his brother. 'This one is Orion's account book,' Jasper said solemnly, opening the ledger. He was aware of Fleur coming to stand beside him, positioning herself to read over his shoulder. He appreciated that she was letting him take the lead on combing through the ledger. He bounced his knee surreptitiously under the table, hoping they found nothing.

There were the usual deposits, the quarterly allowance from the estate, the payments made to tailors, club memberships and other young man's pursuits. He winced at one large payment made to a club off St. James's. There was another further down, and another.

'Is that excessive?' Fleur asked, pointing to the recurring entries.

'Yes. Gaming hells are the vice of many young men.' Jasper grimaced. 'This was seven years ago. Orion had some trouble at a gaming hell.' In customary Orion fashion, his brother had played over his head in an attempt to recoup his losses. When that had failed, Orion had tried to handle the debt on his own, but his allowance was not large enough.

'Who are these people? Brown and Whitaker?' Fleur leaned closer, the scent of her perfume intensifying with its nearness. Jasper swallowed, not against desire, but embarrassment on his brother's behalf. He did not want another to see Orion like this. Orion was his brother, a fun-loving, caring, often short-sighted young man who was still looking for his place in the world. He was not what these numbers suggested. Jasper hadn't even told his mother about it.

'Those are some gentlemen who will make short-term loans at high interest rates to other gentlemen who find themselves short on cash.' Instead of turning to him and asking him for help, Orion had taken a loan from Brown and Whitaker in Cheapside. 'It was the beginning of a snowball of debt that got larger each month until I found out the hard way.' He paused, remembering that horrible night. 'Orion was found in an alley, badly beaten.' Brown and Whitaker had taken their pound in flesh when coin had not been produced in a timely manner.

Fleur's hand squeezed his shoulder. 'How awful.'

'I paid the debt the next morning and put Orion up at a hotel until he was fit for Mother to see him.' Jasper pushed a hand through his hair. 'I cut off all credit for him at the gaming hells. When his own funds ran out, he was not to be allowed to play.' Jasper sighed. 'He was not happy with me. We had many fights that spring.'

'Well, it appears to have worked,' Fleur said as they reached the end of the spring quarter account book. 'There doesn't seem to be any more payments to Brown and Whitaker or other such folks.'

Jasper reached for the summer and then the autumn books. 'You take autumn, I'll do summer. Then we can trade to double check each other.' He hated this. Going through someone's finances was like going through their underwear drawer. Yet it was the only way if Orion was to be vindicated. He'd just finished with summer, having spied nothing, when Fleur looked up. Her expression grim.

'There's a deposit in October of 1846 for seven thousand, eight hundred pounds,' she said in a near whisper. Jasper froze. That was the exact sum request for dam repairs in the August work order.

'Who is it from?' Jasper asked, although it didn't matter. What else could it be? It wasn't Orion's quarterly allowance. The timing was wrong and so was the amount. It was too much.

Fleur shook her head. 'It doesn't say.'

'I'll get Mr Sikes and have him check the bank records.' It was the next logical step. Leaving the room also gave him a chance to get his emotions under control. Good God, Orion had really done it. He'd filed a work order and pocketed the money. And a few years later eighty-one people had died.

Jasper calmly made the request for Sikes to find the

deposit record, but all the while his mind raced. What was he going to do? This would devastate his mother. What had Orion been thinking? Why had he done this? Had he got in trouble again and tried to find his own way out?

He waited until Sikes returned with the bank's record of transactions. 'Here's the cheque.' Sikes showed him the grey and mauve note used by the Huddersfield Banking Company. Jasper studied it, his eyes landing on the signature at the bottom, his gut tightening. It had been issued from Parliament for the express purpose of reservoir repairs. The only saving grace was that it had not been issued directly to Orion. It had been issued to the Holmes River Reservoir Commission.

Jasper furrowed his brow. 'If this cheque was not issued to Orion, how was it possible he was able to deposit it into his account?'

Sikes set down the big book that kept track of deposits. He turned to the date the cheque had been deposited. 'It didn't go to his account. It went to the Commission's account. You can see the amount right here. Then, a day later, one of the commission members transferred the funds to Orion's personal account. I imagine whoever was the drawer at the time did the transfer.' At which point, Jasper surmised, the funds fell out of the public eye. They were mixed with Orion's personal monies and no longer traceable. Or maybe they were. 'Sikes, I'd like the family ledgers for forty-seven.'

Fleur looked up when he returned, new ledgers in hand. 'The cheque was a match, sort of.' He explained how it had been deposited to the commission's account first and the whole sum was later transferred to Orion. 'I want to see if we can find where the money went. Was it frittered away on new purchases?' Jasper tried to remember back that far. Had Orion gone through a spending phase that was over and above his usual? 'Or...' he offered another suggestion fearfully '...did it go to pay more debt?' He handed Fleur a ledger. 'If it went to pay debt, there would be a large outlay all at once.'

After an hour of combing ledgers, they'd come up with little. 'There is nothing except for these four payments, made quarterly,' Fleur remarked. 'They caught my eye because they were regular occurrences, and because when you total up the amount, it comes out to seven thousand, eight hundred.' She shook her head. 'I didn't want it to.'

'It's not your fault.' Jasper slouched in his chair. Perhaps it was his fault. Why had Orion done this and thought he could get away with it? That no one would find out? It didn't make sense. 'Who did the payments go to?' He did not think for a moment the payments had gone for reservoir repairs. At some level, it didn't matter where the money went. The bottom line was that Orion had taken it.

'It doesn't say. Your brother doesn't seem to be a prolific record keeper. He just writes down the basics.'

Perhaps because he didn't want anyone to know. If only he knew where Orion was now. He could get some answers, talk some sense into him. Jasper forced his mind to work. He had to think of next steps. 'You were right. My brother embezzled money from the reservoir commission.' When he looked at Fleur, she was pale, her expression tight.

'I would prefer not to be right about this,' Fleur said apologetically.

'That's not how you felt when this all began,' he corrected. 'You don't need to feel that way now simply because things changed between us.' No, this couldn't be about them. This had to be about Orion. 'What will you do with the information?' It was the last piece she'd been looking for, the piece that proved a single man had been responsible for the collapse of the dam. If the money had gone to repair the waste pit, none of this would have happened.

'The *Tribune* will break the story.' They were speaking in whispers now. If they didn't speak these horrible things too loudly, perhaps they wouldn't become real.

'The board of directors will be pleased. You will sell a lot of newspapers. It isn't every day a peer's brother is caught stealing money from the government.' Just saying the words made him sick to his stomach. How could he tell her not to print the story when she had her evidence? That had been the only condition he'd asked her for, that if she did want to connect the deaths to Lord Orion that she have proof for it. Would it be enough? All that was left was the press of causal arguments. Could it be proven that this money had been given to the commission for the express and singular purpose of the repairing the waste pit? Or had it been meant for other repairs? If so, it was still embezzlement, but at least it wasn't manslaughter.

'How long until the story breaks?'

'A week at most. With something this big, I do need the board of directors to approve it and they will need time.' To her credit, Fleur did not break. He admired that. Perhaps another woman would have given in to the relationship between them and decided not to publish. But Fleur was made of sterner stuff, and he loved her all the more for it—for her conviction, for her strength, for her dedication in doing what was right even when it hurt. This was not easy for her. Nor for him.

He'd chosen the right words in his head a moment ago. He *loved* her, that very thing that brought pain with the joy, that very thing he'd sworn to avoid because he knew that pain first-hand from losing his father and watching his mother fall apart. Fleur had turned his well-protected logical world upside down and he *loved* her for it despite the cost. He would do it all again to have had this time with her, to have *her* in his world no matter how briefly. How ironic he should realise that now, here at the end.

'I do not want to cause you pain, Jasper. I am sorry it didn't turn out another way.' What other way was there? With her losing her papers? Her position? That would not have helped them any more than this did. Perhaps she'd been right last night. A future for them was impossible.

She rose from the table. 'I want to commend you for your integrity. I understand I'd never have been able to access these records without your co-operation. You could have obstructed all this. You could have lied to get what you wanted and you didn't. And I am repaying you poorly.'

'Say nothing more, Fleur. We are past words now. I'll take you back to Rosefields.'

She shook her head. 'No. There's an afternoon train to London. I think it's best that I take it. Good bye, Jasper.'

She made a clean break of it, then, walking out of the room and towards the front doors, the sound of the click of her heels diminishing on the tiles until the door shut behind her and she was gone.

She would go to London and he would go to Rose-fields to plot his next move. He had a week to find Orion, to find a barrister with an impeccable reputation or to send Orion out of the country, which seemed fairly appealing at the moment. The legal system couldn't prosecute a man they couldn't find. Orion would never be able to come home, but perhaps that was better than the alternative. Then, when that was settled, he would try to put his heart back together, perhaps settle for one of the girls on his mother's list, assuming anyone would have him with the taint of scandal on the family name.

Jasper pounded a fist on the table. Damn it. He'd been right all along. Love hurt. Why the hell had he decided to test that hypothesis once more? The results had been the same.

Chapter Nineteen

Rosefields was not the same without her. Jasper wandered the garden at sunset, his footsteps aimless, his thoughts picking over each scene, each moment of the week they'd shared here. How was it possible that a person could make such an impact on a place in such a short time? Perhaps because it wasn't the place they impacted, but the people in it. Wasn't that why he loved Rosefields? Here was where the reminders of his childhood lived, of days spent with his father, of happy summers and snowy Christmases.

Jasper kicked a pebble, watching it roll away. Rosefields was the home of his childhood. By necessity, London was the home of his adulthood at present. But he'd always imagined Rosefields would be the home of his own family when the time came. He'd marry here in the little chapel on the property in the off season, not at St George's in town. His children would be baptised here as he and Orion had been. A family would give him reason to spend less time in London, to run his politics from a distance.

Now, he wondered if that time would ever come. He stopped to watch a bee burrowing deep in a rose. Had that time, perhaps, already come and he'd missed it? Had Fleur been his chance? For a moment he stilled, thinking there'd been a sound in the garden, the crunching of gravel beneath a foot. He looked up, wild, illogical hope beating in his chest. Had she come back? But the garden was empty. There was just him and his thoughts.

Jasper pulled out his pocket watch. She would be in London now. Had she gone home, or had she gone straight to the office? Would she stay up all night crafting her article? He snapped the watch shut. Would she think of him and Rosefields at all? She belonged here with her love of the countryside, with her desire for family and children.

He could give all of that to her here: a country home, children, time away from the paper. These were all things Adam Griffiths had chosen not to give his wife. By doing so, he'd chosen her life for her. Which begged the question: would she give up the syndicate for Rosefields? He supposed the question bore asking in the little hypothesis he was testing. If he ever were to offer her Rosefields and a family, would she take it? Or was she wedded to the ghost of the life she'd had with Adam? Did she stay at the paper for Dead Adam, or did she stay for herself?

He gave a harsh chuckle. What did any of these questions matter? She was gone and Orion was in trouble. Her newspaper was going to expose what he'd done and how that act had led to the Holmfirth flood deaths. He needed to think about Orion now. He couldn't save his relationship with Fleur, but perhaps he could find a way to save his brother.

* * *

Two days later, Jasper had something of a plan. He'd consulted the family solicitor on retainer in Huddersfield, who'd recommended an excellent barrister with ties to the region. Both Jasper and the solicitor felt that a home-grown connection might help if the time came. Or rather *when* that time came. Short of Fleur not publishing the article, that time *would* come and it was coming quickly. The article would not print before tomorrow at the earliest and he hoped that it was more reasonable to assume it would print the day after.

Jasper poured himself a drink and settled in to pass the long evening reading. All that was left now was to go back to London and brace his mother. His trunk was packed, ready to go to the station tomorrow for the morning train.

'My lord,' the butler interrupted shortly after nine o'clock. 'Your brother is here to see you. Shall I show him in?'

'Orion is here?' Jasper leaped up. Despite the trials of the week, his first reaction was one of relief. 'Yes, show him up. No, I'll go down.' He was in too much of a hurry to wait. His brother was home, safe, a bright spot in difficult times.

'Orion!' he called from the top of the stairs, his brother turning to face him. Jasper raced down the stairs and pulled his brother into a tight embrace. 'I was so worried. I didn't know where you'd gone or how long you'd be.' He hugged his brother and then stepped back to look at him, relief giving way to concern. Orion was well dressed as usual, sporting an elegant silk waistcoat of lavender paisley, but he was tired. There were dark circles beneath his eyes and his typically lively gaze was dull concern.

'Jasper, your welcome makes me feel quite the prodigal.' He gave a half-laugh.

'Where have you been?' Jasper asked.

'Everywhere, nowhere. Thinking, or at least trying to think. I keep reaching the same conclusion. I am in trouble, Jasper, and I need your help.' Orion pressed a hand to his mouth in a visible effort to hold on to his control. It took a moment for him to recover himself. 'I am sorry. I am so sorry.'

'Come, sit. You don't look as if you've eaten. I'll have a tray sent to the library and we can talk.' Rather, Orion would talk and he would listen. Jasper led his brother upstairs. He could guess what this was about, but he wanted to hear it from Orion. He poured his brother a drink and settled him in a chair. 'Now, tell me what this is all about.'

'It's about those articles regarding the Bilberry Dam accident, the ones that name me as being primarily responsible.' Orion looked down at his drink. 'I am afraid of what the newspaper will find if they keep digging.'

'Why would you be afraid of that?' Jasper asked carefully.

'Because there was a deposit made to my account for a sum meant to be used for repairs to the waste pit. It will look as though I took the money and the waste pit repair never happened. It's why the dam burst. We need to make sure the paper can't get a hold of my accounts. You can block that, right?' Orion's blue eyes held his in earnest desperation.

'I suppose I could. But it wouldn't be moral, Orion. It would be deliberately hiding evidence.'

Orion's eyes sparked. 'I would think philosophical ethics would be the least of your concerns. Do you know what it would mean? The case could be reopened. I could go to trial and be convicted for embezzlement, for manslaughter.' His voice rose in panic.

'Calm down, Orion. That hasn't happened yet,' Jasper said in careful, evenly measured tones. He wanted to tell his brother it would be all right, that they would fix it. In part because he couldn't—it was too late for that—but also in part because he shouldn't. Perhaps that had been his Achilles heel with Orion all along. He'd been so intent on helping him, on cleaning up Orion's messes instead of making Orion clean them up. He'd made the messes go away without asking for atonement. And Orion had learned a very different lesson than the one he'd intended to impart.

'Since you've been gone, some things have happened. I need to tell you, so please listen without losing your head,' Jasper said sternly. 'The paper has indeed dug deeper and they have found the deposit.'

Orion blanched. 'How did they get my accounts? Surely that is an inadmissible sort of evidence. They can't go get a man's private accounts without a warrant or something.'

'I gave permission. I went to the bank with Fleur Griffiths. I was the one that went through the account book and had the bank cross-reference the cheque with their deposit records.'

Orion exploded out of his chair and began pacing. 'You! Do you understand what this means? You've all but delivered me for trial and admitted my guilt *for* me.' Orion flashed a hurt look. 'All for a woman? She really got to you. But she'll sell you short, too. Do you think you'll emerge unscathed? That you will look like a hero? This will touch all of us. Think what it will do to Mother. She won't be able to hold her head up. Think of what this will do to your marital prospects. Who will want a scandal-tainted marquess for a son-in-law?' Orion shoved a hand through his hair. 'Was she worth it? I never thought you'd throw me over for a woman. I thought you were better than that.'

Orion made him sound like a traitor and Fleur a harlot. 'I will not obscure the truth for you, Orion.' It took willpower to keep his temper on a firm leash. 'Yes, what you have done will have ugly consequences for innocent people like myself and Mother, and that is not fair to us, but that doesn't mean you should be excused of the responsibility. Perhaps I've excused you from too much responsibility in the past.'

'You would see me face a trial? Be sentenced for crimes?' Orion was aghast. 'All to teach me a lesson?'

The leash of his control slipped a little. He'd been desperate to see his brother and relieved to have him here. But now he wanted Orion to accept responsibility for what he'd done and Orion would not. Orion only wanted a way out. Yet, to not give him a way out would be to condemn him. 'Eighty-one people died, Orion. Whole families were killed. Babies drowned in their sleep. Children washed away while parents looked on helpless. Homes were destroyed, mills were destroyed. I saw Holmfirth last week, over a year since the flood. The place still bears scars. Bridges have not been replaced, mills have not been rebuilt, some wreckage has still not been removed. People lost homes, lives and livelihoods. They can't work if the mills don't run. No work means no wages, no way to support families.'

There was a long silence between the brothers, the tray of food untouched. Jasper hoped the import of what had happened was weighing at last on Orion's conscience. 'I have engaged a barrister with an excellent reputation,' he said after a while.

Orion glared. 'You've engaged a barrister? That is your idea of help? Let the newspaper print the opportunity and drag me to trial? And then what? Just throw up your hands and hope for the best? How am I supposed to be vindicated when they've got the cheque and the financial records?'

'We can make arguments of causation. If we can show that the money was for repairs in general, that it wasn't specifically for funding only the waste pit, we can argue you weren't directly culpable. If we can show that there were other problems with the dam that contributed to the accident, we can mitigate the role of the waste pit. We can show it to be one of many flaws in the dam's engineering. Those arguments stand a good chance of being successful since they've already been made and the original findings conclude there were a variety of factors. I do think the burden of proof is on paper.'

Orion shot him a sardonic look. 'And if you're wrong? This is my life you're playing with. It's bad enough you are willing to trot me out into the public eye and let the Griffiths news syndicate attempt to pin this on me.'

Jasper answered with a solemn stare. 'All right then,

let's back up. Did you do it? Did you take the money? Did you place the work order and not see it carried out?'

'Yes. No.' Orion shook his head. 'It's complicated.'

'That's not an answer. Try again. First, have a sandwich. There is no rush. We have all night.' He couldn't save Orion if Orion was not willing to save himself.

Orion sat and Jasper waited patiently while his brother ate. At last Orion was ready to talk and the eating had done its job in settling his emotions.

'I sent in the work order requesting repairs on the waste pit,' Orion began. 'It was a request that came from all three of us assigned to oversee the Bilberry reservoir. My name is on the order only because I drew the short straw and had to fill out the paperwork. It just happened to be my turn. When the money was awarded, it went into the commission's account first. Then, William Hendricks, who was the current drawer and who was also on my subcommittee for Bilberry, asked if the money could be transferred to my account so that the money could be easily accessed by us to oversee our repairs. He said he was concerned that the money would get used by other reservoirs or eaten up by other expenses. He wanted it separate, given the commission's history of insolvency.' Orion gave a tell-tale fidget and Jasper interrupted.

'The ledger shows evenly quarterly distributions over the course of the year that total up to the deposit amount. Did those go to repairs?' Even if that money hadn't gone to the waste pit repair, it would definitely eradicate charges of embezzlement. It would be a start.

Orion shook his head. 'The money went to Hendricks. He volunteered to be in charge of hiring engineers for the repairs.'

'Did he ever hire anyone?' This would also be helpful. If someone had been hired, they could find a contract. It would show that Orion had not wilfully ignored the need for repairs.

'I don't know. Hendricks rotated off the subcommittee at the end of his term. By then, the money had all been transferred to his account.' Orion was nervous. He was bouncing his leg. There was something amiss here.

'Let me understand. You transferred the repair funds to Hendricks once a quarter and yet no repairs were made and no one was hired. Did you question him about that? Make him accountable?'

Orion fiddled with a sandwich. 'No. But neither did our third member.' He let out a sigh. 'What do you want me to say? That I didn't follow up? That I didn't hold another committee member accountable for his actions? That I was lazy? That I didn't take my position on the commission as seriously as you would have? A position, by the way, that I didn't want and you foisted it on me not for just one term, but two.'

'I was trying to give you purpose,' Jasper explained. 'I thought after the engineering corps, that dam work would put some of those skills to use. I thought it was a good fit.'

Orion took a savage bite of his sandwich. 'Except that I *hated* the engineering corps. I was a horrid engineer.'

'It was better than *your* option, which was do nothing,' Jasper shot back, remembering how difficult Orion had been after university—which he hadn't quite finished. The don had felt academics weren't Orion's calling.

Orion gave him a baleful stare. 'I'm not you, Jasper. I don't have answers for everything. I don't have a sense of purpose. I just move from disaster to disaster, or perhaps I am the disaster. I suppose every family has to have one.'

'None of that is true, not even the part about me.' Jasper blew out a breath. If it was, he might not have lost Fleur. They were getting sidetracked now.

'Being incompetent is unfortunate, but it is not a crime,' Orion drawled.

Jasper nodded. 'Where is William Hendricks these days?' He could hunt down Hendricks, make him accountable. Orion had not acted alone.

Orion took a swallow of brandy. 'He's dead. Died last year in April in a hunting accident on the moors, although some say it was suicide because April isn't exactly hunting season, is it?' There'd certainly be no hunting down Hendricks, but Jasper could still get his hands on Hendricks's accounts. Hendricks's accounts could clear Orion while still giving Fleur a story. Jasper made a note of the date of Hendricks's death. Just two months after the flood.

Jasper swirled the remainder of the brandy in his snifter. 'Why did you do it, Orion? Surely, something must have seemed off to you after that first disbursement and no one had been hired to start repairs?'

Orion was silent for a long time and Jasper felt that he'd at last come to the crux of the matter. Orion met his gaze, regret etched in his face. 'Because I owed him money and he offered to wipe the debt clean if I'd just let him park the reservoir funds in my account.' Orion sighed. 'I couldn't really say no. I didn't have the funds to pay him back. It seemed like a good option at the time. It was true that there was concern the funds would be used for other expenses. His argument wasn't illogical. It did make sense to have access to the funds.' Orion shook his head. 'But when he didn't actually disburse those funds for repairs, I couldn't call him out on it.'

'That was a better option than coming to me?' Jasper put in, hurt.

'Yes, given that I had just so recently disappointed you with my little run-in with the moneylenders.' Orion closed his eyes, struggling for control. 'That was eight years ago. I haven't gambled over my means since. You know that.' He opened his eyes and Jasper saw real regret there. 'I told myself it wouldn't matter. The reservoir waste pit was fine as long as the water didn't exceed a certain level. Chances were the waste pit would never reach excess. I took a gamble on that. Who would have thought the whole dam would go?'

'Hendricks was using extortion in order to launder money through your account.' Jasper drummed his fingers on the arm of his chair. 'It would be harder to trace that way. It would have been too obvious if the whole sum had just shown up in his account all at once and then no work materialised.' A hypothesis was forming. Perhaps Hendricks's death had been a suicide after all. Riddled with guilt over the dam deaths, fear of being found out for extortion or connected to the dam accident, and whatever other problems the man had—it would be interesting to find out—Hendricks had taken his own life before he could be discovered.

As the clock chimed one, Jasper came to certain conclusions. Yes, Orion had put himself in trouble's way, yet again. Yes, he'd need to bear responsibility for his part in it. But his part was no longer the role of the per-petrator. He was guilty of negligent oversight, for not calling for accountability, but he was also the victim of extortion. Orion was guilty of many things, but not the failure of the dam, at least not any more so than of the other commission members.

'What are we going to do?' Orion asked.

'We are going to get some sleep. Tomorrow, we are going to London to stop the presses. There's an afternoon train and with luck we'll make it.'

Fleur Griffiths had the wrong man. For his sake and for hers, Jasper hoped they got to London in time.

Chapter Twenty

It was nearly time. Fleur glanced at the clock on her office desk. She would leave herself twenty minutes to take the stairs down to the basement of the *Tribune* building where the presses were housed, far enough away from the daily business of running the paper that their noise didn't interrupt. The feature story on the Bilberry reservoir would go to print and be out in the morning edition. She'd taken the story down this morning for lay out and she wanted to be on hand this evening when the first copy of the paper came off the presses.

She'd stayed late tonight especially for that reason. Last night she'd stayed late for a board of directors' meeting. The night before that she'd stayed late to write. The night before that... She stopped right there. She didn't want to think about that night or the one before it. Suffice it to say, there'd been a lot of reasons this week to stay late. Here, she was busy. She didn't have time to think about anything outside of work.

And why would she? Work had been good this week for the first time in a long time. There had been successes. The board of directors was thrilled with being able to break the Bilberry Dam story. It was going to be the biggest story of the summer and into the autumn once a trial was called for. Circulation would go up and that meant revenues would go up. The board had actually applauded her and complimented her work.

Two weeks ago they'd wanted her head on a pike, blaming her for losing money even though the losses had pre-dated her tenure. And now, they were so pleased. Her position was safe. Adam's newspaper syndicate was safe. She sat back in her desk chair and raised a teacup to the empty room. 'I did it, Adam. I found the culprit and he is going to pay for your death.' She was going to have justice for Adam, Keir, Garrett, Antonia, Emma and herself, just as she'd vowed after the tragedy last year. So why didn't she feel better about it? Why wasn't the thrill of victory thrumming through her? She'd triumphed. Breaking this story would also give momentum to her call for better oversight legislation. By rights, she should be on top of the world.

The higher the pedestal, the further the fall. What a long way down it would be with no one to catch her. It was an incredibly morbid thought and a lonely one, too. But she wasn't going to fall. She'd done her research, she had her proof. Her story was airtight. Adam's syndicate was rallying. Why did none of this fill her with satisfaction? With pride? Why did it all of this good news leave a sour taste?

Was it a sour taste or just no taste at all? Where was the joy? There was no one to celebrate it with. She'd achieved the improbable, she'd discovered what Captain Moody's inquest could not. For her efforts there'd been a round of applause in the boardroom and a perfunctory champagne toast. Then the board had shook

her hand and headed home to their families to celebrate
their own good fortunes with those they loved. It was
what she would have done. In the past, Emma and Antonia would have celebrated with her. But they were
long gone, off to new lives. Adam wasn't here. There
was no one.

'Damn it, Adam. You should be here,' she scolded out
loud. 'I became a reporter for you. I learned about the
newspaper business for you and now you aren't here to
do your part.' This was for him. It had always all been
for him. They'd dedicated their lives to his news syndicate because it had been his dream. She'd kept that
dream alive for him. But this was not her dream, it did
not feed her happiness. She saw that more clearly now.

For so long whatever Adam had wanted, she'd wanted,
too. She'd not stopped to consider her own dreams. Not
until Jasper. He had been just for her because he couldn't
be more. He was a dream she couldn't have. They could
never go out into society. She didn't belong in his circles
and now she was bringing scandal to his family.

Whatever he felt for her would not withstand the
firestorm her article would stir up. He would hate her,
knowing that she'd done this to his brother. He couldn't
possibly love a woman who would strike such a blow
against those he loved. It didn't mean she was doing
anything wrong. This story must be told. It was right to
tell it. But it did mean she couldn't have him.

*'What can your story change? It can't bring anyone
back.'*

His words had haunted her this week amid the champagne and congratulations. She had her success but at
what cost? At the cost of hurting him, of ruining his

brother's life, even though his brother ought to have shown better judgement to begin with. There was cost to her as well. She'd lost Jasper, a man who cared for her. She'd never thought to feel again the way she felt with Jasper: on fire, alive and it was better than anything she'd ever known.

Even with Adam.

Such a thought bordered on heresy. Adam had been the sum of her world for so long it seemed wrong to let anything or anyone challenge his place. Life with Adam had been fiery, passionate, an adventure. There'd been wealth at her fingertips and unique opportunities that appealed to her bolder nature. But there'd also been a limit. She'd never truly been Adam's partner, had she? Their life was Adam's life. She was just invited along for the ride.

With Jasper, she was a partner in truth. He'd invited her into partnership that night at Meltham House and never looked back, knowing the risk he took in doing so. He'd never flagged in that partnership, not even when the account books squarely implicated his brother.

She'd not easily forget the pain on his face when she left him at the bank. Even in his own private agony over his brother, he'd offered to take her back to Rosefields. She'd left because she couldn't bear to see him suffer, knowing that she was the cause of it. She'd not trusted herself to hold on to her principles. One halfway decent argument from him and she would have let the findings go. Now, it didn't matter. She had put herself beyond him with this article.

The last of the clerks were locking up the offices as she walked through on the way to the stairs. Only the print crew would remain throughout the night to have the morning edition ready when London awoke. She stopped and looked about the space. It was quiet with everyone gone. Jasper would like that. He appreciated the value of quiet. Did she really want to give all this up? Could she? She rather thought she could. It would not be easy. The adult years of her life had been spent in these offices. But what and who was she keeping this for? Not for herself, she saw that now. This did not bring her joy, not without Adam.

She thought of the conversation she'd had with Antonia earlier in the spring. She'd urged Antonia to think about why she was holding on to Keir's company. Perhaps she ought to ask herself that question, too. Why was she holding on to the papers? Out of habit? Because she felt she owed it to Adam? Because running the syndicate brought her joy and fulfilment? Two of those answers were not reasons to stay involved. The third one was, though. Could she answer yes to it? The last few weeks with Jasper had caused her to question her choices and reasons. Perhaps it was time to start exploring those answers, and perhaps for the first time since Adam's death she was actually in a mental and emotional place from which to do that exploration.

She was about to turn the knob on the door leading to the basement when the night security guard called out, running towards her, 'Mrs Griffiths, wait. There's a gentleman here to see you. I told him we were closed for the night, but he insisted it was important.'

He panted his message as two men came up behind him, one, an immaculately groomed dirty blond, the other dark-haired and tousled. *Jasper.* Her reaction was physical and real, after almost a week without him. Her pulse raced, the sight of him enough to fluster her. She'd missed him so much.

'Fleur.' Urgency underscored that single word. 'Have you printed the article yet?' There was desperation and hope mixed in his eyes as if everything hung by the thread of her answer.

'Um, no. It runs tomorrow morning. I was just going down to see the first editions come off the press in a few minutes.'

Jasper's hand gripped her arm with a gentle pressure, his eyes intent on her. 'You have to halt the presses, Fleur. That story cannot run.'

She had to be strong here at the eleventh hour even when faced by the temptation of seeing him again, all those feelings of want and need that only he could satisfy surging to the fore. 'Jasper,' she said in low, private tones, 'we've discussed it. You know I cannot ignore the evidence.'

'I know, Fleur. That's not why I'm asking.' She'd never seen him like this, so stern, so intense. 'You've got the right idea, but you've got the wrong man. The story is bigger than you think. Trust me,' Jasper ground out. 'I'm asking for your sake. That story will be the ruin of you. I cannot let you run a piece that I know is false.'

That was when she knew just how much he loved her. This was not a gambit to save his brother or even himself. He'd come to save her. After all she'd put him through, he'd still come for her. Halting the presses was no small consideration. The board of directors would be furious to discover the piece was pulled. They'd have to lay out the front page differently. The paper might even be late. There'd be a price to pay for her decision. But Jasper had come for her. The least she could do was listen to him.

'We'll have to hurry,' she said gravely, making the decision on the fly, hoping they weren't too late as it was and racking her brain for what she was going to use to replace it.

They made it with a minute to spare, Fleur bellowing at the top of her lungs, to stop the presses before tying on an apron and taking charge of the needed alterations. Jasper stepped back, keeping himself and Orion out of the way. As far as he was concerned, he had the best seat in the house. It was impressive to watch her work as she moved from group to group, helping with the typesetting to rearrange the layout and to find a new article to substitute.

'It's not going to run, right?' Orion asked nervously at his side.

'Not that version of events,' Jasper said sternly. He and Orion had engaged in serious discussion on the train trip to London. 'She will run your complete version of events when the time is right. She will want to interview you tonight. You must tell her about Hendricks and the extortion, just like you told me. Then she will want to go out and get proof. When that is done, the story will run.' And Orion would be named. He would have to own up to his part in the debacle, but at least it would be honestly and fairly presented and the backlash for the family would be mitigated. For the Marquessate of Meltham it would be a survivable scandal thanks to her.

* * *

After two hours of work, the presses began to hum and Fleur made the rounds, congratulating the press crew on their effort. At last, she came to join him and Orion. 'We've got it all under control.' She smiled as she wiped her hands and took off her apron. 'Now, you need to live up to your end of the bargain.' She gave him a sly smile that was part coyness, part seriousness. 'I stopped the presses for you, you'd better have a great story for me. Come upstairs to my office and we'll talk.'

After a day of not having enough time, of wanting time to slow so that the train delays would not prevent them from arriving in time to beat the presses, it seemed to Jasper that there was suddenly too much time—too much time between Orion having a chance to tell his story and his being able to have Fleur to himself, to ask her the questions that mattered most to him. It took all of his willpower to sit patiently and quietly—two things he was usually very good at—while she listened and Orion got the lion's share of her attention.

She finished questioning Orion and set her pencil down, turning her gaze in his direction, an appreciative smile on her face. 'You were right. The story is bigger than we thought. I can start tracking down leads on Hendricks right away. We'll need proof before we can print.' A palpable tension crackled between them, neither of them sure what to say next.

Jasper cleared his throat. 'Orion, take the coach back to the town house. I'll find my own way home. Mother will be pleased to see you and you can see to getting our trunks unloaded.' To Fleur he added, 'We came straight from the station. I didn't want to risk waiting too long.'

When Orion departed, he asked, 'Will you be all right? You made an enormous sacrifice for me tonight.'

'You also made one for me. You could have hung me out to dry, let me run the story and then sued the paper for slander. You could have ruined me, could have had a nice piece of revenge,' Fleur said. 'But in truth, I don't know how the board of directors will respond. They will be disappointed. I will have to answer to them. Still, I will have a better story, later, so I am hopeful that they can be pacified with an exclusive interview from Lord Orion Bexley himself.' She gave a tired smile and for the first time, Jasper noted the faint circles about her eyes.

'You've been working late.'

'I didn't want to be home alone. I don't think I've even unpacked yet.' Her gaze flickered over his face, doing its own assessment. 'How are you, Jasper? Are you holding up?'

'I am doing much better now that I've seen you.' He reached for her hand, the first contact they'd had in days, his gaze steady. 'I missed you, Fleur. Rosefields didn't feel right with you gone. I spent a lot of time thinking about you, about what a great team we made—and still make. Not just in politics or in bed, or in problem solving, but in life.' His grip on her hand tightened. 'I want to pursue the possibility of that life with you, Fleur.' He watched a flurry of emotions scuttle across her face, none of them the emotion he hoped for. It would be so much easier if she simply responded by throwing herself in his arms. Instead, her answer was in the form of a question.

'What exactly are you asking me, Jasper?' Her green eyes were sharp and wary.

'I am asking you to marry me.'

Chapter Twenty-One

Wwhat did one say when a fantasy came to life? This was madness, something that was both possible and impossible and she didn't know how to respond. 'After only six weeks? Jasper, are you sure?' She could feel herself trembling with shock and delight, and surprise and, yes, with uncertainty.

'I am sure, but perhaps you are not?' Jasper seemed disappointed with her response. Dear heavens, she was hurting him all over again in a different sort of way. She seemed doomed to hurt him. He made to disengage his hand, but she held on, refusing to let him go.

'It's not that. I am overwhelmed by the asking,' Fleur said hurriedly. 'Perhaps too overwhelmed to think straight.'

'I love you, Fleur.'

Her voice shook a little at hearing the words for the first time from him. 'I know you do. I saw it in your eyes tonight. You came to save me, not yourself. That was an act of true love, an act that was entirely selfless.'

'I want you to be my partner in all things and I want to be yours. I want a life with you in the country at Rosefields, children with you, the family we both want.'

Fleur nodded, unable to speak against the emotion

conjured by his words and the images that went with them. He offered her everything she craved and true partnership to go with it. She understood implicitly that partnership had made tonight's outcome possible. If he'd not compelled her into partnership with him, if they'd remained opposing enemies, tonight could have hurt them both—exposing his brother in an unfair, incomplete light in a way that cast aspersions on him and the family, as well as hurting the paper's reputation. But the honesty of their partnership, their trust in each other, had prevented that two-way disaster.

'It would be easy to say yes, Jasper. But I am not sure it would be right or fair to either of us to jump headlong into this.' She paused. 'I've been doing a lot of thinking since I've been back. This week, I had everything I thought I'd been searching for. I had justice for Adam, validation of my hold on his news empire, recognition. And it wasn't enough. Those things didn't fill me. They were things that were important to Adam and, without him, they were no longer important to me. I still think the values that Adam championed are important—literacy and access to information as cornerstones to a society that practises real equality.

'I still want to fight for those things, promote those things. But I don't know if I need to do it at the helm of a news syndicate. I certainly couldn't run the syndicate from Rosefields. It is too remote. But maybe I am ready to give all of that over to someone else and start fresh with those efforts on a more local level. Perhaps I should take a leaf out of the Huddersfield Banking Company's book and focus on regional literacy efforts close to home at Rosefields.' She leaned close. 'Do you hear what I am saying, Jasper? I just don't know what the right direction is for me. I have to work some things out about what I want and how I want them before I can invite someone into my life on a more permanent level.'

Jasper smiled. 'That doesn't sound like no.'

Something warm blossomed in the vicinity of her heart. Perhaps that was what hope felt like. 'It's not "no". It's "I need a long engagement". I think you do, too. Between the newspapers and Parliamentary legislation, we have a big year ahead of us, Jasper, plenty of time and ways in which to test our partnership.' She could feel relief sweeping him and she let herself be drawn into his arms until she was on his lap. She reached for his glasses. 'I'm looking forward to most of it.'

'What part are you not looking forward to?' Jasper teased, stealing a kiss.

'Meeting your mother. I'm not on her list.' That would be one more item they'd need the year to sort out.

'You're not on the list...yet. But you will be.' Jasper grinned. 'So, this time next year, you'll marry me?'

She twined her arms about his neck, letting her fingers play with his hair. 'Yes, but I have conditions. I want a small ceremony at Rosefields, family only. No big celebration. Just something intimate. Quiet.'

'Perfect.' He laughed against her lips. 'Just as I imagined it. Until then, we'll have one whirlwind of a year.'

One year later

'We made the front page,' Fleur whispered, startling Jasper in the tiny antechamber of the Rosefields family chapel.

'What are you doing here?' Jasper scolded in surprised tones that conveyed more pleasure at the surprise than displeasure. 'It's bad luck to see the bride before the wedding.' But from the look in his eyes, he didn't seem to mind. She gave a twirl in her wedding gown, showing off the delicate raised white roses embroidered at the hem. The gown was made from a pretty white cotton, fresh and simple with its three-tiered skirt and tight-fitted bodice. She'd chosen to wear white even though she wasn't a new bride: white for new beginnings, new chances.

'You've been seeing me all year. I can't think today makes much of a difference.' She laughed, twining her arms about his neck.

'What's this about the front page?'

'We're the headline on the front page of the *London Tribune*. "*Newspaper Mogul Makes Marriage Deal with Marquess*",' she recited happily. 'They ran a whole article about us: how we met, what we've done together this year and our plans for the future.'

'They need a whole special edition for that!' Jasper chuckled.

'It was a pretty spectacular year.'

They'd spent the year lobbying for legislation that would prevent lax accountability on dam commissions. Just last week, they'd celebrated their bill passing the House of the Commons. They'd also spent the year making decisions about life going forward. Fleur decided it was indeed the right choice for her to scale back her active role in the news syndicate.

She still held stock in the company, but her role was now focused on overseeing the regional paper out of

Huddersfield so that she had time working with a local committee dedicated to establishing a public library open to everyone without fees. She even had time now to devote to her own personal writing and had a novel in the works.

Socially, the year had been spent navigating new social circles for Fleur. The Duchess of Cowden and Jasper's mother combined efforts to ease that transition. When she was in town, Fleur enjoyed re-joining the Duchess's charity circles and in November, she and Jasper had attended both the Duchess's Christmas fundraising ball and Lady Brixton's literacy ball. There would always be those who looked down their noses at her and who would think Jasper had married beneath himself, but she'd found many people quite welcoming and even a bit awed by her.

'Thank you,' she whispered to Jasper.

'For what?'

'For this year, for giving me the time I needed to sort through my life so that I could come to you whole and ready to commit to *our* life together.' She kissed him just as Orion poked his head into the little antechamber.

'Ahem. Ten minutes, Brother. Really, you two, could you wait just a little longer?'

Fleur flashed him a look over her shoulder. 'Absolutely not. We were just practising.' The door shut and they could hear Orion laughing. 'Now, where were we?'

'Right about here,' Jasper murmured, picking up their kiss where they'd left off.

'You can tell a lot about a man by how he kisses,' Fleur whispered.

'And what can you tell about me?'

'That you're the one.' She'd come through grief and guilt, anger and resentment to arrive here, to be here with this man. 'What does my kiss tell you about me?'

'That you are worth waiting for.' He hoisted her up on the flat surface of a cabinet built into the wall.

'We're going to be late.' She laughed.

'Not to worry. They can't start without with us.'

Epilogue

1864

The summer of champagne and roses had started. June was well underway, the gardens were in full bloom at Rosefields, and the estate was alive with the sounds of laughter and children. Fleur would not have it any other way. This summer, Emma and Antonia had come to England with their husbands and children for business and for pleasure and Fleur was intent on making the most of the opportunity.

A footman approached with a tray of ice-cold champagne and lemonade, the champagne courtesy of Emma's husband, Julien Archambeau, the Comte du Rocroi. Fleur took a glass of lemonade while Emma and Antonia opted for the champagne as the three women lounged in the shade, stealing a moment of quiet to be together while their husbands taught the children battledore on the court they'd put up for the summer.

'Cheers, dear friends.' Fleur touched her glass to the others. 'Here's to having come thousands of miles for a reunion.'

'And here's to safe travels for all of us,' Emma said

solemnly. 'The distances we've come can't all be measured in miles, especially when it's a journey in love.'

Fleur couldn't agree more. If someone had told her eleven years ago that they would all three find love again, have the families and lives they wanted after such incredible, devastating loss, she would have thought it impossible. And yet, here they were. Out on the battledore court, she caught fragments of instruction as Jasper showed their son, five-year-old Michael, named after Jasper's father, how to hold his racket as they set up for a match against Julien and nine-year-old Matthieu-Phillippe. On the side-lines, Antonia's husband, Cullen, tanned a deep bronze with long tawny locks bleached by the Tahitian sun, stood with Emma's youngest— Etienne—and their own boy, Manahau, ready to play the judges should a shuttlecock go out of bounds.

'There's not a daughter among them.' Emma sighed wistfully. 'I love my sons, but how is it that we didn't conspire to have at least one girl among us?'

Fleur slid her a coy glance, her hand dropping to her stomach. 'Well, maybe this one will be a girl. Jasper and I started after all of you. We're not finished yet.'

'I thought so!' Emma cried joyfully. 'I didn't want to say anything, but then when you didn't take any champagne…'

Fleur smiled, beaming. 'We're halfway there. Just four and a half months to go.' She'd have preferred there be fewer years between Michael and this new child, but that was not to be. There'd been a miscarriage three years ago early in her term and she and Jasper had been careful after that not to conceive too soon. Then she'd not got pregnant as easily as she had with Michael.

Antonia squeezed her hand. 'It's wonderful news. A real blessing.' One Fleur knew, boy or girl, she'd not take for granted.

'This one will be our last, I think. I'll treasure every moment of it.' Fleur smiled at her friends, seeing the echo of her words in their eyes. They all knew the import of savouring each moment. They'd experienced the fragility of life and how quickly that life, the things one thought they could count on, could be swept away. They'd all made the journey to Holmfirth a couple of days past to see the flood marker at the butcher shop and to walk the streets. The homes on Water Street in Hinchliffe Village remained unbuilt, their absence a gaping hole and strong reminder of the power of nature and human vulnerability.

'I am excited for this child, but a little sad, too,' Fleur confessed. 'I wonder if either of you will see him or her? I am happy for us, but I am unhappy that we live so far apart. It's been what? Eleven years since we've been together other than through letters.' Letters that came only twice yearly from Antonia. Tahiti was still a long way off.

Emma smiled, eyes sparkling. 'Perhaps you will be seeing more of us. We've established an office in London as British importation of champagne has grown astonishingly. My brother will handle most of the day-to-day operations, but we'll need to check in regularly. Julien's been talking about a champagne Christmas here in London this year. He wants to give the children the same experience of growing up in both England and France that he had. You and the new baby will be up for visitors by then, I assume?'

Fleur laughed with gratitude. 'If you're angling for a Christmas invitation to Rosefields, you've got it.' Jasper's mother would be in her element with so many children to love, and Orion was perfect uncle material even if he wasn't quite husband material…yet. She could imagine nothing better, unless it was Antonia being here, too, but that was too much to hope for. They would have barely reached Tahiti by December.

'Would there be room for one more family?' Antonia put in with a broad smile. Tahiti agreed with her. 'Cullen told me today that he's decided to stay through winter to work with the Duke of Cowden on expanding the South Seas arm of the company. The good news is that we can be together for Christmas. The bad news is that if Cullen is successful, and I know he will be, we won't be back for another ten years.' She gave a wistful sigh. 'Matthieu-Phillippe will be nineteen by then, practically all grown up.'

'Tahiti is good for you, Antonia. You belong there,' Fleur consoled.

Antonia smiled. 'I love it. I wish you could see our house with its thatched roof and bamboo poles and barely any walls. It's big and airy and unlike anything I ever dreamed I'd live in, and I love it. The water is warm, you can swim all year. It's a little boy's perfect playground. I couldn't imagine Manahau growing up anywhere better. I have everything I want.'

'I'll drink to that.' Fleur raised her lemonade. 'We are the luckiest of women. We have everything we want.' Although there'd been a time, long, long ago, when she'd not thought she was lucky at all, that she hadn't deserved the love of a good man. She was happy to be wrong. Today, she had a man who loved her, who had made her a true partner in that love and in the life they were building together one day after another, through good times and bad. Jasper had been right that night so many years ago when he'd argued for them. They were indeed better together.

* * * * *

HISTORICAL

Your romantic escape to the past.

Available Next Month

A Scandalous Match For The Marquess Christine Merrill
How The Wallflower Wins A Duke Lucy Morris

....

Uncovering The Governess's Secrets Marguerite Kaye
Rescuing The Runaway Heiress Sadie King

Keep reading for an excerpt of a new title
from the Special Edition series,
A SMALL TOWN FOURTH OF JULY by Janice Carter

Chapter One

Where's Jake?

Maura Stuart dropped the pitchfork of hay into the stall trough, muttering at the same time. Stomping down the length of the barn to its opened doors, she stood for a moment, shading her eyes from the early-morning sun. No sign of him anywhere. *Great. Just what I needed today.* And no sign of Maddie, either. Too much to hope that she'd gone looking for Jake—the enticing aroma of coffee was probably just now luring her out of bed. She took a deep breath. Giving in to this constant frustration would gain her nothing, especially if they continued to be business partners. But there were moments—plenty of them—when Maura silently questioned her decision to bring her twin sister on board. Yet there'd be no business at all if she'd had to manage on her own.

She scanned the property, from the two-story farmhouse straight ahead and its adjacent garage, to the shed on the far side of the garage. It was closed up, so no Jake there. She knew the chicken coop behind the barn and the small, fenced riding ring next to it wouldn't be a draw for Jake. Thankfully, he wasn't trotting down the long gravel drive out to the road. Then her gaze drifted east, to their neighbor's fields, overgrown with weeds. No sign of Jake, but she suddenly caught a glimmer of red through the thicket of vegetation separating the two farms.

Maura walked across the drive to the row of cedars along the property line and pushed through them into the adjacent land. She and Maddie used to come this way when they were kids, but the cedars had been newly planted then and only waist-high. Now they were taller than her shoulders.

Stepping onto what was once the Danby homestead felt strange. The elderly owners, Stan and Vera, had passed away several months ago, but the farm had been left derelict since their admission to a nursing home in Rutland two years before. When Maura and Maddie took over their own family farm a year ago, the Danby place was already run-down. The neighboring families had been close when the girls were growing up, but that gradually changed after the sisters left for college.

It was only natural, Maura knew. People aged, withdrew from community and old friends due to health or mobility issues, and lost touch with one another. She and Maddie had experienced a similar loss of contact after being away from Maple Glen for so long. But thankfully, they'd been able to reconnect with former schoolmates and other neighbors since their return.

Maura waded through the field toward the Danby farmhouse, realizing as she got closer that the flash of red was a car—a fancy sports car. When she reached the drive, she could hear the low rumble of a male voice. She paused for a second, debating whether to retreat or continue looking for Jake. The voice pitched nervously as she was rounding the back end of the car to see Jake standing between it and the closed barn door, his stocky frame blocking the object of his interest from Maura's view.

"He won't bite," she said, stifling a laugh as she drew near. "He's just curious."

The man splayed against the barn door grimaced. "Maybe call him off?"

She closed in on Jake, wrapping an arm around his neck and gently pulling him away from his attempt to nuzzle the man. She recognized him then, despite the passage of years and his transformation from teenager to adult.

"Welcome back, Theo." She kept her eyes on him, fighting to ignore the sudden throbbing at her temples, then turned Jake around, slapped him on the rump and ordered, "Home, Jake."

Theo Danby watched the donkey amble off. "Thanks... uh... Maura?"

The fact that he was slow to identify her irked. "Yes," she snapped.

He moved away from the barn door and unzipped his windbreaker. "Warmer than I remember," he mumbled.

So he's going for small talk. "Yeah, climate change and all that. Plus, it's the middle of June." She shifted her attention away from the well-toned chest muscles emerging through his short-sleeved shirt—muscles that the Theo she remembered hadn't had. She felt her cheeks warm up as a trace of a smile crossed his face.

"Are you visiting your folks or...?" he asked.

"No, Mom died about three years ago and my father, last June."

"I'm sorry." His face softened, and she peered down at the ground, hiding unexpected tears.

"We moved back here more than a year ago," she went on.

"We?"

She raised her head, meeting his dark brown eyes again. "Maddie and I."

"Ah."

"So…you're here to…" she continued.

"Have a look at this place before I sell it."

Of course. She'd been expecting that from the day she and Maddie first returned home and had seen that the Danby homestead had been left to ruin. Though she couldn't figure out why it had taken Theo so long to return after his aunt and uncle passed away. She was about to ask him more about his plans when a slamming door and a young voice got her attention.

"Dad?" A boy who looked to be a preteen was standing on the farmhouse veranda, his face wrinkled in disgust. "This place is a dump!" He caught sight of Maura and hesitated before descending the porch steps and walking their way.

Maura shot a glance at Theo. He flushed slightly as he said, "My son."

Maura scolded herself for automatically assuming that Theo might still be single, too. The boy heading their way was a near replica of a young Theo—same thick dark hair and eyes. He sidled up to his father but kept his eyes on Maura.

"Uh, Luke, this is Maura—" The last part of his introduction dropped off, as if he were unsure of her current surname. "Her family owns the place over there." He gestured to his right, though the boy kept his attention on her.

"It's Maura Stuart. Nice to meet you, Luke." She held out her right hand, and after an elbow nudge from Theo, the boy shook it. "My sister and I knew your father years ago, when he used to spend his summer vacations here, with his aunt and uncle."

"Dad told me about that, but he made it sound more interesting than—"

"What you see here?" Maura smiled. She resisted glancing at Theo, but thought she heard a faint sigh.

"Yeah." He looked at Theo and asked, "So now what?"

"Well, uh, I thought after we looked around, we could go into Maple Glen for some lunch and then talk about our plans."

"*Our* plans? It wasn't *my* idea to come here."

Maura took in the disgruntled face and voice. Time to head back to the farm, she decided. "Okay, well, nice to see you again, Theo and Luke... The bakery in the village sells sandwiches and pizzas, but if you want anything substantial, you'll have to drive to Wallingford."

Theo's smile was strained. "Thanks, Maura. I think a bite to eat will help us both. And...uh...is there a place to stay? It's been a while since I was last here."

"Maybe you remember the Watsons? Bernie used to manage the gas station at the junction to Route 7, but he bought the old Harrison place about ten years ago and turned it into a B and B. The Shady Nook. I hear it's quite nice. If you're planning to stay in the area for a few days, of course." When Theo failed to respond, she added, "Unless you'd rather stay somewhere with more to offer, like Rutland or Bennington." Theo was staring, and she realized she'd been babbling. "Okay, well, I better go."

She was about to turn around when he finally spoke. "Thanks, Maura. Um, my plan is to stick around until I can make a decision about my aunt and uncle's place. A few days, anyway—maybe more." He shot Luke a quick look. "Nothing definite yet. But maybe we'll see you around. And Maddie, too, of course. Say hi for me."

"Sure." She managed a smile and headed off, taking the same route across the weed-filled field and through the cedars, feeling two sets of eyes tracking her. Her mind buzzed with random thoughts and questions. *Theo Danby is back. He has a son. Presumably he's married. Or was.*

But the important question was, how long would he be around?

The very thought of Theo spending any amount of time in Maple Glen made Maura's stomach churn. Was it too much to hope that Theo Danby would just drop out of their lives again, as he had twenty years ago, and never discover her secret?

By the time she reached the barn, Jake had instinctively headed for his stall and was munching the hay she'd deposited. She took a moment to inspect the stall door and noticed the hasp was loose enough to give way with a solid push. A small thing to fix, but one more item on the long list of jobs. The other two donkeys, Matilda and Lizzie, were too busy eating to give her more than a half glance, their long ears twitching as she walked by their stalls.

Maura decided that after the encounter with Theo—and his son!—a second cup of coffee was definitely on the day's agenda and headed for the side door of the farmhouse that led through a tiny mudroom into the kitchen. Maddie was sitting at the table eating cereal and skimming through yesterday's Rutland newspaper. She looked up when Maura entered the room.

"What's up?" she immediately asked.

They'd always been good at reading one another, Maura knew. Even though they were nonidentical twins, there was still that inexplicable twin connection. At least, until the summer they'd turned eighteen, when they'd withdrawn from one another and begun new, separate lives.

Maura sighed. There was no point postponing the inevitable. "Jake got out of his stall—it's okay," she quickly put in, seeing Maddie was about to ask how. "I've figured it out. We have to fix the stall gate. Anyway, he'd wandered over to the Danbys', and I followed him." She paused. "Someone was at the house."

Maddie put her spoon down. "Who?"

"Theo."

Their eyes locked for what seemed ages. "He's come to get the place ready to sell," Maura added. "And he has a son who looks to be about eleven or twelve."

Maddie's impassive face revealed nothing. "Okay," she said and resumed eating.

That went well, Maura thought. Clearly her sister was still unhappy with her after last night's disagreement over the ongoing plans for the business, as well as finances. She poured herself a coffee and sat across from Maddie, whose head was still bent over the newspaper. The kitchen filled with the silence that had fallen between the sisters seventeen years ago, and Maura hoped it wouldn't last five years this time around, too. *Not if you do something about it right now*, she told herself.

"Look, Mads, Theo is ancient history. We were all teenagers the last time we were together, and presumably—" she attempted a half laugh "—we're a whole lot smarter now. I got the impression he and his son are here only long enough to sell the farm. Then he'll be gone."

Maddie finally looked at her. "I'm not worried about any of that, Maura. Like you said, that last summer is ancient history. I've moved on, and I hope you have, too."

Maura felt her face heat up under her sister's penetrating gaze. She bit down on her lower lip, quelling an instant rise of hurt. She wasn't going to be drawn into a debate they'd both sworn to put behind them. "Okay," she mumbled. "You're right." She got up from her chair and rinsed her coffee mug, letting the tension seep out. "So, who have we got riding today?"

It *had* to happen. Theo parked the car in front of the Shady Nook B and B and sat, unmoving. He'd known from the start that meeting up with the Stuart sisters—or at least one of them—was a possibility, but he wished fervently that it hadn't happened under such humiliating circumstances. Trapped by a donkey, for heaven's sake! Only to be rescued by one of the sisters. Worst of all, for a second he couldn't recall which was the redhead and which the raven-haired. They weren't identical twins, so it shouldn't have been so difficult. When he was a boy and then a teen, he'd never have made such a mistake.

"Are we going in or what?"

Luke's grumble finally registered. Theo blinked. He was back in Maple Glen. Thirty-six years old, divorced and on leave from his job. With a twelve-year-old son he barely knew who didn't want to be there any more than he did. He sighed. Those few minutes back at the farm with Maura had been a cold-water-shock reminder that time didn't change everything. Her stony expression and clipped voice took him immediately back to his last summer in Maple Glen countless years ago.

"Dad? Jeez!"

"Yeah, yeah. C'mon. We'll leave our stuff here until we know if we can get a room."

"Why don't we go back to the highway? I saw some motels there. Maybe we could get one with a pool, like we did yesterday."

Theo ignored Luke's plaintive tone, which had been incessant since he'd made the decision to take a road trip to Maple Glen and finally deal with his inheritance. Reconnecting with his son was meant to be part of a new, postdivorce direction in Theo's life, but he had a sinking feeling he'd already taken a wrong turn somewhere and now was lost. Like the rookie hikers on the nearby Appalachian Long Trail that the locals used to complain about.

At least the B and B looked like a welcoming place,

with its smoky-blue clapboard siding, white gingerbread-trimmed veranda and wicker chairs and tables. Theo vaguely recalled the original Colonial-style home had been painted white, but any memory of the people who'd lived there—the Harrisons, Maura had said—escaped him. Though come to think of it, had there been a boy roughly his own age?

"Well?" Luke was staring up at him from the bottom porch step.

His expression was a mix of frustration and concern, which made Theo feel a tad guilty. He hadn't been paying full attention to him since leaving Maine. Perhaps their road trip's destination should have been somewhere more exciting than a small place like Maple Glen, Vermont. He reached down and tousled Luke's hair. "C'mon," he said and opened the screen door.

Theo's eyes were adjusting to the cool darkness inside the entryway when a voice called out from somewhere farther inside. "Give me a sec!"

The interior gradually took shape, from the hall table with a vase of flowers and a small display of tourist pamphlets, to the staircase straight ahead. There were rooms to the left and right off the entry, and Theo spotted tables and chairs in one of them. A good sign, he thought. Even if there wasn't a room available, maybe they could get a bite to eat. Breakfast had been early, at a fast-food place on the highway.

Luke was fidgeting beside him, but at least he wasn't complaining. Not yet. Theo was about to reassure him that the next town, Wallingford, was only minutes away and they could always get some lunch there when a large, gray-haired man wearing an apron over baggy pants and a T-shirt emerged from a room at the end of the hall and lumbered toward them.

"Had to pop my bread rolls into the oven," he explained, his big, welcoming smile shooting from Theo to Luke. "What can I do for you folks?"

"We'd like a room, if you have one."

"Aha! That I do. You came at the right time—it's Sunday and I've just had two checkouts, plus the Fourth of July holiday is a couple of weeks away. How many nights are you thinking?" Before Theo could reply, the man headed for one of the rooms leading off the hall and, after a second's hesitation, Theo and Luke followed.

The room still exhibited its early days as a parlor, with a cluster of seating arrangements and an impressive bow-legged table with a Tiffany-style, stained glass lamp in the center of the bay window that looked onto the veranda. The man—Bernie Watson, Theo assumed—was rifling through a drawer in the table. Pulling out a small ledger book and pen, he swung around to say, "Here we go. Have a seat there—" he gestured to a chintz-upholstered wing chair "—and fill in the information I need while I go check on my dinner rolls."

Theo grasped the book and pen that were thrust at him and, casting a quick grin at Luke, sat where he was told. He wrote his name and address on the page headed with the day's date, hesitated over the "length of stay" column before jotting *2-3 nights* and hoped Luke, now standing at his elbow, hadn't noticed. He had yet to tell the boy that his plan was to fix up a couple of rooms in the farmhouse for them until the meeting with the Realtor.

Despite Luke's disparagement of the house as a "dump," the place had been dusted and aired only the week before their arrival by a company from Rutland that Theo had hired. The Stuart sisters obviously hadn't noticed the recent activity there, though the weeds in the fields between the two places could have hidden the cleaning agency's vehicle. Maura's search for her donkey had likely been the only reason for her to discover he was back. A donkey! Theo was pretty certain the Stuarts had never had animals larger than goats.

"Dad? I'm hungry." Luke was pulling on his arm.

Theo roused himself from thoughts that were leading nowhere. He was hungry, too, and the heavy footfalls along the hallway were reassuring. They'd be getting a room and, hopefully, lunch as well.

"Excuse my bad manners," the man was saying as he reentered the room. "I'm Bernie Watson, the owner, general manager as well as cook here."

Theo shook his hand and passed the sign-in book to Bernie, who peered down at it.

"Good heavens," he exclaimed. "Theo Danby!" His beaming grin faltered immediately. "I was sorry to hear about Stan and Vera."

"Thank you," Theo murmured. Luke shuffled impatiently, and he added, "Is it possible to get some lunch?"

"Definitely. Go get your things from your car. It'll be okay parked out front for now. I've got a small lot behind where you can move it later. As for lunch, I don't have any other patrons at the moment, but I can rustle something up for you two." He turned to Luke. "How about a grilled cheese sandwich with fries? I can even manage a chocolate milkshake, if you're up to it."

The smile on Luke's face was the first Theo had seen since the motel with pool they'd stayed at. "I think he's up to it," he said.

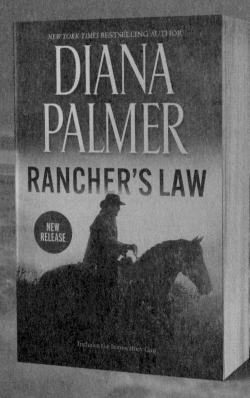

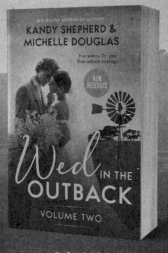